You Can't Always Get the Marquess You Want
"Sensual romance fills the pages of this novel, which is rich with smart, well-rounded characters and an engaging plot."
—*Publishers Weekly*

"The charming characters, tender love story, and fast pace combine to keep readers turning the pages and enjoying every moment. Hawkins delights with another emotional and well-written read."
—*RT Book Reviews*

"Full of torrid trysts, sparkling conversation, and Machiavellian machinations."
—*Fresh Fiction*

"Love in this story does conquer all."
—*The Good, the Bad, and the Unread*

"Alexandra Hawkins is rapidly becoming one of my favorite authors. She doesn't shy away from showing life as it is, and as the reader, I appreciate her emotional and complex storytelling."
—*Kilts and Swords*

"A diverting and spicy forbidden lovers' tale."
—*Affaire de Coeur*

A Duke But No Gentleman
"The attraction between Blackbern and Imogene is intense."
—*Publishers Weekly*

"The first of the Masters of Seduction series will more than satisfy those who savor a dark, richly woven romance."
—*RT Book Reviews* (4½ stars)

"This edgy historical will appeal to romantic-suspense readers looking for darker layers in a Regency love story."
—*Booklist*

"5 stars. This book is everything that a historical romance novel should be."
—*The Reading Wench*

"Sensual and filled with plenty of surprises . . . an excellent summer read."
—*Romance Reviews Today*

"5 stars. The reigning authority of charismatic Regency rogues."
—*Jenerated Reviews*

"A fantastic start to a seductive series."
—*Night Owl Reviews*

"*A Duke But No Gentleman* shows readers that real love always triumphs."
—*Romance Junkies*

All Night with a Rogue
"Hawkins's first Lords of Vice tale calls to mind the highly sensual reads of Beatrice Small and Susan Johnson."
—*Romantic Times*

"Brimming with witty repartee, well-drawn characters, an intriguing plot, sizzling sensual love scenes, and innocence, this story is a delight."
—*Romance Junkies* (4.5)

Till Dawn with the Devil
"*Till Dawn with the Devil*'s romance is first-rate with unusual characters and an underlying mystery that will intrigue readers."
—*Romance Reviews Today*

"Hawkins cements her reputation for bringing compelling, unique, and lush romances to fans eager for fresh story-telling." —*RT Book Reviews* (4½ stars)

After Dark with a Scoundrel

"Hawkins's talent for perfectly merging Gothic elements into a sexually charged romance is showcased along with the marvelous cast of characters taking readers on a thrill ride." —*RT Book Reviews*

"I would recommend this story to anyone who loves an amazingly written romance." —*Night Owl Reviews* (5-star Top Pick)

"Alexandra Hawkins has just cemented herself a place on my 'must-read' author list." —*Romance Junkies*

Sunrise with a Notorious Lord

"Simply spectacular from front to back!" —*Fresh Fiction*

"Regency fans will enjoy the bold heroine and rakish hero." —*Publishers Weekly*

"Charming, fun, and sexy." —*RT Book Reviews*

"*Sunrise with a Notorious Lord* is a fun and lively story." —*Romance Reviews Today*

All Afternoon with a Scandalous Marquess

"Desire in disguise was never so sweet or passionate, and Hawkins hooks readers and draws them in all the way to the perfect ending." —*RT Book Reviews*

Also by Alexandra Hawkins

THE MASTERS OF SEDUCTION novels
You Can't Always Get the Marquess You Want
A Duke But No Gentleman

THE LORDS OF VICE series
Twilight with the Infamous Earl
Dusk with a Dangerous Duke
All Afternoon with a Scandalous Marquess
Sunrise with a Notorious Lord
After Dark with a Scoundrel
Till Dawn with the Devil
All Night with a Rogue

EBOOKS
The No Good, Irresistible Viscount Tipton
The Scandalously Bad Mr. Milroy

WRITTEN AS BARBARA PIERCE
Tempting the Heiress
Courting the Countess
Wicked Under the Covers
Sinful Between the Sheets
Naughty by Nature
Scandalous by Night

ANTHOLOGY
Christmas Brides

Waiting for an Earl Like You

Alexandra Hawkins

St. Martin's Paperbacks

This is a work of fiction. All of the characters, organizations, and events portrayed in this novel are either products of the author's imagination or are used fictitiously.

WAITING FOR AN EARL LIKE YOU

Copyright © 2017 by Alexandra Hawkins.

All rights reserved.

For information address St. Martin's Press, 175 Fifth Avenue, New York, NY 10010.

ISBN: 978-1-250-06474-5

Our books may be purchased in bulk for promotional, educational, or business use. Please contact your local bookseller or the Macmillan Corporate and Premium Sales Department at 1-800-221-7945, ext. 5442, or by e-mail at MacmillanSpecialMarkets@macmillan.com.

Printed in the United States of America

St. Martin's Paperbacks edition / January 2017

St. Martin's Paperbacks are published by St. Martin's Press, 175 Fifth Avenue, New York, NY 10010.

10 9 8 7 6 5 4 3 2 1

Men, some to business, some to pleasure take;
But every woman is at heart a rake
                                    —Alexander Pope

Chapter One

Malster Park, England

It was a typical Netherwood gathering.

His mother, the Marchioness of Felstead, had sent invitations to all of her closest friends and anyone within a twenty-five-mile radius of their country estate. There wasn't a single room in the entire house that wasn't overflowing with guests. To accommodate the individuals who preferred to take part in the numerous outdoor activities, large tents had been erected to provide refuge from the sun and places to feed everyone.

Justin Reeve Netherwood, Earl of Kempthorn—or Thorn as he was called by his family and friends—had lost track of the marchioness hours ago. Nevertheless, he had no doubt his mother was savoring the large assemblage as she discreetly directed the servants with the confidence of any general in the British Army.

He had just left the library where his father and a dozen of his friends were engaged in a heated political discussion that had resolved no issues and given him a slight headache. If the argument had dissolved into fisticuffs, it might have been amusing to linger. However, the fifty-six-year-old marquess was well aware that his wife disapproved of such barbaric displays so he would step in and quell any discord between his friends.

Which was a shame, really, because there was nothing

like a good fight. It dispelled unspoken grievances, fired the blood, and lightened his mood. Fighting made him think of his identical twin brother, Gideon. Thorn ground his molars in annoyance. Although he would rather cut his tongue out than admit it, he regretted his decision to join the family at Malster Park. There was only so much civility he could bear. Perhaps it was time to concede defeat and rejoin his friends in London.

His grievances with Gideon could wait a little longer.

Thorn strolled through the front hall. Liveried footmen were positioned like sentries at each door as they directed guests who lingered to other amusements or awaited direction from their mistress. The shriek of a young child echoed, and he abruptly halted as the two-year-old ran into his legs. He bent down and picked up the blond-haired boy and held him until their gazes met.

"And whom do you belong to?" he inquired, noting the boy wore nothing under his white frock.

In response, the child stuck his thumb and forefinger into his mouth and grinned.

"Unrepentant about the state of your undress, I see," Thorn murmured and was rewarded with a garbled reply. "Let's say we look for your mother before—"

A wet spot appeared on the front of the boy's frock and was expanding at an alarming rate. Thorn groaned as held the child away from him. Bystanders pointed and giggled at his wretched predicament while urine dripped from beneath the sodden frock and onto his mother's marble floor.

Thorn glared at the nearest footman. "A little assistance if you do not mind."

The boy chortled with glee.

"Yes, yes . . . you have made a fine mess, my lad," he said, handing the child to the servant.

From the corner of his eye, he noticed the approach of his nine-year-old cousin. Lady Muriel Oldman was a beautiful child, with strawberry blonde hair and light green eyes. Her parents, who were distantly related to his mother, had tragically perished in a house fire three years earlier. With no immediate family, Lord Felstead had petitioned to be her guardian. Thorn's younger sister, Fiona, had taken the orphaned little girl under her wing, and the child had flourished in the Netherwood household. He had come to regard her as another sister.

"Muriel, do you know this boy?"

The girl nodded as she grimaced at the puddle forming beneath the wiggling child who was attempting to free himself from the servant's grasp. "He is Mrs. Staple's son."

"Be a good girl and fetch his mother," Thorn said, retrieving a handkerchief from his waistcoat. He grinned at the boy. "Before this mischief-maker has a chance to escape again." He leaned down and wiped the wetness from the toes of his boots.

Always eager to help, Muriel was already walking away. Over her slender shoulder, she said, "I will find her for you." She stopped and turned around. "Oh, I almost forgot to tell you."

"Tell me what?"

"Your brother cannot be found." She sent him a knowing glance. "Lady Felstead has tasked you with finding him since you know him best."

Not as well as I should, Thorn thought. "I will see to it immediately."

Her message delivered, Muriel waved farewell and rushed off to find Mrs. Staple.

He glanced at the footman and his soggy burden. "Hold on to the lad until he is reacquainted with his mother."

"You can count on me, milord," the servant replied, grimacing when the boy accidentally kicked him in the ribs.

Thorn winced in sympathy. He avoided the puddle on

the floor and headed for the open front door to find his errant twin.

Forty minutes later, Thorn was in no mood to be polite to anyone, including Gideon. He had searched the grounds surrounding the house, but his brother had managed to disappear without a trace. It did not help that he could not take five steps without someone calling out his name and begging a few minutes of this time. With each delay, his annoyance increased.

He had lost count on how many people stopped him to inquire, *"Oh, where is your charming brother? Or are you him?"*

Thorn and Gideon had been asked similar questions their entire lives. No one could tell them apart unless they deliberately went out of their way to reveal themselves. There were very subtle differences between them, like the faint half-inch scar on his outer thigh from a mock sword duel in his youth and Gideon's small mole on his right buttock. And since his mother frowned on them strolling about naked in public, even she had trouble telling them apart.

From a young age, he and his brother had reveled in the confusion, often using it to their advantage. It had been a mischievous game to them, one they had perfected as they became young gentlemen.

Until the day Gideon had announced that he was leaving England to seek his fortune and he did not require Lord Felstead's heir to accompany him on his travels. His brother's decision had cut him deeply, and had left him wallowing in an unrelenting cycle of ennui that still plagued him.

For the first time in his life, his brother's abandonment had left Thorn alone in the world. Now, after years of separation, Gideon was back in England and Thorn was uncertain he could cast aside his unspoken resentment.

The freshly cut lawn gently sloped into a terrace garden.

As boys, he and Gideon had raced up and down these same gravel paths as they explored the gardens and swam in the lake that had been created a hundred years earlier. The gravel path became cobblestones beneath his feet. The lake occasionally flooded and washed away the gravel, so his mother had insisted that a few changes needed to be made to the back gardens. That was ten years ago. Now the hedge walls that lined the walk to the lake towered over him. Ornate pots overflowed with pink rhododendrons and white azaleas adding a touch of color. Three paths intersected with the main one and led away from the lake. One led to a private garden that was one of his mother's favorite places to enjoy the good weather. Another took the stroller to a cottage that was offered to guests who valued their privacy. The last one led to a Greek-style temple. He and Gideon had held mock battles beneath the folly's Doric columns as they fought with wooden swords.

Thorn should have found the familiar surroundings and the memories that the gardens evoked soothing. Instead, he felt restless. As if he was on the precipice of another change in his life, one he was uncertain he desired or could accept. The pathway opened to the right, and he stepped onto the wooden platform that extended over the water. It was large enough for an orchestra, but it also served as a dock. He used his hand to shield his eyes from the sun and the reflective glare of the smooth surface of the water as he directed his attention to the man and woman seated in the small sailboat in the middle of the small lake. On the other side, sheep grazed on the overgrown grass.

Gideon.

He did not recognize the lady. Her back was to him, and the bright-red parasol she was holding concealed the upper half of her body as she conversed with his brother.

The pair appeared to be engaged in an earnest conversation, and they had yet to notice Thorn's presence as he stood on the white wooden platform. Annoyance tightened the muscles in his jaw and neck. If Gideon had not been so dismissive of family and friends who had gathered to celebrate his homecoming to Malster Park, he might have left his brother alone to flirt with the chit.

However, their mother had put a great deal of effort into planning this house party for his ungrateful twin. The least he could do was show his appreciation—and if Gideon had lost all semblance of civility during his travels, Thorn was more than willing to remind him by beating some manners into his thick skull.

From the sailboat, masculine laughter floated on the warm air, crossing the distance until it reached the dock.

Thorn scowled. He could not recall the last occasion when he had heard his brother laugh. His gaze lingered on the woman as he attempted to discern her identity.

Lost in contemplation, he did not notice the precise moment when Gideon had become aware of his presence.

"Huzzah, brother! What a timely arrival. A fine day, is it not? I did not think anything could pry you from our father's library."

Gideon's mysterious companion turned and slightly elevated her parasol so she could view him discreetly, but her face was still hidden.

Thorn cupped the sides of his mouth with his hands and shouted, "I have been sent to remind you that you are the guest of honor this afternoon. Perhaps you should think more of our mother and less of yourself."

Even from a distance, he noted Gideon's grimace. His twin murmured something to the woman, and she placed her hand on his arm as if to soothe him.

Gideon glanced upward at the sky and shrugged. "It appears we have lost the wind."

Thorn doubted there had been much of a breeze when his brother coaxed his companion into the sailboat. "A pity," Thorn said, feigning sympathy. "I recommend that you remove your frock coat before you paddle back to the dock. It would be a shame if you strained the seams on such a fine garment."

Thorn's lips thinned with grim satisfaction as his brother cursed. A minute later, the sailboat wobbled as Gideon hastily removed his coat and handed it to his companion. With his task accomplished, he could have left the dock and returned to the house. However, his curiosity held him in place. He wanted to meet the lady who had charmed his twin into forgetting his obligations.

Not that Gideon required any assistance. He was quite capable of avoiding unsavory tasks all on his own. This fete was a perfect example. His brother had been on English soil for ten months and only now had he yielded to Lady Felstead's demands that they celebrate his homecoming with a formal gathering.

Thorn crossed his arms and observed Gideon's progress. Once the sail had been secured, his brother picked up the oar and paddled toward the dock. He took his time as if concerned that his efforts might stir the air and ruffle his hair. His casual strokes sliced through the water while he maneuvered the little sailboat until it glided mere inches from the edge of the dock.

Thorn crouched down and reached for the coiled rope at the bow. He cast an inconspicuous glance at the woman as he tied a knot to prevent the boat from drifting away. She pointedly ignored him. Straightening, he held out his hand and waited for her to close her parasol. "Perhaps I may be of service, Miss—?"

Gideon set aside the oar and held on to the dock to minimize the rocking. "Take Thorn's hand, my dear. I promise he will not bite. He will be too busy lecturing me on my rudeness."

"It is the least you deserve," was Thorn's terse reply.

The woman sighed, and Thorn could not decide if she was bored or vexed by his intrusion. She tipped the parasol in his direction and collapsed it, revealing her bowed head. All he could see was the top of her plaited straw bonnet with cream silk taffeta ribbons cascading down the front like a waterfall.

With an air of impatience, he snatched the parasol from her light hold, causing her to gasp in surprise. She lifted her face and their gazes met and locked as recognition gave way to mild dismay.

Almost a year had passed since he had last spoken with Miss Olivia Lydall. Her father, Lord Dewick, owned lands that shared a border with Malster Park to the north. Six years younger than Thorn and Gideon, Miss Lydall had often found her way onto their lands when she was a child. Gideon had befriended her, but Thorn had been more guarded. Even though she had two older brothers, for some unfathomable reason, she preferred to spend her days exploring Netherwood lands and sharing secrets with his twin. He wondered where the little baggage had been hiding all of these months. There was a time when he could not take a step without running into the young woman. Of course it came as no surprise to him that Gideon's homecoming had lured her back on to his family's lands.

Thorn tucked her parasol under his arm and offered her his hand. "Miss Lydall," he said, daring her to refuse. As a boy, he had been envious of her friendship with Gideon and had not always been kind. As they grew older, the only occasions she risked approaching him was when she had mistaken him for Gideon.

He should have been flattered that she was wary of him. Instead it irritated him.

"Lord Kempthorn," she said politely, her cornflower-colored gaze sliding down to his hand. A few stray dark reddish brown curls had escaped the confines of her bonnet.

Catching the sunlight, the hue blazed with an internal fire. Oblivious to his unspoken fascination with her curls, she slowly rose from her seat and struggled to keep her balance.

"Steady," Gideon advised, tightening his grip on the dock. "There is too much slack in the rope."

Thorn switched his attention to his brother. He arched his right eyebrow as the line of his mouth thinned with grim amusement. "Critiquing my efforts, brother?"

"I would not dare," was Gideon's mocking retort. "Everyone knows that Lord Felstead's heir is perfect in all things."

Miss Lydall's nervous gaze switched from Gideon to Thorn. "Ah, gentlemen." She held her arms away from her sides to maintain her precarious stance.

Thorn made a soft chiding sound with his tongue. "I see your insults have not improved with age."

"What does that mean?" Gideon demanded.

"Uh." Miss Lydall reached out her hand, but neither brother was paying attention to her.

Thorn glared at his twin. "Simply put, I thought your time away from England would have seasoned you. I expected to reacquaint myself with a gentleman, not some young puppy who continues to whine over the circumstances of his birth."

"Good god, you are such an arse!" Gideon snarled. In his fury, he lost his grip on the dock.

Miss Lydall cried out, her arms flailing in the air as the sailboat rocked and floated away from the dock.

"No!" Thorn shouted and lunged for one of her arms so he could drag her onto the dock.

Gideon made things worse by throwing his weight to the side in an attempt to catch hold of the dock again.

Disaster loomed. For a moment, time seemed to slow down for Thorn. His fingers brushed against Miss Lydall's arm, but the rocking boat sent her backward. Without thought to his own safety, he made a second attempt to grab her. A soft cry of distress escaped her lips as he seized her wrist while Gideon clutched at her skirt and Thorn's leg in a futile effort to avoid the inevitable.

All three tumbled over the side of the boat and into the water.

Thorn was the first to recover from the shock of the cold dunking, his face breaking the water's surface as he stood. The water level came to his chest, so there was little chance that any of them would drown. Gideon appeared splashing about several yards away.

His brother howled and then shuddered. "Bloody hell, the chill just shrinks a man's—" His jaw snapped shut as he recalled a lady was present and glanced around for Miss Lydall.

Miss Lydall!

Thorn plunged his arm into the water. To his relief, his hand grasped a section of wet fabric and he unceremoniously hauled the lady to the surface.

Miss Lydall choked and batted at the veil of water that was cascading from her straw bonnet. Sputtering, she exclaimed, "Oh, it is wretchedly cold!"

The poor woman lost her footing and would have slipped under the water again if not for Thorn's tight grip on her arm.

"And I think I swallowed a bug." She pushed the soggy taffeta ribbons away from her eyes. "I doubt this day could get any worse."

Thorn glanced at his brother, and the intimate connection they had always shared flared to life. Gideon's slow grin mirrored his own. Neither man could hold back his laughter.

Chapter Two

Olivia was beyond mortified.

Before she had left the house, she had promised her father that she would stay out of mischief. Until the Countess of Grisdale had entered her and Lord Dewick's lives, her father had found little fault in his only daughter. Of late, all he saw were her flaws.

"A lady never drops her mask of gentility and grace, even when she is alone," was one of the countess's favorite sayings.

Before Lord Kempthorn had appeared, she had been doing so well. Even Gideon had remarked on the changes he noticed since he had last seen her, and his manner had been respectful when he had invited her to join him at the lake.

Now she looked like a soggy moppet that the earl had plucked out of the water.

She glared at her companions, but the effect was ruined by the silly taffeta ribbons that were blinding her. "I have had enough humiliation for one day," she announced as she tested Lord Kempthorn's firm grip with a quick tug.

Since no one was paying attention to her, her release earned her another mouthful of lake water. The water was not deep, but she was shorter than the Netherwood twins.

Lord Kempthorn took custody of her arm again. At this rate, she would end up with bruises.

"What the devil are you doing?" the earl demanded.

"You and your brother may be accustomed to bathing in spring lake water, but I am not," Olivia said, struggling not to lose her temper. "If it is not too much trouble, I need some assistance. My skirt and petticoat are too heavy for me to swim to the dock."

She untied the ribbons of her ruined bonnet and removed it.

"You can swim?"

Olivia could not decide if Lord Kempthorn was deliberately baiting her or was amazed that she was capable of something more than drowning. "Of course I can swim. My brothers insisted that I learn."

Not that she was feeling wholly confident in her skills as her wet skirt undulated around her body as her movements stirred the water.

"I will help her." Gideon moved closer.

"No need." The earl brushed his brother's offer aside. "I have her."

The light pull on her arm alerted Olivia of his intentions. "My lord, there is no need to—"

Olivia pressed her lips together to keep from swallowing more lake water as Lord Kempthorn's actions caused her to sink lower in the water as he drew her closer. Water dripped down her nose as she scowled at him. A part of her wondered if he had done it deliberately to silence her.

"Stop fussing," he scolded, pressing her against his chest. His arm slipped under her legs and he cradled her in his arms. "Your lips are not the only thing turning blue in this water."

A soft choking sound erupted from Gideon's throat as he tried not to laugh. "And I thought I was the one who was lacking in manners," he mocked.

Olivia felt her face heat as she tried not to dwell on what part of Lord Kempthorn was turning blue. She clutched her sodden bonnet tighter and was grateful the earl was no longer looking at her. Their proximity was awkward for both of them. Instead, his gaze was focused on the dock as he waded toward it.

"Give me a moment," Gideon said, reaching the dock before them. He braced the palms of his hands on the wooden surface and used his arms to haul himself upward and then his knee to secure his perch. He shook himself to rid his clothing of excess water.

The twins had always been vain peacocks when it came to their attire. *Only the finest tailors and fabrics for the Netherwood twins,* she mused. Her gaze lingered on his arms. The wet linen was clinging to him like a second skin, revealing the muscled contours of his upper arms.

"Stop flaunting your impressive physique to Miss Lydall and lend me a hand," Lord Kempthorn growled.

Gideon winked at Olivia. "Thorn, you are just jealous that I am her favorite."

Appalled by his outrageous boast and the undeniable fact that she had been caught staring, Olivia hurriedly averted her eyes. She could practically hear Lord Kempthorn's teeth grind together as he resisted offering his brother a scathing denial that would likely hurt her feelings.

Fortunately, the earl was too much of a gentleman to stoop so low.

Oblivious to the tension he had created, Gideon crouched down and extended his arms. With an envious display of strength, Lord Kempthorn raised her fully out of the water and handed her to his twin.

"You are a remarkably light burden, my lady," Gideon teased. "And such a pretty one, too. Perhaps you and I should take a stroll into the woods."

"Gideon," the earl said, a clear warning.

Her pulse quickened. "Mr. Netherwood, stop baiting your brother."

"I disagree," Gideon drawled, his heavy-lidded gaze meeting hers as they both became aware that her wet dress was revealing more of her body than was proper. "The notion has merit. When was the last time you were kissed?"

His mouth was temptingly close to hers.

Olivia grabbed Gideon by the chin and turned his face away from hers. "Did you strike your head when you fell into the water? Cease this foolishness and release me at once!"

Lord Kempthorn gracefully climbed up onto the dock. "Put her down. You are upsetting Miss Lydall."

"Miss Lydall, Lord Kempthorn, Mr. Netherwood," Gideon muttered under his breath. To Olivia's relief he complied with his brother's command. "There was a time when we used to be friends. When did we become bloody strangers?"

Olivia felt her throat tighten as a rush of sadness threatened to overwhelm her. To conceal her distress, she frowned and concentrated on squeezing the water from her sleeves.

The earl turned his back on them and knelt down to make certain the rope was secure. Olivia doubted Lord Kempthorn had ever considered her a friend, so she did not expect to hear him deny that any ties they shared had been severed a long time ago.

"We were children," she said softly. At Gideon's look of frustration, she smiled at him. "If you are planning to remain in England, perhaps we can be friends again."

His stern expression eased into mild amusement. "I never stopped, Olivia."

"Here."

Olivia blinked in surprise at the frock coat Lord

Kempthorn held in his hands. It was the one Gideon had removed and abandoned in the sailboat.

"It will ward off the chill and give you a degree of modesty when we return to the main house," the earl explained without looking directly at her.

The wave of heat she felt had nothing to do with the afternoon sun. She glanced down and brought her ruined bonnet up to conceal her breasts. If not for her stays and petticoat, the wet dress was almost as sheer as the gentlemen's linen shirts.

"Good grief!" Olivia glared at Gideon who was grinning at her. "And you said nothing, you scoundrel!"

Unrepentant, Gideon did not bother to hide his appreciation. "Why would I spoil such a lovely view?"

Her response was to shove him into the water.

When Gideon surfaced, he was still laughing. "You don't have to be prudish around us, Olivia. If you think about it, we are all but family."

He climbed back onto the dock.

"You must forgive me if I disagree, Mr. Netherwood." Olivia huffed and snatched the coat from Lord Kempthorn. "And what about you, my lord," she said, her embarrassment making her voice gruff. "Were you enjoying the view as well?"

Holding the bonnet to her chest, she struggled to put her arm into one of the sleeves of Gideon's coat. Without being asked, the earl stepped forward and helped her into the oversized tog.

"I doubt you will find comfort in my answer, Miss Lydall." Lord Kempthorn glanced at his brother, who had water dripping from his long limbs and puddling at his feet. "And I would prefer to avoid another plunge into the lake. Shall we go?"

He gestured toward the cobblestone path.

Unable to think of a clever response, Olivia pinched the edges of the frock coat together and left the two brothers standing on the dock.

That's when she realized that she had lost one of her shoes.

Pity stirred in Thorn's chest as he and his brother watched Miss Lydall struggle to maintain the frayed threads of her dignity as she walked toward the cobblestone path with her chin held high.

By Jove, the lady was a bedraggled mess!

Soaked to the skin, her white muslin dress had molded to her body in a fashion that a Covent Garden nun would have considered scandalous. Gideon's coat covered her from her shoulders to her thighs, but he had held her in his arms. The water had made the front of her bodice almost transparent, giving him a teasing view of her breasts. The soft swells of flesh were generous without being too ample. His body had responded to the tantalizing bounty in his arms. His cock had hardened in spite of the chilly water, which should have dulled what was a perfectly natural response to gazing at the female form.

Even if the lady who had inspired his unruly body's response was Miss Olivia Lydall.

Annoyed, Thorn abruptly turned and punched his brother in the shoulder.

Gideon grunted. "What the hell was that for?"

Thorn shook his head. "Your sins are too many to list, brother. Hurry along."

Neither man had to quicken their pace to catch up to their companion. He winced at the squishing and fart sounds coming from his and Gideon's boots as they walked several steps behind her.

Without acknowledging them, Miss Lydall absently touched her damp hair. She had lost most of her ornamental hair combs when she had pulled off her bonnet. Her dark hair fell a few inches below her shoulder blades. The ends were already drying and beginning to curl into small ringlets. The natural curls were rather charming, Thorn decided as he admired the way her hair gleamed in the sunlight and bounced in rhythm with her steady gait. Of course the lady smelled of lake water, and her curls—as pretty as were—required a thorough combing or her hair would look like a rat's nest when it dried.

A soft cry of pain jerked him from his musings. Miss Lydall halted and inclined her head to inspect her shoeless foot as he and his brother caught up to her. The white stockings she wore were dirty, and her upturned foot revealed a small hole in the delicate silk.

The earl noticed that the ruined stockings encased small delicate feet and attractive ankles. He frowned at the direction of his thoughts.

"What is it? Did you hurt yourself?" Gideon asked before Thorn thought to.

"Just a sharp stone, Mr. Netherwood," she said, expelling a sigh of frustration. "There is no hope for my stockings. It is the third pair that I have ruined in as many days."

Although she had piqued his curiosity, he had resisted asking her to elaborate on her statement.

"Here. Permit me to take a look," Gideon said, kneeling down so he could examine her foot. He bowed his head and gently checked the bottom of her foot for an injury. Without looking up, he said, "Our families are too close to stand on formalities. If you call me by my given name, then I will know you have truly forgiven me for my carelessness."

She cast a nervous glance in Thorn's direction, sensing he would be displeased with her taking such liberties. Undecided on how she should proceed, she tapped Gideon on the shoulder. "There is nothing to forgive. Pray stand, sir.

You are embarrassing me. My foot does not warrant your attention. I was merely startled."

Gideon slowly straightened from his crouched position and stared at Thorn. Both men were aware that she had deliberately ignored his invitation to put aside all formalities. His brother looked slightly annoyed, but not at Miss Lydall.

Thorn sensed his brother was blaming him.

So very typical of Gideon.

"Well, there is no help for it."

Puzzlement shadowed her face. "No help for what?"

"We cannot have you walking about the grounds with only one shoe," Gideon explained. "I will carry you."

"Gideon, I do not—" Thorn began.

"A very generous offer, but not—" Miss Lydall began.

His brother swept Miss Lydall into his arms.

She squeaked in surprise and wrapped her arms around his neck. "Gideon!"

"Ah, sweet Olivia, I knew you couldn't stay mad at me forever," his twin teased. He glanced at Thorn and winked.

Thorn shook his head as they continued down the cobblestone path.

"This is absurd. Put me down at once," Miss Lydall primly ordered. "I am too heavy."

"You are light as swansdown," his brother countered. "With a beautiful lady in my arms, I can walk for miles."

"Then put me down and go find a beautiful lady," she said, kicking her feet to slow him down. "If anyone sees us together, I will never live down the humiliation."

"So you are too good to be seen with us, is it?" Gideon asked.

"Oh, do not twist my words," Miss Lydall spat. "It is going to be difficult to explain why I fell into the lake. Showing up with the two of you will only create more problems for me."

"It was an accident, Miss Lydall. Who will challenge our account? Your father? Your brothers?" Thorn pressed when she said nothing else.

She shook her head. "Lady Grisdale."

"Why would she meddle?"

Thorn had been introduced to the thirty-five-year-old widow last Season. The encounter was so unremarkable he could not recall any details of their conversation.

"The countess has tired of widowhood and has decided my father would make a tolerable husband," she confessed.

"You are joking," Gideon said.

"I dearly wish it was a jest," she said, gazing at the horizon. "My father seems . . . amenable. As a sign of her devotion to him, Lady Grisdale has vowed to take me under her wing to improve my chances on the marriage mart."

For a girl who had been lacking a mother's guidance for most of her life, Miss Lydall did not appear to be overjoyed by the prospect of gaining a new ally to navigate the tricky waters of securing a husband.

"Is that what you want?" Gideon softly asked. "Are you hoping to find a husband?"

Miss Lydall shrugged. "I have not given it much thought until this year. After all, I will soon turn twenty. I have a few more years before I can officially call myself a spinster. Do you not agree?"

Gideon laughed at the absurdity of her question. "Quite so, my dear girl."

"Is your father also eager for you to marry?" Thorn asked in even tones.

Another dainty shrug. "Lord Dewick—my father—is content to leave such matters to the countess." She chewed on her lower lip in contemplation.

"What are you not telling us, Olivia?" his twin asked.

"Please put me down, Gideon. I cannot think with you—just please do as I say," Miss Lydall pleaded.

His brother hesitated as he silently debated if he should honor her request or do what he thought was best for her. It was obvious to Thorn that time and distance had not dimmed Gideon's affection for the chit. If his twin wasn't careful, he would be caught up in the lady's troubles.

Some of the tension in Miss Lydall's slender shoulders eased when his twin allowed her to stand. "Thank you. Shall we go on?"

"You never answered my brother's question, Miss Lydall."

She gave him an exasperated look. "Are you truly interested in my problems, Lord Kempthorn?"

When your problems concern my brother, I am.

"Naturally. As Gideon pointed out, you are almost like family to us," Thorn lied.

"Well," she said, drawing the word out, "in spite of my father's assurances, I do not believe Lady Grisdale has my best interests at heart."

Gideon linked his fingers with hers. "Are you certain? I am not familiar with the lady."

The muscles in Thorn's jaw tightened at the ease his brother was able to slip into the role of friend and protector.

"In private, she is always ridiculing me. I can do nothing right in her opinion," Miss Lydall said, the melancholy in her voice touching even Thorn's heart. She continued down the cobblestone path, and he and his brother followed her lead.

"The devil you say. You are wonderful. Any lady would be honored to have you as a daughter," Gideon said, already her staunchest defender.

"You are too kind." She met Thorn's gaze and held it as if daring him to contradict his sibling.

He expected to see hurt in her cornflower eyes, but Miss Lydall looked bloody furious.

She switched her attention back his twin. "Lady Grisdale does not wish to be my mother, Gideon. I am something of an inconvenience to her. She wants to see me married and out of my father's house."

"Have you spoken to your father?" Thorn asked.

Miss Lydall nodded. "Once. However, he is smitten by the countess and is blind to her faults. Besides, the lady is careful in how she treats me in front of my father. If he is asked to choose between me and the woman he desires to wed, then I will lose."

It was difficult not to feel sympathy for a motherless girl who will soon lose her father to another lady.

Gideon's jaw hardened and his gaze narrowed with determination. "Then we must do something."

No! Thorn thought. His brother had a bad habit of making a fool out of himself when it came to women. He was not going to allow Miss Lydall to involve her brother in her family troubles.

"There is nothing that can be done," she said, appearing resigned to her fate. "This is why I want to avoid a confrontation with my father and the countess. Our accident will bolster her argument that I am an embarrassment to him."

She glanced wistfully at the path that led to the cottage. "Are there any old dresses stored in the cottage? Perhaps I could find a dress and change before we—"

Thorn rejected her suggestion by shaking his head. "Any of my mother's old dresses are given to the servants."

"Ah, one of the guests might have something I could borrow."

"Our mother thought it best to have the unmarried gentlemen reside in the cottage. Discovering a lady's dress in their possessions or you dressing in borrowed breeches would create more talk than the three of us walking into the main house in our wet clothing," Thorn said, amused that her shoulders dramatically sagged as he dismissed the thought of her wearing male togs. Although seeing the lady in breeches would give him a good view of her legs.

Priorities, Kempthorn, he silently chastised himself.

In the distance, the three of them watched a couple crossing the gravel path ahead and disappearing behind a hedge.

Miss Lydall turned around to face them. There was genuine panic in her eyes. "I cannot do this."

Gideon took a step closer. "Olivia, what choice do any of us have?"

"I could return home," she said, warming to her ridiculous plan.

"Don't be a goose, Miss Lydall," Thorn said, ruthlessly dashing her hopes. "You cannot walk several miles wearing only one shoe. Nor will we allow you to do so."

"I am willing to take the risk," she said, too stubborn for her own good.

He scowled at her. "Try it, and I will be entering the main house with you tossed over my shoulder."

"Thorn," his brother murmured.

Miss Lydall stuck her chin in the air. "You would not dare!"

Gideon tried to step between them. "My brother would never humiliate you—"

"I can speak for myself, Gideon." Thorn moved closer to intimidate her with his height. "Test my patience, Miss Lydall, and you will be unhappy with the results."

He waited for her to decide.

"You are a coldhearted gentleman, Lord Kempthorn," she said, her lips set into a mutinous line of defeat.

Satisfaction gleamed in his eyes. "Then we understand each other, Miss Lydall. Just think of all of the misunderstandings we will avoid this Season."

Her lips trembled as she swallowed a scathing retort. Turning on her heel, she wordlessly walked away from the brothers.

Chapter Three

Never in her life had Olivia detested Lord Kempthorn more than in that moment.

He was overbearing, uncaring, and hateful. She pitied Gideon for being tied to such a callous creature.

Her anger gave her the strength she needed to forge ahead. Gideon's apologies and his attempts to soothe her feelings were just an irritating noise in her ears. All she could think about was *him*. She saw only the triumphant gleam in Lord Kempthorn's eyes, the arrogant curl of the corner of his mouth, and the outrageous threat that he would toss her over his shoulder if she did not obey his dictates.

Obey *him*.

Oh, his rudeness was beyond the pale.

"Be reasonable," Gideon cajoled, when the cobblestone walk ended and the gravel path began. "If you think I will permit you to continue—"

"No! Thank you," was her curt reply, her high dudgeon allowing her to endure the discomfort of the rough stones against her unshod foot.

"Stubborn," Lord Kempthorn muttered under his breath.

"And you can go to the devil, my lord," she said, tossing the careless words over her shoulder.

Neither gentleman spoke another word as her gait slowed

and her limp became more pronounced. Olivia walked through the cultivated sections of Lady Felstead's terraced gardens without stopping to admire the flowers. She ignored the stares and soft exclamations from the guests the trio encountered with increasing frequency as they approached the house.

When the gravel path ended and she stepped onto the lawn, she had to stifle a moan of relief. The bottom of her foot was bruised and she doubted the stocking could be repaired, but she took some satisfaction in having made the return to the house without having Gideon carry her like a helpless lamb.

If she had not been so vexed at Lord Kempthorn—

Had he deliberately set out to upset her? The unexpected insight caused Olivia to stumble. Before she could react, she felt the earl's hand close around her upper arm to steady her. She started at his touch. He murmured an apology and released her arm. She had not realized he was walking almost at her heels or that he had observing her so closely.

Olivia glanced over her shoulder, but Lord Kempthorn was staring ahead. Even an unexpected dip in the chilly lake had not taken the starch out of his expression. He looked detached from everything around him.

Including her.

What a daft thought! The man was as cold as the fish in the lake.

"My, my," a middle-aged woman said as Olivia, Gideon, and his twin approached the back terrace. "A bit chilly for a swim. What mischief have the three of you been indulging in?"

"A minor sailing accident," Gideon said, placing his palm against Olivia's back when she froze. "You are so kind to inquire after our welfare."

Olivia inhaled sharply. The woman had done no such

thing. Her knowing glance suggested the three of them had been doing something wicked.

Gideon gave Olivia a little shove to spur her forward.

The terrace was a gauntlet of speculative looks, amusement, questions, and expressed concern for their woeful condition. Olivia edged away from Gideon, with a fleeting thought of escape, but she was boxed in by Lord Kempthorn.

"You are not a coward, Miss Lydall," the earl whispered in her ear. "Prove it."

Olivia stiffened at his words and her chin lifted.

Had she not decided all of this was *his* fault?

No one came too close to them as they moved closer to the open doors of the ballroom. Olivia and her companions moved through the growing crowd of guests like soap bubbles in a washtub of dirty water. The curious flowed around them, but kept a safe distance. She could not blame them since their clothes were still dripping with lake water. Or—she wrinkled her nose as she sniffed her left shoulder—they smelled like rotten fish and old boots.

In the distance, she heard someone order one of the footmen to retrieve some blankets.

"Thorn . . . I cannot believe it. Is it really you?" a gleeful feminine voice halted their progress.

Up until this point, Olivia had not made eye contact with anyone, taking comfort in the slight haze to her surroundings. However, the familiar voice brought an unpleasant clarity that she preferred to avoid—Lady Millicent Atson.

The twenty-four-year-old was Lord and Lady Flewett's eldest daughter. Her family's lands were southeast of Malster Park, so Olivia had been acquainted with the young lady for most of their lives.

Not that she considered Lady Millicent anything more than a distant neighbor—and an annoyance. As a child, she had chased after the Netherwood twins and had taken an immediate dislike to Olivia. Gideon and his brother enjoyed flirting with the dark-haired beauty whenever she came to visit, but it soon became obvious that Lord Kempthorn was the gentleman she had set her cap for.

Slightly wounded by her indifference, Gideon had confided to Olivia one evening as they watched several ladies flutter around Lord Felstead's young heir. *"A beautiful lady with aspirations of marrying a titled gentleman never casts her lure at the second son."*

Of course, many of the same ladies took solace in Gideon's arms when Lord Kempthorn ignored them or moved on to more challenging conquests.

Olivia should have anticipated that Lady Millicent and her family would attend the fete. While the young lady and Gideon had grown less fond of each other over the years, she would not miss an opportunity to flirt with Lord Kempthorn.

"Lady Millicent," the earl greeted her cordially.

"Goodness, it *is* you," Lady Millicent said too brightly for the awkward occasion. "I almost did not recognize you." Her gaze reluctantly moved from Lord Kempthorn to his brother. "Netherwood, it is good to see you again."

"Lady Millicent," Gideon acknowledged her with a slight nod.

"While you were off on your little adventure, my family and I have remembered you in our prayers each day," she said, her gaze drifting back to the earl. "We were so happy when Lady Felstead told us of your return. I cannot tell you how disappointed my mother was that you did not call on us last summer."

Olivia felt Gideon's fingers tense on her back. "Please extend my apologies to your family, Lady Millicent. I regret that I was unable to return home until recently."

The lack of warmth in his voice revealed he was not

pleased by Lady Millicent's attempt to delay them or her determination to ignore Olivia's presence.

"Did you lose your way and fall into the lake?" Lady Millicent teased. "I suppose Thorn lost his footing as well when he rescued you."

"Not quite," the earl said, the chill in his tone causing Olivia to shudder.

She moved to slip away from her male companions, but one of the footmen came up from behind and covered her shoulders with a wool blanket. Two other servants presented blankets to Lord Kempthorn and Gideon.

"Thank you," she murmured, offering the footman a weak smile. "Do you think it would be possible for me to retire upstairs and—"

"After all, Miss Lydall was part of our little misadventure," Lord Kempthorn continued, lightly gripping her upper arm so she could not flee. "You do recognize another one of your neighbors, do you not?"

Assuming the earl was speaking to her, Olivia glanced up, but his attention was focused on Lady Millicent.

The woman pasted an insincere smile on her face as she finally met Olivia's wary gaze. "Of course. Pray forgive me, Miss Lydall. I confess, I did not recognize our little Olive under all that wet hair, male togs, and mud. I thought you were one of Lady Felstead's servant boys."

Several of the onlookers chuckled at her observation.

Olivia lowered her gaze and shifted her stance so her bare foot was concealed behind her muddy shoe. The blanket hid her ruined bonnet, but not the sudden anger and shame burning red flags on her cheeks. "Quite understandable, Lady Millicent. It is your younger sister who is admired for her cleverness, is it not?"

Olivia gently tugged her arm free from the earl's grasp and walked by the speechless woman.

She heard Lord Kempthorn as he coughed into his fist. However, it was Gideon who did not bother to hide his snort of laughter. It was unlike Olivia to be so mean-spirited, but the sting of "little Olive" had not abated. It was an old nickname that Lady Millicent and her friends had not bestowed on her out of affection.

"Miss Lydall, wait."

She disregarded the earl's command and continued her retreat across the ballroom. She headed for the nearest door. Two servants followed in her wake, attempting to mop up the lake water dripping from her hem. Once Lady Felstead was made aware of her circumstances, Olivia was confident that a dry dress could be found for her.

She exited the ballroom and walked straight into the path of the lady who intended to marry her father before the end of the year.

"Olivia Lydall! I want an explanation at once," Nann Mathews, Countess of Grisdale, snapped, already warming to her future position as Olivia's stepmother.

The thirty-five-year-old light blonde widow had buried her husband five years earlier and possessed the confidence of a woman who knew her worth and was unafraid to take what she wanted. Her tall, willowy figure attracted gentlemen who were younger and older than her, and she caused quite a stir when she appeared in London last October with her taste for daring fashions and disreputable men. The gossips had linked her name with numerous gentlemen, but she was often seen with an earl who was ten years younger. He had spent a small fortune on her, which included a sapphire necklace that matched the color of her eyes. A few weeks after their public parting, she was wearing diamond earrings that were a gift from an Italian count. A month later, she was betrothed to a marquis, but she hastily severed her ties with the Spaniard when he beat her for flirting with another gentleman.

In between her torrid affairs and betrothals, Lady Grisdale was introduced to Olivia's father and a friendship blossomed. Although the countess's betrothal to Lord Dewick had not been formally announced, the lady was not about to allow such a trivial detail stop her from taking charge of the baron's household or his family.

Unfortunately, her father seemed too bemused by the woman to deny her anything.

"The dock was slippery," Olivia lied, deciding any explanation that involved the Netherwood twins would not amuse the countess. "I was about to ask Lady Felstead if I could borrow some clothing while my dress dried."

Lady Grisdale had made it quite clear from their first introduction that she was not charmed by Olivia's frivolous nonsense. She found her lover's daughter lacking, although she reserved her more critical remarks for when they were alone.

"You will not trouble Lady Felstead," the countess countered. "She has more important guests to look after than a young lady who trips over her own feet."

"I did not—" She swallowed her protest. Lady Grisdale detested young ladies who whined.

The older woman's gaze dropped to Olivia's feet, and her lips parted in surprise. "Where is your shoe?"

Olivia tried not to wince. "I lost it in the lake."

The countess shook her head. "What is your father to do with you, girl? You have ruined your beautiful dress and look like a—" She gestured with her hands when she could not summon the right word to describe Olivia's appalling condition.

"It was an accident," Olivia quietly explained.

Their conservation was already drawing a small group of curious guests. There were so many people attending Lord and Lady Felstead's fete, she doubted there was an empty room available for Lady Grisdale to scold her in private.

"I apologize for embarrassing you and Father," she said in hopes of appeasing the older woman.

"I vowed to take you under my wing, my dear girl, but even I cannot work miracles," Lady Grisdale lamented. "You will have to be sent home."

Olivia nodded in relief. "Of course. I will change my dress and return shortly."

"There is no need for you to rush. You will not be returning to Malster Park," the countess decreed, her eyes narrowing when Olivia's lips moved to protest. "You have turned yourself into a laughingstock with your clumsiness and there is nothing I can do to spare you from further shame. Thank goodness, you and your father will be leaving for London soon. If we are fortunate, I am certain we can find a few unmarried gentlemen who are not in attendance this afternoon."

As much as she loathed admitting it, the notion of exchanging words with Lady Millicent again held little appeal. She was sure Lord Kempthorn would be also pleased to see the last of her. "You are correct, my lady. I shall return home at once."

"What's this? There is no need for you leave," Gideon said, overhearing her announcement.

Olivia turned around to see Gideon and Lord Kempthorn approaching them. The brothers had identical scowls that might have been humorous if she was not the source of their displeasure. Behind them, she noticed Lady Millicent and several other guests had followed.

Lady Grisdale's eyes widened as she realized Olivia had not told her the entire tale of her fall into the lake. "What have you done, Olivia?"

"And who are you, madam?" Lord Kempthorn asked, staring intently at the older woman.

"Lady Grisdale, my lord," the widow curtsied. "I had the pleasure of being introduced to you last Season. Since our last meeting, Lord Dewick and I have become betrothed, and hopefully you will consider me a valued friend to your family."

The earl raised his eyebrows at the other woman's bold statement. "If you are a friend of the family, then you should know that Miss Lydall is innocent of any wrongdoing, my lady," he said, surprising Olivia by coming to her defense. "I am to blame, I fear."

"You are too generous, brother. In truth, I am the one responsible," Gideon argued. "And we have come to apologize and make amends."

"That is not necessary," Olivia said hastily.

The countess was suspicious, and very little could dissuade her when she had made up her mind about something. "I agree. It is very chivalrous for you to protect Miss Lydall, but we have already decided that it is best for her to return home."

"Nonsense," Gideon said, winking at her. "With a house filled with guests, there is bound to be someone who can loan her a dress. Our mother would insist. Olivia is practically a member of our family."

"Indeed," Lord Kempthorn muttered under his breath, earning him a contemptuous look from his twin.

"Well, she isn't borrowing one of *my* dresses," Lady Millicent said to no one in particular.

It was sweet of Gideon to step in and defend an old friend. However, Lady Grisdale was correct. In a few hours, everyone would know what happened, and the speculation and teasing would only fuel the lady's indignation.

"No, I—" Olivia cleared her throat.

"I just heard from one of the servants that—good heavens, Olivia, *you* were the poor girl who was almost drowned by my boys!" Lady Felstead swept into the hall and wrapped Olivia into a warm embrace as her gaze narrowed on her sons.

Lord Kempthorn and Gideon tried to look innocent.

"It was a silly accident," Olivia murmured against her hostess's generous bosom. "No harm done. I was just leaving for home."

Lady Grisdale stepped forward. "Lord Dewick and I feel it is for the best."

It mattered little that the gentleman was unaware of his daughter's plight.

Lady Felstead stared at the other woman as if she had spoken to her in a foreign language. "You will do no such thing," the marchioness declared to Olivia. "We have trunks *filled* with dresses. There is bound to be something that will fit you."

Without waiting for anyone's approval, she held on to Olivia and led her to the staircase. "You must be chilled. I will have someone send up water for a bath. And tea. You will feel better once you are warm and dry. I will see to it personally."

Olivia glanced over her shoulder, and noticed Gideon was following them. Lord Kempthorn had not moved, but was observing their progress with an unreadable expression. Lady Grisdale, on the other hand, did not disguise her anger at being thwarted by the lady of the house.

"You will need to order more than one bath, Mother," Gideon said cheerfully. "Unless you expect Thorn and I to share Olivia's."

"Share?" The marchioness sputtered at the suggestion, and then she laughed. "That will be the day. You have to watch your step around my sons, Olivia. It appears they have turned into scoundrels."

With a parting glance at the earl, Olivia said, "I will keep that in mind, Lady Felstead."

Chapter Four

Several hours later, the upheaval in the household created by Thorn, Gideon, and Miss Lydall had dissipated as Lord and Lady Felstead's guests drifted away to seek other amusements. A bath and a change of clothes had restored Thorn's spirits. His brother had disappeared into the card room an hour earlier. He had caught a glimpse of Miss Lydall's back as she conversed with his seventeen-year-old sister as he strolled past the drawing room. The blue dress she had borrowed likely belonged to Fiona, although he imagined the maid had struggled with the laces of the lady's stays to fit her generous breasts into the bodice.

Their unexpected plunge into the lake had revealed that Miss Lydall's slender figure had developed some very womanly curves in the last few years. How old was she now? Eighteen? Thorn mentally counted. No, she was six years younger than him and Gideon, and her birthday was approaching. It would be her twentieth. During the years of his brother's absence and his time away from Malster Park, Miss Olivia Lydall had left her childhood behind and had grown into a woman.

He wondered if Gideon had noticed. *Of course he had,* Thorn thought as a soft humorless chuckle escaped his lips. It was just one more thing that he and his brother had in common. Their good looks had always drawn women to them, and some unique adventurous creatures welcomed being overwhelmed by their attentions in and out of bed. There was one widow in particular that he still recalled with a degree of fondness, even though she had cast him and Gideon aside for a duke.

"A man reserves such a look only for a woman."

Thorn's smile broadened as he recognized his cousin's voice. Mathias Rooke, Marquess of Fairlamb, was two years younger, and Thorn remembered Lady Felstead occasionally lamenting when all of them were younger that he had not been a good influence on her twin boys. He turned around and realized Chance—as his cousin was called—was not alone. His beautiful wife, Tempest, and her younger sister, Lady Arabella, had accompanied him.

"Chance, this is a surprise," Thorn said, briefly embracing his cousin and stepping back to greet everyone. "I did not expect to see you and your lovely marchioness until I arrived in London."

Knowing it would annoy his cousin, he clasped the marchioness's hand and pulled her into an affectionate embrace. He grinned unrepentantly over Tempest's shoulder when Chance glowered at him.

"Release my wife, Kempthorn," Chance said, placing his hands around his wife's waist and separating her from his cousin. "If you want a lady to cuddle in your arms, seek out your own bride."

Thorn winked at the twenty-year-old Lady Arabella, causing her to blush. To include her, he said, "And this is the gratitude I receive for helping him kidnap and elope with his lady."

The blonde woman's hazel eyes sparkled with amusement. "You and your friends did make dashing highwaymen."

Chance's courtship of Lady Tempest Brant had been conducted in secret. The marquess's father, the Duke of

Blackbern, and Lady Tempest's father, the Marquess of Norgrave, had severed their close friendship when they were young men, and the animosity between the two gentlemen had divided the *ton*. For years, everyone had speculated on what had caused the two men to come to blows. Most assumed the duke's wife was the reason for their bitter rivalry because she had married the Duke of Blackbern shortly after the two gentlemen had parted ways. However, the Rookes and the Brants were determined to keep their secrets, and for several decades the families kept their distance from each other until Chance met Lady Tempest.

The attraction between the couple had been immediate and all-consuming. Ignoring all advice, Chance had pursued her, and when her family had tried to separate them his cousin had asked Thorn and a few friends to kidnap the lady so the young lovers could marry. Neither the Rookes nor the Brants were happy about the marriage, and Lord Norgrave tried to trick Chance into annulling the marriage. It was possible the two families would never put aside their animosity for the sake of their children. However, his cousin and his wife were determined not to allow their families to ruin their happiness.

Thorn was surprised to see Lady Arabella in the company of her sister and her husband. Attending the Felstead fete was akin to consorting with the enemy. He had heard that Lord and Lady Norgrave had kept the younger sister away from Tempest in the initial months of her marriage to Chance.

"Unfortunately, my days as a highwayman were short-lived. I have vowed to be almost respectable this season," he drily announced.

Chance, Tempest, and her sister laughed at his outrageous lie.

"I wager it is difficult vow to keep, with your brother's return," Chance said.

Thorn shrugged. In an attempt to change the subject, he looked to Tempest for help. "My dear cousin, have you had the opportunity to introduce your sister to the rest of the family?"

The marchioness's hazel-colored eyes narrowed slightly as if she sensed his motive behind the innocent question. "Not everyone. Arabella was looking forward to meeting your brother."

"Tempest!" the young woman hissed and glared, embarrassed that her sister had called attention to her curiosity.

The marchioness leaned closer. "Arabella cannot believe you have an identical twin. She has never met one before, you know."

Slightly puzzled by her comment, Thorn asked, "A brother?"

He was acquainted with Tempest and Lady Arabella's older brother, Oliver Brant, Earl of Marcroft. Since he was related to the Rookes, none of the encounters were particularly pleasant.

Lady Fairlamb giggled, and there was a guileless charm about her that he thought was admirable. Chance must have noted his silent appreciation, because he was frowning at him again.

"Don't be a goose," she teased. "My sister had never met identical twins. I've already warned her that it is impossible to tell the difference between you and Mr. Netherwood."

Perhaps it was wicked of him, but he impulsively clasped Lady Arabella's hand and raised it to his lips. "It will be up to you to discern our differences."

"Thorn," Chance growled in warning as his sister-in-law's face turned a delightful pink hue.

"I-I look forward to it, Lord Kempthorn," Lady Arabella stammered.

"Come along, Arabella," Tempest said, giving him a

measured look. "If our dear Thorn plies any more charm, you will need my silver vinaigrette."

Thorn watched as the two ladies walked away. He glanced at Chance and noticed he was shaking his head.

"Norgrave will castrate you if he learns that you have flirted with Arabella."

"You appear to have survived his wrath," Thorn said, deliberately dropping his gaze to the front of his dark brown breeches. "Unless there is something you will to confess."

"Thorn."

"Should I extend my sympathies to your wife?" he said, lowering his voice with mocking sympathy. "The poor lady. She is too young to be married to a gentleman who has lost his—"

"Enough," Chance growled, but his lips twitched as he tried not to laugh.

Thorn placed his arm around his cousin and led him past the music room and toward the stairs. "In the spirit of keeping these private matters in the family, perhaps I should offer my services to your lady."

"Services?" Chance lowered his voice when a gentleman and his two female companions glanced in their direction. "Keep baiting me, and Norgrave will be the least of your concerns. I will geld you myself."

His cousin used his palm to lightly clout him on the side of the head. Thorn laughed and released Chance as they stood on the second-floor gallery and watched the activity below.

"About Arabella," Chance began.

"You have nothing to fret about, my friend. My affection for Arabella is quite brotherly since she is a new member of our family," Thorn said, though he silently conceded there was a time or two when his thoughts had not been so innocent. "Besides, you have enough problems with Norgrave. I would not wish to become one of them."

The notion of having that scarred old blackguard for a father-in-law was enough to make a man contemplate celibacy.

His expression must have given Chance a hint to Thorn's inner thoughts or perhaps his cousin knew him too well.

"I have no regrets," the marquess softly confessed as he watched three children chasing each other down below.

Thorn turned his head and studied Chance's profile. "Are you referring to your marriage to Tempest?" He braced his forearms on the rosewood balustrade.

His cousin nodded, gripping the wooden handrail. "It has been difficult for her, and I am not just speaking of Lord and Lady Norgrave."

Chance did not elaborate on his cryptic comment, nor was any explanation required. Thorn's mother was close to the Duchess of Blackbern. During his visits home, he had overhead snippets of conversations between his mother and father as they discussed family news. While the duke and duchess had publically accepted their son's marriage to Tempest, in private there was tension between the two couples. The fact that the Duke and the Duchess of Blackbern were not attending the Felstead fete was quite revealing.

His parents loved Chance as if he were their own son. His mother and father were distressed by the strife within the family and had done their best to make certain Tempest had felt welcome.

"Your mother and father need more time," Thorn advised. "Blackbern's feud with Norgrave is older than you. They have accepted your marriage publicly. Take that olive branch and give them the time they need to make peace with the past."

The low derisive snort was unexpected and very unlike

the man who faced life with humor and courage. "Some things cannot be forgiven, Thorn."

If Chance had learned more about what had caused the bitter feud between the Rookes and the Brants, he had decided not to share the details with his friends. He wondered what secrets his cousin had learned when he and Tempest had announced their marriage to the Rookes and the Brants.

"Who is with your brother?"

At first, Thorn thought Chance had mentioned Gideon to distract him from pressing him for answers the other man was obviously unwilling to give. He glanced down at the front hall below, and his gaze searched through the various groups of guests until he saw Miss Lydall. When had she left the drawing room? She must have slipped by him when he had been distracted by Chance, Tempest, and her sister.

Not that he was keeping his eye on her.

And if he had been following her movements, it was only out of concern for the chit. Lady Grisdale had dealt with Miss Lydall harshly, which seemed unfair since he and Gideon were to blame for their unplanned swim in the lake. His association with the countess was limited, but his impression of the lady was not favorable. His mother might have overruled the other woman's decree to send Miss Lydall home like an errant child, but he predicted the woman had unfinished business with Lord Dewick's daughter.

"I do not see him," Thorn replied, sounding distracted as he watched Miss Lydall.

Chance stepped to the left and beckoned him to follow. "The view is better over here. I do not recognize the young lady."

Thorn obliged his cousin by changing his view, and immediately realized he had solved the mystery of his brother's companion.

"Do you see him?" At Thorn's terse nod, Chance added,

"The lady in the blue dress is unfamiliar to me, but from here it looks like Gideon is eager to get to know her."

If they had been discussing anyone else, Thorn would have chuckled at Chance's lewd observation. But realizing that Gideon was attempting to slip away with Miss Lydall again was a troubling development.

"He already knows her. You are acquainted with the lady as well."

Chance lifted a brow at the news. "The devil you say. I thought I knew all of the pretty misses in the parish."

"Not anymore," Thorn replied. "Lest you forget, you are a married gent now."

His cousin dismissed the teasing reminder with a wave of his hand. "I am not speaking in the biblical sense, you arse. I have spent enough summers at Malster Park that I am acquainted with most of your neighbors. Who is the chit your brother is flirting with?"

"Miss Lydall," he replied, his eyes narrowing as Gideon murmured something in the lady's ear to make her laugh. "She is Lord Dewick's daughter."

"Damn me, I cannot recall meeting her," Chance said, leaning forward as if a few extra inches would make the difference.

"Last spring, you were too distracted pursuing your future bride to pay attention to other ladies," he replied wryly, recalling what a lovesick fool his cousin had been and the times he had been a willing accomplice in the other man's schemes. "Though you are likely to remember the slip of a girl who used to chase after us."

Chance considered the small hint Thorn had given him for a minute. His blue-gray eyes widened in incredulity. "Good god, Miss Lydall is that grubby little ragamuffin who used climb trees and spit on us." He stared at the lady flirting with Gideon and tried to reconcile her with the child who had intruded on their adventures. "Someone had come up with a nickname for her. What was it?"

Thorn tensed. "Olive," he said finally.

"That was it. Olive. Oily Olive," Chance replied cheerfully. "A positively dreadful nickname for a girl. Children can be so cruel."

He glanced away from his cousin. "They can be. Do I need to remind you that Gideon was always protective of the chit, so it would be unwise of you to remind Miss Lydall of her unpleasant past?"

"Have you mistaken me for that brute, Marcroft?" Chance grimaced as his thoughts drifted to his brother-in-law. "I have no intention of doing anything other than procuring an introduction from your mother. Besides, Gideon used to be quite handy with his fists when provoked."

"Still is," Thorn said, his hand absently rubbing his jaw.

After years of separation, he and Gideon had displayed their affection for each other within the first hour of their reunion by pounding on each other until both of them were panting and bruised.

When Chance did not reply, Thorn turned his head and noticed the other man's speculative look as he observed the flirtatious discourse between Gideon and Miss Lydall. "Do you think she is the one?"

Thorn's eyebrows lifted at the question. "The reason why Gideon had the sudden urge to seek his fortune?" The muscles in his jaw tightened. He was reluctant to admit that he had asked himself the same question. "I do not know. Maybe. Gideon refused to discuss it with me."

"Or any of us," Chance said. "Rainbault, St. Lyon, and I all approached him before he departed London."

Over the years, he had often wondered about the secrets his brother and Miss Lydall had shared. Thorn had sensed that the lady knew more about Gideon's departure even though she had denied it when he had been angry enough to confront her. Nor had it not stopped him from resenting her.

He and Chance watched as Gideon seized Miss Lydall's hand and tugged her toward the open door behind him. She shook her head, ignoring his playful cajoling, but his brother was determined to have his way. He circled around his quarry and placed his arm around her waist. The lady was still shaking her head and arguing with Gideon as he led her away.

"In those last days before his departure, your brother seemed embittered. It was a natural assumption to conclude that a lady was involved. His fights with you, and his damn secrecy had Rainbault and St. Lyon speculating that Gideon had fallen in love with another man's wife," Chance said. His brooding expression revealed that Thorn was not the only one who had been hurt and baffled by Gideon's decision. "If Miss Lydall was the reason for your brother's rash behavior, it appears he has forgiven her."

"It certainly appears so," Thorn replied. "Though, there is a flaw in St. Lyon and Rainbault's theory. Miss Lydall is unmarried and is not likely to be any man's mistress."

"Then perhaps your brother didn't believe he was worthy of the lady's esteem and sought to earn her heart?" his cousin suggested.

Was Gideon planning to seduce Miss Lydall? It was too disastrous to contemplate.

Thorn punched Chance in the arm and was pleased to see the other man wince.

"What the hell did I do?"

"Marriage has softened your head," Thorn said, walking behind him as he headed for the stairs.

The task would require subtlety, but he intended to separate Gideon from Miss Lydall's influence.

Chapter Five

"Gideon, where are we heading?" Olivia asked breathlessly as the he led her through a short maze of narrow passageways used by the Felstead servants. The walls were unadorned and the color of old parchment, but the well-trodden wooden floors smelled as if they had been recently scrubbed.

"Such impatience," Gideon teased over his shoulder. "Have you grown too old for surprises?"

"Not at all. However, I believe I have gotten into enough trouble for one day, and I have you and your brother to thank for it."

In truth, she was not particularly cross with either gentleman. It was not their fault Lady Grisdale was determined to see all of Olivia's faults and none of her virtues.

"Has the countess been treating you poorly?" he asked, bringing them to the end of a corridor that had two doors. Gideon chose the one on the right.

"It depends on how you define poorly, I suppose," she said, resigned that Gideon was not planning to spoil his surprise. "Lady Grisdale feels my father has been neglectful in my education."

Gideon slowed and came to a halt. "That is a bit harsh. I seem to recall meeting several of your governesses."

She grinned at him. "Well, I did have ten of them." She held up her hands and counted them off with her fingers.

"Two abandoned their posts because they felt too isolated, four of them declared I was too willful and wearing on their nerves and all quit within a few months, three were seduced by my father so he was forced to dismiss them, and I believe it was you who bedded the last of the lot."

Gideon shut his eyes and sagged against the wall. "You know about that?"

"The poor creature cried on my shoulder when she heard you had abandoned her for London and a new mistress." She crossed her arms and frowned at him. "She claimed to be half in love with you."

"Christ, you were a child when I"—he gestured vaguely as he struggled not to be indelicate—"I have no words."

Olivia laughed. "I was twelve years old, so that would mean that you and your brother were breaking hearts at the ripe old age of eighteen years old."

He groaned. "I feel as if I owe you an apology, my dear."

"Miss Hill—that was her name in case you have forgotten." She grinned when he shook his head and muttered something about her impertinence. "She was an emotional creature and prone to melancholy. I doubt she would have lasted more than a year. Besides, if it is any consolation, I suspect she sought comfort in one of my brothers' beds," she said blithely. "I could never quite figure out which one, though it is not really important. Though it was reason enough for my father to sack her."

Gideon covered his eyes with his hand and rubbed his temples with his thumb and finger. "You were too young to be privy to such details."

"What do you expect from a poor motherless girl raised by her father and two brothers?" she said cheekily. Olivia tilted her head. "This door leads to the conservatory, does it not?"

Gideon grinned down at her. "It does."

Olivia stilled. "What did you find for me?"

He placed his hand against the small of her back and gestured toward the door. "You will have to come see for yourself," he said enigmatically.

Olivia did not need a second invitation. She opened the door and entered the Felsteads' conservatory. The hidden entrance was not designed to impress the guests. The walls were aligned with tools for gardening and several long wooden tables. A wall of shelves separated the work area from the plants and trees Lady Felstead tended.

"Where is it?" she asked, eager to see what Gideon had discovered during his travels.

"Near the fountain," he replied, his expression indulgent.

Her eyes gleaming with excitement, she grasped the front of her skirt and hurried to the southeast section of the conservatory. She slowed and clasped her hands together when she saw it.

Gideon came up behind her as she knelt down to admire her gift.

"The fellow who procured it for me called it a coontie," he said.

It certainly wasn't the handsomest plant in the Felsteads' conservatory. The rough woody cycad had a dull reddish hue with a hint of green leaves sprouting at the top.

"I would have sent it to your house months ago, but I thought it had perished during the journey when it lost all of its leaves. Mother suggested it needed some time to recover."

Her hand lightly stroked the fragile leaves. "You brought me a *Zamia pumila*. Where did you find it?"

He lifted his shoulder in a careless shrug. "The West Indies. Do you like it?"

"Like it?" She straightened and faced him. "I absolutely adore it!"

Impulsively, Olivia launched herself into his arms.

Gideon grunted as he caught and embraced her. "So you

are pleased? I know little about plants," he confessed. "Nevertheless, this one had caught my eye. It was so odd-looking, I knew you would love it."

"I do," she assured him. She leaned up and kissed him several times on the chin, making him laugh. "You are so kind and wonderful. Oh, I have truly missed you, Gideon!"

"I missed you, too, Olivia." He stared down at her and gave her a lopsided smile. "Seeing you again makes me wish that I had returned home sooner."

Her earlier enthusiasm dimmed as she savored the firmness and strength of his upper arms. "Why did you—"

The sound of someone clearing his throat startled the couple.

Olivia released her hold and swiftly stepped away from Gideon, and he mirrored her actions. Over his shoulder, she saw Lord Kempthorn standing six feet away. His blank expression gave her no indication to his thoughts, but she sensed his disapproval. The earl's gaze touched briefly on her face before it dropped to the front of her dress. Her cheeks heated as he noted how the fabric stretched tightly over her breasts and then moved to the light dusting of dirt on the skirt.

"Thorn," Gideon said casually.

"Am I interrupting something?" Lord Kempthorn asked.

Olivia bent down and brushed away the dirt. "Not at all," she said, her movements feeling stiff and awkward under the earl's cool perusal.

"Olivia was admiring her gift," Gideon said, oblivious to the increasing tension between her and the earl. "Would you like to see it?"

"I have seen enough," Lord Kempthorn quipped. "Before you embarrass the lady further, perhaps we should escort Miss Lydall back to the drawing room."

Olivia straightened and pasted a cheerful expression on her face as she met the earl's stern gaze. "A very kind offer, Lord Kempthorn, but I can find my way back on my own." She turned her head, and the rigidity in her lips softened as she stared at Gideon. "Thank you for the plant. May I leave it here until I can arrange for one of my father's servants to collect it for me?"

"Of course, my dear," Gideon replied. "Run along. We will see each other before I leave."

"Leave?" The mild curiosity in his brother's voice held a note of censure.

Olivia acknowledged Gideon by nodding. The tension she had sensed from Lord Kempthorn had abruptly shifted from her to his twin. If the two men intended to argue, she had no interest witnessing it.

She curtsied and murmured, "My lords." She could feel the gazes of the two brothers on her as she strolled out of the conservatory through the main entrance.

The second Thorn was convinced Miss Lydall was out of earshot, he confronted his brother. "What's this foolishness about leaving?"

Gideon's handsome features were pensive as he stared off in the direction of Miss Lydall's departure. "Do you do it deliberately?"

Frustration flashed in Thorn's dark green eyes. "You will have to be more specific."

"Very few things manage to upset Olivia. However, you manage to send her scurrying with that disapproving scowl on your kisser." Gideon turned, his gaze ablaze with banked fury. "Have you been treating her poorly since I left?"

"Has she come to you with a complaint?" Anger stirred in his breast at the implication. Never in his life had he mistreated a woman, and his brother knew it.

"No," he admitted with some reluctance.

"Then how I deal with Miss Lydall is not your concern," he countered, unwilling to let his brother goad him into a fight.

"When did you start calling her Miss Lydall?" Gideon asked. "She is a neighbor and friend to our family. We played together as children. She was always Olivia to both of us, and now you behave as if she was a stranger."

"You speak of the days when we were boys." Thorn glanced away from Gideon's doubting expression. "Once we were old enough to be sent away to boarding school, our days at Malster Park could be counted in months. In recent years, my visits have become less frequent. However, when I do join our mother and father, I rarely have the time or inclination to call on every neighbor. Besides, you were always her favorite. I barely spoke to her even when we were boys."

Gideon rubbed his jaw. "Still jealous that she favored me over you, are you?"

"Not in the slightest," Thorn scoffed. "The annoying baggage was too cheeky for her own good, and she had a nasty habit of getting into mischief. You were too indulgent with her then, and it appears nothing has changed. Every time I have sought you out this day, Miss Lydall had been clinging to you like a bloody shadow."

Gideon's green eyes narrowed, and Thorn braced for the storm he saw gathering in his brother's gaze. Instead of rushing to Miss Lydall's defense, he exhaled slowly and shook his head. "Aye, and it took some effort to coax her onto that sailboat earlier because the brave girl I knew has grown into a frightfully skittish miss. Not that I minded the task. If you were paying attention in my absence, you would have noticed Miss Olivia Lydall has grown into quite a ravishing beauty. It's a blessing you never called on her and her father. You might have had a chance to steal her away from me."

The not-so-subtle taunt annoyed Thorn. He had always prided himself in possessing a keen eye for the bold and exotic when it came to women. Unlike their friends St. Lyon and Rainbault—and Chance, before he had married Lady Tempest—Thorn was in command of his passions and carnal appetites. His affairs were discreet and satisfying. There were no tearful recriminations from his lovers when their affair ended because he never made promises that he could not keep.

He avoided emotional, willful females who were ruled by their heart rather than their heads. Miss Lydall was such a creature, and he had done his best to avoid the charming disorder that surrounded her.

"I highly doubt it," Thorn said, glancing at the odd-looking plant his brother had given Miss Lydall with a slight sneer on his lips. It was ugly and not worth the enthusiasm and chaste kisses she had pressed against Gideon's chin. The women *he* courted and bedded would have spurned such an unappealing gift. "I do not covet the lady."

"I would be relieved if I believed you." Gideon walked toward the large double doors.

His brother was wrong. Thorn was not attracted to Miss Lydall. He trailed after Gideon. "You are deliberately trying to provoke me."

"Perhaps," his twin drawled. "However, I am still calling you a liar."

It wasn't until he and Gideon had returned to the house that Thorn remembered that his brother had not explained why he had told Miss Lydall that he was leaving.

Chapter Six

"You have been behaving oddly all evening." Chance pulled Thorn aside after the evening meal. "You are beginning to worry me."

The dining room was too small to accommodate all of Lord and Lady Felstead's guests, so long tables had been set up in the ballroom. To manage the overflow, several tents had been converted to serve anyone who preferred to eat outdoors with their family.

"There is nothing to worry about."

Thorn had expected to see his brother to join him at the main table, where he intended to finish their conversation. Instead, Gideon had secured a seat at the same table as Miss Lydall. Although they were not sitting together, Thorn observed on more than one occasion the silent exchanges between the couple.

"This is about Gideon," his cousin said, eyes shadowed with concern. "I assume your conversation with your brother did not have a productive outcome."

Thorn scratched at his left eyebrow to conceal his annoyance. "He is avoiding me," he confessed, unwilling to let even Chance see the depth of his hurt. "And he is up to something, and it involves Miss Lydall. Nothing good can come of it."

"So do something about it," Chance encouraged.

"What do you suggest?"

"Speak with Miss Lydall," the marquess said. Both gentlemen had noticed the lady had left the ballroom a few minutes earlier to avoid conversing with Lady Grisdale. "Perhaps she can give you the answers you seek about Gideon."

It did not sit well with him that his twin was sharing secrets with Miss Lydall. Thorn wondered what other mischief his brother was engaging in with the chit. "The lady is not fond of me."

"When have you not charmed a lady into revealing her—uh—secrets?" Chance asked, grinning at him. "It is obvious to me that Miss Lydall likes your brother well enough. Your handsome visage should soften her disposition."

"You are not helping, Chance."

"If the lady dislikes you, then approach her as Gideon," the other man said carelessly.

"You speak of a child's game," Thorn said, scoffing at the idea. "Gideon and I have not tried to fool anyone since we were boys."

"Is that what you tell your sweet mother?" Chance slapped him on the shoulder as he laughed heartily. "What a bouncer! I recall a particular spring fair where Gideon, Rainbault, St. Lyon, and I were besotted with a pretty redheaded wench. Christ, how old were we? Fifteen or sixteen?"

Thorn's lips quirked. "Too young to have any sense."

"Ah, so you do remember how Gideon panicked when the wench invited him to escort her about the fair." Chance shook his head in dismay. "You would have thought he had learned a thing or two from St. Lyon and Rainbault when it came to handling females, but your brother turned an unflattering shade of green."

"You and the others had not set your sights on a shy innocent miss," Thorn said, who had been flirting with a comely brunette when his brother and their friends had run off to chase after the redhead. By the time he had caught up to his companions, Chance, St. Lyon, and Rainbault had ganged up on his brother for politely rejecting the woman. "Gideon was unaccustomed to a brazen female."

"Neither were you," his cousin said pointedly.

No, he had not been, but after the brunette had not encouraged his advances, his pride needed a little soothing. If Gideon had coveted the redheaded wench, Thorn would not have been so eager to step into his brother's shoes.

"It would have been rude to abandon Miss Jacobs to the rogues and rascals attending the fair," Thorn said, looking back on that afternoon with a degree of gratitude and fondness. "I was only doing my brotherly duty."

"Duty, my arse!" Chance punched Thorn's upper arm. "We spent half the night searching for you when you disappeared from the fair."

"Miss Jacobs was five years older and she possessed knowledge of the carnal arts that left me in a befuddled state for weeks." Thorn grinned when his cousin brought his hand to his face and groaned. "I didn't forget to thank all of you properly, did I?"

"No," Chance replied, his hand falling to his side. "St. Lyon still occasionally grumbles about your good fortune. Oh, and let us not forget that bit of mischief with Lady Spicer."

"Ah, yes, Lady Spicer," he drawled. "A delightful woman. She wasn't even angry when she figured out there was two of us."

"You and Gideon never did tell us if you succeeded in bedding the young widow."

"A gentleman doesn't speak his private affairs," Thorn said, striving for a little dignity. Egad, his cousin was correct. He and Gideon switched places when it suited their purposes. Although they had vowed never to discuss the details with anyone, Lady Spicer had developed a taste for multiple lovers, and he and Gideon had shared the lady's bed for several months. "Fine, you have proven your original point. Gideon and I did not leave our games behind in childhood."

"So let's tell Gideon—"

Thorn scowled at his cousin. "We tell Gideon nothing. In fact, I may need you and your wife to distract my brother while I speak with Miss Lydall."

Lady Fairlamb must have overheard part of Thorn's statement as she strolled up to her husband's side. With a quizzical look, she said, "I assume Lord Felstead taking charge of the fireworks isn't adventurous enough for the two of you. What can I do to help?"

Lady Felstead would have accused her of hiding.

Olivia silently disagreed as she strolled down the torch-lit gravel path that led to the marchioness's Greek folly. Even after her humiliating stumble into the lake with the Netherwood twins, she had returned to the gathering in a borrowed dress that did not quite fit her while she ignored the disapproving glances Lady Grisdale cast in her direction. Later, when everyone had adjourned to the ballroom for supper, her father—much to his credit—laughed when she recounted to him her unexpected dunking in the lake. Gideon had been seated within earshot, so he had embellished the tale for their rapt audience until her father's hand shook so much he spilled his wine.

She had a few words for Gideon for his bit of mischief.

The gentleman had a gift for storytelling. His additions had made the incident more humorous than embarrassing while casting her in a favorable light. When everyone at the table laughed, there was no malice or blame.

Olivia wondered if Lord Kempthorn would have approved of his brother's retelling?

She had forgotten how exciting Malster Park could be when Lord and Lady Felstead's sons were in residence. It was a pity occasions such as this were rare these days.

Humming along to the song the orchestra was playing in the distance, she savored the coolness of the night air, the steady rhythm of her borrowed shoes on the gravel, and the earthy scents of the surrounding woodlands.

Much to her relief, no one else had thought to walk to the folly. Olivia walked up the three steps and wrapped her arms around one of the marble columns. Keeping the palm of her hand against the cool surface, she circled around it and then moved to the next one. Most of Lady Felstead's guests were too stuffed from their evening meal to wander farther than the lake, where the orchestra played on the large wooden platform while the servants prepared with the assistance of Lord Felstead to set off the fireworks. The trees obscured most of her view of the lake, but she could sit and enjoy the music and fireworks.

Olivia was content to be alone. The quiet gave her time to gather her thoughts. She had had enough excitement for one day.

A soft, almost musical whistle floated on the night's air, the source coming from the shadowed path. The notes heralding the arrival of one of the other guests. Of someone who knew her habits.

"Who is it?"

The soft footfalls abruptly halted as if she had surprised someone by announcing her presence. The light from the nearby torches and the soft glow of the lanterns illuminating the folly prevented her from seeing too deeply into the shadows.

Her pulse quickened in anticipation to learn the identity of the man approaching the folly. She knew Malster Park as well as her father's lands. She was acquainted with most of the Felsteads' guests, but if she encountered an amorous drunken fellow, she was confident that she could slip away before he became a nuisance.

"What are you doing out here alone, Olivia?" a voice demanded, the barest trace of anger hardening it.

She grinned down as the familiar face emerged out of the surrounding darkness. "Gideon! You gave me such a fright," she said, meeting him at the bottom of the steps.

"And I can see it taught you nothing," he growled, taking her hand and pressing a kiss to her fingers. The tenderness of the action was an intriguing contrast to his tone. "You are too old to be running about at all hours."

Hands still clasped, she led him up the three steps so he could appreciate their view. "When Lord and Lady Felstead invite the entire parish to Malster Park, everyone is running about at all hours. I am perfectly safe. What are you doing here? I thought you would be sitting with your family near the lake."

"I could ask you the same question."

Lord and Lady Felstead had illuminated the garden walkways and connecting paths with torches. Paper lamps glowed from every tree limb, adding warmth to the darkness. Gideon sat down beside her and leaned against one of the marble columns.

Olivia shrugged. "This seemed a good spot as any to watch the fireworks."

She adjusted the shawl on her shoulders to conceal the front of her borrowed dress. The marchioness's daughter was smaller in the chest, and Olivia worried the top of the bodice was showing too much flesh. When she had expressed her concerns to Lady Felstead, the older woman had assured her that she looked quite lovely. However, Lady Grisdale's disapproving scowl at supper and the admiring glances she had noticed from several gentlemen this evening proved that her worries were not unfounded.

Gideon scratched his jaw and glanced in the direction of the lake. "There are better views," he said, politely not mentioning the trees that closed in around the folly. "And you are missing the revelry."

She turned slightly so she could admire his profile. Gideon and his brother were breathtakingly handsome. It was no hardship to stare at the gentleman seated close to her. "How did you know where to find me?"

He braced his elbows on the tops of his thighs. "When I could not find you near the lake, I thought I might find you here."

Olivia laughed. "Well, after our little accident, it seemed prudent to stay away from the water."

Gideon cocked his head and gave her a rueful grin. "Angling for another apology, Olivia?"

"Not at all," she said, circling the column as if it were a dance partner. "I have already forgiven you."

"And my brother?"

The curious note in his inflection made her pause and stare at him. "Of course. I have no quarrel with Lord Kempthorn."

"Are you certain? I sensed some tension between you and him when he found us together," he said, watching her gracefully move between the marble columns.

Her full lips formed a contemplative pout as she considered her words. "Well, he did catch us in a slightly compromising position. Knowing your stiff-necked twin, he was likely offended by our familiarity."

"Is that how you see him?" Gideon said, humor glimmering in his eyes. "Stiff-necked?"

"Pompous could apply too. Though to be fair, I prefer not to gain his attention. I am not one of your brother's favorite people." She stilled and tilted her head as she concentrated on the music playing in the distance. "I adore this Scottish reel."

"What?" He looked slightly baffled when she held out her hand.

"I cannot dance alone, Mr. Netherwood," she said, leaning down to take his hand.

"I have not danced in years," Gideon protested.

"Then you have not been living," she answered, pulling him to his feet.

Gideon shook his head, but did not try to ruin her merriment. Olivia was practically bouncing on her heels as they descended the steps and made their way onto the gravel path. She clasped both of his hands, inclined her head, and curtsied.

"We are missing a few people for our reel."

Gideon bowed his head. "There are plenty of people near the lake."

Olivia rolled her eyes as they circled clockwise twice around and then reversed directions. Gideon rested his hand on the small of her back as she extended her right arm outward as if she were taking part in a dance position that would have included other ladies. She and Gideon moved in step to the energetic tune. Then they reversed direction.

"Do you know how ridiculous we look?" he asked, resigned that he could not discourage her.

Olivia released his hand and turned toward him. She grabbed the front of her skirt and gave him a flash of her ankles as she hopped from side to side, alternating her feet. "Why? Because we are dancing under the stars and moonlight?"

It pleased her that Gideon had not missed a single step.

"One of many reasons," he teased as he gripped her elbow and tugged her closer for a quick turn.

Olivia felt her breath catch in her throat as their gazes

locked as he whirled them about four times. The air warmed and her chest grew tight. This was Gideon, of all people. She would never live it down if she fainted at his feet. To clear her head, she danced away, her hand positions and feet moving as if in step with other dancers.

"Olivia, you do realize you are dancing alone?" Gideon said. His hands were planted on his narrow hips as he watched her with a hooded gaze.

"Am I?" was her cheeky reply, but she dutifully danced her way back to his side. "I had not noticed."

She had intended to dance around him, but he caught her elbow and clasped her other hand before she could break away. Gideon turned them in a tight circle.

"You never change," he said with a laugh. "I have missed your mad, wild ways, Olivia."

"Have you?" Her right brow arched. "Perhaps the next time you plan an adventure, you will invite me along."

Gideon stared down at her with a thoughtful, too serious expression on his face. "Maybe I shall."

Before she could reply, several large popping sounds caught her attention. "Oh look, the fireworks have begun," she said, moving away from him as she stared above the trees. "Lovely."

"Aye."

Olivia glanced over at him and was startled to see that he was staring at her instead of the sky. Flustered, she shifted her gaze upward. "Can you see the fireworks from there?"

The orchestra had moved on to another musical composition that might have been played specifically for the fireworks, but the timing was off. Still, it was a beautiful piece that added to the festive mood.

"Come along. We will have a higher perch if we stand at the edge of the portico," Gideon said, grabbing her hand and tugging her back to the folly.

Olivia happily indulged him. If she had been alone, she would have selected the same spot. She was surprised how easily she and Gideon had slipped into their old friendship, even though years apart should have made them strangers.

"Shared history, I suppose," she muttered under her breath.

"What?" Gideon halted at the edge and tucked her into his side. His hand touched the small of her back as if he was prepared to catch her if she was clumsy enough to fall.

His lack of faith in her sense of balance was embarrassing, but it was a sweet gesture.

"It's nothing," she said, staring above the line of trees. Distant cheers and crackling noises indicated she and Gideon were missing some of the spectacular display illuminating the night sky. "I guess this wasn't the most ideal location to watch the fireworks."

"I agree."

She winced at his bluntness. "Well, I do not recall inviting you to join me."

"Truly?" Gideon waited until she looked at him. "I could have sworn that we had plans to meet again."

Olivia placed her hand on the column to steady her stance. "What are you talking about? A *clandestine* meeting?" She fluttered her eyelashes at him. "Why Mr. Netherwood, I do not believe my father would approve of your conduct."

"Your father would never know," Gideon said, his hand moving from the small of her back to her left hip. "You do understand what it means to meet in secret."

"I do, you clodpole," she said sweetly. "Nevertheless, there is no reason for us to keep our visits a secret. Unless you are worried that your brother will not approve."

He frowned. "My brother has no influence over me."

Olivia snorted indelicately. "He is your twin. If his

opinion did not matter so much, you would not chafe against the restraints you feel he has imposed on you."

"You have no notion of what you are talking about," he said through clenched teeth.

"Clearly I have overstepped my bounds," she said, unapologetic and undaunted by his anger. "There." She pointed at the sky. "Did you see it?"

"You speak of old rivalries," Gideon continued, not paying attention to the fireworks. "What do you know of my relationship with my brother? It has been years since we have lived in the same household."

"The moment you and Lord Kempthorn were in spitting distance of each other, I ended up in the lake," she countered. His open-mouthed expression had her swallowing her annoyance. "So you must forgive me if I do not wish to be placed in the middle again. I doubt your sister has another clean dress that will almost fit me properly."

Gideon noted the uncomfortable way she had pinched the edges of the shawl together with her fist. When they had been dancing together, she had forgotten about the tight bodice or the indecent amount of flesh revealed. Had he noticed? He had not mentioned it, but that did not mean he had not looked.

"Are you cold?"

The change of subject threw her off-balance. "Cold? Uh, I—no."

"Here. Allow me," Gideon said, gently prying her fingers from the shawl. "If you keep tugging on the shawl, you'll end up strangling yourself."

He brushed her hand aside and adjusted the edges so he could see a small portion of her bodice. "Better?"

Olivia nodded, acutely aware of the warmth from his hands, of the light tingles his touch created as his knuckles grazed her skin. She swallowed to ease the dryness in her throat. "We are missing the fireworks."

"Are we?" he softly asked. "Look at me, Olivia."

Butterflies battered the walls of her stomach as she stared at his hands. No, that was not helpful at all. She shut her eyes. Unable to explain her reluctance, she shook her head. She heard several explosions overhead. Fireworks.

"You are missing—"

Olivia dutifully tilted her chin upward and opened her eyes. Without speaking, Gideon blocked her view of the sky as his mouth descended on hers. Her body started at the first brush of his warm lips. It was a revelation. The awareness. Her body came alive as his lips pressed against hers. The heat. It was not just her cheeks that burned. She felt like she had taken her first sip of liquid fire. It flowed over her tongue and down her throat and spread through her entire body. She leaned into him, wishing for—what? Olivia was uncertain of what she was yearning for.

Gideon groaned against her mouth, and that seemed to break the enthrallment.

She took a step backward and he caught her to him. Otherwise she would have fallen off the portico. She tried to push him away.

"What is this? What are you doing?" she demanded, feeling off-balanced and slightly betrayed.

"It's called a kiss," he said, sounding amused.

"I know what a kiss is," she hissed, pulling away from him. "That was not my first kiss."

"I should hope not," he teased. "You are almost twenty years old. You are too young to forget your first kiss."

Damn him. He would pick this moment to remind her that she had shared her first kiss with him. It had taken place the year Gideon had seduced her final governess. He and his brother were leaving Malster Park the next day for London. Olivia had not expected to see him again until autumn. He had come to bid her farewell. To this day, she did not know what possessed him to kiss her.

Nor had he mentioned it until now.

She took a fortifying breath. "Not all kisses are memorable, Mr. Netherwood."

"Is that a dare, Miss Lydall?"

The ice in his voice reminded her of Lord Kempthorn. She already felt muddled by Gideon's kiss. "Not in the slightest. Once is enough."

"You mean twice, my dear lady."

The look she sent his way was one of utter loathing. She pushed him, and this time he moved out of her way.

"Where are you going?"

"Back to the main house," she said over her shoulder. "You are not invited to join me."

"Was it something I said?" he said, causing her shoulders to stiffen at his mocking tone.

Olivia ignored him and kept her eyes focused on the dimly lit gravel path as she increased the distance between her and Gideon. Her hearing felt muffled, but if she concentrated, she could hear the crackling and hiss of the fireworks and the cheers from the crowd gathered around the lake.

Olivia tried not to think about Gideon's kiss. Her mouth tingled and burned. She had almost forgotten about their first awkward kiss, and she could not fathom why he had decided to kiss her again. It was the tight bodice, she thought as she brooded, recalling the undisguised heat she had glimpsed in his eyes.

The borrowed dress had brought her nothing but trouble.

Olivia had been too angry to notice the man who stood in the shadows. Gideon stared at her departing figure, and waited until he no longer heard her footfalls. Thorn had much to explain for his latest mischief. He stepped onto the gravel path and headed toward the folly.

Chapter Seven

"Well, this is quite unexpected. How long have you been playing our favorite game with Olivia?"

Seated on the lowest step, Thorn pulled his hand away from his face and glared at his brother. His twin had lousy timing. He had tried several times to pull Gideon aside to have a private conversation with him all day, and now he wished his brother would leave him alone. "What the devil are you doing out here? I thought you were holding court with our mother."

Gideon strolled closer, and the flickering light of the nearest torch revealed the hard angular lines of cold fury and his eyes burned with the promise of retribution. "I was restless."

"You were bored," Thorn said flatly, unfolding his body and standing. "Our mother spared no expense in your homecoming. Have you considered for a moment how your indifference has made her feel?"

Gideon kicked a stone with the toe of his boot. "Mother understands."

"Does she? Or is she afraid that you will run off again?" Thorn said, taking an intimidating step toward his brother.

His twin squared his shoulders. "Are we speaking of Lady Felstead's fears, or yours?"

Thorn was the first to glance away. "This is not about us, damn you!"

"No it is not," Gideon agreed. "I want to talk about what I witnessed between you and Olivia. She seemed rather upset when she walked away."

"It was nothing," Thorn insisted. "I—"

He did not anticipate Gideon would lunge for him and seize him by the front of his evening coat. "Do not lie to me, Justin! I watched you dance and flirt with Olivia."

"The chit has no sense of propriety," Thorn said, worried about the jealousy he sensed in his brother's accusation. "When I realized she was not heading to the lake with the others, I decided to follow her. You should be thanking me for looking after your little friend."

Gideon tightened his grip on Thorn's coat before he shoved him away. "So I should be thanking you, is that it? Christ, you are an arrogant arse! I may have not been able to hear the conversation between you and Olivia, but I know the lady believed she was with me."

"Now who is arrogant?" Thorn mocked. "You have been absent from England for many years. Perhaps the lady has developed a *tendre* for me."

His brother shook his head. "I doubt it. You had little patience for her when she was a young girl, you cannot convince me that you have developed a fondness for the lady she has become. As for Olivia, she would never flirt with Lord Kempthorn. She definitely would not *kiss* him. No one knows you as I do, and as your twin I demand a favor from you. Whatever you are planning with Olivia, it stops this evening."

"You have been out of Miss Lydall's life for a long time, brother, and yet you are quick to play the chivalrous knight," Thorn said softly, disliking the stab of jealousy he felt in his chest. "Would it bother you if she prefers my kisses instead of yours?"

"Olivia will always have my loyalty and friendship. You also might want to remember that because of your mischief, *I* am the man she believes she has kissed," Gideon said, the corners of his mouth curling with smug satisfaction at Thorn's grim expression. "I would thank you for it, but I do not trust your intentions toward the lady."

"Worried I might steal her away from you?"

Gideon's face became shuttered. "You can't steal something that is only valuable if it is given freely. However, you could hurt her. I will not stand for it."

"Are we quarreling over a woman?" Thorn asked, unable to keep the surprise out of his voice.

His brother expelled a weary sigh. "Stay away from Olivia. She is too innocent for the types of games you like to play."

"You used to like to play them too," Thorn said, curious to see how far he could push his twin.

"There hasn't been much point in the last few years," Gideon said, a hint of regret in his eyes.

"Whose fault is that?" Thorn challenged.

Gideon threaded his fingers through his dark hair. "I am not rebuking you for indulging in our old game, Thorn. Just the lady you approached."

Miss Lydall was off limits. Gideon's warning was clear, though Thorn had not made up his mind if he would respect his brother's wishes. "Care to recommend another lady?"

His brother released a snort of disbelief.

"You can approach her first as me," Thorn said, crossing the short distance between them. "If you behave like an arse, I will certainly be the one who gets slapped for it."

"It is tempting," Gideon said, his expression lightening as the tension in his shoulder's eased. "Though, I believe I will reserve that bit of revenge for another evening. It pains me to admit it, however, you are correct. I have been neglecting my duties as the guest of honor of these festivities. If I return to Mother's side before the fireworks end, there's a chance she may have not noticed my departure."

"Care to wager on it?" Thorn asked, capturing his brother's jaw with his right thumb and fingers and affectionately squeezing his chin before he released him.

"Only a drunken fool would consider that bet," Gideon said, hooking his arm around Thorn's neck. "Very few things escape her notice."

"I agree. She will expect an apology *and* an explanation."

Gideon added a little slack to his hold until his arm rested companionably across Thorn's shoulders. "I can provide both. I will simply blame you for my absence."

"A delightful plan," Thorn said, more amused than offended. "It took you all of three seconds to come up with it."

"Well, to be fair, whenever Mother is vexed at me, I always blame you." His brother grinned, and it was contagious. Thorn found himself matching it.

"Excellent."

"There's no reason to discard a solid plan when it always works," Gideon said. "Come on, you can join me. Seeing us together should soften the marchioness's disposition."

"I suppose I can grant you this small favor," he said. They both of them fell silent as they followed the gravel path that led to the lake.

Thorn listened to the music and allowed his thoughts to drift to Miss Lydall. In front of the Greek folly, her movements had been graceful and relaxed. She had danced up to him with a coy smile teasing her lips, and he knew that he was going to kiss her.

"Thorn?" his brother said in a quiet, thoughtful voice. "Something on your mind?"

"Olivia—" Gideon began.

Thorn closed his eyes and let his arm slip away from his brother's shoulders. "I suppose you want me to apologize for kissing her."

"No," was his brother's curt reply. "I suppose you had your reasons. Just refrain from kissing her again."

Would it count if I kissed her as Lord Kempthorn?

"I will do my best to resist the lady's charms," he replied dryly.

Gideon sent him a questioning glance, but he appeared to be satisfied with Thorn's answer.

He was quite certain he was not telling the truth, but what was one more lie shared between brothers?

Lost in thought, Olivia had reached Lady Felstead's back gardens before she recognized her surrounds. Several cheers rang out from the nearby guests who had decided to watch the fireworks display from the numerous benches positioned throughout the gardens. Closer to the house, the servants had set up additional tables and chairs. She could continue up the path to the terrace or remain in the garden and find a quiet alcove to watch the fireworks.

I could join Lady Felstead and her friends.

Olivia knew the older woman would find a place for her, but she dismissed the idea. It was too risky. She could run into Lady Grisdale, who was still displeased that their hostess had overruled the countess's decision to send her home. There was also Lord Kempthorn. Even when her back was turned, she could feel his disapproval whenever his gaze settled on her. Sitting next to his mother would only earn his annoyance.

In truth, she was not in the mood to verbally fence with the Netherwood twins.

Olivia stopped in front of a large fountain with a circular base and a half-naked marble maiden rising from the center of the shallow pool. Water poured from an oversized seashell the maiden had braced on her hip. Olivia stared up at the marble face to admire its beauty, but her thoughts were turned inward as she thought about her friendly exchange with Gideon and the joy she felt when they danced together.

The last time she had danced with him, she had been a girl.

She grimaced. "Why did you have to ruin it all with a kiss?" she asked, voicing her lament into the surrounding darkness.

"A kiss with the stars overhead sounds exceedingly romantic."

Olivia tried to conceal her astonishment as she turned her head and recognized the lady.

"Lady Arabella, where—I had not realized anyone was paying attention to me," she said, greeting the lady with a curtsy. The young woman mirrored her actions. "How are you this evening?"

Olivia had been first introduced to Lady Arabella Brant last season, since they were the same age and their hostess had thought two unmarried young ladies could find something in common. Initially, she had had a few doubts. To be fair, it was not Lady Arabella's fault that Olivia always felt like a plain, uninspiring dunnock when she stood next to the delicate blonde who possessed a beauty that would inspire artists and poets. She had expected her to be as vain and unkind as Lady Millicent, however, she had discovered the young woman to be friendly and well versed on numerous subjects. Her older sister, Lady Tempest, had married Lord Fairlamb—Lord Kempthorn and Gideon's cousin. That had caused quite a stir in London because the lady had been practically betrothed to another gentleman, and the feud between the Brants and the Rookes was longstanding and oftentimes violent. Or so she had heard. She had not paid attention to the gossip until she had been introduced to Lady Arabella.

"I am splendid." The other woman's hazel eyes sparkled with merriment. "And so are you if you are kissing strangers—"

"Oh, he was not a stranger," Olivia corrected. In an attempt to change the subject, she asked, "Why are you not at the lake with most of the other guests?"

"I was for a while, but I thought my sister and her husband might enjoy a quiet moment without me underfoot," Lady Arabella said airily. "However, what I was doing is less interesting than you and your mysterious suitor. I want to hear all the details."

She frowned. "He is not my suitor, and there is nothing to tell."

"If there was a kiss, then there is definitely a tale to share." Lady Arabella took Olivia's hand and pulled her away from the fountain to a small alcove where she had a direct view of the fountain. "Sit and tell me everything. I will begin. Have I met him?"

Gideon was family to Lady Arabella, albeit by marriage. Olivia assumed her friend had been introduced to him at some point since his return to England. If not, Lady Felstead had introduced her to him when she had arrived at Malster Park.

"Yes."

Lady Arabella considered her next question. "You said that your suitor was not a stranger. Is he one of your neighbors?"

Olivia gave her an exasperated look. "He is not my suitor. And, yes, he is someone I am acquainted with in the parish."

"Is he handsome?" her new friend asked, her right brow arched in a clever, knowing manner that Olivia could have never duplicated even if she practiced in front of a mirror for a solid year.

"No, he is quite ugly," she managed to deliver in a serious tone.

"I do not believe it!"

Olivia's lips twitched in response to Lady Arabella's disbelief. She lasted another fifteen seconds before she started giggling. "Of course I consider him handsome. I would have not permitted him to kiss me otherwise."

Lady Arabella's eyes widened. "So, he was the one to kiss you first."

"Do you think me so forward as to kiss an unsuspecting gentleman?" Olivia straightened her shoulders and tilted her face upward to admire the latest round of fireworks. "I cannot believe your opinion of me is so low."

"I did not mean to—" Lady Arabella began hastily before she noted Olivia's smirk. She laughed and leaned against her friend. "So it was an exceptional kiss?"

"I barely noticed," she replied, rising from the bench. "And I will not be kissing him again."

It was a promise she intended to keep. Gideon was her friend, but the gentleman was as much of a rake as his twin. Unlike the women who had fallen in love with him, she had no interest in adding her name to his collection of broken hearts. Good grief, what had he been thinking? He had just come back into her life. She was not going to lose him again over a kiss.

"Why not?" Lady Arabella asked.

It seemed unfair to place her friend in the awkward position of defending a new member of her family. Olivia shrugged as the other woman stood and walked to her side. "The gentleman is a charming scoundrel. He kissed me on a whim." She scowled as a darker thought occurred to her. "Or on a bet. I do not see him as the type who would be content to settle down and marry a baron's daughter."

Lady Arabella placed her hand on Olivia's shoulder to stop her from walking away. "You are fond of him."

"More than he deserves," she admitted, giving her a wistful half smile. "However, there is no reason to worry about me. I am not so foolish as to give him my heart."

"I think I know the name of your mysterious suitor."

Olivia rolled her eyes. "I told you, Lady Arabella, he is not a—"

"Is it Lord Kempthorn?"

Olivia's mouth fell open in surprise, and her hand absently tugged on the edges of her borrowed shawl. "Lord Kempthorn? Your skills at deduction have failed you, my friend. I would not have that cold, arrogant man if you trussed him up and shoved a damson in his mouth," she said with a breathy laugh. "My throat is parched and I could do with a glass of punch. Would you care to join me as I return to the house?"

"Yes, I would," Lady Arabella said. "It will give me another chance to guess the name of your gentleman."

"He isn't mine," Olivia reiterated.

"Hmm," was her friend's response.

As Thorn and Gideon walked along the edge of the garden path, Thorn spotted Miss Lydall in the distance. She and Lady Arabella strolled arm in arm, and the two ladies were laughing. When had she become friends with Tempest's younger sister? It was another connection to his world that he had been unaware of, he realized with some consternation.

"What is it?" Gideon asked.

Thorn had no intention of mentioning Miss Lydall to Gideon. "Nothing. Shall we visit with Mother or do you want to light some fireworks with father?"

Excitement glinted in his brother's eyes. "What do you think?"

"It seems a bit unfair to allow the marquess to have all of the fun," Thorn replied.

To his thinking, handling and igniting fireworks seemed safer than kissing Miss Lydall again.

Chapter Eight

Treversham House

Three days after the Felsteads' fete, Olivia was spending her afternoon inspecting the household accounts in the small breakfast room. When she was finished, she was planning to reward herself with a walk in the garden so she could read Mr. Chauncey's letter. She had met the gentleman last spring, and they had exchanged several letters since they had left London. If the handsome gentleman had intentions of a romantic nature, he was taking his time about it. In his last letter, he had expressed a desire to see her again when he was in Town, so she was hopeful. She heard a soft knock and someone opened the door.

"I beg your pardon for the intruding, Miss Lydall. Lord Dewick requires your presence in the library."

"Thank you, Martha," Olivia said, adding another item to the household ledger. "You may tell my father that I will join him once I have finished."

The maid hesitated at the threshold. She was young, about sixteen years old and new to her position, so she was eager to please her employer. "His lordship anticipated this would be your reply so he also wanted me to impress a sense of urgency to his request."

"With Mrs. Henders tending to her ill daughter, someone must see to her tasks," Olivia muttered under her breath as she dipped her pen into the small pot of ink and finished her notation. She set the pen aside and reached for the pounce pot and sprinkled the page. "Very well. I can finish this later. You may tell his lordship that I have received his message and I am on my way."

She picked up the ledger and tipped it so the loose pounce slid back into the pot.

"I mean no disrespect, miss, but if you were on your way, wouldn't you be following me to the library?" the maid asked.

Olivia sighed and stood, while giving the ledger a final shake. "I suppose you are right. Carry on with your duties, Martha. I will head to the library."

The maid curtsied. "Very good, miss," she said, and quietly slipped out of the room.

Olivia tucked a narrow silk ribbon in the crease of the ledger and closed it. She brushed the residual pounce from her fingers and then placed the lid on the inkpot. It was a rare occurrence for her father to be home in the afternoon, but the rain had caused him to delay his plans for the day.

She stepped out of the breakfast room and into the main hall. Until the fateful day that Lady Grisdale married Lord Dewick, she was the mistress of the household. Built in the early 1770s, Treversham House was a long building with a Pantheon-like façade featuring an Ionic portico and blind bows above the main entrance and windows. The house was not as grand as the Gothic-style Malster Park, but she adored the simple, understated elegance of its design.

There had been little alterations to the interior since her mother's death. It was rather comforting to be surrounded by the furniture, rugs, and pictures that had been chosen and enjoyed by her mother. She was too young to have any memories of Lady Dewick, but there was a painting of her in the music room. Olivia shared her curly chestnut hair and her chin. Her mother looked too delicate and finely boned in the picture to have given birth to two sons and a daughter. Giving birth to Olivia had weakened her, and had made her vulnerable to illness that eventually claimed her life.

Olivia wondered if her mother's painting would be removed from the music room once Lady Grisdale became mistress of Treversham House. It was, of course, a reminder that Lord Dewick had loved and mourned another lady. Perhaps she was misjudging Lady Grisdale, but the countess did not seem to be sentimental about the past. Her mother's painting would be removed from the wall, covered, and hidden away until it was forgotten, she was sure of it.

Getting rid of Lord Dewick's daughter would take a little more effort.

One of the wide oak planks beneath her feet creaked as she walked the short distance to the library. The floor had been recently washed, but it needed a thorough scrubbing and airing. Their housekeeper would oversee the task when she returned to her duties and Olivia and her father had left for London. Olivia frowned at the dirty smudges and paw prints near the library door. There was evidence of a trail that led to the front door. Someone had allowed her father's dogs outside while it was raining, but no one had cleaned up the mess.

Olivia glanced around, but found herself alone in the front hall. Where was their butler, Hopps? He usually assigned one of the younger servants to look after the dogs when they were in the house. She raised her fist and knocked on the door.

"Enter."

She opened the door and stepped into the library.

"Papa, have you seen, Hopps? Dancer and Trouncer have made a small mess in the hall," Olivia said, striding by the large bookcases at the entrance and turning left.

She halted and gaped with surprise.

Her father was not alone. On her arrival, Lord Kempthorn and Mr. Netherwood rose from their chairs. Their cousin Lord Fairlamb was positioned near one of the large windows.

The greyhounds had been resting in front of her father's desk, but they lifted their heads when they saw her. Trouncer barked, and both animals were wagging their tails as they unfolded their lean limbs with the intention of greeting her.

"Good afternoon, my dear," Lord Dewick said, giving her an apologetic look. "I confess I am responsible for letting the dogs back into the house. I realized, much too late, their muddied condition."

Fawn-colored Dancer did a tight circle before he bound toward her with Trouncer behind him.

"Could one of you—"

The dogs reached her before any of the gentlemen could react. Dancer jumped up on his hind legs and braced his front paws on the front of her dress. Trouncer circled around her and furiously sniffed at her skirt. Olivia had no clue what scent had captured his interest. She had been in the kitchen earlier, so it was possible she brushed up against something that smelled like food to him.

"Dancer and Trouncer, come here," the baron sternly commanded.

Neither animal listened.

"Uh, Dancer," she said, gripping the dog's paws so they were almost dancing. She would have laughed, but she was too busy keeping her face turned upward to avoid the dog's enthusiastic tongue. "This is no time for kisses, you oaf."

At the mention of "kisses," Trouncer also jumped up, slipped, and dropped to the floor several times. On his third attempt, he remained on his hind legs and Olivia staggered back at the weight of both dogs pushing to unbalance her. "Some help, if you please!" she said, noting the Netherwood twins were moving toward her though she was too distracted to tell them apart.

In the background, Lord Fairlamb was laughing while Lord Dewick shouted at the dogs to heed his order.

"Behave! Both of you," she said, taking another step backward and bumping into a pedestal that displayed a Chinese porcelain vase. "Oh dear!" She didn't have the heart to glance over her shoulder.

The pedestal tipped and the magnificent vase wobbled from its perch.

One of the brothers made a sharp turn to the right and fell to his knees, catching the vase before it struck the floor. The dogs thought it was a new game, so they began to bark.

Another bump from her backside sent the painted wooden pedestal crashing to the floor.

The other brother—she still couldn't tell them apart—grabbed Dancer, lifted the dog up, and set him down away from Olivia. "Stay!" he said sternly, and the animal whined before he collapsed into a crouched position.

Already anticipating trouble, Trouncer dropped his front paws to the floor and rolled onto his side. He sniffed at Olivia's hem, and then his black narrow angular head disappeared so he could rest his head against the top of her shoe.

Trouncer sighed.

Warily, Olivia glanced up at the Netherwood in front of her. Her brief tussle with the dogs had shaken a few delicate hair combs loose, leaving her hair disheveled. The front of her bodice had smudges of dirt from the dogs' paws, and there was a good chance that she smelled like wet dog hair.

The gentleman standing in front of her took note of every detail.

"You have a talent for causing trouble, Miss Lydall," he observed while the other gentlemen laughed around them.

"Ah, so it is you, Lord Kempthorn," Olivia said brightly. She gently slipped her shoe free from underneath Trouncer's dark head. "I knew I could count on you."

To bear witness to yet another humiliating moment in my life.

She offered him a vague smile as she stepped around him and the dogs to greet her father.

Thorn shook his head as he righted the fallen pedestal.

"Here," Gideon said, thrusting the blue and white vase up at Thorn.

Thorn turned to the pedestal and carefully placed the vase back on its base. "Are you finished shining the oak boards with your backside?"

His brother stared up at him in disbelief. "I caught the vase, did I not? And no one has bothered to thank me for it."

The black greyhound with a patch of white on his right shoulder climbed to his feet and went to Gideon. The dog began licking the side of his face. Gideon patted the dog. "That's enough, Trouncer. I stand corrected. Someone in this family appreciates my efforts."

"Trouncer is not the only one who appreciates that you sacrificed your dignity on my behalf," Miss Lydall said, shifting her stance so she could divide her attention between Lord Dewick and Gideon. "The vase belonged to my great-grandmother. I would have never forgiven myself if I had been responsible for breaking it."

"I must admit, I am impressed," Chance said, crossing the room and offering his hand to his cousin. "I would not have believed you were capable of such speed and grace."

"At least not without the benefit of a proper incentive, like your breeches ablaze," Thorn teased.

"Or being pursued by an angry mob," Chance quipped.

Gideon gave his cousin a lopsided grin and accepted the other man's hand. Once he was standing again, he retrieved a handkerchief from the inner pocket of his frock coat and wiped the residual wetness from his cheek.

"Well, I thought you were quite heroic, Mr. Netherwood," Miss Lydall said crisply, feeling the need to defend him. The annoyance in her face faded when the door opened and the butler appeared. "Oh good, it is you, Hopps. I was searching for you earlier."

Hopps had joined the Lydall household ten years ago. His last employer had a large household that included sixteen children. The old butler liked to lament to anyone who would listen that he had ruined his back climbing up and down the stairs at all hours. He had been searching for a more tranquil household, and Treversham House seemed agreeable since Lord Dewick's sons were away at school.

Although Thorn was certain Miss Lydall had tested the servant's patience a time or two over the years.

"My apologies, miss," the sixty-year-old servant said. "I noticed the mud in the hall so I went to fetch some rags and water to clean it up."

Miss Lydall's brow furrowed with concern. "You are taking on too much in Mrs. Henders' absence. You should not be cleaning the floor, Hopps."

The servant expelled a heavy sigh. "Well, my knees aren't as sturdy as they used to be, but I am not too old to carry out my duties," the butler said, his mouth thinning as he noticed the mud on the carpet and wood flooring. "Of course, my lower back does give me trouble when it rains."

Familiar with the servant's complaints, Lord Dewick said, "Hopps, there is no reason for you to see to the task yourself. Have one of the maids scrub the floor."

The gentleman was too polite to mention that he was a year younger than the butler.

"You are too kind, milord," the servant replied.

Miss Lydall sent her father a look of gratitude. She moved closer to Thorn, and a curious tension settled in his shoulders as she gestured toward the greyhounds. "I fear the dogs are too high-spirited for company. Would you mind taking them out of the room before you serve refreshments?"

"Of course, Miss Lydall. I will return shortly with the tea," Hopps said. He clapped his hands to capture the dogs' attention. "Trouncer, Dancer—come."

The butler grabbed Trouncer's collar the moment the animal was within reach. Dancer collided into Miss Lydall as he raced to join Trouncer at the servant's side, causing her to stumble into Thorn.

His arm came around her as he tried to steady her grasped left forearm. To the casual observer, it might have been mistaken for an intimate embrace.

Her lowered gaze lifted, revealing a flustered mix of shyness, awareness, and finally embarrassment. Thorn stood there open-mouthed, feeling the impact of her cornflower blue eyes in his gut.

"My apologies," she murmured, and slipped out of his embrace. "You must forgive Dancer for his exuberance. He assumes he will be receiving a treat."

A somewhat predictable reaction from a male.

What treat would you offer me, I wonder?

"Of course," he replied, his throat strangling on his words.

Miss Lydall nodded, and left him to give Hobbs some additional instructions.

For a few seconds he stood there, distracted by the gentle sway of her hips. Appalled that he was ogling Lord Dewick's daughter while the gentleman was in the same room, he deliberately looked away, his gaze colliding with Chance's. His cousin's lips curved in amusement as he walked by—as if he could read the other man's thoughts.

Miss Lydall closed the library door and turn to face the four gentlemen in the room. "So Papa," she said, striding toward her father, "was there a reason why you wished to see me?"

Thorn and Gideon moved closer as Lord Dewick returned to his desk to pick up a handwritten note.

"Yes, I almost forgot the reason why I had summoned you." The baron handed her the paper. "Our guests were so kind to deliver an invitation from Lady Felstead."

"Is she planning another gathering?"

Thorn sat down and watched Miss Lydall as she unfolded his mother's note with curiosity. A slight pout formed on her lips as she read it. He had expected her to be overjoyed by the marchioness's invitation, but the lady managed to surprise him again.

Her expression was solemn as she handed the letter back to her father.

"It is very thoughtful of Lady Felstead to include me in her plans," Miss Lydall said in neutral tones. "However, I must politely decline her invitation."

Thorn concealed his mild surprise at her announcement.

Gideon, on the other hand, had no compunction of expressing his opinion. "My dear girl, if you believe a polite refusal will satisfy the marchioness, you are sorely underestimating her."

The baron's gaze narrowed on his daughter. "I do not see why there is a problem. We were planning to leave for London in a fortnight."

Miss Lydall sat stiffly in her chair, her body as unyielding as her decision. "You expect me to leave in three days when I have not packed a single trunk? And what of the household? With Mrs. Henders away tending to her daughter, someone is needed to oversee—"

"Hopps will see to everything," her father said, dismissing her argument.

"Hopps cannot see to everything," Miss Lydall protested. "There is too much work to be done and it would be unfair to place such a burden on him. Lest you forget, the poor man has a weak back." She lowered her voice at the end just in case the butler was eavesdropping at the door.

"Hopps is strong as an ox," Lord Dewick replied, addressing Thorn, Gideon, and Chance. "He just has a propensity to complain about his health. That is all."

"That is *not* all," his daughter said, leaning forward in her seat. "There are a thousand and one things to be done, and you expect me to do them all *and* pack for Town?"

Thorn had not expected to benefit from the lady's stubbornness, and for once he was happy to lend his support. "It is a common lament uttered by your sex, and you have my sympathies," he said, and was rewarded with her complete attention. He anticipated that Miss Lydall might take offense, so he lifted his hand to delay her response. "Whether you join our little group in three days or leave in a fortnight with your father, I see little difference. Both decisions lead to London."

Miss Lydall's mouth softened as she sent him a look of gratitude. "I concur. I have no business rushing off to London while the household is in disarray."

A sensible decision, Thorn thought.

"I disagree," Lord Dewick said, staring at his daughter as if he was just figuring out that she was rebellious child.

"As do I," Gideon added, earning a frown from Thorn.

Miss Lydall abruptly shifted her body and head to glare at Lord Fairlamb.

"Do you have an opinion as well, my lord?"

Chance raised his hands in surrender. "I was in the mood for a brief ride so I joined my cousins on their errand. Do what you will," he said, absolving himself from the argument.

Satisfied that not everyone in the room was trying to

bully her into accepting Lady Felstead's invitation, she turned her attention back to her father. "There is no reason why we cannot go forward with our original plans."

"Three days is more than enough time for you to pack, Olivia," Gideon countered. "As Mother mentioned in her letter, you will need to be fitted for dresses for Town. You would be foolish not to take advantage of her expertise."

Thorn's thoughts turned inward as Gideon and Lord Dewick debated Miss Lydall on the merits of changing her plans. Although he was not prepared to admit it, he agreed with his brother. The floral pattern of Miss Lydall's morning dress appeared to be several years old and too matronly for a young lady. It was all too apparent that she could benefit from having someone with a critical eye and a sense of fashion to guide her. Otherwise, she might be ostracized and mocked by certain members of the *ton*.

But it was not his concern if Miss Lydall's drab fashion choices and awkwardness turned her into a wallflower for yet another season.

But her vulnerability will draw Gideon to her side.

Thorn had come to Treversham House with the hope of discouraging the lady and her father from accepting Lady Felstead's invitation. Now he was reevaluating his decision. Perhaps it was a bit shortsighted of him to stifle his mother's efforts to help Miss Lydall. The lady had been denied her own mother's affection and guidance and had suffered for it. With a little encouragement, the lady could make a respectable showing with the *ton*. Her dependence on Gideon would fade once other gentlemen paid her compliments and courted her. His brother would step aside because he was too good of a fellow to stand in the way of Miss Lydall's happiness.

And if he forgets, I will remind him.

"There is Lady Grisdale to consider," Lord Dewick said, the name returning Thorn to the conversation.

"What about the countess?" Miss Lydall asked.

Thorn was not fooled by the lady's cheerful curiosity. Neither was Gideon.

"Well, your decision not to join Lady Felstead's party puts me in a bit of a quandary," the baron confessed.

"How so?" she asked, her expression guarded as if already anticipating that she would not like his answer.

"As I explained earlier to our guests, I am not planning to head to London directly since I must travel to Bristol," Lord Dewick said.

Miss Lydall stared at her father. "How does this involve Lady Grisdale?"

Her father seemed flustered by the question. "Bristol? Oh, nothing at all. That is a bit of unfinished business. Lady Grisdale confided at the fete that she has also been forced to abandon her original plans to travel with friends and expressed a desire to join us. Naturally, I could not refuse."

Miss Lydall closed her eyes. "Naturally. You are too kind, Papa." Her shoulders sagged in defeat.

A warm rush of triumph flowed through Thorn. It would have been rude to gloat. He managed to conceal his elation, though Gideon sent him an odd glance. While he could not fathom the reason for Miss Lydall's reluctance to join his family, he was confident that she would do anything to avoid spending a few days confined in a coach with Lady Grisdale.

Even if that meant spending time with him.

Chapter Nine

Three days later, Olivia sat rigidly on the dull green leather–padded bench of the stagecoach. They were already ten hours into their breakneck eighteen-hour journey to London and she had watched the midnight landscape slowly transition from muted shadowy hues and silhouettes to a brilliant dawn sky of reds, oranges, and yellows. She had taken a moment to admire the sunrise when they had stopped at a coaching inn so the ostlers could change their horses for fresh ones. It had been a truly spectacular sight.

The brief respite from the stuffy interior and the endless jostling lasted only minutes before the stage was ready to depart. Olivia sat beside Lady Felstead while the marchioness's daughter, Lady Fiona, was seated near the window. Lord Kempthorn and Gideon sat across from them. In the stage following them, Lord and Lady Fairlamb were sharing the compartment with the marchioness's sister, Lady Arabella; the marquess's mother and father, the Duke and Duchess of Blackbern; and their eldest unmarried daughter, Lady Honora. There was little time for pleasantries between the two stagecoaches, however; the passing hours had drained Olivia of the fortitude of being sociable.

It was difficult enough to conceal her discomfort from her companions.

Thankfully, their evening departure assured her some

privacy since the stuffy interior and the rocking of the coach lulled most of the Netherwoods to sleep.

Except for Lord Kempthorn.

More than once, she had felt his gaze linger on her. She was not about to admit her humiliating weakness to a man like him.

"Are you unwell, Miss Lydall?"

Her eyes were closed, and she wondered if she could feign sleep so she did not have to answer him.

"I know you are not sleeping," he continued, pitching his voice low so he did not disturb the others. He stretched his leg so his boot brushed against the side of her half boot. "I doubt you have nodded off once."

Annoyed that he was paying so close attention to her, Olivia opened her eyes and their gazes locked in the morning light that was filtering through the window. "I was unaware that you suffered from insomnia, my lord," she said, matching his soft inflection. "Or is it a symptom of a more troublesome condition?"

"What the devil are you talking about?"

"Ennui, Lord Kempthorn," she replied as she brought her handkerchief to her lips.

"Who told you that I suffered from ennui?"

"No one in particular that I can recall," she admitted. "It was something I overheard last Season. You are aware of how gossip is bandied about a ballroom."

"You are too intelligent to listen to gossip, Miss Lydall. I am not afflicted with ennui or anything else," he said crisply.

"Then why are you not sleeping?"

"Who can sleep when the coachman is doing his damnedest to bump and rattle my brains into mush?" he complained.

His quarrelsome grumble teased a brief smile from her lips. "I always feel like my limbs are being shaken loose," she confided, trying to ignore the nauseating heat that had been washing over her for the last few hours.

"Is that why you look so pale? You are uncomfortable?" he pressed.

"Among other things," she vaguely replied. Olivia strived to change the subject. "It appears we are making good time."

"Aye, the coachman is comfortable with his bone-jarring pace," he said, staring at her as if she were a puzzle he was determined to solve. "If we can avoid rain, we will keep to his schedule."

The sleeping marchioness interrupted their conversation with a loud snort. Her chin bounced against her chest and a soft snore rumbled in her throat.

Olivia struggled not to laugh. After all, the lady was the gentleman's mother. When she glanced over at Lord Kempthorn, she saw that there was a pleasant upward curve to his lips and his eyes gleamed with silent amusement.

"You must be looking forward to returning to London."

The earl cocked his head to the side and gave her a considering look. "You have not answered my question."

She blinked, feigning innocence. "What question?"

He muttered something under his breath. "Your pallor concerns me, Miss Lydall. I asked if you were unwell."

Now that she was committed to the journey, she refused to give Lord Kempthorn a reason to abandon her at one of the coaching inns. "I am fine, my lord."

"Liar."

Her eyes flared at his rudeness. She ignored the small fact that she was lying to him. "Are you deliberately trying to provoke me?"

The earl shrugged and leaned back against his seat. "Perhaps. It is a side of your character that I have never witnessed."

"Really."

"I have always considered you appallingly honest," he said, deliberately baiting her.

"And you disapprove," she said, resisting the urge not to kick him in the shin.

He gestured with his hand. "A clever lady wields lies as agilely as a fan to get what she wants."

"It is not my honesty that should concern you," she said, clasping her handkerchief in her hand. "It is your atrocious taste in deceitful women. I grant you, some ladies have a talent for lying, but it does not make them exceptionally clever."

"I have offended you. Pray, forgive me for speaking so bluntly."

Lord Kempthorn did not seem particularly repentant for his comments.

"Perhaps I will when you offer me a sincere apology."

He softly chuckled. "There is no reason for you to sharpen your claws on me, Miss Lydall. I happen to like deceitful women."

If he thought to appease her with his explanation, he was sorely mistaken. "I suppose this is why your mother laments that you will remain a bachelor."

"Why do you say that?"

"Because no decent lady will marry you," she said flatly.

Lord Kempthorn brought the back of his hand to his lips to muffle his mirth. "Paragons are a bore, Miss Lydall. I prefer a devious creature who will entertain me in public as well as in private."

A soft gasp escaped her lips. His expression was one of anticipation, as if he dared her to respond to his impertinent declaration.

"Then it is fortunate the *ton* has many ambitious coquettes in its ranks," she said, offering him a smile that held little warmth. "I would wish you luck, but I shall reserve it for your future bride."

"Claws . . . and now teeth," Lord Kempthorn mused out loud. "Gideon worries you do not have the temperament for Town life, but I predict you will surprise all of us."

"Your brother need not watch over me," she muttered, offended that the earl and his brother viewed her as a guileless child. "I can manage on my own."

"We will save that debate for another time," he said carelessly. "Your coloring has improved. Why don't you close your eyes and try to sleep a little before our next stop."

Olivia was about to protest, but Lord Kempthorn shut his eyes, signaling that their conversation had come to an end. She could not believe the audacity of the gentleman, she thought, even as she leaned back and complied with his order.

As she settled down to sleep, it occurred to her that arguing with the earl had restored some of her strength, and most of the nausea seemed to have faded. She wondered if Lord Kempthorn had deliberately set out to distract her to ease her discomfort.

She was still puzzling over the possibility when she finally drifted off to sleep.

The rigid schedule of the stagecoach had doused the high spirits of the occupants, even that of Lady Felstead. Mercifully, their current stop would last longer than five minutes and included a brief repast at the Salty Briar, though he doubted anyone would complain about the quality of the food. Everyone was too damn weary to summon the strength.

Thorn was the last to disembark from the stagecoach. Gideon stood several yards away from him and stretched. Both of them watched their mother and sister greet Chance's wife, Lady Arabella, and the Duke and Duchess of Blackbern in the courtyard. Chance and his sister were not with the others, but there were other personal needs that required attention besides an empty stomach.

"I am starving," Gideon said, covering his mouth with the back of his hand as he yawned.

"We have less than twenty minutes," Thorn cautioned, his gaze settling on his mother and the others. He observed them as they entered the inn.

His brother yawned again. "Plenty of time to fill my stomach and empty my"—he glanced around to make certain there was no female within hearing distance—"well, you know what I mean."

"Tend to your needs and be quick about it," Thorn advised. "The ladies will also require a few moments of privacy and I do not want to leave any of them without a male escort."

Between the coordinated efforts of Thorn, Gideon, Chance, and the duke, the four gentlemen had managed to watch over the ladies and discourage any man who wandered too close.

"What are you planning to do?" Gideon asked.

"Join the others," Thorn replied. "Unless you need an escort?"

"I will pass on your generous offer," his brother said, looking up at the sky. A drop of rain struck his cheek and he wiped it away. "It appears we will not escape the rain after all."

"It is all the more reason for us to be ready to depart when the horn blows."

Gideon waved dismissively at the mere hint of an impending lecture and wandered off in the direction of where he assumed he would find the outhouse.

Several raindrops splashed against his hat and his shoulders. Nodding to the coachman, he headed in the direction of the inn when it occurred to him that one lady had been missing from their party.

Miss Lydall.

Leave it to the independent miss to amble about the inn on her own.

Olivia sagged against one of the outer buildings as she struggled not to retch. Pressing her handkerchief to her lips, she closed her eyes and willed her unruly stomach not to rebel. In that moment, she could not recall ever feeling this miserable in her life. The long hours in the stagecoach had given her aching muscles and a head stuffed with cotton.

Her eyes snapped open in distress. She wrapped her arms around her abdomen and leaned forward to retch.

"Dear god, are you ill?"

Olivia groaned. Naturally, it would have to be *him*. Her humiliation was complete. "Go away," she pleaded without glancing in the direction of the approaching gentleman. "Let me suffer with my dignity intact."

She leaned forward and retched again. The muscles in her throat constricted to rid her stomach of its contents, but nothing came up. She flinched away from the masculine hand on her back.

"Please," Olivia mumbled, her body trembled and strained. "I cannot fight you and my stomach."

A strong arm curled around her waist and pulled her against a solid front of unyielding male. "Then don't," he murmured, his lips against her ear. "Permit me to lend you my strength until you regain yours."

"Oh god."

A few tears were squeezed from her tightly shut eyes as she bowed and retched again. The muscles in her abdomen continued to spasm until her stomach felt like a fist. A few minutes later, she straightened and allowed her unwelcomed companion to hold her.

"When was the last time you had something to eat or to drink?" he quietly asked.

"I do not remember," she replied weakly. "Nor do I care."

He remained silent for a minute.

"You cannot continue without eating something, Olivia."

Olivia. Not Miss Lydall. Well, it appeared fate had sent her Gideon instead of Lord Kempthorn. Her relief gave her the strength to stand without her companion's assistance.

"I am not an invalid, Gideon," she muttered, gently pushing his arm away and stepping out of his embrace.

"You could have fooled me," he said, his voice sharpening in anger. "You should have told one of us that you were ill."

Lord Kempthorn had suspected that she had fallen ill during their journey. For some unfathomable reason, he had refrained from revealing her weakened condition to the others.

"I am not sick," Olivia said, moistening her dry lips with her tongue. "I do not possess the constitution to travel long distances by coach. I never have."

"Why the devil did you not speak up when we discussed this in your father's library?" Gideon thundered, sounding too much like his brother for her sensibilities.

"I tried." When he remained silent, she felt compelled to add, "I did try to decline your family's generous invitation, but no one listened to me."

She extended her hand, noting it was raining.

Gideon was not satisfied with her explanation. "I was there. I do not recall you telling us that traveling by stagecoach would make you ill."

Olivia glared at him. "I was ashamed to admit such weakness." *Especially, in front of your brother.* "Nor did I wish to offend your mother."

"Or travel with Lady Grisdale," he added.

A faint smile lightened her grim countenance. "I saw that as a boon as well."

Gideon did not return her smile. He studied her face in silence. After a minute, he said, "It appears the spell has passed. You need to come indoors and eat something."

"I cannot." She anticipated the protest rising within him and met it directly. "There is little time left and I would prefer that the others did not learn that I feel unwell."

She was too embarrassed to have Lady Felstead fuss over her, or for Lord Kempthorn's annoyance that she was hindering their journey.

"Olivia—"

"I will eat at a future stop. I promise," she said, hoping she could keep her word. "If you have no objections, I wish to return to the coach and wait for the others there."

Gideon looked as if disagreed with her decision, but took a deep breath and released it. "If I cannot dissuade you, then I shall escort you to—"

She wrinkled her nose and shook her head. "That is very kind of you, but it is hardly necessary since our stagecoach is in view."

"I do not do it out of kindness, Olivia," he said tersely. "I do it out of necessity. It is not entirely safe for you to be wandering about on your own. This is not your lands or even Malster Park."

"Very well," she sighed. There was no point in explaining that her distress had prompted her to leave their party in search of some privacy. "Although, I do not want you to feel obliged to remain. Once you are discharged of your duty, pray join your family for the meal. I promise not to leave the stage again."

Gideon inclined his head. "As you wish."

"Thank you." Olivia started to turn away from him, but she hesitated as another concern surfaced. "Ah, one more thing. I would consider it a small favor if you would not tell the others the true reason I did not join them indoors."

His eyebrows lifted in mild puzzlement at her request.

"My family would understand, Olivia," he said gently.

She was certain Lady Felstead would be sympathetic to her plight, but she did not want the marchioness to fuss over her. Nor was she in the mood to share confidences with Gideon on why his brother's opinion mattered to her.

"I have no doubt they would," she said firmly. "Nevertheless, there is no reason to disturb anyone. Do you not agree?"

He gave her a measured look. "I will collect on this favor one day."

"I expect you will." Her wry grin seemed to startle him. "When you do call in your favor, you will be gentle with me, will you not? Try not to be too onerous."

He grasped her arm above the elbow to prevent her from slipping on the gravel. "The cost will be as painless as another kiss from your sweet lips," he assured her.

Was he teasing? A quick glance did not assuage her curiosity. "There is nothing to be gained by kissing me again, you charming rogue. The least you could do is demand something of value."

"I did not say that I will claim another kiss from you as my prize. I merely pointed out that it will be just as painless as one," he said before he released her.

It was ridiculous to feel insulted, but she was. "Oh."

"Besides," he drawled, allowing her to step away from him, "kissing a lady of quality always comes with great risk. I usually avoid such temptations."

"An excellent rule," she said, not looking back at him. "I am certain your restraint has served you well."

"Not of late," he replied darkly. "What shall I tell my mother when I join the family?"

"Do what you will."

Her careless comment made him chuckle.

"I always do, my lady."

Olivia felt the weight of his gaze on her back as she

crossed the remaining distance to the stagecoach. Their conversation had taken an uncomfortable turn, and she welcomed a brief respite from her companions to regain her composure.

It seemed only minutes had passed when a nearby horn blared, a warning to the occupants within the inn that the stagecoach would be departing with or without them. Before the final note had faded, Olivia could hear Lady Felstead's distinct voice as she conversed with her children.

The door opened and Olivia grasped the marchioness's extended hand and tightened her hold as she assisted the older woman until she was seated.

"You have my gratitude, my dear." Lady Felstead exhaled loudly as she pulled her skirt closer to her legs so her daughter would not step on the hem. "The stiffness in my limbs has not eased and it has made me quite clumsy."

"Rubbish," Olivia said, too devoted to the lady to allow her to diminish herself in front of her family. "I have never seen anyone more graceful than you, my lady."

She exchanged a quick friendly grin with Lady Fiona as she settled in beside her mother.

"Did you not vow at the table that you were done with complaints?" her daughter teased.

Lady Felstead huffed, mildly annoyed that she had already broken her promise. "My vow does not count until our departure," she said, impulsively amending her vow. "Uncharitable child. You could learn a thing or two from Olivia. She has always possessed a sympathetic heart."

Gideon stepped into the compartment. "Passing out compliments, Mother? Have I earned a few?"

His warm gaze met Olivia's, and she was relieved that he was willing to feign ignorance about her illness. He sat down opposite her.

"Not of late," the marchioness declared with a frown

marring her pleasant features. "You neglected to join us in the inn."

He sent her a hooded look. "I wasn't hungry."

Lord Kempthorn took that moment to enter the coach. "Excellent. Everyone is here. We are leaving and I have been warned by the coachman that he will not tolerate a delay."

"You may assure the man that we are ready," Lady Felstead said, content to believe she was the one who was in charge of their journey.

The earl turned his back on them as he spoke to the coachman standing near the open door.

"And what of you, young lady?" the marchioness asked, staring at Olivia.

She brought her hand to her bosom in a nervous gesture. "Me?" she squeaked.

"You were also absent from the morning repast. And pray do not tell me that you were not hungry," she said, her eyes sharpening when she noticed Olivia's grimace. "You have barely eaten this entire journey."

She had not realized the marchioness had been paying such close attention to her.

"I desired a walk more than a meal, my lady," she explained, resisting the urge to glance at Gideon. "You are not the only one who is suffering from stiff limbs."

"Were you with Gideon?"

Olivia visibly flinched when a servant shut and secured the coach's door. "Ah—"

"No, Olivia was not with me," Gideon said. Leaning forward, he braced his hands on his knees as the coach lurched and rocked as the horn sounded. "My business was my own and it was private."

"Do not give me that look, Gideon Netherwood," his mother ordered in stern tones that she must have used often when the twins were young boys. "Your business is your affair. I am just concerned that Olivia was wandering about the courtyard without an escort."

Now it was Olivia's turn to bristle. "With all of the activity in the courtyard, finding a moment of privacy is more of a challenge than you would think."

Noting her expression, Lady Felstead explained, "I am well aware that you are used to looking after yourself. However, we are far from home and while most of these inns are relatively safe, there could be unsavory characters lurking about in hopes of robbing an unwary passenger."

Olivia had not been worrying about thieves when she headed for the nearest building. "Forgive me, Lady Felstead, I had not thought my absence would cause you to worry. If it makes you feel better, I did not stray far from the stagecoach."

"There's no need to apologize," the marchioness said, dismissing the subject with a wave of her hand. "No harm has been done. The next time, I will have one of my boys watch over you."

"The next time, Miss Lydall will join us in the inn," Lord Kempthorn interjected, causing Olivia and his mother to gape at him.

"Of course," Olivia hastily replied. The earl did not wish to be tasked with providing her with a respectable escort. "I am certain I will be hungry for the next meal."

She smiled to conceal her small lie.

"What is wrong with you?" Gideon asked abruptly.

Her smile dimmed with her annoyance. "Nothing."

"You get this line"—he brought his finger and lightly touched the space between his eyebrows—"right here—lawks!" He swallowed the rest of his observation when she kicked him in the shin.

"Oh, *do* forgive me, Mr. Netherwood," Olivia replied with false sincerity. "I was not braced for that last bump. Did I hurt you?"

Gideon scowled at her as he reached down to rub the sore spot. "Only enough to make your point, wench."

Olivia glanced in surprise at Lord Kempthorn's soft chuckle. Bemused, she watched him reach into the inner lining of his coat and retrieve an object wrapped in a linen napkin. He unceremoniously dropped it into her lap.

"What is it?" his sister inquired.

"Some bread from the table," Lord Kempthorn said, sounding bored with the subject. He adjusted his hat so it covered his eyes. "Stiff limbs are no reason to starve, Miss Lydall. We cannot have you getting sick."

Olivia glared at Gideon, but he seemed bemused by his brother's reluctant act of kindness, so she shifted her attention back to the earl. If he sensed her perusal, his slouched posture and expression revealed nothing.

"How very thoughtful of you, Thorn," his mother said.

"Thank you, my lord," she murmured, her gaze dropping to the linen-covered bread. Her fingers caged the bread as she struggled to sort out her feelings.

Good heavens, it was *him.*

Gideon had not been the one to find her. It was Lord Kempthorn who had held her while she had been ill. He was the one who had promised to keep her secrets, and then had made certain she had something to eat.

She could not fathom why the earl had not corrected her when she had called him by his brother's name. Nor did she understand why he had followed her and offered comfort to someone he considered beneath his notice.

Perhaps it was cruel of her to view his charitable actions with suspicion, but Lord Kempthorn rarely did anything that did not benefit him.

It was a puzzle that kept her amused throughout the rest of their journey together.

Chapter Ten

London

"Rainbault, did you lose a bet with St. Lyon during our absence?" the Marquess of Fairlamb complained as he deliberately selected the most uncomfortable chair in the private room their friend had procured for the evening.

Thorn could sympathize with his cousin's discomfort. The Acropolis was one of the more notorious clubs in Town. Its origins were murky, but it was generally accepted the building was built after the Great Fire of 1666. Over the decades, the ownership changed numerous times and had even gained some respectability as a gentleman's residence. However, one of the heirs turned it into a gambling hell and some enterprising proprietor began to rent rooms to the famous courtesans of the day. Its notoriety was established long before Thorn and his friends were born when the Acropolis became a private gentleman's club that excelled in decadence and perverse pleasures of the flesh.

It was not much of a stretch to assume that generations of young gentlemen had strolled through the club's doors in search of adventure and the forbidden. Thorn had been seventeen years old when he and Gideon had joined Chance, St. Lyon, and Rainbault for a memorable evening of drunken revelry. There were newer, more refined establishments scattered about London that were more aligned to his and his friend's tastes, but the Acropolis was a part of London's wicked past. Old traditions could not be ignored.

"You disapprove of the Acropolis's Bird Room?" Antoine Sevard, Duke of Rainbault and exiled prince of Galien, said in mocking tones as he looked very much like royalty in the mahogany throne chair with its scrolling gilt and a dark blue velvet cushions. At six foot one, their friend wore his straight blond hair unfashionably long and untethered. Dressed in black evening attire, his white linen shirt and intricately tied cravat lightened the severity of his unadorned coat and emphasized his muscled chest. Eschewing formal evening pumps for leather boots, and with a sheathed dagger secured near his hip, Rainbault looked like a handsome privateer rather than a gentleman who had blood ties to multiple royal houses. "I will grant you, the bird décor has not improved much with age, but it was one of the first rooms we rented and I seem to recall you enjoyed the enthusiastic wench dressed only in feathers."

A slow sheepish grin banished Chance's brooding expression. "It wasn't her lack of dress that impressed me. It was how she employed those feathers." His cousin glanced at Viscount Bastrell, or St. Lyon as he preferred, who was reclining on a red sofa with green, gold, and blue silk pillows. "It was St. Lyon who spent the evening trying to pluck her."

Gideon laughed and handed the viscount a glass of the Acropolis's best brandy. "By night's end, the carpet was littered with feathers. I thought St. Lyon had murdered the poor girl." His twin nodded in his direction. "Brandy?"

Thorn raised the glass of wine in his hand. "This will do for now."

"There was no cause for violence, though the wench was willing," St. Lyon replied, too used to their teasing. "She was running about the rooms naked with those leather straps crisscrossing her body. Her breasts were plump and bounced in a delightful way."

"I thought it was Chance who bedded the little bird." Rainbault interrupted the viscount's musings. "After all, his ears are quite red at the moment, and then there is his fondness for her skills with a feather."

Chance laughed. "I might have caged her a few times in the bedchamber, but she fluttered away and landed in St. Lyon's lap."

The viscount sent him an apologetic look. "Your little chick was impressed with my cock."

All four men sputtered and heartily laughed at St. Lyon's quip.

"The wench ended up in my lap as well," Gideon admitted as he poured more brandy into Rainbault's glass. "Though I ended up spending the evening with one of her non-feathered companions. I believe she was a brunette."

"I was the one who put those leather straps to good use," Thorn said with a hint of a sly grin. At her urging, he had bound her wrists and ankles to the bed and with her encouragement had pleasured her with a hard spanking, and later with his cock. She had been the first woman he had bedded who required pain to be thoroughly pleasured.

"Well, that explains the screams," Rainbault said dryly, who often dabbled in dark carnal pleasures.

After all, out of the five of them, the duke held an exclusive membership at the Acropolis.

"And all of the scattered feathers," Chance teased. He held up his hand. "Have mercy on me, gents. I am a married fellow now. Any recollections of me shagging a wench that is not my wife shall be forgotten." He shook his head. "If Tempest ever learned of a woman dressing in nothing but leather straps and feathers—"

"She would wish to make a sketch of her," Chance, Thorn, St. Lyon, and Rainbault uttered in unison.

Gideon seemed stunned by the suggestion. His next statement clarified his concern. "Chance, you are *not* thinking of bringing your wife here. No respectable lady should walk the halls of this establishment."

Fairlamb grimaced. "I shudder at the mere thought. It is bad enough that her mentor at the Royal Academy has hinted that her skills with a pencil could be improved if she were to attend classes where male and female models would be present."

"Would these models be naked?" St. Lyons arched an inquiring brow.

"Naturally," Chance replied, sounding mildly annoyed.

The viscount peered over his glass of brandy. "Fascinating. Well, if you need someone to escort your lady, I will happily volunteer for the task."

His cousin was not amused. "So you can seduce the female models while my wife and the other artists sketch your debauchery? I think not."

Before St. Lyons could protest, Rainbault said, "Respectability is making you tense, Chance. If your wife wishes to sketch naked models, you should not discourage her. However, I do agree with you on this point. St. Lyons should not be the one to escort her."

Thorn and others murmured their agreement. There was nothing wrong with St. Lyons. He was a loyal friend and fierce in a fight. However, he was too handsome for his own good. Ladies of all ages were attracted to him and the rogue often accepted their invitations, which inevitably led to broken hearts and unfortunate incidents.

"All of you call yourself my friends. I resent your lack of faith in me," the viscount said, scowling at them.

"I am capable of escorting my own wife," his cousin announced. He finished his wine and set down the fragile glass on a small round table.

"True," Rainbault said soothingly as he turned to Gideon

in a halfhearted attempt to change the subject. "Since we have been without your refined company for numerous years, Netherwood, you may be unaware that the club enjoys the patronage of several notable ladies of the *ton*. These individuals carry full privileges, so it would be unwise to view all of the females you encounter here as common stock."

From Gideon's expression, Thorn deduced his twin was intrigued about the possibilities of encountering a respectable widow or matron whose carnal appetites were as insatiable as a man's. He sent the duke a meaningful glance, but the other man rejected the unspoken warning with an elegant shrug. Already frustrated by his brother's secrecy, Thorn did not want Rainbault and St. Lyons to lure his brother into their shadowy world of overindulgence and vice.

"How do you tell the difference between a patron and a whore?" Gideon asked.

Thorn scowled at his twin but he remained silent.

Rainbault gestured broadly with his glass of brandy. "There is no rule to forbid someone from being both patron and whore."

Gideon's face was impassive but it was obvious he was considering the duke's words. "The next time we attend the same ball, I hope you will introduce me to these ladies."

"Gideon," Thorn snapped.

His friends chuckled, amused by Thorn's need to protect his twin rather than Gideon's undisguised curiosity.

"Perhaps I will," the duke said magnanimously. "Although, it would be more entertaining to watch you discover them without my assistance."

Chance bowed his head and pressed his fingers into his forehead as he shook his head. "Tell me again, Your Grace, why I gave up an evening with my beautiful wife to spend it with you lusty sots." His hand fell away as he glanced at his surroundings. "Not to mention at the Acropolis."

"We always celebrate the first night in Town together," St. Lyon said, raising his glass to gain Gideon's attention.

Not always, Thorn thought as he watched Gideon refill the viscount's glass. His twin had missed many of their first nights and he appeared to have few regrets about his decision.

"You will have countless evenings with your lady, Chance," Rainbault said, stretching his long legs in front of him. "You may be obliged to sit through every ball this season, but I have other plans."

"Here, here." St. Lyon raised his glass to toast the duke's vague plans, while Gideon tried not to pour brandy on the carpet.

"All of us have obligations," Chance said with a slight edge to his voice. "Even you, my friend."

"True," the exiled prince conceded. "Though like a swimmer in a large river, I prefer to float and savor my fated course rather than tire myself by going against the current."

The neck of the decanter clanked against Rainbault's glass. "You speak as if living a good life is simple," Gideon said, filling the duke's glass to the top.

Thorn envied his friend because nothing ever seemed to ruffle his composure.

Rainbault stared at him, and for an unsettling moment Thorn wondered if he had spoken his thoughts out loud. The gentleman gave him a smug knowing look and winked.

"For some, it is, Netherwood," he said, replying to Gideon's remark. He leaned back on his throne chair. "However, most of the *ton* would accuse us of living a wicked life, so it would be a lie to claim familiarity with goodness unless it applies to a well-filled stomach or a sated cock.

"You are an expert at both," Chance said with a grin on his lips.

"I will drink to that too," St. Lyon called out.

Thorn raised his empty glass as a tribute to Rainbault. With his other hand, he picked up the wine bottle and filled his glass. " 'Simple' is too bland for the likes of us."

The duke slammed his fist down on the carved armrest. "Agreed. Anything easily won has no value and is tossed aside. What we covet, we take!"

All five raised their glasses high and cheered as they had the first evening nine years earlier when they stood together and pledged their unfaltering loyalties to one another. None of them wanted to admit that their lives were already changing. For one evening, they could forget that time had made them wiser and fate was gradually placing them on different paths.

Six hours and countless bottles of wine and brandy later, Chance batted at Thorn's knee. It took him three tries to land a blow.

"What?" Thorn grumbled. At some point, sitting in a chair had become too troublesome, so he was sitting on the floor reclining against the cushion.

Chance hit him again. "Wake up. I need to leave before Rainbault returns."

Thorn blinked and stared blearily at the room. Over Chance's shoulder, Gideon was lying on his stomach with his face buried in the cushions. He was snoring softly with an empty bottle clutched in his hand.

He rubbed the corner of his eye. "Where did Rainbault go? Did St. Lyon leave with him?"

"No," the viscount said over his shoulder. On the other side of the room, he stood in front of the rosewood commode table as he relieved himself into the concealed chamber pot. "Still present. His Grace decided we needed a new amusement since you are too drunk for whist."

"I am not drunk," Thorn hastily denied before it struck him that his statement was precisely what an inebriated gentleman would say. "Well, not overly much. What time is it?"

"Late enough," Chance said, using the sofa to assist him as he stood. He leaned over and slapped Gideon on the arse. "Wake up."

His twin muttered something unintelligible.

His cousin held out his hand and wiggled it in front of Thorn's face to gain his attention.

"Why are you in a rush to leave?" Thorn asked, and was rewarded with a hard slap on the cheek. "Stop that or I will hit back."

"Drinking always makes Rainbault affectionate," St. Lyon said, fastening his breeches. "He left in search of some females to join our gathering."

Understanding seeped into Thorn's wine-soaked brain. "Ah, I see. Did you remind His Grace that Fairlamb is married? I doubt his wife will approve of her husband committing debauchery." He grabbed his cousin's hand and was pulled until he could stand on his own.

"That's adultery, you arse," Chance said. He scrubbed his face in annoyance. "And, aye, Tempest will not approve of either one, so let us depart before he returns."

"Did you even attempt to talk Rainbault out of this?" Thorn demanded. St. Lyon was close to their family, and he adored Lady Fairlamb and her sister.

The viscount turned around. "Why would I?" He reached out and grabbed a small towel to wipe his hands. "No one is expecting Chance to shag any of the wenches. Christ, the man is married and if Norgrave doesn't geld him, Tempest surely will."

Thorn glared at St. Lyon in disbelief. "You must be

drunker than you look." He grabbed Chance by the upper arm before he could cross the room and punch their friend. "You will feel bad if you hit him while he is cup-shot."

His cousin glared at the viscount. "I can live with the guilt."

Gideon rolled over and fell off the sofa. St. Lyon snorted as the three of them watched his twin sit up. "What happened? Did I miss anything?"

"Not yet, but you will," Thorn said, hauling his brother up. "Say farewell to St. Lyon."

"You're leaving?" Gideon asked, stifling a yawn. "I thought we were leaving Acropolis for some new gambling hell Rainbault was telling us about."

Thorn fought down the urge to throttle his sibling. "You have amassed a small fortune during your travels. Do you want to lose it all at cards when you are so drunk you can barely stand?"

"Am not," Gideon said with a touch of defiance in his voice.

Chance grabbed the man's other arm so he didn't lose his balance. "Tell Rainbault I will call on him tomorrow when we can review some of the changes since last spring. Such as the small detail that I now have a *wife*!"

Immune to the marquess's anger, St. Lyon scratched at the beard stubble under his jaw. "There is no cause to be upset with Rainbault. He knows you are married to a paragon."

Thorn groaned. With a soft curse, he sensed his cousin had reached the end of his tether.

"Perhaps you are concerned that you cannot be faithful to your lady wife," St. Lyon taunted.

Chance released his grip on Gideon and charged like a maddened bull at one of his closest friends. Too drunk to fully comprehend the danger, St. Lyon stood there like a wooden post until the marquess's fist slammed into his jaw. Both men went down with a furious Chance on top.

"Bloody hell," Thorn muttered as he let go of his brother's arm.

Gideon sank to his knees and made no effort to stand as he watched Thorn march over to the two fighting men.

"Damn it, Chance." Thorn bent down and wrapped his arms around his cousin and dragged him off the viscount before he could do any real damage. "Stop fighting me. You don't really want to hurt him."

"Aye, I do," Chance growled, kicking at the prone man.

"He was baiting you and you fell for it," Thorn said, tightening his hold as he laced his fingers together and pressed hard against the other man's neck. He dragged his cousin backward another few steps.

The corner of St. Lyon's mouth was bleeding. He dabbed at it with his thumb as he sat up. "Fill his belly with enough brandy and he would fight his own shadow."

His cousin strained against Thorn's hold while he glared at the viscount. "Stop baiting him, you arrogant arse, or I will let him beat you bloody." He bowed his head until his lips were close to Chance's ear. "If you behave, we can leave."

"Aye, my thoughts exactly," Chance said, his feverish gaze on St. Lyon. "He isn't worth bruising my knuckles on his hard head."

"I—" the viscount began.

"You have said enough for one evening," Thorn said, cutting him man off. "You can convey my thanks to our royal friend for another unconventional evening."

Simmering annoyance gleamed in St. Lyon's dark blue gaze. "Such restraint, Thorn. You are an example for us all."

"You and your caustic tongue can go to the devil," he bit out. Once he was assured his cousin would not attack St. Lyon again, Thorn released his hold.

Chance stepped away from him and rubbed the stiffness out of his neck. "Are you coming with us, Gideon?"

"Of course he is," Thorn replied.

"Let the man speak for himself," St. Lyon advised. "You treat Gideon as if he is your son rather than your twin."

Thorn glanced over at his brother, who sat listless on the sofa. "Now you are spouting rubbish. Gideon, Chance, and I arrived together, it only makes sense that he leaves with—"

"I'm staying."

With a silent promise of retribution for his interference, Thorn turned his back on St. Lyon to deal with his stubborn twin. "I need you to help me get Chance safely home."

His cousin headed for the door. "If we are going to fight again, I may have to throw up first."

Gideon looked drunk and weary as Thorn felt. "You don't need me to tend to Chance. Nor do I need you."

The muscles in his abdomen rippled as if he had taken a physical blow. "So what are you planning to do? Plant your nose in the cushions and go back to sleep?"

"Perhaps," was his brother's sullen reply. "As I see it, what I do is not your concern."

Another crushing blow. It seemed as if everyone was determined to pick a fight with him this evening.

"Fine. Do what you will," Thorn said coldly, refusing to show his friends how much his brother's refusal had stung him.

"I always do," Gideon replied, matching his brother's harsh demeanor.

A blistering curse from Chance forced Thorn to break eye contact with his twin. "What is wrong? Has Rainbault returned?"

"Not quite," his cousin said, quietly shutting the door and turning the key in the lock. "Tempest's father is speaking to someone at the end of the corridor."

Chapter Eleven

Chance leaned against the door and rubbed the nape of his neck. It was miraculous how quickly a gentleman sobered when his father-in-law was patronizing the same notorious club.

"Did you know he was a member?" St. Lyon asked.

His cousin shook his head. "I may have married his daughter, but we are not confidants. He leaves the room whenever Tempest and I call on her mother and sister. If he discovers me at Acropolis, he will assume there is trouble in my marriage and he will do everything to exploit it."

Gideon rose from the sofa and joined them near the door. "You have witnesses who can attest that we have done nothing but drink and play cards all evening."

"And friends will not lie to protect one another?" Chance groaned. "And while the four of us are explaining our presence at Acropolis to the man who detests me and my family, swearing that I am faithful to his daughter, that is when our lusty friend will join our little group with his collection of handpicked courtesans in his wake. Curse Rainbault and his unruly cock!"

"Norgrave is married, too. If he accuses you of betraying your marriage vows, then you can make the same charge. He cannot touch you."

His cousin scowled at St. Lyon. "You of all people have

heard the rumors about Norgrave. The man has no honor and shames his wife by taking mistresses and fathering bastards," he said, dispassionately observing his friend's wince. "He would take pleasure in hurting the daughter who betrayed him and calling my own honor into question. My family would not believe him, but there are other members of the *ton* who will."

Thorn knew Chance did not care a pittance about the *ton* or anyone else's opinion of him. He was worried about Tempest. She did not deserve to be ridiculed for aligning herself with him or to be used as an instrument of revenge against the Duke of Blackbern and his family. Nor did Chance wish for her to have any doubts about his commitment to her.

"Be at ease, cousin," Thorn said, clasping the marquess's shoulder. "Even if someone has told him that you are here, he will need more than rumors to cause mischief for your family. The feud with your family and Norgrave's unhappiness with your marriage to his daughter will only prove he is spiteful."

A knock at the door caused them all to tense.

"My lords?" an unknown man queried. "I have a patron with me who desires a brief moment of your time."

Thorn silently motioned for Chance to hide in the bedchamber, but the marquess vehemently rejected the suggestion by shaking his head. He soundlessly mouthed something. It could have been an explanation on why the bedchamber was a poor choice or he could have been cursing Rainbault and his carelessness. St. Lyon was in no mood to debate the issue, so he abruptly seized a fistful of his friend's evening coat and steered him toward the open balcony and a Chinese Coromandel screen large enough to conceal three grown men.

Chance shrugged off the viscount's grip and crossed to the dark lacquered folding screen unaided. St. Lyon rejoined Thorn and Gideon and tipped his head toward the shut door. The anger that had heated the viscount's eyes had cooled with the knowledge that they had a common foe waiting for them to open the door. Taking a deep breath and releasing it, Thorn turned the key in the lock and opened the door several inches.

"Is there a problem?" he asked, deliberately roughing his voice to convey his displeasure.

The man glanced nervously at Thorn and then at his companion, who Thorn couldn't see. He was a short portly fellow with small dark eyes and a once-broken nose that had healed crookedly. "Forgive me for intruding, my lord. Is your name Fairlamb?"

Thorn glanced at St. Lyon, who was positioned behind the door. "I was under the impression that names are not offered or shared in this establishment," he answered, the servant's nose reddening as his meaning was clear.

"N-Naturally," the other man stammered. "The Acropolis prides itself on discretion. There has been a bit of confusion on the size of your party, Your Grace. We were not expecting another guest to join you."

So the servant thought he was Rainbault. Thorn decided not to correct the man. "I am not expecting anyone else. You have my permission to turn him away."

"That would be rather awkward since I am a longstanding member of this club," the Marquess of Norgrave drawled as he stepped into view. Recognition widened the older man's eyes as he stared at Thorn. His familial ties to the Rookes made him an enemy. "You fool, this is not the duke. Good evening, Lord Kempthorn. This is most unexpected. I had not heard you were joining Rainbault this evening. It is rare that you do. I have heard several ladies speculate if you live the chaste life of a monk, dedicating yourself to intellectual pursuits rather than those of the flesh."

Thorn glanced at the servant before he responded to the marquess. "His Grace will be touched that you have taken an interest in his private affairs. I, however, do not, so I have little interest in satisfying your curiosity."

"A shame," the marquess said with feigned disappointment. "I view myself as something of a mentor, and I would relish the opportunity soaking some of that starch out of your inflexible scruples. It is truly quite liberating."

"I will accept your word on it."

He was quietly contemplating Rainbault's demise. It was no secret that his friend was on friendly terms with Norgrave and, much to Chance's frustration, His Grace had never taken sides on the feud between the Rookes and the Brants.

"Rainbault values his alliance with me and my supporters," the marquess explained.

Norgrave spoke with an air of confidence that had a ring of truth. A tiny seed of doubt took root in Thorn's chest as he silently wondered if their friend was amusing himself by offering his friendship to both families. To maintain the delicate balance, had Rainbault sent word that Chance would be present this evening?

No, such a betrayal was utter rubbish and only proved he had had too much wine this evening.

"You seem surprised. My friendship with His Grace can be traced back to when he first arrived in England as a child," the older gentleman explained. "I went to the king and pleaded on the lad's behalf that he be offered sanctuary from his enemies."

"I have heard the tale from Rainbault's lips, Norgrave," Thorn said, not concealing his derision. "Many were sympathetic to the orphaned prince, and six men argued on his behalf. Although not all of the gentlemen were impelled by magnanimity. A few, it is rumored, sought to use the boy to improve favor with the royal court." Thorn smirked. "I have been told that you might be one of these men."

Norgrave pushed the servant aside and stepped closer to the narrow opening. "You are too young to be so jaded, Kempthorn. Or may I call you Thorn?"

Thorn held the other man's gaze. "Why? Do you hope to sway me with your charming tale of love and fatherly devotion to an orphaned boy?"

Norgrave's light blue eyes narrowed in annoyance. "Perhaps your disposition could be improved on if you chose new friends. I could be persuaded to make a few introductions on your behalf. After all, through my daughter's marriage to your cousin, you are distant family."

Kinship to Norgrave? It was too appalling to contemplate even in jest. "I believe I will respectfully decline your generous offer and keep my current friends."

"A man can never have enough, in my humble opinion," the marquess said, his shrewd gaze taking the measure of everything in front of him, including the fact that Thorn had not altered his stance. "I would assume we have a few friends in common."

"It seems unlikely."

"Now you are just being difficult. What about Rainbault? And then there is Chance," he added.

The gentleman was playing games. Thorn did not risk glancing behind him, but he prayed his cousin had enough sense to remain hidden and not lose his temper. "You have an odd sense of friendship, Norgrave. I heard you were furious when you learned Chance and Tempest had already married. It ruined your plans for her, did it not? Still, you refused to give up. You tried to tear the couple apart with outrageous lies and if you had succeeded, their marriage would have been annulled and Tempest would be married to some gullible fool you could easily manipulate."

Lord Norgrave showed little reaction to Thorn's accusations. "Would you believe that I was protecting my daughter from the scoundrel who kidnapped and married her?"

Thorn grunted in disbelief. "No."

The marquess sighed. "Then I will not waste my breath trying to convince you that I was vilified by Blackbern and his son. I understand family loyalties. You do not wish to accept that your cousin seduced my daughter and then filled her head with ridiculous accusations to turn her against her family."

Thorn remained silent. He had been present the day Chance and Tempest had first met. Once his cousin had learned Norgrave was Tempest's father, he had tried to keep his distance, knowing that nothing could happen between them. Thorn had watched as love blossomed between them. He also had witnessed the upheaval their marriage had created in the two families. Like his father before him, Chance had become Norgrave's enemy. In the marquess's jaded world, people were either gullible pawns or obstacles.

Thorn wanted Norgrave to understand one important detail. He was standing in front of a six-foot-three-inch obstacle.

"The last time I spoke to Lady Fairlamb she was in the company of her sister, and both ladies appeared quite happy as they visited with my family."

Norgrave leaned closer and sneered. "Stay away from Arabella. I will not lose another daughter to your depraved family. Defy me, and I will demonstrate that I am wholly capable of hurting you in ways you cannot contemplate." His mouth curved into a fiendish grin. "Talk to your cousin or Blackbern if you do not believe me."

His eyes slid away from Thorn's face and sharpened as they heard the sound of breaking glass coming from inside the room. "Where are your manners, Kempthorn? You have neglected to invite me in for a drink."

Without warning, Lord Norgrave struck the door with the palm of his hand with enough strength to widen the opening. Thorn glanced at St. Lyon before he stepped back and allowed the marquess to enter the room.

The man's expression darkened as he noted Gideon crouched down picking up the large glass shards that remained of the wine bottle he had knocked off the table and St. Lyon who stood several feet behind Thorn.

"What's this?"

"The demise of a private gathering, Norgrave," Thorn said, dismissing the servant who lingered at the threshold with a stern look. "I regret I cannot offer you a drink. It appears my friends and I have imbibed every drop while we played cards all evening."

"Cards?"

The three men watched as the marquess strode angrily to the bedchamber and peered inside. The interior was softly lit with oil lamps and a large unused bed. He walked back into the main room.

"Where is everyone? Where is Fairlamb? My spies tell me that he is here." Norgrave picked up several of the playing cards on the table and discarded them. His anger and frustration that his son-in-law had outwitted him was palpable.

"Is Chance here, St. Lyon?" Thorn asked while he stared at the marquess.

"I do not see him," was the viscount's cool reply. "What about you, Netherwood? Any sign of your cousin?"

"He is not hiding in the sofa cushions," Gideon said, warming to their game of words. "Has anyone checked the folding screen?"

Thorn turned and openly glared at his twin. In that moment, he could have strangled Gideon for mentioning the damn screen.

The one that was presently concealing Chance!

Noting Thorn's mute fury, Norgrave cocked his head and with a jaunty swagger in his stride he walked to the black-lacquered folding screen. "An excellent suggestion, Netherwood. Or do the lads still call you Thornless. An unfortunate nickname, but the cruel ones tend to stick."

"Never for long," Gideon murmured silkily.

Norgrave peered behind the screen and Thorn, Gideon, and St. Lyon held their collective breaths as the older man froze. "Where the devil is he?"

Relief flowed through Thorn as he exhaled. "You have lousy spies, Norgrave," he drawled. "Shall I see you to the door? If you are quick, you might catch one and demand your coins back."

Just then Rainbault walked into the Bird Room with a comely woman gripping each of his arms plus two more women following behind them, and they had brought refreshments. The blonde was cradling bottles of wine in the front of her gathered skirt and the other held a tray of food. "Excellent, all of you are awake. I thought I would have to arrange—" He paused when he recognized the marquess. "Norgrave, what are you doing here? Have you stumbled into the wrong room?"

Thorn walked up to greet Rainbault. With his back to the marquess, the warning in his gaze was obvious. "I suspect your old mentor has had too many pots of ale. He mistakenly thought Chance was dallying with whores at the Acropolis."

The duke laughed, and gently pushed the two women toward the bedchamber. "You must be drunk, Norgrave. You have been a member of this club for decades. When have you ever encountered Fairlamb here? If Blackbern's son was a frequent visitor, you would have used the information to blackmail him and that would have displeased me."

Norgrave did not seem to hear the duke. "I was told—"

Rainbault's expression hardened. "Go back to your rented rooms or find your way home. This is a private gathering. I know you understand and will respect the rules."

The marquess shook his head as if to clear it. "Of course . . . of course."

Thorn followed him to the door. "I see no reason to mention your visit or your suspicions. Chance is less forgiving than I am when his honor is impugned. Nor would I wish to humiliate Lady Norgrave."

"A pity since it is my favorite pastime," Norgrave said with a gleam in his eye. "I pray Rainbault hasn't taken it into his head that you and your brother are prime candidates for the Acropolis. I deduced years ago that neither one of you were worthy to be a member."

"It is a disappointment I struggle to live with each day," Thorn mocked.

Norgrave nodded at the viscount. "St. Lyon, on the other hand . . . well, the apple does not fall far from the tree, eh?" he said enigmatically and winked at the other man.

St. Lyon stiffened.

Thorn shut the door in the marquess's face and gave the key in the lock a vicious twist.

He turned around and was in the mood to punch Rainbault for his carelessness. The duke was speaking quietly to the other two women as he guided them to the bedchamber door to join the others and closed it.

Viewing his friend's thunderous expression, Rainbault said, "Are you planning to beat an apology out of me, Thorn? In my defense, I was not expecting Norgrave to make an appearance this evening. He has not visited the club in months. Rumor has it, he has been distracted by his latest mistress."

"I will let Chance deal with you," he said, heading to the folding screen. "Tell me, Gideon. What possessed you to encourage Norgrave to look behind the bloody screen? Christ, you are an arse!"

His brother was stirred, anger goading him forward. "Ignoring an obvious hiding place would have made him suspicious. He was so certain he would find Chance, he would have checked it with or without my assistance," Gideon replied, joining his brother.

"Next time, keep your mouth shut!" Norgrave wasn't lying. No one was behind the screen. He tugged at the nearest curtain and released it. He scowled at his brother. "So where is he?"

Rainbault and St. Lyon also moved closer.

"Chance slipped out the window," the viscount volunteered.

Thorn gaped at his companions. "In his inebriated condition, Chance will break his neck if he falls." He opened the window and squinted into the darkness below. The putrid scent of sewage and rotten food filled his nostrils. "Chance?" he called out, resisting the urge to raise his voice.

Norgrave could be listening at the door.

All four of them had crammed their heads through the opening of the window and waited for their friend to reply. After a tense minute, the men heard, "Is he gone?"

Thorn's shoulders sagged with relief. "How did you find your way to the street? Did you fall? Are you hurt?"

"So little faith," was Chance's indignant response. "How do you think I managed it? I climbed down, though the last part was tricky since I couldn't see the street. I might have reconsidered Gideon's plan if I had gotten a good look at the distance and my precarious perches."

"Stay there. I am coming down," Thorn ordered stepping away from the window. The duke, St. Lyon, and Gideon mimicked his actions.

From below, they faintly overheard, "Hurry. There are rats scurrying in the weeds and garbage. Not to mention, it smells like a damn chamber pot down here."

Thorn looked at his brother and felt the urge to apologize for yelling at him. "This was your plan?"

Gideon shrugged. "With you distracting Norgrave, it seemed sensible to come up with a plan of escape before the man demanded to search the rooms."

"You broke that bottle deliberately."

"Aye," his twin said, nodding. "I thought the marquess would take advantage of your divided attention and force his way in. He would have never taken your word alone that Chance was not here."

"Impressive," the duke said, staring at Gideon with new appreciation.

His brother shrugged off the praise, but he was obviously pleased. Hell, even Thorn was proud of his twin's quick thinking.

"This calls for a toast," St. Lyon said, wandering over to the table that was laden with wine bottles and a tray of refreshments. He selected one of the bottles and inspected it.

Thorn was not staying. Norgrave was correct about one thing. He did not possess the temperament for the Acropolis.

Rainbault picked up Thorn's discarded hat and tossed it at him. "Extend my apologies to your cousin. Tell him I will grovel later."

Thorn caught his hat and chuckled. His Grace was too arrogant to grovel to anyone. "Are you staying?" he casually asked his brother.

"Aye," Gideon replied. "I will find my own way home."

"Very well," he said, acknowledging St. Lyon by raising his hand. "Next time we meet, I vote someone other than Rainbault picks the establishment."

"Agreed," Gideon and St. Lyon said speaking over the duke's halfhearted protest.

"Has everyone forgotten that I am stuck down here with the rats and filth?" Chance's voice drifted into the room through the open window.

Chapter Twelve

The town house was ready for Lord Dewick's arrival.

Olivia strode through the library. The owner's book collection was not as grand as her father's, but it was diverse. When she had joined her father last spring, she had selected over twenty books that she planned to read during her stay. She had gotten through twelve of them, which, according to Lady Felstead, was eleven books too many. The marchioness had scolded her about turning down the scores of invitations that arrived at her doorstep each day.

It was pride that kept Olivia from admitting she and her father were often overlooked by the matrons of the *ton*. After her mother's death, Lord Dewick had shunned the ballrooms and chose to spend his evenings at his favorite clubs. Spurned matrons struck his name from their guest lists and, over the years, everyone had forgotten that he had a daughter. Oh, she attended a few balls last spring and the theater on four occasions. She visited the museums and sat in on a few scientific lectures. She had been content with her quiet evenings at home, while other young ladies her age were caught up in the whirlwind of nightly social events.

Nevertheless, Lady Felstead was practically apoplectic when she gradually deduced that Olivia's father had done nothing to rectify the situation. Her father and the marchioness had several fiery discussions behind closed doors that ended with the older woman marching out of the house with her generous mouth a straight line of disapproval and the heat of indignation in her eyes. At the end of their stay, her father had pulled her aside and vowed that next Season would be better.

Olivia had her doubts.

Oh, she was certain that between her chastened father, Lady Felstead's efforts, and Lady Grisdale's determination to be mistress of Treversham House this spring would be different than last year's. As she hired servants and readied the house, Olivia mentally braced herself for stepping into the social whirlwind that everyone expected her to enthusiastically embrace.

No one seemed to appreciate the simple pleasure of reading a good book.

Lady Arabella had told her that reading was best done in winter or when foul weather limited a lady's choices of amusements. Perhaps she was correct. However, it would not deter Olivia from selecting a few books during her stay just in case London's whirlwind tossed her into the Thames.

Olivia giggled at the thought.

She tugged off her lace cap and scratched the back of her head. The curly ends of her chestnut hair tumbled and bounced against her shoulders. Placing her cap on a bust of a Roman emperor, she playfully rubbed her nose against his marble one.

"I require your opinion, kind sir," she said to the statue. "Would it be untoward for me to have a glass of wine at this late hour? The servants are in bed. No one will know."

Olivia titled her head and waited for his response. "You agree. How wonderful! I knew there was a reason why I like you," she said flirtatiously over her shoulder as she walked to the cabinet and opened it. "Just one glass, of course . . . and none for you. The last time I allowed you to have one, you spilled it—"

"Who the devil are you speaking to?"

Olivia jumped and let out a shriek as she turned around and saw one of the Netherwood twins standing near an open door that led to the back gardens. Her hand fluttered up to her throat and then slid over her heart. She could feel it pounding in her chest.

"If I drop dead from fright, I hope the magistrate hangs you!"

"I never realized what a bloodthirsty creature you are." He stepped inside without asking her permission.

He was drunk.

The Netherwoods were so proper about everything that it was rare to see any of them in a state of undress. Her midnight visitor wore a wrinkled white linen shirt with the three buttons at his throat unfastened. His shirt was partially untucked from his dark brown breeches and he wore boots. Was this Gideon? She could not imagine Lord Kempthorn so disheveled. Even when he fell into the lake with her and Gideon, he had been wearing a waistcoat.

Gesturing to the marble bust, he asked, "Were you speaking to this fierce-looking gent with a lady's cap on his head?"

Why did I place that silly cap there? "Ah." She glanced at the door, contemplating her escape.

"Does he ever answer?"

When Lady Felstead had told her that Gideon and Lord Kempthorn had rented the town house behind hers, she had declared it happenstance. The earl had seemed less enthused, but he and his brother had agreed to check on Olivia while she waited for her father to join her.

"Well, does he?"

"It is a marble bust," she said warily. "If the Roman spoke, I would be sleeping at your mother's house."

He gave her a lopsided grin that was so endearing the knot in her stomach eased a degree. "A very wise decision," he said solemnly. "Talking statues will cause you nothing but trouble."

Olivia giggled at the odd remark. Her lips parted to ask him how often he chatted with statues, but she resisted because he was likely teasing her.

This had to be Gideon. Lord Kempthorn was too dignified to approach her in such an outrageous and informal manner.

With a sigh of delight, he noticed the glass decanter she had been reaching for when he had startled her. "Ah, the wine!" he said, picking up the decanter and removing its glass stopper. He sniffed the wine and nodded with approval. "Since the emperor will not be drinking this evening, do you mind if I drink from his glass?"

"But I was not really—oh, never mind," she said, deciding that his head was too muddled to appreciate her explanation on why she was chatting with the marble bust. "Before your arrival, I was planning to pour myself a glass of wine."

Olivia selected two wineglasses and placed them on the narrow shelf. She tried to take the decanter from him, but he waved her off. His hand was surprisingly steady when he filled the first glass and then the second one.

"Do you often imbibe wine at midnight?"

"It seems like a dreadfully personal question," she teased. "I will give you an honest answer if you tell me which twin visits his neighbor in the middle of the night?"

He sent her a disappointed look. "Can't you tell?"

She shook her head.

"No, you never could. Have you considered wearing spectacles?"

"I do not need them. Besides, even if I did, Lady Grisdale would not approve," she confessed as she picked up her glass.

"Why not?" He returned the decanter to its proper place.

"Well, according to the countess, spectacles are for wall-flowers. It is better to be lovely and blind than to observe another lady win your handsome suitor with your new pair of spectacles."

He frowned down at her. "That is atrocious advice."

"No gentleman wants to marry a lady with flaws," she said with a shrug. "Poor eyesight would definitely be considered one, and if there are discernable imperfections, there are likely hidden ones as well."

"Another one of Lady Grisdale's misguided observations?"

Olivia peered over her glass. "I will have you know that the countess is a fount of information when it comes to the subject of gentlemen and marriage."

"And most of it should be shoveled into a dustbin and burned."

Olivia privately agreed. "We are speaking of my father's future bride, so I will politely ignore your insulting comment and answer your question. I occasionally imbibe wine at midnight."

He blinked owlishly at her, so she turned away and resisted the urge to comb her hair with her fingers. This afternoon she had absently stuffed it under her cap, and it must look like a squirrel's nest.

"Just like you occasionally dance under the stars," he said, trailing after her.

Olivia closed her eyes and smiled. "Gideon." She tried not to think about their kiss.

He came up behind her and placed his hand on her waist. "Who else could it be?"

Most definitely, not Lord Kempthorn.

"What are you doing here? Did you attend a ball this evening?" she asked.

"Not a ball," he replied, not elaborating on what he had

been doing. "As for why I am here. I noticed the lamps were lit in the library so I thought you would like some company."

"That was very sweet of you," she said, feeling a bit warm with him standing so close to her. "Did your brother object? After all, it would be unseemly if anyone caught you slipping through the iron gate that connects the two gardens."

"I am not worried about the gossips. As for my brother, he is not at home."

She supposed a gentleman like Kempthorn kept a mistress in Town. He might not return home until dawn. Olivia heard the clink of glass and turned around. Gideon was refilling his glass.

He raised the decanter. "More?"

"I am fine," she assured him.

He took a hearty swallow of his wine and gave her a considering look.

"What?"

Hooking the neck of the decanter with two fingers, he walked toward her. "Come on. Let's take a stroll in the gardens."

"There is not much to admire in the dark," Olivia said, feeling her arms tingle at the thought of an adventure.

"You would be surprised," he said, handing her his glass. He walked to the double doors and opened one side. "I left my lantern on the terrace."

Olivia did not hesitate in following him outdoors. If another gentleman had issued the invitation, she would have declined. However, she trusted Gideon. She glanced up at the dark sky.

"I see the clouds have cleared," she said, admiring the moon.

"There is enough moonlight that I could have navigated the garden paths." He leaned down and picked up his abandoned lantern. "The hedge maze is still unfamiliar to me and cast in shadow upon shadows. Never fear, I have a good sense of direction." There was a flash of white teeth as he grinned in anticipation.

"You have no sense at all," she said cheerfully, matching his pace. "I am not wandering into a dark maze with you, Netherwood."

"Where is your sense of adventure, young lady? What happened to the girl who set out to explore every inch of Malster Park and the surrounding lands with me and my brother?"

Tiring from his swift pace, she halted near the fountain at the heart of the garden. She leaned against the edge of the stone basin. "My governesses began to order my maid to tighten my stays to discourage my outdoor adventures," she confessed.

Gideon sputtered and struggled not to laugh. "You are joking." He placed the lantern on the narrow lip of the fountain. Next, he crouched down until he could brace his back against the basin. He slid down and stretched his long legs out in front of him. "Wine?" He held up the decanter.

Olivia stared down at the two glasses in her hands. "You might need this. She handed him his.

He took the glass and filled it, and placed the decanter next to him. "Since you have refused to explore the maze with me, you might as well sit down beside me. There's no point in straining my neck when I don't have to, you know."

She had always enjoyed Gideon's irreverence for formality. He had always treated her as if she were part of his family. "If I must," she said with an air of reluctance. She offered him her empty wineglass.

"Cheeky brat," he replied as he took her glass. Switching the glass to his other hand so he held both in one, he extended his empty hand so he could assist her. "Careful. You will get a smudge on your ugly dress."

He spoke so matter-of-factly, she had almost missed his

insult. She slid on the gravel and landed with a slight bounce. "How rude! My dress is not ugly." Although she conceded it was not immaculate. She had worn one of the housekeeper's aprons, but it had not spared her dress from getting smudged with dust.

Gideon filled her wineglass and returned it to her. "Here. Drink some more wine. You will feel better for it."

"No, really," she said, leaning toward him. "I have received many compliments on this dress."

His eyes widened. "You have actually greeted visitors wearing this dress?"

Olivia sensed he was teasing, but this was not the first time he had commented on her attire. "You are an awful man. If you persist in these insults, I can no longer be your friend."

"If I spared your feelings, I would not be a very good friend," he said, his voice roughening. He sipped his wine and stared off into the distance. "You will never capture a gentleman's eye by wearing dresses like that one."

Bewildered, she glanced down at the bodice. "It is perfectly respectable."

"Precisely," he said, stabbing a finger in her direction. "That high neckline should be worn by an eighty-year-old maiden aunt. You are too young to be hiding your breasts."

"Gideon!"

Truly, the man had no sense of propriety at all.

"I am sure your breasts are remarkable, but it is difficult to tell when you have covered them in that ugly floral print. What type of flowers are a muted reddish brown anyway? They look like misshapen toadstools."

"I am not discussing my breasts or my dresses with you," she said, covering her face with her hand.

"Come now, Olivia, you are made of sterner stuff. No subject is forbidden or shameful when it is just the two of us," he said, tugging her hand away from her face.

She peered at him through her splayed fingers. "Lady Felstead would take a wooden spoon to your head if she overheard how you speak to me."

"Only if you tell her."

One by one, he pried her fingers away from her face. His gaze was hooded as he leaned closer and tenderly kissed each fingertip. Against her will, her nipples hardened into peaks and she was acutely aware of a spreading ache in her breasts. Her breath quickened.

"My dear Netherwood," she sighed. "What am I to do with you when you persist in being wicked?"

His beautiful mouth was inches from hers. "Indulge me." The hope in his voice made her grin.

"That would be unwise." Olivia pulled away, but he caught her by the arm.

"Where are you going?" he demanded.

"To find a very large wooden spoon," she said. "Someone needs to knock some of the arrogance out of you."

Olivia was half teasing, but he seemed to take her threat seriously. Before she could take her next breath, his lips captured hers, and the connection was exhilarating. Netherwood's kisses reminded her of the days when she was a young girl and would hang upside down from a sturdy tree limb and let her body swing like a pendulum. The blood would rush to her head, making her hot and dizzy. Her face would tingle and her heartbeat would pound in her ears. She loved the sensation, and would cling to her precarious perch until her fingers ached and her vision dimmed.

It was Lord Kempthorn who put an end to her mischief. One day, he had caught her dangling upside down like damp bedsheets tossed over a taut line of rope. Muttering a curse, he had grabbed her by the waist and hauled her off the tree limb. For a boy, he had seemed exceptionally strong. When her feet had touched the ground, he had done the unthinkable. He delivered a hard smack to her back-side and told her that he would use his father's horsewhip if he ever caught her dangling from another tree.

His fury and rough handling had frightened her. Her backside burning from his hand, she had kicked him in the shin and ran back to her father's lands. She expected the young Lord Kempthorn to follow her home and report her unladylike antics to Lord Dewick. However, he never mentioned the incident and went back to ignoring her.

Just one more secret she shared with the Netherwood twins.

Now it was Gideon turning her world upside down and quickening her pulse. She giggled against his firm lips, wondering if Lord Kempthorn would walk out from the shadows and spank her for kissing his brother.

"You find kissing me amusing?" he murmured as he reached for her again.

"I was thinking about your brother."

Her confession had him drawing back in surprise. "What?" he asked, strangling on the word. "You have been kissing him too."

"Oh no," she said. Her nose wrinkled in consternation as she wondered if the earl's kiss would feel the same as his twin's. "He caught me once, you know."

He stared at her as if she had sprouted horns.

"Your kisses reminded me of when I used to hang up-side down from a tree branch and let the blood rush to my head. I felt dizzy and wonderful—"

"That's how it feels when I kiss you?" Gideon caressed her cheek.

"Well—yes," she shyly admitted, and then her thoughts drifted to Lord Kempthorn again. "However, your brother disapproved and he threatened to take a horsewhip to me if he ever caught me risking my neck again."

She omitted the part about the earl spanking her.

Gideon's caressing hand moved to her shoulder. "Did he frighten you?"

"Of course not," she lied. "I was angry he stepped in where he was not wanted and ruined—" She took a deep breath. "What are we doing, Netherwood? What are *you* doing? Here . . . with me."

Gideon shifted and leaned against the basin of the fountain. "I worry about you, Olivia. Don't tell me that you are fine on your own. You haven't seen enough of the world to comprehend its dangers." He pinched his nose. "You are so fierce, so innocent."

The heat his kisses had created within her chest cooled. "So you kissed me because you were worried." She picked up her wineglass and took a contemplative sip.

Arrogant jackanapes.

His hand fell away from his face and he pulled her closer. She spilled some wine on her dress. "I kissed you because I cannot seem to keep my hands off you. I have no business touching you. It will not happen again."

"Oh good. I am so glad we have that settled."

Swine.

Olivia shoved him away and climbed unsteadily onto her feet. Without looking at him she finished the remaining wine in her glass.

"What have we settled?" he warily asked. He gripped the edge of the fountain to pull himself up.

"That I am not the only one who is afraid of your brother." Olivia headed for the house, leaving Netherwood to find his way home. She did not require the use of his lantern. The light spilling from the interior of the library was her beacon.

"Olivia, don't run off," Gideon called after her. "It wasn't my intention to hurt your feelings."

"Do not worry about my feelings, Netherwood." She gritted her teeth together. "You never have."

His arms wrapped around her waist and he dragged her backward a few steps before she left the garden. "I care, Olivia," he murmured into her hair. "Always have, but it's not enough. I am not the man you think I am, and you are too damn innocent for someone like me."

"Then stop kissing me." She brushed off his embrace. "With a little patience, I am certain I can find a gentleman who will not regret putting his hands on me."

He shackled her slender wrist and held her in place. "London is filled with them, you little fool! That is why you need a keeper. You are too naïve for the sophisticated flirtations too prevalent in Town life. You should beg your father to send you home to Treversham House. There must be an unmarried squire or clergyman who would marry you and keep you tucked away in the country."

Olivia's eyebrows came together in puzzlement. Gideon looked tormented, as if she was the one hurting him. "You have been out of my life for a long time, my lord. I am no longer the girl of your fond recollections. I crave adventure as any other lady."

"Prove it," he growled and pulled her into his crushing embrace.

Her entire body hummed with anticipation as his mouth slanted over hers. His lips were hot and firm as he kissed her ruthlessly, a chastisement for challenging him, for testing the limits of his restraint.

Olivia kissed him back, a potent mix of desire and anger. She had provoked him, and a part of her reveled in the feminine power awakening within her. Netherwood was determined to keep her at a distance, but she had the ability to break down his resistance and enthrall him with a kiss.

His hand moved up from her waist and followed the curve of her breast. He squeezed and her breath caught in her throat as he devoured her lips. Her hard nipples ached and she idly wondered what it would feel like if he kissed those tender buds. His hand slid up toward her throat. There was a harsh tug and the sound of ripped fabric.

Olivia gasped against his lips as the night air seeped between them and cooled her flesh. She abruptly turned her face away to end their kiss. "You tore the front of my bodice?"

"A fitting end to your ugly dress," he said smugly. He stepped back and stared down at the damage. "Have your maid toss it in the rag bin in the morning."

She glared at him in disbelief. "You kissed me," she said, the pitch of her voice increasing with each word, "so you could get close enough to ruin my dress?"

He exhaled. "Yes. I told you that you were too naïve to play such games. I will call on you tomorrow. If you behave, I will escort you to Mother's favorite dressmaker where you can benefit from my advice."

Ill-mannered savage.

"I do not require your assistance, Mr. Netherwood," she said, seething. He had kissed her as if he was dying for her mouth, and he had felt *nothing*. It was all a game to him.

He hesitated when he noticed her biting her lower lip to quell a slight tremor. The fierce satisfaction in his gaze softened to something appallingly close to pity.

"Ah . . . Olivia."

"The hour is late, Netherwood. You should return to your town house before your brother realizes that you are not in bed."

Leave before I cry, you heartless beast!

"I will call on you tomorrow." His expression hardened when she did not reply. "Do not behave like a silly goose, Olivia. You could benefit from my advice." He frowned down at her. "My brother's as well."

She preferred death to begging Lord Kempthorn for his help.

"Farewell, Mr. Netherwood. Watch your step in that hedge maze. It would be a shame if you tripped and broke your neck," she said, unable to conceal the mute anger simmering in her eyes.

Gideon shook his head and muttered something under his breath. He slowly backed away from her. "Don't forget to get rid of that dress."

She held her chin high. "I will do what I please."

"Careful, Olivia. Wear that dress again, and you will not like the consequences."

"How will you punish me? With a kiss?" she taunted. Her lips still stung from his last kiss.

"Perhaps," he said, turning away and heading back into the garden. The darkness swallowed him whole. "Or I might spank you."

Olivia's mouth fell open in surprise. By the time she had recovered her composure, he was gone.

Thorn used the servant's entrance to enter the town house. The house was dark, but he had remembered to collect the lantern he had left near the fountain after he had kissed Olivia Lydall.

I should have never sought her out.

Never kissed her. Again.

There was some comfort in blaming the bottles of wine he had consumed during the long hours at the Acropolis. He had laughed until his stomach had ached while St. Lyon regaled them with tales of his latest conquests. Rainbault spoke of the duel he had almost fought a few days earlier, and Gideon had surprised everyone by sharing a harrowing story about a sea battle and a narrow escape from French pirates.

It had been an enjoyable evening until Norgrave had shown up and demanded to see Chance. Of course, it could have been worse. His cousin could have broken his neck when he escaped out one of the Acropolis's windows and dropped down into the back alley. Marriage was supposed to tame a man, not make him more reckless.

He could have returned to the Acropolis once he had escorted his cousin home. Eight months had passed since he had bedded a woman. Although his friends would not understand, Thorn savored his periods of celibacy almost as much as he loved quenching his lust. Denial heightened his instincts and proved he was in control of his appetites and his emotions. Food and drink tasted better. He took in his surroundings and studied everything. Intellectual pursuits filled his soul. Music and art became a solace as his carnal needs sharpened and taunted him in his dreams.

Encountering Miss Lydall at Malster Park had reminded him that eight months was a long time to deny himself the pleasure of losing himself in an eager woman. Of savoring the taste and texture of her skin, the scent of her arousal intermingling with his own, and the keening cries of her rapture.

Thorn had not denied himself so long to find brief pleasure in one of the Acropolis's courtesans. When he took a lover, the affair usually lasted months to a year. There was no jealousy or bitterness when he ended their arrangement. Emotions rarely played a part in his affairs. He chose women who were similar to him in temperament and appetites. Ladies who understood that he was not seeking a wife, and that he was the one in control. He was loving, devoted, and generous with all of the mistresses. He was also the one who walked away when their passions cooled.

Olivia Lydall was too innocent, too emotional to understand his world.

The realization that he was drawn to her was humiliating. It revealed a weakness within him and he resented her for it. Slipping into Lord Dewick's library while she unknowingly charmed him by flirting with that damn marble bust had been foolhardy.

Luring her into the back gardens so he could steal a few kisses bordered on lunacy.

Perhaps he should follow St. Lyons and Rainbault's example and work off his lust for Olivia Lydall between the fleshy thighs of a skilled courtesan.

"Where were you?"

Thorn had reached the main hall and discovered Gideon sitting halfway up the staircase. He had an empty glass cupped in his hands. His twin had discarded his evening coat, but he still wore his waistcoat. His cravat was tied, but the knot was loose and hastily retied.

He paused at the bottom step. "How long have you been here?"

Gideon shrugged and squinted at the ceiling. "Slightly less than an hour."

"I assumed you wouldn't return until morning."

His twin grimaced and rubbed his chin. "There was little point in staying. Lust like a paphian's love fades once a man spends his seed into the rumpled bedding."

Thorn did not know how to respond. His brother had the demeanor of a well-pleasured man, but there was an air of melancholy in his posture. As if he had regretted not leaving with Thorn and Chance.

Thorn climbed up the stairs until he was standing in front of his brother. "How drunk are you?"

Gideon groaned. "Exceedingly." He gave Thorn a considering glance. "You?"

"Somewhat, but less than I should be." He thought about his next words. "How long has it been?"

His brother lifted his head. "For what?"

Thorn simply stared into Gideon's eyes and waited. Sharing a womb had tied them together in ways unlike other siblings. He refused to believe their time apart and his twin's stubbornness had destroyed their unique bond.

Understanding flashed in Gideon's bloodshot eyes. "Ah, that." He grimaced and shook his head. "Must we discuss this? Out loud?"

Thorn grinned at his brother's reluctance. "We could use hand gestures but that seems a bit vulgar and confusing since neither one of us is at his best."

Gideon scratched at the beard stubble along the line of his jaw. He stared ahead, unable to look at Thorn while he spoke. "Let's just say that it has been a long while since I—uh, have been close to a woman. It wasn't that I didn't have opportunities over the years. Was tempted a time or two." He shrugged as if at peace with his choices. "When Rainbault arrived with those women, I thought it was time. I have spent so many years driven by my anger, by my demons, that it has made me a very rich man. I saw the greed in those wenches' eyes and I figured I had earned the right to take. I was certainly willing to pay for it."

Thorn reflected on his own bouts of celibacy, and the needs unfulfilled. "You were disappointed."

"No, she was rather extraordinary." Gideon glanced over and grinned. "Of course, it has been a long time and my expectations were very low."

Thorn punched him on the arm.

His brother sobered. "Afterward, the wench was curled around me and whispered that she loved me. I felt nothing but a hollowness in my chest."

"The wench wasn't interested in your heart, brother. She enjoyed your cock and the notion of you filling her reticule with gold."

Gideon did not seem to hear him. "A coldness washed over me. The silky flesh I had savored thirty minutes earlier repulsed me. The scent of what we had done curdled my stomach. I left the bed without a word. I was so angry I did not trust myself."

Thorn braced his hands on his knees. "At yourself?"

His brother made a slicing motion with his hand. "At me . . . at her. It wasn't her fault that she wasn't the one I wanted, but it didn't stop me from shagging her."

His hand moved from his knee to his brother's. "There is no need to feel guilty."

Gideon expelled a sound of weariness. "That's the problem, Thorn. I don't feel any guilt. Not about her anyway."

"You said that she wasn't *the one*. Who is?" Thorn asked, dreading his brother's response. If he mentioned Olivia Lydall by name, then his suspicions would be confirmed.

Gideon stood up. "There is no other woman." He rolled the empty glass between his two hands. "Are you heading to bed?"

Thorn was happy to change the subject. "I have had enough adventure for one evening."

His brother snorted in agreement. He and Thorn climbed the stairs. He abruptly halted. "Wait. You never answered my question. Where were you?"

He contemplated lying to Gideon. However, if his brother spoke to Olivia, she would innocently reveal Thorn's deception. "I saw a light in Lord Dewick's library and decided to check on Miss Lydall."

"At this late hour?" He gestured at Thorn's informal attire. "You look like a carriage rolled over you and smell like the floor of a tavern."

"We promised the marchioness that we would look after her," he said, pushing by his brother to continue his ascent. "Lord Dewick isn't scheduled to arrive for a few more days so when I saw the light in the library, it seemed wise to investigate."

Gideon followed him up the stairs. "She must have appreciated your concern."

He thought about how her mouth felt against his. Shy, sweet, and wholly off limits. Of how he tore the front of her dress and allowed her to believe the kiss had meant nothing to him.

Miss Lydall believed it was Gideon who had deceived her. If she figured out that she had kissed Thorn, she would be furious with both of them.

"Perhaps I should call on her tomorrow," his brother said, interrupting Thorn's thoughts.

"She won't be at home." At Gideon's look of askance, he explained. "She told me that her days will be filled with errands as she prepares for Lord Dewick's arrival."

"I see," his brother murmured. "I know you and Olivia have had your differences, but I appreciate that you have been watching out for her in my absence. In truth, I have not been a very good friend."

Neither have I.

"Don't worry about Miss Lydall," Thorn assured him. "The lady herself tells me that she can take care of herself."

Since she unknowingly kept ending up in Thorn's arms was proof that she was ripe for every fortune hunter and rogue.

"In London?" Even Gideon sounded unconvinced. "This is Olivia."

"Then for our mother's sake, we will continue to watch over her." Ignoring his twin's look of astonishment, he added, "The sweet lady is practically family."

Chapter Thirteen

Perhaps she should have one of the servants place a sturdy lock on the gate in the back gardens. According to Lord Barthorpe, the current owner of the town house she and her father were renting, the original owner, Mr. Verdon, had installed the gate at the border of the property so he could discreetly visit his neighbor. The lady in question had married well, but it had been an unhappy marriage. Her only solace had been her gardens, and that was how she had met Mr. Verdon. Every afternoon, the gentleman took a walk in the garden at the same hour as his neighbor. The couple walked together with the stone wall separating them as they discussed gardening, her children, and the latest gossip in the papers.

Five years later, Mr. Verdon commissioned the iron gate.

Lord Barthorpe could not confirm if the couple eventually became lovers, but it seemed likely. Their friendship spanned forty years until the lady's death. Mr. Verdon lived another eight years before he succumbed to a long-standing illness. During those final years, the gardener had a standing order to oil and repair the gate as if Mr. Verdon expected his dear love to return to him one day.

When Lord Barthorpe had told Olivia the tale three years earlier during one of his visits to Treversham House, she had declared it a rather sweet testament to Mr. Verdon's devotion to a lady he could never claim as his own.

Olivia pursed her lips as she thought about how furious she had been when she had returned to the library and caught sight of her reflection in the mirror with her hair disheveled and the front of her dress torn.

Curse it all, Gideon had been correct. The dress she had been wearing was ugly. It just infuriated her that he was a better judge of what was fashionable than she was.

I will not ask for his help!

"It would be too humiliating," she muttered. "I will not do it."

Olivia started at the sound of a knock.

She turned away from the window and cleared her throat. "Yes? You may enter."

The butler opened the door and stepped inside. "Miss Lydall, are you receiving visitors this afternoon?"

She immediately thought of Gideon. He had told her that he would call on her today.

Probably to make certain I got rid of that ugly dress.

Olivia moistened her lips. "Is it a gentleman?"

"No, miss. The footman waiting downstairs presented me with five calling cards." The butler glanced down at the silver salver in his left hand. "A Lady Felstead and her companions, which includes the Duchess of Blackbern, Lady Fairlamb, Lady Arabella, and Lady Fiona. Are you receiving?"

Had Gideon sent them? Lord Kempthorn? Lady Felstead had already been so generous with her time. Olivia had no intention of imposing on the lady so soon. "Yes. You may send them up right away."

Thorn had debated which Netherwood twin would be best received by Miss Lydall. As Gideon, he had promised to call on her, and he had intended to do it properly so none of her neighbors could whisper to Lord Dewick that there had been a hint of impropriety.

However, Gideon was no longer her favorite.

Thorn felt a twinge of regret for bruising Olivia's feelings, but it was for the best. She was too generous not to eventually forgive his brother. It was time someone had scrubbed some of that innocence and adoration from her eyes. No man, not even Gideon, could live up to the lady's expectations.

Gideon's solemn confession last evening was also revealing.

His brother was definitely keeping secrets. There was a woman in his past, someone he had perhaps loved. Someone, a small part of him was still waiting for. Thorn rejected the notion that the lady who owned his twin's heart was Olivia Lydall.

Gideon wouldn't have left England without declaring his intentions to her. Why would he? Olivia was already in love with him. Why hadn't he come to Thorn and asked him to guard her and make certain no man claimed her in his absence.

No, the lady who haunted his brother's dreams was not Olivia Lydall.

Nevertheless, the knowledge would not stop Gideon from turning to her for comfort. Why should he deny himself the boundless warmth and affection when he felt so cold? He might even convince himself that he returned her love.

With ruinous consequences!

Thorn was determined more than ever to distract Miss Lydall and keep her away from his brother.

He had come to a decision at breakfast.

Instead of calling on her as Gideon, he would approach her as Lord Kempthorn. He intended to use her annoyance with his twin to his advantage. Although Olivia was not overly fond of him, he was confident that he could gain her trust. She needed an ally to navigate the perils of London's Polite Society and he was an expert. With a little polish and some new friends, the lady's infatuation with Gideon would fade as other suitors vied for her attention.

He might even earn Lord Dewick's gratitude if he found her a husband.

Thorn was too engrossed with his schemes to pay much attention to the carriage in front of the Lydalls' town house. He disembarked from his equipage and strode to the front door.

The butler opened before he could knock.

"Good afternoon," Thorn began, peering into the hall's interior as he could hear the chatter of feminine voices as descending the stairs. Miss Lydall already had visitors. "I am—"

"Good heavens, is that you, Thorn?" The door opened wider, revealing his mother. She separated from his sister and the other women and walked toward him. "I thought I recognized your voice. What are you doing here?"

The butler stepped out of Thorn's way, allowing him to step indoors and greet his mother. "Good afternoon, Mother." He dutifully kissed her on the cheek that she had presented to him. He removed his hat and inclined his head to acknowledge her companions. "Ladies."

He was related to all of these women by blood and marriage. Miss Lydall's household had been invaded by his family. The development was unexpected, but he could use a few allies.

"Am I intruding?"

"Not at all," his mother replied. "In fact, your visit is providence since we could use your assistance."

Concern furrowed his brow as he touched his mother on the arm. "How so?"

"Lord Kempthorn?" Miss Lydall interrupted.

"Miss Lydall." Thorn looked up and his gaze rested on the lady's face. Olivia didn't look happy to see her front hall filled with people, but she appeared resigned as she descended the stairs. She wore a pale yellow spencer over a walking dress of jaconet muslin. The Angoulême bonnet gipped in her hand was small and the same color as her spencer. Her attire was moderately stylish, but he suspected she had purchased it last season.

Thorn walked to the bottom of the staircase and waited for her. She looked perplexed when he offered her his hand, but she knew the other ladies were watching so she laid her hand over his. He tightened his hold and led her down the final few steps. Before she could pull away, he brought her hand to his lips and brushed a kiss across her knuckles.

The color in Olivia's cheeks deepened as she shifted her gaze from her hand to the marchioness. "Did Lady Felstead summon you?"

"I am not responsible," his mother replied. "Though I am curious. What has brought you to Olivia's door?"

Thorn had yet to release her hand, and his reluctance had not gone unnoticed by his family.

"Gideon sent me." He gave her an apologetic look. "He asked me to convey his regrets. The early arrival of a merchant ship and some confusion about the manifest has forced him to alter his plans. While he deals with business, I have the pleasurable task of keeping his appointment with you."

Tempest and Lady Arabella appeared amused by his explanation while his sister gaped at him in open disbelief. The Duchess of Blackbern exchanged a knowing glance with the marchioness.

Olivia took a step backward, and she would have stumbled if he had not been holding her hand. "That is very gracious of you, Lord Kempthorn. However, as you can see, I am about to leave the house. You are released from your obligations." She tugged her hand free from his grasp, causing her gloves to tumble out of her bonnet where she had stuffed them and onto the steps.

"Oh dear," she sighed, unhappy with her clumsiness.

"Allow me," Thorn said.

Both of them leaned down at the same time to retrieve her gloves. She seized the first glove, and he moved closer to her as he reached for its mate. He took advantage of their proximity to whisper into her ear.

"You can't get rid of me that easily, Miss Lydall."

She inhaled sharply and straightened, while he took his time. He offered her the glove.

"T-Thank you, Lord Kempthorn." Olivia edged away from him, walked over to the side table, and concentrated on putting on her bonnet and gloves.

Tempest strolled over to him. "What mischief are you engaging in with Miss Lydall, dear cousin?" she asked, keeping her voice low so the other ladies would not overhear. "Or is it your brother?"

"Gideon is innocent," Thorn answered truthfully.

"I doubt the same can be said about you," she teased.

"No," he said, a slow grin curving the corners of his mouth. "Even so, what is the harm in flirting with a lady?"

"Nothing at all," Tempest said. "However, you are making the lady skittish with your intensity. For a moment, when you bent down to collect her gloves, I thought you had intended to kiss her."

"In front of my mother and sister?"

He sounded genuinely offended by her accusation. When she simply smiled, he reminded himself that she was married to Chance. Thorn was certain that his cousin had been guilty of worse sins than kissing a lady in public.

And Tempest was correct. As his lips brushed against

Olivia's ear, he had had a sudden urge to trace the delicate outer shell with the tip of his tongue.

"I have always made Miss Lydall nervous. Gideon was always her favorite," he said as he and his cousin's wife watched as his mother offered Olivia her opinion on the proper positioning of her bonnet.

"You hope to change her opinion, do you not?"

Thorn nodded. "I intend to devote myself to the task."

She had been unable to get rid of him.

When Lord Kempthorn learned that the ladies were anticipating an afternoon of shopping, he insisted on offering the use of his carriage and his protection.

Lady Felstead was thrilled by the news. With their party increasing with each stop, the marchioness needed another carriage, and her sons' nearby town house had been her next planned destination to borrow theirs. The dear lady had never imagined she could persuade one of her sons to join them.

It was no accident Lady Felstead had insisted that Olivia ride in Lord Kempthorn's coach. Was the marchioness trying her hand at the little matchmaking? Olivia glanced at the earl's profile as he expertly handled the ribbons to guide the pair of horses through London's streets and wondered how much Gideon had told him about last evening.

"I can see your health has improved in the passing days," the earl said, his attention focused on his task. "The color has returned to your cheeks."

"Thank you. It is kind of you to say so." If there was a rosy hue in her cheeks, she credited the Netherwood twins and their tenacity to exasperate her. "I confess, the stagecoach was dampening my spirits, but I revived quickly with a hearty meal and a night's sleep in a decent bed."

He absently nodded as if he was not listening to her. Which was utterly typical of Lord Kempthorn. He had little tolerance for idle conversation or silly chits. She was certain he considered both applied to her. Not for the first time did she wonder why he had volunteered to join their shopping jaunt.

"Lord Kempthorn—"

He glanced at her. It was brief, but she felt the impact of his dark green eyes, and her stomach fluttered in response. "Thorn. It is ridiculous to stand on formality when you call my identical twin by his first name."

Thorn. She mouthed his name, tasting the word as her tongue touched her teeth. This was not the first time she had been encouraged to use his nickname by him or his family, but she had resisted, preferring to keep in place the distance he had erected between them when they were children. There had been no boundaries with Gideon. He had always been her friend, and even when she called him Netherwood, it was done out of affection.

Her relationship with the earl had been different. Even at an early age, she could sense he viewed her as something of a nuisance. Someone who had distracted Gideon and ruined their fun. Olivia stole another glance and sighed. Gideon had said that she was too naïve for the sophisticated games the *ton* played, and he was right.

What game was Lord Kempthorn playing with her now? Could she afford to lose?

"Have I been so rude to you that it so difficult to say my name?" he asked.

"Not at all," she lied, embarrassed that she had failed to acknowledge his attempt to befriend her. "I guess I never think of you as Thorn."

He chuckled. "Dare I ask what names you do use when you speak of me?"

Olivia responded to his teasing question with a grin. "When I was a little girl, you and your brother were Justin and Gideon." She thought for a moment. "I cannot recall when you became Lord Kempthorn. Likely one of the adults impressed upon me the importance of you being Lord Felstead's heir."

Thinking of him as Lord Kempthorn had allowed the young girl to cope with his unspoken disdain for her intrusion into his life and that of his family.

"Do you always do what's proper?"

"Not always." She gave him a measured look. "I have no doubt your mother wrote to you when you were away at school and shared some of the more outlandish tales. And let us not forget your twin. Gideon probably recounted all of our adventures."

The amusement in his expression was replaced with an inscrutable expression. "There are few secrets between brothers. Even less with twins."

Olivia straightened at his nonchalance. "Blast it all. Gideon told you that he kissed me!"

For the first time, Thorn was uncertain on the best tactic to charm a lady. Miss Lydall was proving to be an exasperating mix of stubbornness, innocence, and spirit. She was also furious as a wet cat that he knew about the kiss— How could he not, since he was the gentleman who had kissed her senseless?

Unfortunately, Thorn's strategy to impress Miss Lydall was faltering. Not only was she vexed with Gideon for kissing and telling—charges he was innocent of—she was also not speaking to him for knowing about the kiss. He was doubly damned for his sins and he only had himself to blame.

Tempest had deduced immediately that not all was well between Thorn and Olivia. The meddling wench sidled up to him when no one was paying attention.

"Trounced by your own arrogance," she said, clearly amused. He would never hear the end of it when she told her husband that Miss Lydall had been so eager to escape Thorn's company that she had practically leaped out of the carriage. Or she would have if he hadn't seized her arm.

"She likes my twin well enough." He sulked as he watched his sister and the source of his frustration admiring a bonnet. "She should like me, too."

Olivia purred in my arms when I kissed her.

Tempest's amusement melted into sympathy. "Have you considered that you are going about this wrong, Thorn?" she asked. "You and Gideon grew up reveling in your similarities. With Miss Lydall, you need to show her the differences. You may share the same face, but you and Gideon are not the same man."

Lady Fairlamb's logic was insightful, and he was chagrined that he had overlooked this angle. "How much has Chance told you?"

"About your infatuation with Miss Lydall?"

Was that how it looked to her? "It is not infatuation—not exactly. It is—"

She dismissed his fumbling denial by rolling her eyes. "Say no more. It is your affair. What does concern me is what happened at the Acropolis last evening."

"Chance told you what transpired?" *What was the man thinking?* Admitting that he had gotten drunk at the notorious Acropolis would have placed many marriages in peril. A spiteful lady would have locked her husband out of her bedchamber for at least a month. "As his cousin and friend, I feel compelled to speak in your husband's defense. The Acropolis was Rainbault's harebrained idea, but I swear the only reckless thing your husband did was tell you the truth."

Tempest intently studied a pair of kid gloves on one of the tables. "I have faith in my husband, Thorn. Though, in the future, I would prefer anyone but Rainbault selects the amusements for the evening. The man is wholly without principles."

Thorn did not bother defended the duke. The man was the consummate scoundrel.

"His Grace is repentant. In truth, he chose the Acropolis because of its familiarity and privacy."

"I see." Tempest frowned as she traced the pattern of seed pearls on the gloves. "I assume my father frequents the Acropolis for the same reasons."

Thorn had misunderstood the young marchioness's distress. He had addressed her as an angry wife, when it was the daughter who sought answers about her father. "I do not know. I am not a member of the club, and my—our—family generally avoids most Brants."

"My sister and I are honored to be the exceptions."

She lifted her gaze, and Thorn was aghast to glimpse a hint of tears in her misty gaze. Chance would not let blood ties prevent him from pummeling any man who made his wife cry.

Thorn reached into his coat and retrieved his handkerchief. "Here. Dry your eyes before my mother notices. I have angered enough ladies for one day."

Tempest's lips trembled as she struggled not to laugh. "You know, Thorn, you can be awfully sweet," she said, discreetly dabbing at the corner of her eyes. "I suppose that is why I adore you."

"Naturally, I learn this after you marry my bounder of a cousin," he said, affectionately hooking his arm through hers as he steered her toward a life-sized painted wood female mannequin so she could admire the dress on display.

From the other side of the room, Olivia observed Lord Kempthorn—no, Thorn, as he strolled about the dressmaker's shop with Lady Fairlamb. His affection for his cousin's young wife was obvious, but he was respectful and teased her like he would his sister. He had never been so relaxed and caring in her company.

As if he sensed her regard, the earl turned his head and winked at her.

Startled, she turned away and collided into a low table that held a variety of trimmings for the partially finished bonnets. Fortunately, only one basket fell on impact. Unfortunately, it was filled with colored glass beads that sounded like pellets of hail striking a window as they hit the floor. She cried out as the beads merrily bounced in every direction.

Olivia sank to her knees and gathered the nearest ones to return them to the empty basket. Behind her, she could hear the earl choking on his muffled laughter while Lady Fairlamb whispered fierce admonishments for his boorish conduct.

Chapter Fourteen

Thorn had been tempted to procure some brandy for Olivia and insist that she drink it, but he settled on tea. They had walked to a nearby tea shop and he found a small table near the window.

"I will have to find a new dressmaker." It was the first time she had spoken since Thorn had hauled her to her feet and guided her out of the shop.

"I will be fortunate if she finishes the dresses that I've ordered." She offered a weak smile and thanks to the elderly woman who served them tea and a plate of almond biscuits. It was another indication that she was recovering from all of the excitement.

"No shop owner turns away business. I will wager you aren't the first lady to knock over one of those baskets," Thorn said, feeling a bit guilty that he had laughed at her, though it had been an amusing sight watching her trying to stop all of those damn glass beads from escaping.

Miss Lydall was upset, but no harm had been done. His mother would soothe the proprietor's ruffled feathers. After all, she would not want to lose such a wealthy client.

"Try one of the biscuits. Almond is your favorite, is it not?" he said, taking a sip of his tea.

Olivia frowned at the plate. "How did you know I like almond biscuits?"

Thorn choked on the tea he had swallowed. He shouldn't have known that she liked almond biscuits. When he had ordered their tea, an old recollection of his father rewarding a very young Olivia with almond biscuits if she promised to behave had surfaced in mind. He shrugged. "Everyone likes almond biscuits. If I am wrong, I will order another flavor."

"No," she said hastily. She picked up a biscuit and delicately nibbled the edge. "I adore them. Thank you."

What else do you adore, Miss Lydall?

They sipped their tea in silence. As the minutes passed, Thorn could see the tension seep out of her shoulders as she finished her biscuit. They watched the pedestrians who strolled by the window.

"I cannot believe we just ran off," Olivia said, shaking her head in disbelief. "The Duchess of Blackbern must have thought I was a clumsy ninny."

"You must have encountered the duchess once or twice over the years when her family stayed at Malster Park," he drawled. "As the mother of six children, no doubt she has seen her fair share of broken porcelain, scattered beads, and spilled tea. One incident will not ruin her good opinion of you."

She was not cheered by his opinion. "If she ever had one."

It was rare for the duchess to utter an unflattering opinion about someone. However, there was something rather endearing about Miss Lydall when she sulked. "Are you so determined to find a reason to remain miserable?"

"I suppose so," she said as she picked up her teacup.

A mischievous grin curved his mouth. "Of course, we could always go back to the dress shop."

"No," she replied quickly, and then caught on that he was teasing her. "That was unkind of you."

Olivia Lydall smiled shyly at him, and Thorn felt the

air leave his lungs. He often thought this particular smile was solely reserved for Gideon. It was demure with a hint of flirtation and affection. Thorn traced the rim of his teacup with his finger, pleased with his efforts to endear himself to the lady.

This would be easier than he had thought.

"Miss Lydall?"

Thorn and Olivia turned their heads at the same moment. Olivia's face brightened in recognition, while Thorn scowled.

Olivia rushed to her feet and took several steps forward to greet Oliver Brant, Earl of Marcroft. He was known by his friends as Croft, but Thorn never forgot that he was Lord Norgrave's son and heir. At five foot eleven, his wide shoulders and thick muscles roped around his arms gave him the appearance of a pugilist rather than a gentleman. His thick dark brown hair was shorter than what was deemed fashionable, and there was a coldness in his hazel eyes that intimidated the casual onlooker.

However, his companion did not seem to notice. When she moved forward, Thorn instinctively wanted to draw her back.

When had Olivia encountered Marcroft?

"Lord Marcroft," she said warmly, and lowered into a curtsy. "It is a pleasure to see you again."

The earl clasped her hand gallantly and bowed. "Miss Lydall, how lovely you look this afternoon. Did you just arrive in Town?"

"I have been here a week," she said, pleased and slightly flustered by the other man's compliment.

"A week," Lord Marcroft said, his thick dark eyebrows rising with surprise. "And this is the first time we meet?"

The earl was deliberately ignoring Thorn's presence, and if Marcroft's intention was to annoy him, he had succeeded.

"There was much to be done to prepare the town house for my father's arrival," she explained in apologetic tones.

The way Marcroft's eyes narrowed on her face made the back of Thorn's neck itch. "Lord Dewick isn't in Town?"

"Business has delayed him. However, I expect him any day now," she confided.

Thorn ground his teeth. The little fool! He did not know what game Marcroft was playing with Miss Lydall, but did not believe the gentleman's interest in the lady was genuine.

Thorn moved forward and curled his fingers around Olivia's upper arm. Her gaze shot up to his face in surprise. "Marcroft, I do not wish you to leave with the erroneous impression that Miss Lydall is without friends or protection," Thorn said, deciding to put an end to their joyful reunion.

The earl was more amused by Thorn's defensive stance than worried. "Kempthorn," he drawled. "I did not realize you and Miss Lydall were together."

"Oh, Lord Kempthorn and I are not together," she said hastily, but at Thorn's thunderous expression felt compelled to add, "not as a couple. Most definitely, not as a couple."

"I believe you have resoundingly made that clear to Marcroft," Thorn growled in her ear.

"I was shopping with Lady Felstead and—" Her cornflower blue eyes gleamed with excitement. "How could I forget to mention your sisters? They are with our party, too."

The earl seemed startled by the news. "Tempest and Arabella are here?" Marcroft asked, searching the tea shop for his younger siblings.

"They are with Lady Felstead a few streets over in a little dress shop. If you hurry, I am certain you could catch up to them." Olivia gave him a sympathetic look. "They would be overjoyed to see you."

"Perhaps I will," Marcroft said, his expression shuttered for the first time since he had approached Olivia. "Are you rejoining them?"

Thorn sensed Olivia's discomfort and her reluctance to explain why she had separated from the other ladies. He subtly moved closer to her. "I am escorting Miss Lydall home, so you will have to find your sisters without the lady's assistance."

"A pity," Marcroft said, giving Thorn a speculative glance. "I look forward to speaking with you again, Miss Lydall."

"As do I," Olivia sad quickly, finally noticing the tension between Thorn and Marcroft.

The earl clasped her hand again and bowed. "I will make certain of it." With a stern nod to Thorn, he turned away and headed back to his companions.

"Shall we depart?" Thorn asked. "Or would you like more tea?"

Olivia retrieved her reticule from the small table. "No, I am finished."

"Excellent."

Thorn felt some of the tension in his muscles ease at her light touch on his arm. Without glancing in Marcroft's direction, he still felt the man's piercing gaze on his back as he and Miss Lydall departed.

It was a lovely day for a drive. The blue sky was relatively free from clouds, but any pleasure Olivia could have derived from the pleasant weather was diminished by Lord Kempthorn's gloomy disposition.

"How are you acquainted with the Earl of Marcroft?"

It was a question that Olivia had anticipated after she had observed the friction between the earls. A different lady might have assumed the two gentlemen were vying for her affection. However, knew she was not the kind of lady who inspired jealousy or duels.

"We were introduced last spring," she said, not understanding his interest.

As their carriage passed several shops Olivia had been anticipating to visit, a lady crossed in front of her view and slipped into a small shop that belonged to a jeweler. A sense of familiarity tickled her senses. She had only glimpsed the woman from the back, but her clothing was the height of French fashion, reminding her of the Countess of Grisdale.

Olivia craned her neck to get another look, but the lady was gone. Was the countess in Town? If so, it could mean her father was waiting for her at the town house.

"I would decline all future invitations from that hostess," he advised.

"I beg your pardon?" Then she recalled they had been discussing Lord Marcroft and his influence on her good character. "Good heavens, why?"

"No sensible creature would introduce a respectable young lady to Lord Marcroft." He cast an unreadable look in her direction. "You are a ripe prize for such a scoundrel."

"Lord Kempthorn—"

"Thorn," he corrected automatically.

"Thorn, there is no reason for you to be concerned. I have spoken to Lord Marcroft on several occasions and we have danced twice." Noting his frown, she added, "And it was his sister, Lady Arabella, who introduced me to her brother. Are you telling me that a sister does not know her own brother's heart?"

The revelation did not seem to mollify him. "Sisters are devoted to their brothers. They are unable, nay, unwilling to see a man's flaws, his dark nature."

"If I followed your advice, I would have to avoid most of the gentlemen in Town, and that includes you and your brother."

Thorn grunted. Olivia watched with fascination as the muscles contouring his jawline tightened. "You may be correct. Nevertheless it does not refute the truth that Marcroft cannot be trusted. If he approaches you again, I want to know about it."

"See here, Lord Kempthorn. I already have two older brothers, I do not require another. Not to mention, you are being unreasonable," she protested. "Lord Marcroft—"

"Would seduce and discard you without hesitation," Thorn said succinctly. "As for your errant brothers . . ."

Olivia knew the direction of Thorn's thoughts and tried to cut him off. "Leave Adam and Joseph out of this. They are fighting for King and Country. You have no right to criticize them!"

"Of course. It was unfair for me to judge them," he said, her sudden outburst subduing his temper. He made an intelligible noise with his tongue. It was difficult to tell if the soothing sound was for her or for his horses. "Your brothers would be grateful that someone is looking after you in their absence."

"I do not need a keeper, Thorn."

A reluctant smile softened the harsh angles of his profile. "Aye, you do, but we will save that argument for another day."

The earl halted in front of her town house.

"Give me moment to tend to the horses," he ordered, his attention already directed to the task.

Olivia waited with an air of impatience. Like everything else, the earl handled the carriage and the horses with the competence and ease of practice. She also noted affection for the animals. Although he had the privilege of being Lord Felstead's heir, he was not a spoiled aristocrat as she often liked to believe. This was a man who did not mind getting his hands dirty when it was necessary.

"Allow me," he said, striding to her side of the carriage and holding out his hand.

"Thank you," she said politely as she stood to disembark.

Lord Kempthorn had other plans. Instead of allowing her to step down, his hands encircled her waist and he lifted her. Her feet dangled briefly in the air, and Olivia had to place her hands on his shoulder. A flash of his teeth revealed that his actions had been deliberate.

The rogue!

Her feet touched the ground before she could utter a single coherent word.

"I am fully capable of descending a carriage, my lord," she said, twisting in his embrace. Her head came up, and their gazes locked when his hands lingered on her waist.

"My way was more enjoyable," he replied, releasing her waist but capturing her left wrist. Before she could reclaim it, he placed her gloved hand on the crook of his elbow. "I will escort you to the door, Miss Lydall."

Seeing no reason to argue with him on the street, she and Thorn strolled to the front door.

"Thank you again for coming to my rescue this afternoon," she said, her annoyance fading as she recalled the incident at the dress shop and his attempts to ease her humiliation.

The dark green color of his eyes deepened as he studied her face. "My pleasure. Why do I get the distinct impression that you believe our association has come to an end?"

"Has it not?" she countered. "In a day or so my father will arrive, and you and your family will be released from your promise to look after me."

"Have you forgotten that we are neighbors?"

Thorn reached out and knocked at the door.

How could I? "It makes little difference. We do not share the same interests or friends, so it is unlikely that we will see each other again."

"I disagree," he managed to hold her in place with the enthralling intensity of his gaze. "When I called on you earlier, the front hall was filled with my family. You have strong ties with the Netherwoods. It would be foolish for you not to take advantage of them."

Olivia glared at him. "Is that what you believe I do? Use your sweet mother and your family for gain? How dare you!"

Thorn winced at his misstep. "Miss Lydall—Olivia, I did not intend to—"

The front door opened and the butler greeted them.

"Good afternoon, Miss Lydall." If he detected the animosity between Olivia and the earl, he was too polite to acknowledge it. "Will Lord Kempthorn be staying for tea?"

"Good afternoon, Tink," she said briskly, crossing the threshold and entering the front hall. "No, his lordship will not be staying."

"See here, Olivia," Thorn said, following her into the hall. He spared the butler a glance. "You may return to your duties."

"You have no right to order my butler about. Remain where you are, Tink," Olivia commanded. "I may require you to toss a certain arrogant earl out on his ear if he persists in behaving poorly."

The butler was twenty years older, and Thorn bested him in height and strength. The servant would need assistance if he thought he could get rid of him.

"Damn it, will you stop fussing with your bonnet and give me a chance to apologize," Thorn said, pursuing her to the other side of the hall. "I did not mean to imply that your friendship with my family was for personal gain and nothing more."

"Are you positive?" She untied the bow under her chin and removed her bonnet. Chestnut curls sprung free to frame her face. "You have often questioned my friendship with your twin. Perhaps I hope to influence Lady Felstead into lending her support as Gideon and I form a romantic attachment."

Lord Kempthorn froze. "You cannot deny that there are advantages in marrying my brother."

"Because he has returned to London supposedly rich as Croesus? You insult me as much as your brother." She slapped her bonnet into his chest as she walked by him. "Tink, you will need some assistance with our unwelcome visitor. Two footmen should be enough for the task."

The butler glanced at the earl and nodded. "Very well, Miss Lydall. I will only be a minute."

"For god's sake, Olivia!" he said, grabbing her and turning her around to face him. "Are you telling me that you are not attracted to my brother?"

"Is that why you took Gideon's place this afternoon?" Olivia became incensed at the thought. "Was this his idea or yours? Do you know what? I do not even care. I want you to leave or I will order the servants to throw you out."

"No one has ever thrown me out of a house!"

Olivia sneered at him. "Of course, no one would dare touch a single hair on the noble head of Lord Kempthorn. Much admired by the ladies of the *ton,* and a coveted drawing-room visitor. Persist, and I will introduce you to a new and humbling experience."

"Outrageous little imp," he said, torn between amusement and exasperation. "When was the last time your father took a leather strap to your backside?"

"Never," she spat. "My father is a decent man, a gentleman."

Olivia stuck her chin out.

"Be forewarned. I am *not*." Thorn grasped her chin

before she could pull away and lowered his head. His lips covered hers, smothering her protest. It was a hard, punishing kiss that filled her with heat. Within seconds her entire body felt engulfed in flames.

He abruptly dragged his mouth from hers. "I will see myself out."

Olivia touched her bruised mouth with her fingers as she watched the door shut behind the earl. She should have been appalled at Lord Kempthorn's loutish behavior, but it was her response to his kiss that concerned her.

She had accused Thorn of not being a gentleman. What kind of lady was she to be attracted to two men?

Chapter Fifteen

"Telling stories about me again?"

Thorn tipped his head back so his valet could finish tying his cravat. "Why should I bother when you seem adept at spinning your own tales?"

"Father sent one of the servant boys with a note. He seemed concerned that a business transaction had gone awry." Gideon moved closer until Thorn could feel the heat of his body as he stood behind him. "How very incompetent of me to allow myself to be swindled by a disreputable ship's captain."

His valet tugged on the knot at Thorn's throat, causing him to grimace. "Mother must have mentioned it to Father. What did you tell him?"

"What do you think?" Gideon leaned against one of the bedposts and crossed his arms. "I told him that there was some confusion with the paperwork, but I was able to straighten everything out. "

So Gideon had covered for him. It pleased Thorn more than he was prepared to admit, even to himself.

The valet stepped back and picked up a rectangular handheld mirror with a silver frame. He presented it to Thorn so he could admire the servant's efforts for the knot. "Excellent, Mr. Zouche. Nicely done as always. You may leave us and retire for the evening."

"Very good, milord," the man murmured, turning away to return the mirror to its proper place. His swift movements as he cleaned up indicated that he preferred to leave before the conversation between him and his brother degenerated into an argument. When he was finished, he bowed to the gentlemen. "I bid you a good evening, Lord Kempthorn . . . Mr. Netherwood."

Thorn faced his brother, who was still leaning against the bedpost. "Are we fighting?"

Gideon straightened from his slouched position and let his arms drop to his sides. "It depends."

"On what?"

"Why did you lie to our mother?" his brother demanded.

Like Thorn, he had dressed for the evening. Both men wore black evening suits, but Gideon had selected a wine-and-blue-striped waistcoat with his cravat fashioned into a barrel knot. Thorn wore an ivory brocade waistcoat. Gideon had styled his hair like Thorn's. He could have walked into a ballroom and fooled everyone into thinking he was Lord Felstead's heir.

"I confess I have wasted a few hours pondering the reasons for the deception."

"Forgive me, brother," Thorn said. He walked to the dressing table and opened a small jeweler's case. He removed his signet ring and slipped it on his finger. "When I encountered the marchioness, I had no idea that she would be so concerned with my white lie about your whereabouts that she would tell our father."

"You have failed to mention the reason for this lie."

Thorn picked up his watch fob as he silently debated on how much he should tell his twin. He was not as secure in his brother's loyalties as he once had been. "I called on Miss Lydall this afternoon. She was not alone. Mother and Fiona were there, and she had brought reinforcements by including the Duchess of Blackbern and Lady Fairlamb. Lady Arabella was also present."

He attached his watch fob and absently touched his hair when he bowed down to inspect his face in the small dressing table mirror.

"You never mentioned that you were planning to visit Olivia," Gideon said, following Thorn as he left the bedchamber. "I could have joined you if you had thought to ask me."

"It wasn't possible," Thorn said evasively. "Would you like to join me this evening or do you have plans?"

"I am meeting a friend."

His brother did not expand on who he was meeting or where he was planning to spend the evening. Nor was he required to, but he thought—no, he had hoped—that Gideon would join him and his friends this evening.

"Very well," he said lightly. They were not parting in anger, so there was no reason why he should push his luck. He reached the bottom of the staircase, his brother not far behind. "I will bid you a good evening then."

Gideon seized him by the arm. "What are you not telling me?"

Thorn accepted his hat from the butler.

He sighed. "I thought we were not going to fight?"

His brother's dark green gaze narrowed. "Did you call on Olivia as me?"

"No," Thorn replied, relieved he could answer his twin honestly. "I swear, it was Lord Kempthorn who called on her." He took a moment to place his hat on his head and adjusted it until he was satisfied.

"I do not understand."

Thorn glanced up. With his hat still in his hands, Gideon was staring at him with a puzzled expression on his face.

"Why would you need to lie to Mother about my business dealings?"

Thorn grimaced. "I had to give the marchioness an

excuse on why I was calling on Miss Lydall. I lied and told her that I was there on your behalf."

"My behalf? Why would you do that . . ." Gideon's voice fading into silence as he contemplated the reasons for his twin's strange actions. His mouth thinned and his head tilted to the side. "This is related to your midnight visit to Lord Dewick's library the other evening. When I suggested that I pay Olivia a visit, you told me that she would not be at home. Why would you do that, I wonder? Could it be that I had already called on her? Is that why you lied to me and approached Olivia as yourself?"

"It is less nefarious than it sounds in the retelling," Thorn said.

Gideon stroked the edge of his hat. "What exactly happened in the library?"

Thorn placed his hand over his heart. "On my honor, nothing untoward occurred in the library."

Gideon looked down at the hat in his hands. "Your sense of honor has lost its rigidity during my absence. Or perhaps, you are more skilled at parsing your words to avoid the truth. Should I approach Olivia and ask her if I owe her an apology?"

His lies had turned as brittle as burned bones, and he was clutching mere ashes. "There might have been a kiss."

"Thorn!" Gideon groaned.

"I was still feeling the effects of the wine I had imbibed earlier in the evening," he said in his defense. "It was a kiss under the stars. It was harmless."

His brother stared at him in disbelief. "She believes I kissed her."

"Well, *I* could not kiss her," Thorn countered. "She would have slapped Lord Kempthorn. She actually likes you so she is more forgiving when you misbehave."

Gideon rubbed his eyes with his fingers. "I cannot believe you kissed Olivia. What made you to do such a thing?"

"I would gladly blame the wine, but truthfully I do not know what possessed me." It had been the worst course he could have taken, since Thorn wanted to discourage her from viewing Gideon as a potential suitor.

"When I kiss a lady, I want to be the one who does it. Not you."

Thorn nodded, accepting that he deserved his twin's anger. "Quite understandable." He refused, though, to promise that it would not happen again. The brief kiss in her front hall proved he could not keep his hands off her when she provoked him.

"We should tell her the truth."

"It serves no purpose in revealing our deception," Thorn said.

Gideon's nostrils flared and his gaze hardened. "Yours, brother. Not mine."

"Aye, but what of the lady's tender feelings?" he asked, pressing the advantage when his brother scowled. "The kiss meant nothing to either one of us. A brief romantic trifling under the night sky. Besides, there was an altruistic reason for my deception."

His brother snorted. "You amaze me, Thorn. Not only do you parse your lies, you season them to make them more palatable."

"Your suspicions wound me, brother," Thorn said. "I did not intend to deceive Miss Lydall. She mistook me for you, and I saw no reason to correct her when I decided that she could benefit from my advice."

"Your advice," was his twin's dry retort.

"You should have seen the dress she wore. The silly chit dresses like a matron and has no head for the current fashions."

"And you do?"

"My opinion is an improvement," Thorn said, refusing to allow his brother to goad him into losing his temper.

"Lord Dewick plans to marry Lady Grisdale, and it was obvious to both of us that the countess will encourage the first gentleman who shows any interest in the young lady. I thought we could improve her odds of making a good match by giving her the polish she sorely needs."

"We?"

Thorn shrugged. "Well, mostly me. I never realized how stubborn Miss Olivia has become. She was such a biddable child. When we were residing at Malster Park, I deduced that she tends to heed your advice over mine, so there are times it is convenient to be you. "

Gideon's eyebrows climbed to meet his hairline. "This has occurred more than once?"

The storm had passed. His brother might be unhappy about the deception, but he would not interfere. "Once, twice—does the amount really matter?"

"It might if you begin courting the lady."

Thorn froze, his mind stumbling over the absurd suggestion. "I am not courting Miss Lydall," he said firmly. "Though, if others believe you and I have an interest in the lady, it could be advantageous for her. Most gentlemen covet what others desire."

Gideon's concerned expression became thoughtful. "For your plan to work, I would refrain from telling anyone in the family. The family adores Olivia. Their approval of the potential match between you and her will encourage gossip. Matrons all over Town will send Lord Dewick and his daughter invitations so they can inspect the lady who has captured your high esteem."

It was Thorn's turn to frown. "That was not my original plan. I think—"

Gideon clapped him on the back. "Why bother when you have me to improve on it? And one more thing—the next time you decide to kiss Olivia under the midnight sky, do it as Lord Kempthorn."

Chapter Sixteen

Olivia entered the Countess of Purles' ballroom, her eager gaze taking in its opulence from the painted mural of Helios crowned with the aureole of the sun driving his chariot pulled by four winged steeds across the sky to the land of the Hesperides. Huge chandeliers of gold blazed like tiny suns. The polished floors gleamed and reflected the candlelight, and the white marble columns along the walls were lined up like warriors reaching for the heavens.

"I am so happy you joined my mother and me this evening," Lady Arabella said, clasping her hand as they strolled into the ballroom.

"After Lord Kempthorn drove me home, I took a walk in the garden and contemplated my reasons for politely declining your invitation. With my father still out of Town, it seemed sensible to wait for him to arrive."

"A prudent decision," the young woman said. "I likely would have come to the same conclusion."

"Thank you," Olivia said, feeling a frisson of nervousness. "Then I recalled Lady Felstead's lament that I was too young to be sitting at home like a spinster aunt, and then there was your brother."

Lady Arabella's lips parted in wonder. "You spoke to Oliver? When?"

"Briefly at the tea shop this afternoon," she confided.

"He seemed pleased to encounter me. To be truthful, I was amazed he recalled our conversations last spring."

"What nonsense!" Lady Arabella teased. "The moment I introduced you, I could tell that he liked you. My brother rarely speaks more than once to a lady who bores him. Nor would he ask such a creature to partner him in a dance on several occasions."

"Oh, do not weave romantic tales about me and Lord Marcroft, dear friend," Olivia cautioned. "He was being polite, but seeing him again reminded me that I have already missed so many outings. My father has no patience for balls and would have placed me in the care of Lady Felstead or another respectable lady he trusted, so there is no reason to deny myself an evening out. I am perfectly safe in the company of you and your mother, Lady Norgrave."

"Marcroft cannot be trusted."

Thorn's words whispered in her mind, but she dismissed his warning. Olivia had done nothing wrong in politely acknowledging Lord Marcroft at the tea shop. It was not as if she had arrived at the ball with Lord Marcroft at her side. Nor had she given the gentleman any encouragement earlier. Lady Arabella's genuine surprise when Olivia had mentioned that she had encountered the earl was proof that her friend was unaware of her brother's plans for the evening. Even if he strolled into Lady Purles' ballroom, it was not due to any scheming on her part.

Olivia had not accepted Lady Arabella's invitation in hopes of meeting Lord Marcroft again. It was Lord Kempthorn who had driven her out of her house for the evening. How dare he tell her who she should call her friend, bully her, and then kiss her senseless when she disagreed with him.

After her stroll through the hedge maze, she had stared at the iron gate separating the two properties. What if the earl had decided to continue their quarrel? What if Gideon visited her again at midnight?

What if he kisses me again?

Lord Marcroft was not her problem. The Netherwood brothers were.

She had returned to the house and immediately wrote a brief note to Lady Arabella to accept her invitation to Lady Purles' ball.

"You will not regret your decision," Lady Arabella said, raising her hand in greeting to a few ladies she recognized. "And who knows, my brother may be in attendance this evening as well."

Olivia halted. "You did not contact him on my behalf."

Espying her friend's concern, Lady Arabella shook her head. "I received your note so late, there was no time to tell him. After my sister married Lord Fairlamb, Oliver decided not to reside with the family when we stay in Town."

Olivia wasn't privy to all of the details, but she had heard about Lord Fairlamb and Lady Tempest's elopement last Season. The news had been discussed in every ballroom throughout London. From the gossips and the tidbits of information she had gleaned over the years visiting Lord and Lady Felstead, she had learned of the discord between the Norgraves—Lady Arabella's family—and the Duke and Duchess of Blackbern—Lord Fairlamb's family.

Family secrets.

Every family had them. The Netherwoods were cousins to the Blackberns, which explained why Thorn was distrustful of Lord Marcroft. She assumed the dislike was mutual. Still, his cousin had married Lord Norgrave's eldest daughter, and Lady Arabella had been welcome at Malster Park. Her Grace, the Duchess of Blackbern, had tolerated the presence of Norgrave's daughters, so perhaps the animosity between the two families had been exaggerated by the *ton*.

Olivia could only speculate. It was not her place to dig into the past since she was not related to either family. What mattered was Lady Arabella's friendship, and the quiet acceptance she had been granted by several members of the lady's family.

"You must miss him," Olivia said, sliding her fingers free from her friend's so she could open her fan. "As I have told you, I have two older brothers. I have not seen them in years, but occasionally they send my father letters."

That was the way of brothers. Younger sisters were easily forgotten.

"I do," Lady Arabella said, her beautiful face growing wistful. "Oliver was closer to Tempest when we were growing up, but he has tried to visit more now that my sister has married."

"How lucky you are!" Olivia said, meaning every word. She quietly envied the strong bonds she saw between brothers and sisters. She had been denied such a relationship with her older brothers, but they were war heroes. She could not be bitter that her brothers had restless spirits.

Olivia was so distracted by her own thoughts, she missed her companion's shuttered look. "So my father often reminds me."

"Arabella, there you are," Charlotte Brant, Marchioness of Norgrave, said, joining them.

It was obvious her friend favored her mother in appearance. In her mid-forties, the marchioness shared the same hazel eyes as her daughters, although her gaze lacked their warmth and clarity. Her fuller figure was attired in a dress the color of red wine with garnets and diamonds dangling from her earlobes and around her neck.

The marchioness acknowledged Olivia with a polite albeit

vague smile. "I am pleased you were able to join us, after all. Arabella, did you introduce Miss Lydall to the countess?"

"Yes, Mama."

"Excellent. Good manners should not be neglected, even when the countess is a very good friend," Lady Norgrave said, her gaze already drifting to another group. "Ah, there is Lady Henwood. I must have a private word with her, and then I shall be in the card room. Do you ladies wish to join us?"

"Perhaps later, Mama," Lady Arabella said demurely, earning her friend's gratitude.

Olivia had little patience for cards.

Lady Norgrave hesitated and seemed to reconsider her decision to leave the two young ladies. "Very well. I trust both of you will conduct yourself in a respectful manner during my absence."

"Yes, Lady Norgrave," Olivia said, curtsying.

Lady Arabella inclined her head. "Of course, Mama."

The marchioness dismissed them with nod and walked away to join Lady Henwood and her friends.

"Has your mother been drinking?" Olivia whispered, when she was certain Lady Norgrave could not overhear her.

"Most likely," Lady Arabella said lightly. "Shall we continue our stroll? My sister and her husband will be attending, but I do not expect them to arrive until later. To amuse ourselves, if you like, we can play a game."

"What sort of game?"

The young woman wrinkled her nose as she thought about it. "We could deduce how many guests are titled."

Olivia surveyed the ballroom with dismay. "I will wager that covers most of Lady Purles' guests."

"Giving up already, Miss Lydall?" her friend taunted. "Whoever finds a duke or a prince will be declared the winner."

Olivia arched her brow. "Would this game be considered respectful by your mother?"

Lady Arabella laughed. "Absolutely not."

Several gentlemen glanced in their direction, which often happened.

Lady Arabella Brant was a first-water diamond, whereas Olivia barely qualified as third water. Or perhaps she could liken herself to a pretty pebble found at the edge of a pond—a lovely, colorful stone with a few rough edges, but not particularly valuable.

Not that their differences seemed to matter to her friend.

"Come along," Olivia said, grasping the other woman's hand. "I see a gentleman with false calves."

"Where?"

Olivia stepped in front of Lady Arabella to block her view. "No, do not stare. We do not wish to chase away our quarry. If he is not titled, I will eat a farthing and my right shoe."

Her companion's hazel gaze shimmered with excitement. "Lead the way, Miss Lydall. Perhaps we can deduce what other false items the gentleman is wearing."

Thorn stood near one of the double doors that led to the garden. The overcrowded ballroom was filled to capacity and hindered his view as he searched for Chance and his wife. After he and Gideon had parted ways, Thorn had intended to meet Rainbault and St. Lyons at a particularly boisterous gaming hell on King Street called the High 'n' Low that was owned by Mr. Scheets. It was a greasy little room where a young rake could literally lose his shirt if he had already lost everything else.

When Thorn had arrived at Rainbault's town house, he found St. Lyon sitting in the drawing room flirting with three women His Grace had been entertaining that day. The duke's stamina in and out of the bedchamber was legendary, and his residence received a steady flow of visitors each day. Thorn doubted anyone was ever turned away.

It had been St. Lyon who had told him that their plans had changed. Rainbault was still feeling guilty about the debacle at the Acropolis, so he had accepted Chance's invitation to join him as he escorted his wife to several balls. Later, the four of them would head to the gaming hell.

"Leave it to you to find the one place in this stifling odorous box where you can actually feel the air stir," St. Lyon said, standing beside Thorn.

"Did you lose Rainbault?"

The viscount was attired in a dark blue evening coat with gilt buttons, a pale-blue-and-gold-striped waistcoat, and ivory silk breeches. The ladies of the *ton* adored him, and that had caused a certain amount of distrust with certain married gentlemen. It was St. Lyons's handsome face and charm that had opened their hostess's door even though none of them had an invitation.

"His Grace is holding court upstairs," his friend announced. "We have orders to collect him when we are ready to depart. Where is Chance and Lady Fairlamb?

"I lost sight of them," Thorn shouted over the orchestra. "Lady Arabella is supposed to be in attendance with her mother."

St. Lyon blinked at the news. "Lady Norgrave, eh? Do you know if the Blackberns will be attending the ball?"

"I do not know."

The strained civility between the Blackberns and the Norgraves was often discussed by the gossips. Wagers had been placed in the betting books on whether Chance and Tempest's marriage would put an end to the old feud once and for all or would simply open old wounds. Much to the frustration of the *ton,* neither family seemed willing to publicly air their grievances for the bloodthirsty lot.

For Chance and Tempest's sake, Thorn hoped that the

two families could find some way to live with their old secrets.

"I expected to see Gideon and the rest of your family here," St. Lyon continued. "The countess must have invited half of London to draw this crowd."

Thorn shook his head. "I never bothered to ask the marchioness her plans for the evening." He had been too distracted by Miss Lydall.

"And Gideon?"

He tipped his head closer. "He had other commitments," he replied vaguely, still aggrieved that he was as in the dark about his twin's evening as the viscount was.

St. Lyons' casual stance straightened as something in the distance caught his attention. "There may be a few seconds for you to slip into the garden."

"Why would I do that?" Thorn asked, peering in the same direction as his friend. "Who is—"

To his right, the crowd parted for Lady Millicent Atson. The twenty-four-year-old dark-haired beauty wore a short-sleeve blue satin dress with a stomacher decorated with diamonds and small pearls. She wore small white flowers in her hair and a transparent veil arranged like the hood of a cloak.

"Thorn," Lady Millicent said, her light brown eyes alight with pleasure as she admired him from head to toe before switching to his friend. "And Lord Bastrell." She dipped low and curtsied, offering both gentlemen a glimpse of her low bodice. "When a friend of mine told me that Thorn, St. Lyons, and Rainbault had arrived without an invitation, I called the lady a liar. Now I owe her an apology."

"When we learned of Lady Purles' ball, we immediately altered our evening plans," St. Lyons said, always eager to engage in a little flirtation.

"I am overjoyed that you did," Lady Millicent said,

adjusting her veil, a subtle gesture to draw the gentlemen's gazes to the soft swells of her breasts.

Her attributes were considerable and worthy of tribute.

His mother had warned him before they had departed for London that the latest on-dit was that the young lady was eager to find a husband this Season after the gentleman she was engaged to had cried off and then eloped with his mistress before the banns could be posted. Her family was furious. According to the marchioness, very few people were privy to the details of the gentleman's true fate. Lady Millicent was telling everyone that her betrothed was obliged to leave the country because he had fought a duel in her honor to garner sympathy.

Lady Felstead also had predicted that Lady Millicent would look to add Thorn to her list of potential husbands. It explained why she had been so happy to encounter him at Malster Park.

Although he could barely recall speaking to the chit. Miss Lydall and their accidental swim in the lake with Gideon had been in the forefront of his mind that day.

"I heard congratulations are in order, my lady," St. Lyon said, amused by the young woman's artful wiles. The viscount considered himself something of an expert when it came to seduction and had often stated that true beauty required little adornment or trickery to draw a gentleman's eye.

Of course, St. Lyon rarely resisted the feminine nets cast to capture his heart. The rewards were too pleasurable to deny himself and the lady. As far as Thorn could tell, there had not been a silken lure fashioned that his friend couldn't wriggle and escape from if he desired.

"Someone told me that you are betrothed."

Thorn tried to quell St. Lyons with a look.

Lady Millicent's light brown eyes flared and a hint of vulnerability seeped into her expression. "It is an old rumor and decidedly false." Her attention switched to Thorn. "Though I do have high hopes for this Season."

"I have no doubt of your success," the viscount said, noting her undisguised interest in his friend. "What man can resist such an enchanting creature as you? At this late hour, I suppose all of your dances have been claimed."

St. Lyons, the scoundrel, stepped closer, until the lady had no choice but to pay attention to him. He clasped her hand lightly and brought it to his lips.

There was a slight hitch to her breath as she held the viscount's gaze. There was an unspoken invitation. Would the lady accept?

"I regret all of my dances have been claimed, St. Lyons," Lady Millicent sighed. "Dare I hope you will ask me again?"

St. Lyons lowered their clasped hands, his gloved fingers caressing hers before he released her hand. "It is my personal motto to never disappoint a lady."

Thorn covered his mouth with his clenched fist to cover his laughter. His friend's double entendre was squandered on Lady Millicent, but she appeared to be pleased that she and St. Lyons would be partners in the near future.

Knowing his friend well, he would claim more than a dance from the lady.

This was a good time to come up with an excuse to leave the couple to their discussion. Before he could speak, Lady Millicent slid her light brown gaze from St. Lyons to Thorn.

"My lord, would you honor me with a turn around the ballroom?" she asked, and then turned to his friend. "Forgive me, St. Lyons. It is of a personal nature."

"Of course." St. Lyon bowed. "I will take my leave and look for Chance and his lovely wife."

He maneuvered his way carefully so as to avoid colliding with the elbows of the guests surrounding them. Over Lady Millicent's shoulder, St. Lyons sent a silent apology to Thorn, revealing his flirtation with the lady had been a ruse to distract her from her original target.

Him.

Thorn inclined his head to acknowledge his message. "We will speak later."

Chapter Seventeen

Olivia could not recall when she had not enjoyed herself more at a ball.

For a solid hour, she and Lady Arabella had moved about the ballroom as they amused themselves with the games they had invented. In spite of Lady Purles' attempts to open more windows and doors, the ballroom was too stifling to dance. The guests had taken refuge outdoors or had sought less-stifling rooms throughout the house.

When four ladies had collapsed from the heat in front of her and Lady Arabella, her companion declared the countess's ball a huge success. Everyone would be talking about it at the breakfast table.

Lady Arabella had introduced Olivia to her family's friends and acquaintances, and Olivia wished she could have returned the kindness. She recognized several of the guests from last Season, but she had either forgotten their names or felt it would be too rude to claim familiarity.

Things will be different next spring, Olivia silently vowed.

She was already changing. Gone was the little girl who used to dance barefoot in the woodlands. She hadn't even recognized her own reflection when she had admired the new dress that had been delivered from the dressmaker's shop.

It must have been Lord Kempthorn's doing. Even after she had ordered him from her residence, he must have returned to the dress shop to ensure her purchases would be finished.

He had kept his promise.

Olivia shrugged, content not to dwell too much on the earl. For some reason, he likely would not approve of her attending Lady Purles' ball with Lady Arabella and her mother, so she had no intention of telling him.

Her enthusiasm had waned slightly when she and Lady Arabella had searched in earnest for her sister and it was apparent that Lady Fairlamb was not in the ballroom. After one of the footmen had confirmed the marchioness and her husband were present, the two ladies had gone upstairs to check the open gallery that encircled the grand staircase and led to various rooms.

"Tempest might have been overwhelmed by the heat too," Lady Arabella had reasoned and Olivia had agreed.

It wasn't until the two ladies had approached Lady Purles' informal parlor and overheard a man and woman arguing that Olivia regretted their decision. When she recognized Lord Fairlamb's angry voice, she touched her companion on the arm to restrain her.

"You cannot intrude," Olivia whispered.

From within the parlor, they heard the young marchioness's soft sobs.

"Tempest needs me," Lady Arabella said, her beautiful face in torment. "I sensed something was wrong when we went shopping, but she denied it."

"How long did you plan to keep this from me?" Lord Fairlamb's muffled fury made both ladies on the other side of the closed door flinch.

"I was not trying to deceive you, Chance," his wife tearfully replied. "At first, I was not certain—"

"And later? Christ, woman, you have known for at least two months and you kept it a secret from your own husband!"

"You are not guiltless, my lord. You knew and yet you did not confirm your suspicions," Lady Fairlamb shouted back. "You remained silent."

There was a thud, as if someone had knocked something over. "Aye, I suspected. How could I not? However, it was your right as my *wife* to tell me that you are anticipating our child." There was an ominous silence. "Unless you taking steps to rid yourself of it. Is this why you have been visiting your mother?"

"You go too far, Fairlamb," the marchioness thundered.

Lady Arabella looked as thunderstruck as Olivia felt.

"I have to find my mother," she whispered, her eyes filling with tears. "She will know what to do."

"Wait," Olivia hurried after her friend. "What we overheard was private, between a husband and his wife." She caught up to Lady Arabella and caught her firmly by the arm. "You cannot interfere. Neither your sister nor Lord Fairlamb will thank you for telling your mother. Besides, I do not understand why your sister is concealing the news of her condition. This is good news for the families."

Lady Arabella's expression was bleak. "For some, perhaps. Not all."

"I do not understand."

"This is family business," her friend said coolly. Olivia felt as if she had been slapped. "If Tempest and Chance are fighting, my mother will want to know."

"I will come with you—" Olivia began.

"No." Lady Arabella pulled her arm from Olivia's grasp. "Remain here and watch the door."

"I will not!" Olivia said, stepping away from her friend.

"What if I am caught? If your sister and brother-in-law see me, they will know I was eavesdropping."

Her friend grimaced as she stomped her foot in frustration. "Then be discreet about it. If Chance leaves my sister alone, I want you to watch over her. If she tries to leave, tell her that Mother and I are on our way to her."

"I am not comfortable with this." Olivia felt awful for disappointing a friend. "This is meddling."

"Very well, then don't help me." Lady Arabella turned away and marched down the passageway.

With guilt suffocating her, Olivia trailed after her friend until she reached the open gallery. She bit her lower lip as she watched Lady Arabella descend the staircase.

"This is wrong," she muttered to herself. "If the Fairlambs catch me spying on them, I will never live down the gossip. Lady Felstead will ban me from ever visiting Malster Park again. Thorn and Gideon will never speak to me again, and my father will likely send me back to Treversham House for the rest of the season."

Lost in thought, she did not realize she was standing alone until she suddenly became aware of three gentlemen surrounding her.

One of the men nudged his closest companion with his elbow. "I told you that not all of the amusements were downstairs."

Lady Millicent had coyly suggested they could admire the countess's gardens instead of remaining in the crowded ballroom. In their youth, Thorn recalled a time or two when he and the lady walking beside him had slipped away into her family's gardens and shared a few stolen kisses. Curiosity and the excitement of indulging in something new and forbidden had spurred him more than genuine attraction. Not long afterward, he had left for boarding school, and those innocent kisses had been forgotten.

"I recommend we explore Lady Purles' open gallery. I have heard her art collection is quite extensive," he said as he steered her toward the main entrance of the ballroom. He knew very little about the countess's art collection, but Rainbault had told him and St. Lyon that she had recently renovated the upper gallery in time for her ball.

"Are you worried about my reputation, Thorn?" Lady Millicent lightly mocked.

"Mine is the one likely to be questioned," he replied with sincerity. "I was certain that your father had discouraged you to avoid the Netherwood twins a long time ago."

"It was the one bit of advice that I choose to ignore."

Thorn and Lady Millicent slowly threaded their way through the main hall. Several of the young lady's acquaintances smiled and nodded as they strolled by, making him acutely aware that they were on display. His mother would be pestering him with questions in the days to come when she learned of it.

"What is this family business that you wished to discuss privately with me?" he asked.

The lady hesitated. "We will speak upstairs."

Thorn was willing to indulge her for the sake of the families, but there were limits to his patience. "My friends will be expecting me to return to them soon. We have other plans for the evening."

Instead of commenting on his obvious ploy to disentangle himself from her clutches, her gait slowed as they ascended the staircase. "Your brother did not attend the ball this evening?"

"No."

"Isn't it strange," she mused out loud. "When I conjure a mental image of you and your twin, he is always at your side."

"Not always." *Not for a long time.*

"That is the way of life, I suppose," Lady Millicent said wistfully. "As we grow older, we spend less time with those we love."

The casual observation put him on edge, as did most conversations that involved Gideon.

"It is the nature of things."

Once they reached the top of the staircase, Thorn surveyed the area. Lady Purles' guests had found their way upstairs and the gallery was filled with small groups admiring the paintings, marble statues, ancient weaponry, and tapestries that covered the walls and filled the alcoves. The circular gallery was connected to at least three other corridors and a large rectangular saloon.

Lady Millicent looked displeased by the number of guests who had assembled in the area, but she had selected their destination. "Shall we go left or right, my lord?"

The lady was stalling. "It hardly matters since we will eventually return to this exact spot."

She gestured away from the large saloon. "I prefer the right."

"Very well."

After a few steps, he and Lady Millicent halted in front of a painting that captured the moment when Castor and Pollux rescued their sister from the King of Attica. She stood beside him, and for a few minutes he wondered if she had forgotten him as she studied it.

She sighed and walked on. "It was kind of you not to correct me when I told St. Lyons the news of my betrothal was false." She sent a wry glance in his direction. "Oh, do not bother denying it. Your expression gave you away. How long have you known?"

"Since Lady Felstead's fete at Malster Park," Thorn admitted. "Rest assured, I have no interest in spreading gossip. It is your private business and it will remain as such."

"I do not mind speaking of it with you, my lord. After

all, you were the first boy who was brave enough to steal a kiss, and thus I credit you for the beginning of my perilous journey of meeting gentlemen of questionable character."

"You honor me"—Thorn paused and then threw back his head and laughed—"and insult me in the same breath. Well done, my lady."

Lady Millicent was two years younger than Thorn, and though he could not recall if she was the first girl he had kissed, she had been his second or third. He had kissed many girls that summer.

"When I was introduced to Mr. Howard two and a half years ago, my family declared he was perfect for me. We shared similar interests, or so he led me to believe. It was later that I learned of his affection for actresses and Hazard." Lady Millicent walked ahead of him and stopped in front of a Venus reclining for eternity in marble. "A magnificent piece, do you not agree? Look closer and inspect the small details."

Thorn dutifully obliged and bent down to study the marble lady. One of Venus's hands partially covered her left breast as if to shield her nakedness. The sculptor had tangled her legs with a sheet, giving him a glimpse of the shadowed hollow at the apex of her thighs. It was a provocative piece that invited the observer to caress the marble flesh.

Thorn was beginning to notice a dedicated theme to Lady Purles' art collection, forcing him to reevaluate his opinion about the elderly countess. Lady Millicent moved closer, but he sensed she was staring at him instead of Venus. Her proximity made him want to loosen the knot at his throat. He stared at the statue, deliberately keeping his hands at his sides. "Exquisite."

"I agree."

At five foot two, Lady Millicent was shorter than Miss Lydall and was not burdened with the shyness that seemed to tongue-tie the other lady. With their heads so close together, she placed her hand on the nape of his neck, pulled his mouth to hers, and kissed him.

"Good evening, my lords," Olivia said genially as the three gentleman positioned themselves around her to block a quick escape. "Have you lost your way in this grand old house?"

Their faces were youthful, so she assumed they were a few years younger than her. One had flaxen-colored hair that curled around his ears. The other two were dark haired. The fellow to her right wore his hair tied at the nape of his neck and had light blue eyes, and the other wore his hair loose and his eyes were dark brown. All three were handsome in their own way, but she could smell the alcohol on their breaths.

The blond standing in front of her bowed with an exaggerated flourish. "Good evening, m'dear. How clever of you to deduce we have turned ourselves about. Maybe you would be so kind as to assist us. We are looking for the card room."

Olivia discreetly glanced around her. There were other guests in the gallery, but they were on the far end, closer to the saloon and the main staircase. Straight across, on the opposite corridor, she caught a glimpse of a couple but could not see them very well from her viewpoint. A large wooden post and her companions obscured her view. She cocked her head and noticed they were kissing.

In public, no less. Quite shameful.

Unfortunately, the passionate couple was oblivious to their surroundings. Olivia silently considered her choices. She could scream. Surely, she was bound to draw someone's attention. Nevertheless, she was not positive her predicament warranted the humiliation.

"I confess, I have not visited the card room so I cannot

offer much help." She gestured to a point over the man's shoulder. "You might appeal to someone in the saloon or any of the other guests strolling along the galley. And if not on this level, you could always head downstairs. Someone must know where the card room is located."

Olivia flinched as the dark-haired gentleman with his hair tied in a queue touched her on the arm. "I have lost my taste for cards," he told his companions. "Go on without me if you like, but I prefer to stay here. What is your name, my sweet?"

"Miss Lydall," she said, and could have bit her tongue off for her honesty. She should have told the gentlemen that she was Mrs. Lydall. The threat of an angry husband would have cooled their ardor.

The blond leered and seemed unsteady on his feet. "Why stand on formality when we want to be friends. What is your given name?"

Enough was enough. "Some other time, perhaps. My companions are late, so I am returning to the ballroom."

The man who touched her groaned. "You don't want to go back there."

"Stand aside," she said in her firmest voice.

The gentleman with the loose dark hair exchanged a look with the blond. The three of men had come to a decision.

Olivia gasped as the two dark-haired men seized her arms. "What are you doing? Unhand me!" She struggled and looked for the couple on the opposite side.

Just her luck, the man and woman were no longer in sight.

She inhaled to scream, but one of the men covered her mouth with his hand.

"There is no need to invite anyone else to our private party," the fair-haired gentleman sneered. "Let's take her down the back stairs. Then we can—"

"Do absolutely nothing but release the pretty dove you have ensnared," a stranger announced nonchalantly as he walked toward them.

"Who are you? Her father?" the blond said, his chest puffing with belligerence.

Olivia had never met him, but he was an older gentleman. As old as her father, or perhaps a few years younger. He had been fair in his youth, but age had darkened and silvered his hair. His face bore a discernible scar. It began near his left eye and traveled down his cheek. He was a striking figure in black, and his light blue eyes were merciless and cold as he surveyed the trio as if he were an avenging angel.

"I am not acquainted with the young lady," the older gentleman said, his gaze narrowing on the hand covering her mouth. "Are you deaf, my young puppies? I told you to release her and step away."

"Why would we leave our dear friend to your tender mercies, old man?" the young man standing behind her said.

Amusement curled the man's lips. "If you don't, I will take immense pleasure in proving to you that I have no mercy. I will start with you." He raised his walking stick to point at the man who had silenced her. "Have you ever had your fingers broken one by one? How many snaps will it take before you cry and wet your breeches?"

The firm hand covering her mouth fell away.

Olivia wiped her mouth to rid herself of the taste of sweat and leather.

"These *gentlemen* are not my friends," she said, noticing that her entire body was beginning to tremble. "Feel free to break as many skulls and fingers as you like, my lord. What's left, we will surrender to the watch."

"You are a fierce little creature, are you not?" her rescuer drawled. Some genuine humor surfaced in his pale blue gaze.

"You can't take all of us," the one with the unbound dark hair said.

Without warning, the older gentleman swung his walking stick low and swept the blond off his feet. He pressed the end of the stick into the young man's throat as he choked him. "Do not allow the silver in my hair to mislead. I am a dangerous adversary. On second thought, be the drunken fools that you are and attack me. I promise you, I won't show you any mercy."

The blond rolled away and climbed to his feet. He rubbed his throat. Glaring at the stranger, he said, "We're done. She's yours, old man." He nodded to his friends and they disappeared through the connecting corridor.

Her companion wore a grim smirk on his haggard albeit handsome face. He almost seemed disappointed the three young men ran off. His expression smoothed as Olivia locked gazes with her rescuer.

He stabbed the walking stick into the carpet with each step as he strode toward her. "So what am I to do with you, my pretty dove?"

Chapter Eighteen

It was an ingenious trap.

Thorn tried to straighten to end Lady Millicent's kiss, but the single-minded lady snaked her other hand over his shoulder and around his neck to hold him in place. He had no desire to hurt her so he did not use his full strength to free himself from the lady's clutches.

Unfortunately, her triumph only encouraged the chit.

He turned his face away. "Damn it all! Give a gent a moment to breathe, woman!"

Lady Millicent giggled, her eyes bright with joy and mischief. "I have waited too many years for that kiss, Lord Kempthorn."

His shoulders hunched, Thorn managed to partially straighten up, which dislodged the young woman's fingers from the nape of his neck. Her fingers clawed down the front of his evening coat until she could only grasp at the edges.

"You cannot wander off without me." She tilted her head to the right. "We could go someplace private."

The lady was feverish in her excitement as she pursued him to an alcove. Thorn was used to being the hunter, not the quarry, when he engaged in amorous pursuits. He found himself hesitating, as he had known Lady Millicent for half of his life and his family and hers were neighbors. He was truly conflicted on his course of action. His mother and Gideon had warned him on separate occasions that the young lady was harboring an infatuation for him, and he had dismissed their concerns. Nothing would happen between them unless he had decided to pursue *her*. He had not expected her to declare her passion for him so aggressively.

All the better for me to flee the damn woman's clutches, he thought with some amusement. Never had he been brought so low by a lady's cunning. He knew Rainbault, Chance, and St. Lyons would laugh until their ribs ached when he recounted the tale later.

He grabbed her wrists and pushed downward. "For god's sake, strive for a little dignity. Anyone could come upon us at any time."

Lady Millicent pouted. "You have always held yourself at a distance. It concerned me that you might think I was beneath your regard. I never considered that you might be shy."

Shy? The insult could not be borne. Thorn was tempted to wipe the word from the lady's mind, when it struck him that was precisely what she wanted him to do.

"Very clever." Thorn scowled at her. "How many gentlemen have fallen for that ruse?"

Confidence filled her light brown eyes as she stroked the gold cording that tethered the dark green curtain to the door molding. "Countless," she said, and tugged one of the ends. The knot released and the curtain fell, concealing half of the doorway. "Gentleman and their pride, you know."

Ah, yes, pride. It was the downfall of too many men.

"Is this more private?" Lady Millicent strolled to the other side of the doorway.

"No!" Thorn raced for the dark green drapery still tied up to stop her from releasing the other gold cord.

But Lady Millicent tugged, and the cording gave way. "Oh dear, what shall we do?" She fluttered her eyelashes. "I have a thought."

"Behave yourself," Thorn scolded. He grabbed the loose cord from her hand and moved to the other side. "Does your father know you have turned into such a brazen minx?"

He gathered up the fabric and concentrated on tying the cord.

"My father adores me," the young woman said, slipping her arm around his waist.

"Stop it," he said through clenched teeth. He gave her a weak push so she would remove her nimble fingers from his waistcoat pocket. "You are embarrassing yourself."

Lady Millicent's expression darkened. "If you tell my father, I will just tell him and Mama that you lured me upstairs so you could seduce me," she threatened.

"Tell him." Thorn glanced right and then left to see if anyone had noticed the young lady's antics. "See how far that gets you. If the man has any sense, he will lock you in your bedchamber for a month."

No one was nearby, which was a blessing. Lady Millicent was preparing to throw a tantrum, which seemed fitting for his lousy evening. Activity from the other side of the gallery froze him in place.

Miss Lydall was the last person he expected to encounter as he admired the art displayed in Lady Purles' gallery. Even at a distance, he recognized her curly chestnut hair. She was pulled back by someone, and he lost sight of her behind one of the large wooden posts. There was some sort of disagreement between an older man and three young rakes who surrounded her.

"Are you listening to me?" Lady Millicent said, her voice rising.

"Quiet," Thorn commanded and ignored Lady Millicent's pain-filled gasp.

Thorn watched with increasing distress as the older gentleman used his walking stick to take down one of the men. Angry words were exchanged, and the three young men left Miss Lydall alone with the older fellow.

Lady Millicent finally noticed the squabble that had captured Thorn's attention.

"Who is it? The lady seems familiar."

Her companion glanced over his shoulder, and Thorn forgot to breathe. It was Lord Norgrave. What mess had Olivia Lydall stumbled into this evening?

Thorn cursed. Was the young woman mad? She was leaving the gallery with Norgrave!

He wasn't aware that he was walking away from Lady Millicent until she said his name.

"Where are you heading? Do you know that couple?"

"Return to the ballroom," he said, dismissing her. His gaze was fixed on the empty doorway that Miss Lydall had walked through with the marquess. "If I hear about you practicing your wiles on another hapless gentleman, I will speak to your father."

"You would not dare!" She stomped her foot, furious that he was abandoning her.

"Go!" he shouted over his shoulder.

Lady Millicent cried out, and her footfalls confirmed that she was obeying him.

With fury simmering in his blood, he made his way to the other side of the gallery.

Thorn did not know what Miss Lydall had done to

intrigue the old scoundrel, but he intended to put an end to it.

"I am fine," Olivia said, touched by the gentleman's concern. "I am not prone to hysterics or fainting, so you do not have to fuss over me."

She half-expected the gentleman to then pursue the three gentlemen who had cornered her, but he seemed content to let them escape. Instead of escorting her to the informal parlor, her avenging angel guided her to a pleasant alcove that included a sofa and several chairs. It was a cozy little area with large potted plants and brass wall sconces to provide lighting for the three paintings that hung from the three walls.

It was perfectly respectable to sit here with her male companion, since anyone who walked down the wide corridor could see them.

He handed her a glass of wine. "A few sips to calm the tremors in your hands."

Olivia held up her hand and stared at it. "See? I am made of sterner stuff, my lord."

"So you are." Her companion nodded with approval, then sat down in one of the chairs. "If you had possessed a walking stick when those scoundrels had approached you, I wonder if you would have required my assistance at all."

"I was absolutely weak with fright," she leaned closer to confess. "No, I will not diminish your part in my rescue. Nor should you. I owe you my life."

He seemed mildly bemused by her statement. "I am old enough to let you believe it. I am honored that I could be on hand when you required assistance." He sipped his wine. "Do you have family here? Did you slip away from your chaperone to flirt with your favorite suitor?"

Olivia giggled. "No, it was nothing like that." At his encouraging nod to continue, she said, "My father has not arrived in Town as of yet, though I do expect him any day now."

"Who is your father?"

"Lord Dewick," she readily answered. "Are you acquainted with him?"

He tapped the edge of his wineglass as he mentally tried to connect the name with a face. "I believe I have encountered the gentleman once or twice." He frowned. "If your father isn't here, then you are attending the countess's ball with your mother."

"My mother died when I was young," she said, wishing she could remember the lady. The sadness she felt was more for her father's loss than her own. Eager to change the subject, she added, "Actually, I am attending the ball as Lady Norgrave and her daughter's guest this evening."

The gentleman gaped at her in disbelief. Before she could question his odd behavior, he slapped his hand against his outer thigh and laughed. Her revelation amused him immensely.

"Are you acquainted with Lady Norgrave and her family, my lord?"

"Aye, I know the lady well," he said, his light blue eyes glinting with intent and something akin to delight. "Permit me to introduce myself. I am Norgrave."

Thorn rushed into the corridor. Dread flooding his body as he realized none of the ladies present were Miss Lydall. Turning left, he headed for the nearest closed door. He did not bother to knock. He strode in, not caring who he disturbed.

Chance whirled halfway around and glared at him. Tempest was sitting on the sofa. Thorn did not have to step into the informal parlor to note that she had been crying.

"Forgive me, cousin," Thorn began, not bothering to conceal his agitation. "St. Lyon and I—"

"Later," Chance said. "This is not a good time."

"Is something wrong, Thorn?" the young marchioness asked as she stood. In spite of her misery, she appeared eager for a distraction from their argument.

"It's Olivia," Thorn said, then added at their blank looks, "Miss Lydall."

Chance scrubbed his face with his hand as he struggled to hold on to his temper. "Has something happened?"

"There was some sort of confrontation that involved three gentlemen. I was too far away and didn't see everything—"

Tempest came up to him. She looked so miserable, Thorn intended to have a few private words with his cousin.

"Why were you not with her?" she asked.

"I was unaware Miss Lydall was here," Thorn said, his concern for the lady mingling with his increasing annoyance. He had a few words for her as well about wandering about London without her family and friends looking after her. "If Lady Millicent hadn't kissed me—"

Chance's eyes widened. "Since when have you been interested in Lady Millicent?"

"I am not," Thorn growled. "The lady lured me upstairs under the pretense of discussing her betrothal."

"To you?"

Thorn scowled at Tempest. "No. Forget about the betrothal."

"I would like to hear more about the kiss. Do you not agree, Tempest?" Chance held out his hand, and there was an indecipherable message in his eyes that was meant for his wife.

Thorn had been forgotten.

The marchioness nodded and she walked to her husband. Her fingers brushed the palm of Chance's hand, and then he pounced. He grabbed her hand and pulled her against him. She buried her face into his chest as he wrapped his arm around her waist. He murmured something to her and she nodded.

Chance kissed Tempest on the top of her head and held her tightly.

"I clearly am intruding on something private, so I will take my leave," Thorn said. He needed to find Olivia.

"Wait, cousin," Chance called out. "We are the ones being rude."

"Did Miss Lydall run off because she saw you kissing Lady Millicent?" Tempest asked.

"No. Forget I even mentioned Lady Millicent. The kiss meant nothing." Thorn inhaled and strived for patience. "This isn't even about the three gentlemen I saw speaking with Miss Lydall. I am worried about the gentleman who chased them off. She strolled off with him before I could reach her."

"We haven't seen her, Thorn," his cousin said.

"Did you recognize the gentleman?" At his nod, she asked, "Who is it?"

"She is with Lord Norgrave."

Tempest paled as Chance's expression turned grim.

Meeting Thorn's gaze, the marquess said, "We will help you find her."

Thorn, Chance, and Tempest exited the informal parlor and stepped into the corridor.

"Miss Lydall could not have gone far, Thorn."

"Unless she and your father took the servant's stairs," Chance said, glancing in that direction.

"I cannot fathom what he could have said to convince her to leave with him," Thorn said, taking a few steps forward before halting. "Perhaps we should separate. I will check the stairs and you and Tempest can check the rooms in the opposite direction."

"Tempest?"

"Mama? Arabella," the young marchioness said, and embraced her mother and then her sister. "Forgive our late arrival. We were planning to—"

"Your sister said that you and your husband were arguing," Lady Norgrave said, glaring at Chance. She had already come to the conclusion that her son-in-law was at fault. "She thought you needed me."

Tempest sent her husband a helpless look before she met her sister's worried gaze. "How could you know?" The marchioness sighed. "You must have overheard—"

"Where is Miss Lydall?" Lady Arabella abruptly asked.

Thorn crossed over to the young lady. "Miss Lydall was with you? Why did you leave her alone?"

Lady Arabella flinched at his anger. "It was only for a short time. I asked if she would remain here while I sought my mother. Why? What is wrong?"

"What is wrong?" Thorn heard his cousin say his name but ignored the other man's plea to calm down. "Your friend was waylaid by three scoundrels."

Lady Norgrave's mouth thinned at the news. "Where is she?"

Lady Arabella looked to her sister in hopes she would deny his charge. Tempest shook her head. "This is my fault. I must speak to her at once."

Thorn wanted to verbally lash out at the young woman's foolishness, but whatever she and Miss Lydall had overheard when they approached the parlor had worried Lady Arabella enough that she left to find her mother.

"You can help us search this floor. The last time I saw Miss Lydall, she was with your father."

Lady Arabella gasped. "My father!" She turned to address her mother. "Did you know he was here?"

Lady Norgrave slowly shook her head. "Norgrave can be unpredictable."

It was exactly why Thorn was worried about Miss Lydall.

Marriage had not prevented the older man from bedding other women. Thorn had heard rumors that Norgrave had particular tastes when it came to his lovers, and he preferred them to be young.

Had Norgrave stepped in to rescue Olivia so he could claim her for himself?

It was a sickening thought, and a quick look at his companions' faces told him he was not the only one familiar with the older gentleman's perversions.

"I will join you," Chance said. "Tempest will remain with her mother and Arabella."

Thorn nodded and turned away before he could say something to Lady Norgrave that he could not take back. Silently he strode down the wide corridor, aware that his cousin was matching his long stride.

"I know what you are thinking and I hope you are proven wrong. It would be a bold move, even for Norgrave," Chance said, keeping his voice low. "He would not take such a risk with so many witnesses."

"You know the man well?" Thorn mocked.

His cousin winced as both of them recalled the lengths he had gone to avoid Norgrave's machinations. "Well enough to know he isn't a fool."

As they walked by a small alcove, Thorn and Chance halted at the sight of Olivia sitting like a queen in the middle of the sofa while Lord Norgrave sat in a chair beside her. The corner of the older man's mouth curved as he recognized them, and there was contempt in his pale blue eyes.

Miss Lydall stood up when she saw them. "Lord Kempthorn and Lord Fairlamb." Her gaze slid to her companion, and Thorn could read from her expression that she was uncertain how to proceed given the unpleasant history between Norgrave and Chance's father. "I believe you know Lord Norgrave."

Tempest, Lady Arabella, and Lady Norgrave joined them.

"Oh, there you are, Lady Arabella," Miss Lydall said cheerfully. She was either oblivious to the animosity between the Rookes and the Brants or she had decided to brazen her way out of an awkward situation by feigning ignorance. "While you were looking for your mother, I managed to run into your father. It is quite an amusing tale."

"Not quite how I would describe it, my dear," Lord Norgrave said, casting an affectionate look at his new friend. "However, watching everyone's faces when you tell the tale will be entertaining."

Lady Norgrave's stared down at her husband. "I should warn you, Miss Lydall. The only tales my husband relishes are the ones that revolve around him."

Unmoved by the coldness in his wife's voice, Norgrave took a sip of his wine. "Those are the only ones worth retelling, my love."

Chapter Nineteen

"I saw no reason why I could not have remained with Lady Arabella and her mother," Olivia said, breaking the silence between her and Thorn on the drive home. The earl had not allowed her out of his sight since he and his cousin had discovered her in the company of Lord Norgrave.

Lord Kempthorn had looked positively intimidating when she had explained the details of how the marquess had rescued her. He expressed a keen desire to find the drunken ruffians who had frightened and roughly handled her, but Lord Fairlamb had stopped him from leaving. Next, the marquess had dragged the earl away from their little group and the two gentlemen had a fierce albeit brief whispered discussion. His cousin had won the argument, but she had been the one who was suffering the brunt of Thorn's brooding anger.

"You had enough adventure for one evening, do you not agree?"

Ah, the man speaks!

"Granted, those three gentlemen startled me—"

The earl's head lifted, and what she saw in his glittering gaze dried her throat. Olivia swallowed.

"Even so, I recovered quickly."

Lord Kempthorn brought his hands to his face and shook

his head. "Those three men were the least of your troubles, Miss Lydall."

Olivia sensed the earl was struggling to leash his temper. "You are distressed about Lord Norgrave."

His hands moved from his face to the tops of his thighs. Thorn gripped the firm muscled flesh as if he needed to throttle something—or someone. "Aye, you could say I am a bit distressed—about finding you and Norgrave together and sipping wine as if you and he were old friends."

"There is nothing scandalous about showing my gratitude to the gentleman who ran off some fellows who were clearly set on mischief. I did not even know his name until I—"

"And what did you do when you learned he was Lord Norgrave?"

None of this was Olivia's fault, but he was acting as if she had committed some grave sin by speaking to the man. "What do you think I did? The man is Lady Arabella's father, Lady Norgrave's husband. I thanked him."

Humorless laughter filled the interior of the coach. "The devil saves you and you thank him for it."

Olivia was swiftly losing patience with him. "See here, Lord Kempthorn."

"Thorn."

"I *know* your accursed name," she shouted at him. "I am not as muzzy as you believe. I am just not very pleased with you at the moment."

"You are vexed with me." The earl chuckled. "That's rich. I chase after you when I discover that you are alone with one of London's most infamous scoundrels, and he is the gent you thank."

"You saw me," she said, just realizing in all of the excitement that he had not explained how he had known she was with the marquess. "You were in the gallery when those gentlemen approached me?"

"Aye, but I was on the opposite side and I—I was distracted," he said, his expression thoughtful as he carefully selected his words. "I did not even notice you until Norgrave had confronted those ruffians. And you were gone by the time I reached the other side of the gallery."

"You were on the other side?" Olivia said, wondering how she could have overlooked him. She could not recall seeing anyone on the other side except for the couple who had been— "I noticed a man and woman. They were passionately kissing."

Lord Kempthorn flinched. "You are mistaken. What you witnessed was me fervently attempting to escape my companion."

"You did not seem to be struggling," she said, feeling an unexpected prick of jealousy.

"Considering the distance and your poor eyesight, forgive me if I do not give your opinion much merit," he said bluntly.

"Who was it?"

"I beg your pardon?"

"Do not be coy," she said, leaning closer as he straightened. "Do I know this mysterious lady who can outmatch you in strength and agility?"

"I was not—the lady took me by surprise," he said, sounding defensive. "I have known Lady Millicent—"

"Lady Millicent!"

The earl nodded. "She asked to speak privately about a family matter. I did not expect her to behave"—he brought his fist to his forehead and rubbed the ache away with his thumb—"I misjudged her determination."

It appeared everyone was aware of Lady Millicent's affection for Lord Kempthorn except for him.

"How ridiculously delicious," Olivia said with a laugh. "If those three gentlemen had not approached me, I might have been the one to rescue you from Lady Millicent's greedy clutches."

"I will agree about the ridiculous part," he said sullenly.

"It also explains why Lady Millicent was glaring at me when we returned to the ballroom to find St. Lyons. Knowing how vindictive she can be, the lady likely blames me for ruining her attempts to seduce you."

There was an audible gnashing of his teeth. "For the last time, there was no seducing."

She gave him a superior look. "From what I had glimpsed, Lady Millicent had landed you in her silken net, and you were flopping about on the floor like a turbot."

"A tur—I will show you what it feels to be landed like a fish!"

Lord Kempthorn lunged forward and pulled Olivia onto his lap. As he shifted her body against his, the back of her head bumped against the side of the coach and she gasped. His hot mouth covered hers. This wasn't a swift, bruising kiss designed to shut her up or punish her. His lips were teasing, light brushes of warm flesh and soft licks from the tip of his tongue. She wiggled against him, feeling unbalanced because of the way she was draped across him and the sudden movements of the coach. The earl cradled her head with his hand while his other hand caressed her hip and backside.

There was no escape for her unless she wanted to be unceremoniously dumped on the floor. *Thorn would do it,* she thought. Unlike Gideon, her reckless ways maddened Thorn and he often tried to bend her to his will.

Not that he had much success.

As they grew older and distance separated them, it had been simpler for both of them to ignore each other.

Then how did I end up in his lap?

He leisurely released her lips. "You never react the way

I expect." He nuzzled her cheek and kissed a sensitive spot near her ear.

Olivia had always been different. On most days, she was untroubled by the notion, but some of the warmth and humor faded. She stiffened in his embrace. "How so?"

Thorn nibbled around her earring. "You are grinning up at me when most ladies would be slapping my face."

"There is still time for me to rectify my error." Olivia reached for his shoulder and attempted to sit up. She wobbled on his lap. "Will you give me a little assistance?"

She had managed to dampen his ardor. His grim expression revealed as much, but he did not seem inclined to comply with her cool demand.

"You started this," he said, causing her to gape at him in astonishment. "You should not goad a man if you are not prepared to face the consequences."

"I was not doing anything!" she denied. "I was merely teasing you because the mighty Lord Kempthorn was overwhelmed by a foolish little chit who has decided that she would like to be your countess."

"Lady Millicent did not best me," he grumbled.

"You forget I caught a glimpse of your torrid embrace." Olivia was pleased to see him wince. "She is probably telling everyone that you tried to ravish her."

"For god's sake, nothing happened!"

"That is your account," she said, taking advantage of his divided attention. Olivia slid off his lap and onto the bench beside him. "You can be certain there were other witnesses who will swear you were kissing her."

Olivia waited for Thorn to lose his temper. He had bruised her feelings by telling her that she didn't behave like a lady, so she had pointed out that his actions were not that of a gentleman. She smoothed a strand of hair and tucked it behind her ear as if she was unconcerned.

The earl remained silent.

Unable to bear another minute of silence, she risked a side-glance. Thorn did not look angry at all. In fact, there was a degree of smugness in his posture that worried her.

He leaned forward and used his arms to cage her against the bench. "And what will the gossips say about you, Miss Lydall?"

"I am beneath the scandalmongers' notice," she said, pressing her back against the firm leather cushions.

Thorn made a soft chiding noise with his tongue. "You drew attention this evening with those ruffians and with Lord Norgrave. Then you left the ball with me."

"You insisted!" she hissed, her voice ripe with accusation. "However, it is insignificant. Everyone will assume you offered out of a sense of duty since you are a gentleman and we are neighbors."

"Ah, but that is the rub, Olivia," Thorn said with soft menace. "While you keep insisting I am a gentleman, I will confess that I have not always behaved in such a fashion."

She glared at him. "You are trying to frighten me because I teased you about Lady Millicent."

"You are correct about the kiss. Lady Millicent is eager and almost as reckless as you in some ways. I could have led her to a place more discreet than the open gallery and done more than sample her lips. I might have even touched her . . . like this."

Thorn traced the delicate line of Olivia's collarbone with his finger.

Peasant!

"Did you?" she huskily whispered.

The earl's finger dropped lower, trailing downward to the cleft between her breasts. "Did I what?"

She could not meet his gaze. "Touch her like this."

"Look at me," he harshly ordered, and her gaze jumped up to meet his. "I could have. Perhaps another time, I would have accepted what Lady Millicent so enthusiastically offered."

His fingers captured her chin to stop her from looking away.

"However, another lady has been dwelling in my thoughts," he confessed. "She is a stubborn, reckless, infuriating creature who is so unlike me in temperament that the sensible thing to do is shun her company."

"Your control is admirable, my lord." The gentleman was controlling, thoughtlessly cruel with his bluntness, and deemed anyone who was ruled by their passions as beneath him. A sensible lady would shun *him* and his arrogant opinions. "You are an example to us all. I wish you luck with your lady."

Thorn slowly shook his head. "I do not require luck, Miss Lydall. I have already caught you. Much like the turbot you accused me of being."

Chapter Twenty

Olivia shouldn't have teased him.

Thorn could tell by her slack-jawed expression that she still did not understand that her innate womanly defiance and affection for him and his twin had battered at the defenses he had erected to resist her.

Although he refused to admit it to himself, Olivia Lydall had always been a temptation.

While everyone around him yielded to his title and family, she had never been impressed. Gideon had been her friend, and he could have been hers as well, but in his youthful arrogance he had turned away. He was Lord Felstead's heir. She had seen only the boy, the one who came in second to her Gideon.

The wild reckless girl had wounded his feelings but not acknowledged his importance, so he had shunned and mocked her. Thorn had quietly resented her friendship with his twin. He had tried to control everything and everyone in his life. His grip had been so fierce and uncompromising; Gideon had slipped free and abandoned him. Olivia had learned to avoid him. He had managed his lovers and his passions with a ruthless efficiency, feeling nothing when he ended his affairs. Over the years, he had even kept his friends at a distance.

He had not understood the depth of his feelings until he watched helplessly as she walked away with his cousin's enemy. Even now, the exasperating woman did not comprehend how dangerous Lord Norgrave could be.

She trusts him, but not me.

Another contradiction. Something to contemplate later when he was alone with his thoughts.

"Have you not received enough kisses for one evening?" she whispered, her eyes softening even though she was likely unaware of it.

She sees Gideon instead of me.

Well, Olivia would see him. She would feel him. When she entered her town house, there would be no confusion about which of the Netherwood twins she had kissed.

"Why should I limit myself?"

She slipped an inch lower. Did she think she could escape the consequences she had wrought? "Lord Kempthorn—"

Thorn dropped to his knee and leaned toward her until his mouth was a hairsbreadth from hers. "Do you desire my kiss, Olivia Lydall?"

To his amazement, she nodded her head. "No."

Thorn grinned, finally understanding that he had the ability to befuddle her too.

"Liar," he said, rubbing his lower lips against hers. "How many gentlemen have kissed you?"

Olivia huffed. "Your question is rude. I have no intention of answering it."

The tip of his tongue emerged, and with a featherlight lick he tasted her lips. Salty and sweet. "That many, eh?"

"Certainly not," she primly replied.

He nipped her lower lip with his teeth and she shivered. "Have you kissed Gideon?" he asked, curious to see if she would be honest.

Olivia glowered at him. "You already know the answer."

She was being evasive. While she might not have initiated the kiss, the man she thought was Gideon had. "Not always. Gideon likes to keep secrets. I will wager, he has told you things that he hasn't shared with me."

Her chin came up and her mouth trembled. "Leave Gideon out of this."

"I agree. Let's keep this just between us," he said before crushing his mouth to hers.

The abrupt movement expelled her warm breath against his lips. He breathed in her scent, drawing it deep into his nose. His mouth had sipped the sweet nectar from her lips, now he wanted to glut himself on the taste of her.

Olivia's hands glided up the front of his evening coat. He grabbed one of her hands and directed it to his waistcoat. A more experienced lady would recognize it as an invitation—for her to unfasten the buttons, and breach another layer. To work her way under his linen shirt and touch his bare chest.

She tentatively stroked the front of his waistcoat as he made a growling sound of approval in his throat. "Thorn," she whispered, her voice filled with wonder and wariness. "None of this makes sense. You and I—"

Their attraction defied all reasoning.

The rational side of him agreed. Olivia had every right to question his motives. Thorn was uncertain how far he was willing to take this. His head and the demands of his body for a physical release battled for control, and the lady he had pinned against the leather-cushioned interior of the coach was to blame for his whetted appetite.

"Are you not curious?" he asked, lightly kissing her lips.

Her cornflower eyes were large, dark and luminous in the shadowed interior of the coach. "I have wondered—" She wetted her lower lip with a swift flick of her tongue. "There was—"

Thorn silenced the rest of her admission by coaxing her

parted lips to widen with his tongue. He stroked and circled, deepening their kisses. His hand cupped one of her breasts and he kneaded the soft globe, offended by the layers of barriers from his gloved hand to her layers of dress, stays, and chemise. She had tensed at his initial touch, her hand covering his as if to stop him.

"Do not deny me," he murmured against her mouth, as he persisted in his bold caresses until she relaxed against him.

Olivia tipped her head back and exposed her bare neck. Another area to explore with his tongue and lips. She shivered in his arms as he nibbled on her shoulder.

Immense pleasure was coupled with acute discomfort. He was wholly aroused. His cock was full and his testicles drawn tight and aching for release. It was exquisite torture to brush his virility against her hips and belly even though she was oblivious to the growing demands of his body. He had always loved to delay his pleasures. While his head was filled with fevered visions of him unfastening his breeches and filling the lady with his eager cock, there were other ways to seduce an innocent miss.

Thorn drank from her lips as if she were his favorite wine. He breached and penetrated with his tongue. She gasped and shuddered in his arms as if he had filled her with his hot seed.

"No more," she panted. "It is too much!"

Olivia moved restlessly against him. Her questing hands had found his back, and she dug her fingers into his flesh to hold him close.

"This is the prelude to passion," he murmured against the heated flesh just above her breast. "There are so many ways a man can give his lover pleasure. Your scarlet blush would cover you from head to toe if I whispered the wicked details in your ear."

Thorn had ripped the bodice of one of her dresses.

Would she scold him if he tore this one so he could suckle her nipples and bury his face into the fragrant soft swells?

"The town house," she said, groaning as he licked a sensitive spot with his tongue. "You need to stop kissing me. I cannot collect my thoughts."

He preferred keeping her off-balance as he seduced her.

He gently cupped her breast and nipped the flesh spilling out of her bodice. "Has anyone ever given you a love bite?"

"Oh, my goodness gracious!"

He smiled as he kissed the tiny mark he had left behind with his teeth. When she dressed in the morning, she would see it and remember the pleasure she had discovered in his arms. "You liked it, did you not? Can you fathom all of the intimate places on your body you could feel that mild sting?"

Olivia expelled a nervous giggle. "Don't you dare—"

"How can I resist when you are so generous with your responses," he teased.

His cock throbbed, almost too sensitive to be touched. He had never been so aroused as to spill his seed in his breeches like an untried lad, but if any lady was capable of shattering his control it was Olivia.

Without conscious thought, he brought his gloved hand to his mouth. He used his teeth to tug on each leather tip. The sheath of fingers gave way and he peeled off the glove with his other hand.

Olivia met his impatient gaze. "What are you doing?"

"I need to touch you," he said, his bare hand moving to her skirt. "Nothing too brazen. A light caress so you will think fondly of me when you dream."

Her cornflower blue eyes widened and her knees locked when he slipped his hand under her skirt and petticoat and his fingers touched her bare calf. "Thorn! You cannot—"

He straightened so he could kiss her lips. "I can, and I will if you allow me to love you properly. Now relax your knees," he ordered and she reluctantly obeyed. "There is no risk in letting me pet you. I may intend to deny myself, however, there is no reason why I cannot give you some satisfaction from this torment."

Olivia gripped a portion of her skirt to still his hand. "No one"—she cleared her throat—"no man has ever touched me like—"

Thorn's harsh expression eased with understanding. He knew when he had kissed her as Gideon that she was innocent in all ways. "I know. You have nothing to fear. Let me show you."

He had held more flexible boards in his arms, so he concentrated on her mouth. Her lips had reddened and lightly puffed from his kisses. He resisted the urge to slip his hand into his breeches and cup the hard stones drawn tight against his cock. A good squeeze would help him soothe the ache, and then his hand would move to the rigid length. As his hand glided to Olivia's thigh, he thought about pushing the crown of his cock against the wet folds between her legs. He suckled her lower lips, and imagined breaching her maidenhead and filling her.

The desire to cover her body with his and ease the lust pounding in his blood was a siren call. The sharp intake of her breath pulled him out of his musings and he became aware of the warm honey of her arousal as it spilled from her sheath.

"A woman's lust is addictive," he murmured, marveling at the wetness coating his fingers as he stroked her. She trembled and her breath hitched in response. "It inspires a man to touch and to taste. What if I buried my face between your legs and satisfied you with my tongue? Would you let me touch you so brazenly?"

"No one is that wicked," she said hoarsely.

He grinned because she looked scandalized. "Little innocent," he affectionately teased. "The look on your face almost makes me want to forget my good intentions."

Of course, he was not feeling particularly "good" as he tormented himself with Olivia Lydall's virginal body. He was selfish and sinful, and when she climbed into her bed this evening, he wanted her to think about all of the things he had done to her.

There were so many things he could teach her.

A part of him wanted to wash that look of innocence from her cornflower eyes. Preferably as he covered her pale body with his, and thrust his cock into her.

One finger, slick with her desire, circled the opening of her womanly sheath. Olivia arched against him, her body tense with unknown needs and anxiety. She was tight, and the thought of being inside her almost sent him over the edge. Perspiration dotted his forehead and headed down his entire body. If he touched the tip of his cock, he would likely feel wetness. Another sign of his acute state of arousal and need to fuck.

Restraint.

His shoulders were taut as a bow as he directed his energies toward pleasing Olivia. The pad of his thumb rubbed the swollen bud of flesh hidden in the silky nest of her slit. He listened to the changes in her breathing, adjusting the pressure and duration of his strokes until she was shaking and her skin was damp as his.

"I can no longer bear it," Olivia said, rising up and hugging him so her cheek rested against his shoulder as Thorn relentlessly teased her with his fingers.

"Aye, you can," he said fiercely. "You are hungry for my cock, are you not?"

She buried her face and a soft choking sound came from her lips. His crude speech aroused and embarrassed her. He shallowly dipped two fingers into her sheath, when he wanted to slide them deeply into her. He growled as he fought his instincts.

Olivia gasped and Thorn tightened his grip on her.

"That's it, Olivia," he crooned into her ear. "Show me how much you want my cock."

She cried out in surprise as he zealously stroked her as she rubbed against him. Her fingers had curled into fists as she held on to the back of his evening coat. He felt the swollen, drenched flesh beneath his fingers spasm and he whispered bawdy words into her ear.

Thorn held her as he felt the tension fade and she slumped against him. Although he was tantalized by the thought of seeing her passion rise within her, he was a mere mortal and his restraint had reached his limits. He slipped his hand free of her skirt.

"How do you feel?" he said, enjoying the feel of her in his arms. Once she came to her senses, she probably would not want him to touch her again.

"I do not know." Olivia shuddered and sighed. "My head feels like pudding."

"I did my best," he said, trying not to sound too arrogant.

She pulled away so she could meet his gaze. "Striving for compliments, my lord?"

With a knowing smile on the curving corners of his mouth, he brought his bare fingers to his lips. His tongue lapped at the wetness before he deliberately inserted his fingers into his mouth so he could savor her arousal.

"Words are unnecessary, when I can taste your gratitude."

Even in the dim interior, he could see the heightened color in her cheeks. The coach had stopped at some point, but Thorn had been too distracted to care. His coachman was well paid and he would wait until he received a signal to open the door.

"You go too far, Thorn," she said, attempting to push him away. He shifted so she could sit up, but within his embrace. "Whatever you did—we cannot do that again."

"Then I did something wrong," he said, feigning disappointment. "I will not have it said that I leave a lady in distress."

Thorn reached for her. He was utterly content to lay his hands on her again since he had yet to find relief to his own torment.

"I will not—I did not say—oh! You are twisting my words!" Olivia slapped at his hands on her waist. "Stop that!"

He dragged her closer and she tipped her head back as if she was anticipating his kiss.

I will oblige you, sweet Olivia.

"Perhaps I will tell the coachman to keep driving until you are satisfied," he said, kissing her throat. "Or, if you insist, we can remain until I am."

"Thorn!"

The door opened and Thorn's frustration boiled into anger at the intrusion.

"I have not signaled—" he snarled.

An oil lantern was thrust into the doorway and Olivia gasped. It wasn't his coachman who had opened the door at an inopportune time. A very angry Lord Dewick scowled at Thorn and Olivia. Gideon and the coachman were standing behind him.

"Papa!" Olivia cried with joy as she struggled to disentangle herself from Thorn's embrace. "When did you arrive?"

"I arrived hours ago," her father said, his hard gaze sharpening as Thorn nonchalantly smoothed down a portion of her skirt that revealed more of her calf than was proper. "When I questioned the servants, no one could tell me where you had gone. I sent a boy to Lord Kempthorn's residence to make a few inquiries to your whereabouts. Gideon was about to call on a few residences on my behalf."

"Forgive me, Papa," she said, trying to edge away from Thorn. "I did not expect you this evening so I accepted Lady Arabella's invitation to join her and her mother since they were attending Lady Purles' ball."

Thorn applauded Olivia's composure. He would have never thought her capable of deceit, but she was doing her best to brazen her way out of an awkward predicament. Nevertheless, he saw the truth burning in Lord Dewick's and Gideon's gazes.

He and Olivia had been soundly caught in a very compromising position.

Chapter Twenty-One

Olivia wanted to pinch Thorn.

His casual pose was not fooling anyone. Her father and Gideon—not to mention the coachman—had caught them in an improper embrace and the earl did not have the decency to remove his arm that was still wrapped around her waist. The gentleman was behaving as if nothing had happened.

The things he had done to her!

Her face felt hot and the walls of the compartment confining. She would slide away from Thorn but his fingers dug into her hip. It was a warning to keep calm. They had been caught kissing. Nothing could be done. In private she would apologize to her father for her indelicate conduct.

Lord Dewick stared at the earl. "If my daughter was with Lady Norgrave and her daughter, how is it that you are the one who is escorting her home?"

"I am just being a good neighbor."

Olivia winced at Thorn's sarcastic response.

"Thorn," Gideon said, silently cautioning his twin to not make the situation worse by provoking her father.

"There was a—" Olivia felt the earl's fingers again at her hips. She turned her head and frowned at him. She was not a horse that needed someone with a firm grasp of the ribbons to guide her in the proper direction.

"I was unaware of Lady Arabella's invitation or that your daughter had accepted," Thorn interjected as if she could not speak on her own behalf. "When I encountered Miss Lydall at Lady Purles' ball, I offered to see her home."

Olivia fumed. Her father was not an unreasonable man. He had no quarrel with Lord Norgrave. She could not fathom why Thorn was reluctant to tell her father the entire truth.

"Very generous of you, Kempthorn," Lord Dewick said, his face cast in uncompromising shadows. "I had no idea you had taken such a keen interest in Olivia."

"You are mistaken, Papa," Olivia said, comprehending the direction of her father's thoughts. "Lord Kempthorn was only following Lady Felstead's orders."

A strangled laugh erupted from Gideon at the same moment the coachman suffered a coughing fit. Thorn's fingers pressed deeper into her flesh. Olivia moved her hand until it covered his.

She gave his fingers a hard squeeze.

"No, it is true," she said, radiating sincerity. "Lady Felstead was unhappy that I had decided to wait for you here while the preparations for the town house were under way so she asked her sons to visit from time to time."

"Daughter, I highly doubt the marchioness would approve of Kempthorn's conduct," Lord Dewick said sternly.

She blinked. "Oh, you are referring to the kiss? It was nothing."

Thorn stirred beside her.

Olivia flinched as the earl's hand tightened like a vice on her hip. The man was going to give her bruises.

She smiled serenely at her father. "I fear, Lord Kempthorn drank too much wine this evening. He lost his head and it amused him to kiss me."

Gideon covered his face with his hand.

"Your account is not very flattering," Thorn muttered. "Nor is it helpful."

"My father—"

"Has good eyesight and a better understanding of young gentlemen than you, daughter." Lord Dewick handed the lantern to the coachman and then held out his hand to Olivia. "Bid Kempthorn farewell, and come along. You must be weary from your evening."

Olivia turned to Thorn. His enigmatic expression gave nothing away, so she could not tell if he was angry about the lies she had told her father about him being drunk. "Good evening, my lord."

"Good evening, Miss Lydall," Thorn replied. "It was an honor to *have* you in my coach."

Olivia bit her lip but had the good sense not to reply.

She clasped her father's hand and shifted as Thorn's hand on her hips eased. She was a bit unsteady on her feet. As she moved, the flesh between her legs felt wet and tender from his touch. She noticed her father's gaze seemed to be focused on the front of her dress. It was then that she noticed the tiny reddish bruise just above her breast.

A "love bite," Thorn had called it.

Olivia stifled a sigh. She could not imagine how this evening could get worse.

Thorn observed as Lord Dewick embraced his daughter. The man murmured something to Olivia. She nodded and replied, but her voice was too soft for him to eavesdrop. Having said her farewells to Thorn and Gideon, she walked toward the house with his coachman providing an escort. Any lady who had almost been thoroughly ravished in a coach might have been tempted to glance over her shoulder for some reassurance from the gentleman who had touched her until she was overwhelmed by the pleasure. Not Olivia. There was no hesitation in her gait.

This did not bode well for him.

When Lord Dewick had opened the door to the coach, Thorn had reached for his hat and placed it on his lap to conceal his erect cock from the baron and his innocent daughter. He need not have bothered. The older gentleman's mute outrage and hard condemning stare had cooled Thorn's ardor within minutes and withered his virile member.

"Did you wish to speak with me, my lord?" Thorn drawled.

"I do," the baron bit out. With Olivia out of hearing range, the man did not bother to hide his anger. "This business with my daughter—"

"There is no need to thank me for looking out for her as if she were a member of my family," Thorn said, his mouth quirking upward at Gideon's expression of absolute shock. He was too old to receive a lashing like an errant child. "I assure you the pleasure was all mine."

"Christ, Thorn," Gideon said, sounding as indignant as the lady's father.

Lord Dewick leaned into the coach, and for the first time Thorn questioned the wisdom of baiting the gentleman. It angered him that Olivia's father was so careless with his only daughter. Instead of being treasured, she was wandering about Town while the baron dallied with Lady Grisdale or anyone else who caught his fancy. Any clever rogue could have seduced her.

He knew this firsthand. The taste of her orgasm still teased his lips and coated his tongue.

"Pleasure and sin. Oftentimes entwined . . . and yet very few people comprehend there is always a price to be paid," Lord Dewick said, thankfully unaware of Thorn's thoughts. "You will honor me with a visit tomorrow."

It was not an invitation.

Thorn gave him a measuring look. "We could speak now."

"No, I confess, this evening is not a good time for me. I am weary from my journey and I wish to see my daughter."

Fair enough. Even so, the heat in the baron's gaze revealed that there was more to his refusal than exhaustion. "How is early afternoon?"

"I will be expecting you, Lord Kempthorn. Pray do not disappoint me." Lord Dewick inclined his head and moved to leave.

Something caught his eye, causing the man to hesitate. He leaned down and when he straightened he had something in his hand. "Just one more thing." The baron tossed the leather glove Thorn had removed earlier into his lap. "You should have more care with what belongs to you."

Lord Dewick said farewell to Gideon and departed.

Without waiting for an invitation, his brother climbed into the coach. His gaze dropped to Thorn's bare hand and his expression became even more foreboding as he considered the reason for it.

"You are home early," Thorn said lightly.

"And you are a bit late. It is obvious you had an adventurous evening," Gideon said visibly striving not to lose his temper. "And you have managed to include Olivia, too. I cannot wait to hear all of the details."

Olivia was waiting for Lord Dewick in the front hall.

She crossed to meet him halfway. "How angry are you?"

"Have you done something for me to be angry about, Olivia?"

"Well, no, not really. Though as my father, you might feel differently when it comes to Lord Kempthorn." She trailed after her father as he headed in the direction of the library. "I will not be able to sleep until we discuss what happened."

"What do we need to discuss?" he politely inquired. Lord Dewick opened the door to the library and waited for her to enter the room. He shut the door and went straight to the cabinet where several glass decanters and wine bottles were stored.

Olivia recalled the night Gideon had caught her talking to the marble bust. Later, he had kissed her in the back gardens. She brought her hands to her cheeks to hide the blush from her father.

"A little port should help both of us sleep," he said.

She waited as her father poured the port into two glasses and handed her one. "Papa, it would be foolish for me to deny that Lord Kempthorn kissed me."

"Aye, daughter, it would."

"A kiss," she said, refusing to meet her father's gaze. "There is nothing to be upset about. It happened once. I cannot fathom it occurring again." Olivia frowned down at the glass of port in her hand.

"You have always been a sweet, dutiful daughter," Lord Dewick mused out loud. "However, you are dreadfully naïve when it comes to the intentions of a gentleman. You also lack the ability for deceit. Whatever happened between you and Kempthorn was more than a kiss."

"Papa—"

Lord Dewick walked over to her and kissed her on the forehead. "Finish your port and then go to bed. I will settle this with Kempthorn tomorrow."

A frisson of unease twisted in her stomach. "But—"

"Lady Grisdale warned me about the Netherwoods, and I did not listen," he said, turning away from her. "I thought Gideon was the one you favored, which proves I have not been paying enough attention to you."

Heartening words, to be certain, but she did not wish for him to take the earl to task about what her father thought he witnessed. "Lord Kempthorn will not tolerate being lectured by you or anyone."

"And my daughter is not to be trifled with by any

gentleman," her father replied angrily. "I know how to deal with young Kempthorn."

"And if I asked you to cancel this meeting?" she said, giving him a steady look.

"If you ask, then I will consider the matter much worse than I had assumed," the baron coolly replied. "Perhaps I should be calling for pistols at dawn rather than a conversation with your young gentleman."

Thorn was not *hers* in any fashion.

"If I cannot dissuade you then I will take your suggestion and retire. Welcome home, Papa."

Olivia handed her glass of port to her father and fled the room.

Chapter Twenty-Two

Thorn was surprised to find St. Lyons, Rainbault, and Chance in his game room when he and Gideon had arrived at the town house. His cousin and friends had probably been there for at least an hour, since St. Lyon and Rainbault had discarded their evening coats and were playing a game of billiards.

"I thought we were meeting at the gaming hell to play Hazard?" he asked, entering the room. "Chance, would you mind sharing some of that brandy. My throat is a bit parched."

He glanced at his twin, who was far from finished with their argument. His ears were still ringing from his brother's accusations.

Was it your intention to ruin Olivia? Do you despise her so much?

It hurt that his brother had such a low opinion of him.

"A change of plans," Rainbault said, studying the billiard table as he pondered his strategy.

"Did Dewick find his daughter, Gideon?" Chance picked up the half-filled bottle of brandy and poured some in a glass for Thorn. "I assume she is well, but this business with Norgrave has unsettled all of us."

"Ask my brother," Gideon said, walking over to the marquess and claiming the glass of brandy that had been poured for his twin. "After all, he was the one who insisted on seeing Olivia safely home."

St. Lyons, who was leaning against the wall while he waited for his turn at the table, appeared amused by the tension between the brothers. "What have we missed?"

"Nothing," Thorn said, plucking the bottle from his cousin's hand and pouring his own glass of brandy.

"Lord Dewick caught Thorn with his hands on his daughter," Gideon revealed.

His friends started at the news, and then everyone looked at him with humor and curiosity in their eyes.

"I do not believe it," St. Lyon said as he pressed the butt of his cue stick just under his chin as he denounced Gideon's accusation.

"I confess, I am not convinced either," Rainbault said, bending over the table as he positioned himself to strike the billiard ball.

Gideon sputtered in disbelief.

"Dewick is mistaken. Thorn is too discreet with his affairs," Chance added.

"I am relieved someone in the family does not believe I am a villain," Thorn said to annoy his brother.

He lifted his glass and saluted him. *Righteous bastard,* he thought uncharitably.

"I do not believe this!" Gideon muttered.

"You have been gone too many years to remark on Thorn's habits," Rainbault said, straightening. He glanced at the viscount. "Your turn, St. Lyons."

The gentleman stirred and moved away from the wall. "He is very particular about his lovers. How long has it been since you bedded a woman, Thorn?"

"Considering my brother's accusation, you will forgive me if I do not answer your question," Thorn said, taking a hearty swallow of his brandy.

St. Lyon motioned dismissively with his hand. "I will wager it has been months."

"At the very least five months," the duke said.

Chance chuckled. "If we are placing bets, I wager it's been more than six months."

He mumbled an expletive that would cause even a sailor to blush. "Nosy gossips . . . all of you. Keep out of my business."

"Lives like a monk, if you want to know my opinion," St. Lyons teased. "Tell me, Thorn, do you have to shake off the dust when you present your cock to a wench?"

"At least I have one. You have dipped yours in so many females, I am amazed it hasn't fallen off," Thorn taunted back with affection infusing his voice.

"I am particular about my lovers," the viscount said in feigned outrage.

"He limits to himself to females," Chance said, his mood lighter since he had left Lady Purles' residence. "I suppose one could call that being particular."

"I disagree," Rainbault said. "St. Lyons, do you recall that one night when we—"

Gideon threw his empty glass to the floor. It shattered and effectively silenced everyone as his brother charged at Thorn. His twin seized him by the front of his coat and drove him backward. The back of Thorn's legs struck and knocked over a rosewood gaming table, sending the concealed contents skittering across the rug. Chance, St. Lyons, and Rainbault were shouting and slowly moving toward the brothers. However, none of it mattered to Thorn. He and Gideon had been avoiding the unspoken issues between them for a long time.

Thorn's back hit the wall with enough force to rattle the paintings, armor, and swords mounted on it. He gritted his teeth. "Are we fighting, Gideon?"

"I do not like the games you are playing with Olivia Lydall," his brother said, holding Thorn against the wall. "First you visit her under the guise as me—"

"Really," St. Lyons drawled. "You have been keeping some very intriguing details to yourself, Kempthorn."

Chance stood within arm's reach but did not interfere. "Your mother is fond of Miss Lydall, cousin. As is Tempest and her sister. You will have half the ladies in our family furious with you if you break that girl's heart."

Gideon retreated an inch so he could batter the back of Thorn's skull with the wall again.

"Damn it, Gideon. Will you calm down and listen to me," he said, struggling not to laugh. There was nothing humorous about his predicament, however, his brother's anger reminding him of the countless fights that had occurred in their youth.

"I am Lord Dewick's witness, you arrogant blackguard!" Gideon shouted at him. "There are countless females in Town you could have used to knock the bloody dust off your cock, but you had to chase after Olivia."

"My apologies for belittling your appetites for lechery, Thorn," Rainbault said, clapping his hands. "Even I would not stoop so low as to bed an innocent miss for sport."

"Olivia is untouched!" Thorn glared at all of them, then returned his attention to his brother. In his mind, he recalled all of the things he and Olivia had done, even though they had barely scratched the surface of depravity. "Well, untouched is not quite accurate. Nevertheless, the lady departed with her maidenhead intact."

Chance expelled a low whistle to convey his surprise and turned away. He seemed content to allow Gideon to mete out the appropriate punishment.

Gideon's green eyes darkened in pain and disgust. "If Dewick wants to put a bullet in you, I will not stop him."

"The baron is a reasonable gentleman. He will mostly issue a warning to Thorn to court his daughter in a decorous fashion or stay away," Rainbault said casually. "No one mentioned a duel."

As if his twin could not bear standing so close to Thorn, he sneered in his face and released him. Gideon turned away.

Thorn's chest constricted as pain made it difficult to breathe. "You readily defend the lady. Have you told her that you love her or are you just annoyed that I trifled with her first?"

From the corner of his eye, he noted St. Lyons's wince.

The momentary distraction was all that Gideon required. He whirled halfway around and buried his fist into Thorn's abdomen.

"Merde!" Thorn's hand covered his stomach as he doubled over. His brother had not held back his strength, revealing the depth of his fury.

Rainbault had grabbed his arm to prevent him from punching Thorn again. "That's enough."

Gideon shook off the duke's hand and pointed at Thorn. "I expect you to keep that appointment with Lord Dewick tomorrow."

Thorn angled his head and gave his brother a sullen look. "And if I do not?

"Then I will offer my services as the baron's second, and I will happily load his dueling pistols," Gideon threatened. Without another word to their friends, he left the room.

Rainbault gazed contemplatively at the door Gideon had just slammed.

"It is unlike you, Thorn, to handle your affairs so messily."

Thorn flinched as he rubbed his bruised stomach. His

friend was correct. He felt as if his tidy life was unraveling and he was angry enough at the moment to blame his brother and Miss Lydall.

"This profound observation coming from a prince who has no people, no country," Thorn said, ignoring the murmurs of objection from Chance and St. Lyon. "Concentrate on your own problems, Your Royal Highness. Leave me to mine."

Olivia paced her bedchamber unable to sleep.

She had never seen her father so angry, and she was to blame. If she had only stayed in this evening, but she had been so worried about Thorn returning to the house that she had taken a risk and accepted Lady Arabella's invitation. In the end, everything had circled back to the earl anyway and she had ended up in his arms. She had allowed him to touch her intimately. It was wondrous and embarrassing, and a part of her wanted Thorn to do it again.

However, she was too sensible to permit such boldness and intimacy with him again. After catching her and the earl in a very telling embrace, her father was certain to order Thorn to stay away from her. It was for the best. She understood it intellectually, but her heart was reluctant.

I may have to stay away from Lady Felstead and the rest of the family, too.

In his anger, her father might have come to the conclusion the Netherwoods were not a good influence on his daughter. Olivia's chest tightened at the thought of never visiting Malster Park again.

She walked to her open window and stared down into the dark back gardens that would take her to Thorn and Gideon's town house if she was daring enough to traverse the land in the dark.

Olivia started at the loud crack as something struck one of the panes of glass in the window. Frightened, she stepped back, but then heard someone whisper her name. She moved closer to the window and peered into the shadows.

Thorn.

Olivia stuck her head out of the window and realized there were subtle differences in the gentleman's attire from when she last saw him. "Gideon?" she whispered. "What are you doing here?"

"I wish to speak to you," was his reply. "Can you come outdoors without alerting your father?"

If her father caught her speaking to Gideon, he might order her to return to Treversham House. "Can it wait until tomorrow?" There was a sense of urgency in his voice, and she assumed he wished to discuss what he had glimpsed in the coach.

Unless Thorn confessed everything to him.

"I need to see you now."

Olivia sighed. "Very well. Give me a few minutes."

Olivia slipped out of the town house fifteen minutes later. To cover her state of undress, she wore a brown silk cloak over her linen nightdress. She was covered from her neck to her feet, but it did not negate the impropriety of meeting Gideon.

He strode over to her and clasped her bare hands within his gloved ones.

"Is something amiss, sir?" she asked innocently.

Gideon led her away from the door where they might be overheard to a nearby wooden bench. "Are you well?"

The query surprised her. "Of course. Why do you ask?"

"Your father was upset when he left us," Gideon said, his face a dark mask. "I was concerned that he would have reprimanded you for the offense that should be laid squarely on my twin's shoulders."

"You need not have worried so," she said, lightly touching him on the arm. "Papa was distressed and I did my best to console him, but he remains resolute in speaking with Lord Kempthorn."

"As well he should," Gideon said fiercely. "Thorn went too far this evening, and I intend to make him pay for it."

Was Gideon jealous? After all, she had kissed him first. Olivia glanced away, troubled that she had come between the brothers. Gideon and Thorn would weather their difficulties. However, first she needed to ease his concerns that his twin had taken advantage of her.

"For a few kisses?" she asked blithely. "How can you condemn your brother when you are guilty of the same indulgence?"

"What are you talking about? I have not"—he swallowed his protest—"aye, you have the right of it."

Gideon looked uncomfortable.

"You are one of my dearest friends and I have loved you for most of my life," she confessed. "I could not bear it if I was responsible for the rift between you and your brother."

"I love you too, dear friend," Gideon said huskily. "I have missed our talks. During my travels, your letters comforted me, especially when I questioned my decision to leave England."

"I am happy for it."

"I do not understand this business between you and my brother." He exhaled heavily. "I do not trust Thorn."

Olivia's lips parted as if to reassure her friend, but she hesitated. In truth, she did not wholly trust the earl either. He felt some sense of duty to watch over her. It still did not explain the growing attraction between them.

"Your brother would not hurt me," she said, knowing the words were the biggest falsehood she had uttered all day. By opening her heart to the earl, she was giving him the power to break her heart. "Do you believe your twin will keep his appointment with my father?"

"I will make certain of it."

"Tempers were high this evening; let us pray cooler heads will prevail tomorrow afternoon," Olivia said. "I will speak to my father again at breakfast and assure him that nothing untoward happened in the coach."

"I do not understand why you are so determined to protect my brother."

"I see no reason for him to be punished for kissing me," she replied. "I know I am not the first lady he has kissed."

Gideon chuckled. "No, you are not." He stroked her cheek with the back of his hand. "You are too good for him, Olivia. I would not see you wounded because of his selfishness."

Olivia brought her hand up and placed it over his. "I am not a child, Gideon."

He nodded. "It was easier to ignore a child."

"I do not—"

Gideon's hand fell away and he stood. "You should return to the house before someone discovers that you have slipped out of your bedchamber."

Olivia rose from the bench. "Will you advise your brother not to bait my father? I love your family. It will be awkward if I am forbidden to speak to anyone with the Netherwood name again."

"I vow, it will not come to that." In a small gesture to comfort her, Gideon bowed his head and kissed her lightly on the lips.

Olivia stilled.

Gideon drew back and his dark green eyes met hers that likely reflected her shock. "I should not have done that. Do you want me to apologize?"

"No," was her weak reply. "No harm done."

She blindly reached out for his arms and firmly grasped his limbs as the ground beneath her feet rolled. Or at least that is how she felt at the moment. Hot and dizzy, and perhaps a little nauseous.

He mistook her response as encouragement so he lowered his mouth to hers again. Gideon's kiss was sweet and tentative as if he was kissing her for the first time.

The first time.

"Good night, Olivia," he said, backing away from her.

Her throat was too tight for her to speak. Olivia raised her hand to signal her farewell and turned away.

After Gideon strolled away and Olivia slipped into the town house, Thorn stepped out of the shadows. He had been too far away to eavesdrop on the couple's conversation, but he watched how his twin had touched her cheek so lovingly. The kiss had been unexpected. It had taken all of his control not to explode out of the shadows and tackle Gideon to the ground. No words would have been necessary when his fists smashing to his brother's face would have conveyed his displeasure.

Nor was he happy with Olivia Lydall.

His brother tossed a few pebbles at her window, and she rushed down to meet him. It was difficult to discern her attire under her silk cloak but the late hour suggested that she wore her nightclothes. What if his brother had desired more than a kiss? Would she have shed her cloak and allowed his twin to pleasure her with his fingers?

Thorn was jealous. It didn't seem to matter that Gideon's kiss was chaste and brief. Olivia was not overwhelmed by the kiss. He should have been comforted by that realization, but he was not feeling particularly reasonable when it came to Olivia and his brother.

After Gideon had stormed out of the gaming room, Thorn had not expected his twin to leave the house and head directly to Olivia's window. What had they discussed? Him?

The speculation would likely keep him up the rest of the night.

* * *

It wasn't until Olivia had reached her bedchamber that she started to shake. Her distress was not over Gideon's kiss. It was what it confirmed—Gideon was not the one who had kissed her in the garden. It had been Thorn. He had pretended to be his brother.

Why?

Olivia sank to the floor of her bedchamber. Her fingers touched lips still tender from the earl's earlier kisses. She was indecisive on what she should do with this newfound knowledge.

Chapter Twenty-Three

"His lordship is in the library, Lord Kempthorn," Tink, the Lydalls' butler, announced as Thorn entered the front hall.

"And Miss Lydall?" he asked, mildly curious if Olivia would also be waiting for him in the library.

"I believe Miss Lydall is in the drawing room." The butler escorted Thorn to the door and knocked.

"Enter," the baron's muffled voice could be heard from within.

Tink opened the double doors and strode into the library. "Lord Kempthorn, milord."

Thorn walked past the butler and bowed to the baron who was seated at the French mahogany pedestal desk. "Good afternoon, Lord Dewick."

The older gentleman stood and inclined his head. "Lord Kempthorn." He nodded to the servant. "You may leave, Tink. See that no one disturbs us."

Was the baron worried that his daughter might interfere? He was learning that Olivia was not as timid as he had once thought.

"Very good, milord."

Thorn listened to the butler's footfalls and then the door closed.

"Sit down, Kempthorn," the baron said gruffly, pointing to red-upholstered walnut fauteuil a few steps away from Thorn. Lord Dewick took his seat. "I will get right to business. What are your intentions toward my daughter?"

Thorn had anticipated such a question would be asked by an irate father who had come across his only daughter in a compromising position, but he still felt like an insect pinned to a board.

"My intentions?" He was stalling.

After stroking Olivia's sweet, honeyed quim last evening, he had several plans for the lady—not one could be shared with her father.

"It is no secret that I would like to see my daughter settled with a husband," Lord Dewick said. "I am intending to marry Lady Grisdale and she—uh—we feel that Olivia would be more content setting up her own household. With this in mind, I have increased her dowry to encourage ambitious gentlemen who are seeking a sweet-tempered lady to marry."

Sweet-tempered? Olivia was stubborn and opinionated. *Though she purred for me when I kissed and stroked her with my fingers.*

"Increasing her dowry will draw fortune hunters, my lord."

"It is a concern," the baron conceded as he clasped his hands in front of him and rested his arms on the desk. "Or it was, until you decided to dally with my daughter."

"Lord Dewick," Thorn began.

"Do not deny it. I know what I saw and I have witnesses, which includes your twin brother." The baron's harsh expression would have made most men falter in courage. "You have ruined my daughter and I will have my pound of flesh. Can you guess which part of your anatomy I plan to start with, Kempthorn?"

Lord and Lady Felstead would not approve of their son facing Lord Dewick, a friend and neighbor, in a field at dawn. His father might shoot Thorn himself if he heard the baron's version of events. His mother and father adored Olivia. A dalliance with her would be frowned on. Gideon barely spoke to him at breakfast.

"Lord Dewick, your daughter is not ruined," Thorn said, attempting to calm the gentleman. "If you summon your physician—"

The baron slammed his fist on the desk, toppling a silver candlestick over. "I would never humiliate Olivia in such a fashion." He slowly stood and braced the palm of his hands on the surface of the desk. "You and I both know that the gossips do not quibble with facts. Olivia was compromised the second she climbed into your coach alone with you. With most of the *ton* crammed into Lady Purles' town house, did you not consider that someone was bound to notice and speculate on your relationship with my daughter?"

The question had him straightening in his chair. He had not considered that anyone had noticed his and Olivia's departure. Her fright at the hands of the drunken ruffians and Norgrave's timely rescue had knocked him off-balance. Once she had been found, all he wanted to do was separate her from the older gentleman. Thorn had been troubled by Norgrave's interest in Olivia. No one seemed to notice when he and Olivia had exited the countess's town house.

Unless someone had deliberately set out to spread rumors about him and Olivia.

It could have been Norgrave.

Olivia's reputation could have been an unfortunate casualty of the marquess's attempt to hurt anyone connected to the Duke of Blackbern and his family.

"This is my fault," Thorn said finally. "My family and I will quell any rumors—"

"By god, it is your fault, you arrogant whelp!" the baron said, his voice thundering. "You will quell this mess by announcing your betrothment to my daughter."

Thorn tugged at his cravat. "You wish for me to marry Olivia?"

Lord Dewick's eyes narrowed. "As your betrothed, Olivia will have certain protections. No one will question your interest in my daughter and many will forgive your eagerness to steal her away for a kiss," the older gentleman said, his grimace revealing his feelings on the subject of Thorn kissing Olivia. "Once the rumors die down, you and Olivia can discreetly end your arrangement."

Thorn thought of Lady Millicent and how her young gentleman had abandoned her.

"Olivia will never agree to such a ruse."

"My daughter will obey me in this." Lord Dewick cocked his head to the side. "And this will not be a ruse, Kempthorn. You will be betrothed to my daughter. Everyone, including your family, must believe your affection for my daughter is genuine. Otherwise, any hint of deceit will lend credit to the rumors circulating last evening at Lady Purles' ball."

Thorn considered walking out of Dewick's library. The wily gentleman was pushing his unmarried daughter at him, and he resented it. What stopped him was Gideon. If Thorn was betrothed to Olivia, his concerns that his brother had a *tendre* for Olivia were moot. His twin was an honorable gentleman. If Olivia belonged to Thorn, Gideon would stay away from her.

I will not have to witness another clandestine kiss in Dewick's back gardens between Gideon and Olivia.

"What if at the end of the season, I do not wish to end our arrangement?" he quietly asked.

The baron snorted in amusement. "I have not decided if you are worthy of my daughter, Kempthorn. Protect my daughter, and we will talk again."

As Thorn departed Dewick's library, he did not feel particularly triumphant. Olivia was betrothed to him. Temporarily.

Her alliance with Thorn would discourage Gideon from pursuing Olivia. If the lady desired a Netherwood, she would have to settle on his company.

Thorn paused at the bottom of the staircase, his head filling with the possibilities.

Perhaps the baron had done him a favor, after all.

I cannot wait to share the good news with my betrothed.

The butler appeared from one of the doorways. "Are you leaving, Lord Kempthorn?"

"No, I need to have a private word with Miss Lydall. Is she still in the drawing room?"

"Yes, milord," the older man said. "Although she does have a visitor."

Thorn hoped Lady Felstead wasn't upstairs. He would have his hands full explaining their arrangement to Olivia without witnesses.

"You do not have to announce me," Thorn said, heading up the stairs. "I am practically family."

"May I be the first to offer my congratulations, Lord Kempthorn," the butler said, thawing a little of his polite reserve. "Miss Lydall runs a solid household and she treats the staff fairly. You could do worse in selecting a countess."

Thorn almost missed a step but swiftly recovered. He halted and stared down at the butler. "How did you know that Miss Lydall and I are betrothed?"

"It is difficult to hide such important news from the servants, milord."

Lord Dewick was rather loud when he ordered Thorn to marry his daughter.

Not marry—their arrangement would last a month or two and then he and Olivia would go their separate ways.

Thorn's pace slowed as he headed upstairs to the drawing room. The ramifications of his agreement with Lord Dewick were beginning to take root in his head, and any sensible gentleman would have politely declined before he escaped the eccentric household.

Fortunately, he had some experience with the unconventional and he had the discipline in handling individuals who were prone to emotional outburst and reckless decisions. If the baron could not manage his daughter, then Thorn was up to the task. Unbeknownst to either of them, he had been laying the ground rules to their relationship since the day he had stepped out onto the Felsteads' wooden dock at Malster Park.

The door of the drawing room was open, so he walked through it as if he were already a member of the family. Although Olivia could not be credited for the interior design, the Rose Room suited her. The walls were crimson with large floral accents that included exotic birds and butterflies. The rococo-styled furniture complemented the silk wall hangings, and the white ceiling was decorated with extravagant plaster medallions. Gilt accents gleamed in the sunlight.

Olivia was seated in a chair with her back to him. Beside her, a gentleman had moved his chair closer to hers. Thorn arched his brows as he took in the intimate pose. Olivia's slender shoulders were bowed as she leaned forward and quietly conversed with her companion.

"My apologies for my tardiness, my dear," Thorn said, taking grim satisfaction in how swiftly Olivia and her friend started at his intrusion.

Olivia glanced over her shoulder and frowned as she squinted at him. It was not the sort of welcoming a man expected from his betrothed. She redeemed herself seconds later by immediately standing and crossing the room to greet him.

"My lord, this is most unexpected," she said cheerfully, and extended her hand. She dipped into a graceful curtsy as he clasped her hand and bowed.

"Did you forget that I had an appointment with your father?"

"Not at all," she countered. "I just did not expect you to honor me with a short visit as well."

Thorn looked expectantly at Olivia's guest. "It appears you have already found someone to amuse you."

The gentleman was already standing and waiting for an introduction. He was an affable-looking fellow. Standing at five foot ten, there was a fragility in his slender, elegant frame and jaw that gave him a boyish appearance, even though he was likely close to Thorn's age. His full lips left him with a permanent pout. His curly blond hair and large blue eyes would be deemed attractive by many ladies.

Thorn disliked him at first glance.

Olivia's cornflower eyes grew wary at Thorn's pleasant expression. "My lord, may I present Mr. Martin Chauncey." She motioned for her companion to move closer. "Mr. Chauncey, may I present Lord Kempthorn. The earl's parents, Lord and Lady Felstead, have lands that border Treversham House."

"Lord Kempthorn," Mr. Chauncey acknowledged and bowed. "It is an honor to meet one of Miss Lydall's neighbors."

"Miss Lydall is more than a neighbor," Thorn said silkily. Olivia and Chauncey looked askance at him. "The lady and her father are almost family."

Olivia's smile faltered as she stepped aside so he could sit down. "If you have a few minutes, Mr. Chauncey and I would be pleased if you joined us."

Thorn considered taking Olivia by the hand and leaving Chauncey to find his own way downstairs. Olivia undoubtedly would not approve of his highhanded tactics, so he decided to bide his time. Nevertheless there was no reason why he could not make a silent declaration. As he walked past Olivia, he shackled his fingers around her delicate wrist so she had no choice but to follow him to the crimson upholstered sofa.

Her expression was one of puzzlement when she and Thorn sat down. Mr. Chauncey returned to his chair.

"You appear to be in good spirits," she said to Thorn. "I trust your meeting with my father went well."

"Your father is fair-minded," he said, ignoring her astonishment. Thorn motioned to the large book on the table. "What is this? Some kind of pocket book?"

Mr. Chauncey leaned forward, enthused to share his treasured book. "Yes, I was showing Miss Lydall my recent acquisitions that I had collected during my stay in Wales." He opened the book, which contained pressed leaves. This is my *Hieracium tavense* or Black Mountain Hawkweed."

Thorn glanced down at the dried leaves and the hastily written notations the man had scribbled on the page with little interest. He knew Olivia had filled her father's conservatory at Treversham House with plants she had collected over the years. What Chauncey possessed was less impressive. One good sneeze and his pressed leaves would end up beneath a broom.

"Very nice," he lied, when Olivia discreetly drove her elbow into his ribs.

"Thank you," the other man said, pleased by the compliment. "I was fortunate to collect several different species of Hawkweed. I also have a fine example of *Centaurium scilloides*."

Thorn nodded absently, trying not to appear bored as the gentleman elaborated on his discoveries. Olivia, on the other hand, was attentive and interrupted the man from time to time with questions. Mr. Chauncey warmed to his subject.

If this gentleman was a rival for Olivia's affections, Thorn felt he was doing her a favor by saving her from long hours of tedious lectures.

"How did you meet Miss Lydall," Thorn asked, after the other gentleman had gone through his entire book.

"We met last spring," Olivia replied. "We attended the same botany lecture."

The other man confirmed her declaration with a nod. "It was quite an unremarkable speech. The speaker's delivery was so dull, he fell asleep at the podium."

Olivia and Mr. Chauncey laughed.

"However, fate placed me two seats away from Miss Lydall, and our friendship flourished from that day forward," he said, his blue eyes gazing at Olivia with fondness.

It was obvious Olivia liked the young gentleman, even if his character was as flat as his pressed leaves and flowers. "Mr. Chauncey was kind enough to write to me when I returned to Treversham House."

Did he? It was a shame Thorn was about to dash the man's aspirations for acquiring Olivia for his collection.

"Then it seems fitting that we share our news with your good friend," Thorn said smoothly.

Mr. Chauncey's forehead furrowed. "News?"

"What news?" Olivia echoed.

"My meeting with your father," Thorn said. "Lord Dewick has granted his consent. We are betrothed."

Oliva abruptly stood. "What?"

"You have been courting Miss Lydall?" Mr. Chauncey also stood. He was so shocked by the news that he did not conceal his disappointment.

"I do not believe it!" Olivia sputtered.

"I know, my dear," Thorn said, enjoying his part. He rose from the sofa and grinned down at her. "You thought it would take months to earn your father's approval. This calls for a celebration, does it not? Shall we go downstairs and share a glass of wine with Lord Dewick?"

"No," Olivia whispered.

"Allow me to be the first to offer my congratulations. I should take my leave so you and Lord Kempthorn can have a private celebration," Mr. Chauncey said, sounding sad and confused, to no one in particular.

Please do, my good man, and take your pocket book with you.

"A pity you have to go," Thorn said, his fingers encircling Olivia's elbow to stop her from walking to the other gentleman. "The butler is just outside the door. He will escort you downstairs."

Mr. Chauncey picked up his book and clutched it to his chest as he stared forlornly at Olivia. "Yes, I must leave. Miss Lydall, please give my regards to Lord Dewick, and once again, I wish you and Lord Kempthorn good tidings."

"It was so good to see you again, Mr. Chauncey," she said, sounding as if she was strangling on her words.

Mr. Chauncey raised his hand in farewell. "Lord Kempthorn," he muttered, sending Thorn a quick look of resentment before he stalked out of the drawing room.

Her tight smile fell as soon as the gentleman departed. Olivia turned to confront him and proved her annoyance by poking her finger into Thorn's chest. "What have you done?"

Chapter Twenty-Four

"This is a prank of some sort," Olivia declared. She strode to the drawing room doors and shut them so she and Thorn could speak in private. "Though I cannot fathom how you convinced my father to participate."

"You wound me, my sweet," Thorn said. "If I am not speaking the truth, why would I allow Mr. Chauncey to leave with fresh gossip ringing in his ears? He is bound to tell someone what he learned and that person will tell twenty of his closest friends. By nightfall, a third of London will know."

Oh dear, poor Mr. Chauncey. She could not fathom what the gentleman thought of her now when she had given him permission to call on her just minutes before Lord Kempthorn's arrival.

Olivia passed by Thorn and sat down on the sofa. She brought her hands to her face. "How did this happen? You were supposed to convince my father that nothing happened in the coach."

Thorn dropped down next to her, causing her bounce on the plump cushion. "Something did happen in the coach. Do you recall when I slipped my hand beneath your skirt—"

"Stop!" She groaned into her hands and then let them

drop to her lap. "My father saw us kissing. Nothing more. He would not demand that you marry me."

"Well, we did more than kiss, Olivia," he said, looking rested and cheerful. So much so, she longed to throttle him. "We must have given ourselves away or your father understands the nature of young couples better than we have given him credit. And if you doubt that we are betrothed, all you have to do is go downstairs and Lord Dewick will confirm it."

"Why are you not furious?" she demanded. "You have no desire to be leg-shackled to a wife."

"Calm down, Olivia," he advised. "Another man might think that you do not want to marry me."

How could she be Thorn's countess? The man's moods were similar to the tides, ever shifting from amusement to displeasure. Olivia sensed that he viewed her as another duty to oversee, but was there friendship? Affection? Oh, to be certain, the gentleman enjoyed kissing her. Though the news did not ease her fears. Thorn had kissed countless ladies.

She tried to stand, but the scoundrel reached out and grabbed her arm. Irritated, she sat down. "I do not wish to marry you, Thorn." She rushed on, "Any more than you have a desire to marry me. We must speak to my father and talk him out of his nonsense."

"Are you brave enough for such a frank conversation?" he pressed. "In your father's eyes, you are ruined."

Her shoulders slumped. "Oh, this is most unfair," she cried out. "No one is telling you that you are ruined for kissing a lady. Otherwise, you would have been betrothed as a boy."

Thorn laughed. "Very true, though it does not alter your circumstances. Did you not find satisfaction when I intimately caressed you?"

Her face burned with the knowledge that she had enjoyed every minute of it. "I do not wish to discuss it."

Thorn leaned closer. She inhaled and held her breath as he brushed his lips against her earlobe. "When I was lying in my bed last evening, I thought about you. How your tongue tasted against mine. The wetness that coated my fingers when I slipped my hand between your thighs and stroked that sensitive slit."

She refused to look at him. "Your words are as coarse as your manners," she said, feeling her nipples constrict at the reminder.

"We took a risk and were caught," he whispered into her ear. "I have agreed to pay the price for our night's mischief. What about you? Especially, when I cannot wait to put my hands on you again."

Olivia felt a wave of heat wash over her. The flesh between her legs ached as if her body was anticipating his touch. "You dare to tease me. In my father's house?"

"Aye, I dare. I will tease and torment both of us until you cannot think of another man touching you." He paused. "Kissing you."

Gideon's kiss.

Olivia turned her head and stared at him. Had Gideon told Thorn that he had kissed her? Or was this just another one of the earl's games. The kiss she had shared with Gideon was restrained and a bit tepid. It lacked the spark and the excitement she had felt when she had kissed Thorn within the dark interior of his coach. Or the earlier kiss she had thought she had shared with Gideon.

Malster Park.

It had been Thorn who had kissed her in front of Lady Felstead's folly.

She gritted her teeth. "What do you want from me?"

"Everything."

The single word crackled in the drawing room like invisible lightning and rumbled through her entire body like thunder.

"Or nothing." Thorn shrugged. "Though if we are betrothed, I see no reason why we should deny ourselves."

Of course, he was already weighing the advantages of their arrangement.

Thorn's face sobered. "You should know why your father is upset. My cousin and my friends told Gideon that there was some ballroom gossip about us."

"Gossip?" She was disheartened by the revelation. "Is this about Lord Norgrave?"

Thorn gave her an impatient look. He obviously was recalling his unhappiness at discovering her in the company of the marquess. Shaking his head, he said, "No, though I would not be surprised if a few individuals are commenting on your appalling taste in friends."

"Lest you forget, you may add yourself to that growing list," she shot back.

He quelled her with a stony look. "Regardless, there is some speculation about the nature of our friendship. When your father came to our town house, Gideon repeated the gossip told to him by St. Lyons, Chance, and Rainbault."

Good grief, why had Gideon revealed such news to her father? Of course, she and Thorn had compounded the problem by allowing themselves to be discovered together in the coach.

"This announcement will only confirm the rumors."

"It will dispel any nasty gossip and restore your good name. You know, you should be grateful that I agree with your father," he reminded her.

"Did you have a choice?"

Thorn hesitated. "Not really, but that is beside the point."

Olivia sighed as her spirits reached a new low. "Let us be honest, Thorn. We are not a good match."

"No, we are not."

She winced at the ease with which the earl confirmed her declaration. "I was supposed to be seeking a husband so I did not end up with one handpicked by Lady Grisdale," Olivia said, marveling at how much trouble she had gotten into in less than a day.

"There is no reason why you cannot continue to search for him," Thorn drawled.

Olivia locked gazes with him. There was not a hint of teasing in his dark green eyes. "Why should I look for a potential husband when I have you?"

"My thoughts exactly," was his wry reply. "Most ladies in your enviable position would consider me quite the catch."

"So this is a ruse," she exclaimed and then punched him in the arm for teasing her. "How could you go on and let me think—"

Thorn silenced her with a kiss. He indulged himself by spearing his tongue between her teeth. Playfully, he coiled and uncoiled his nimble tongue against hers until she had forgotten what they were discussing.

"The engagement is real. You are my betrothed, and by nightfall, my family will learn of this joyful development," he said. His green irises were thin rings, inflamed by a simple kiss. "Neither one of us should give anyone a reason to think otherwise. However, you are not the only Lydall who believes I am unworthy to marry you."

"I did not say you are unworthy," she said crossly. "It is my opinion that we are not a good match."

Thorn kissed her again. Both of them were breathless when they separated. "Definitely not a good match," was his husky reply. He smirked at her. "Where was I?"

Olivia gave him a weak shove and stood. "I am heading downstairs to speak with my father since you are making little sense."

He also climbed to his feet and trailed after her. "Lord

Dewick is committed to this course. You will not dissuade him."

"We will see," she said, not feeling as confident as she sounded. Olivia crossed the threshold. "Besides, I doubt anyone will believe you have been courting me in secret."

"We have known each other since we were children. With the support of my family and Lord Dewick, no one will question my interest in you," he said, unmoved by her misgivings. "With a little effort, I can be quite convincing."

As Lord Kempthorn or as Gideon?

Olivia's mouth thinned at his arrogant statement but she refused to be goaded. Holding her head high, she ignored Thorn and went downstairs to find her father.

Ten minutes later, Thorn was leaning against the wall with his arms crossed as he watched father and daughter argue over the merits of announcing their engagement. Lord Dewick was unyielding in his decision and the banked fury in the baron's eyes was a reminder that he blamed Thorn.

"Papa, if you would consider—"

"No. I will not alter my opinion on the subject," Lord Dewick said, unwilling to let his daughter's emotional appeal sway him.

Thorn was sympathetic. Olivia lived a sheltered life, but no one had interfered and she had freedoms most ladies would envy. Now everyone had an opinion about all aspects of her life from how she spent her afternoon to the gentleman her father had betrothed her to without her knowledge. He moved his shoulder as leverage to push himself away from the wall and crossed the room to where Olivia was standing.

She stiffened as she became aware of his proximity.

"It isn't fair to Lord Kempthorn," she protested.

"Lord Kempthorn can speak for himself, my dear lady,"

Thorn murmured into her ear, startling her. "Would you care to join me when I tell my family?"

Olivia stared at her father. "What if I promised to heed all of Lady Grisdale's advice without complaint?"

Lord Dewick's lips twitched. "An impossible feat. Though I would appreciate it if you were kinder to her since she will one day be your stepmother."

"You are stuck with me, sweeting," Thorn teased. He was tempted to kiss her shoulder, but the lady was flustered and feeling cornered. If he touched her, he might lose a tooth.

"Only temporarily if I deem you unworthy to marry my daughter, Kempthorn," her father said, his countenance darkening.

"How so?" she asked. "Lord Kempthorn mentioned that I could use my time in Town to seek a more like-minded gentleman. None of this makes any sense to me."

Naturally, his betrothed was planning her escape.

"From what I saw in the coach, you and Kempthorn seem compatible enough," the baron said bluntly. "However, I told him that I would not fight him in the courts if he broke the engagement."

"You gave him permission to abandon me at the marriage altar?" she wailed. "I will be a laughingstock!"

"Stop being dramatic," Thorn ordered. "When it is time for us to end our engagement, it will be you who will cry off."

"You are serious."

"Do not fret, Olivia, I will come up with a good reason for you and I to part ways that will appease even the most hardened critic. By the time I am finished, you will have the *ton's* sympathy," he said, lightly touching her on the upper arm.

Olivia whirled halfway to confront him.

She frowned. "And your reputation as an utter bounder will be secured."

He acknowledged her observation by inclining his head. "You would deny me a small reward?"

Olivia's hands came up in surrender. "I cannot talk sense into either of you. Do what you will." Without bidding her father farewell, she marched out of the library.

"I always do, my dear," Thorn softly replied.

"Olivia rarely loses her temper."

He shrugged. "I can handle your daughter." What astonished him was that he was relishing matching wits with the lady.

Lord Dewick cleared his throat. "This arrangement is to protect her reputation and quell the gossips, Kempthorn. It does not give you license to continue your dalliance."

Thorn slowly exhaled. "No one will believe our engagement isn't genuine if we do not behave like a besotted couple."

"I will not see her hurt."

The baron was as stubborn as his daughter.

"I have no intention of causing Olivia pain, my lord," Thorn said with an air of impatience. "However, I will gain her cooperation by any means. Do not interfere."

"Are you threatening me, Kempthorn?" the baron sputtered in outrage.

"Aye, I am," Thorn replied. "I have agreed to this engagement because it suits both of our purposes. You have done your part. Let me do mine."

Chapter Twenty-Five

"You have proposed to Olivia?" Lady Felstead stared in astonishment at her eldest son. At his brisk nod, she switched her attention to Olivia. "Marriage?"

"Aye, mother," he replied wryly. "Why else would I have proposed to the lady?"

It had taken a day and a half to assemble his family into his mother's drawing room to share the good news. Lord and Lady Felstead held court in the middle of the room as they were seated on the sofa. Chance and Tempest sat opposite his parents on another sofa. His sister Fiona and his father's nine-year-old ward, Muriel, had claimed two of the chairs. Gideon had distanced himself from the family as he stood near a window.

"Nothing that can be uttered in front of the children, I wager," his twin drawled, and was rewarded with a glare from Thorn, Chance, and Lord Felstead.

"Enough, Gideon," the marquess growled, ignoring the Duke of Blackbern's soft chuckle.

Without telling him, his mother had invited the Duke and Duchess of Blackbern to join them. Their numbers increased with their children. Chance's brother Benjamin was absent due to another commitment and Frederick was away at school, but the Blackberns' eighteen-year-old daughter,

Honora, sixteen-year-old Mercy, and eight-year-old Constance were present.

Thorn had decided not to include St. Lyons and Rainbault in this first meeting. The two gentlemen were like brothers, but he could not trust them not to question his lack of courtship and hasty engagement to Miss Lydall. They had witnessed Gideon's outburst at their town house, and were too intelligent not to draw their own conclusions of Thorn's meeting with Lord Dewick. He would speak to them later in private.

He had considered inviting Lady Arabella. Not only was she Tempest's sister, she was also Olivia's friend. Unfortunately he was uncertain if she would approve of his engagement to Olivia so he eventually discarded the notion of adding her to the guest list. The Duke and Duchess of Blackbern's unexpected arrival affirmed he had made the right decision.

Lord Dewick had also offered to attend with Lady Grisdale, but Thorn had politely declined. Olivia was skittish. Her first glimpse of the drawing room filled with his family had sent her fleeing in the opposite direction. It had taken a sip of brandy, a little fanning to cool her face and neck, and a few sniffs from the ornate vinaigrette box he had retrieved from her reticule to restore her courage.

Thorn and Olivia stood side by side in front of Lord and Lady Felstead as he announced to his stunned family that he had spoken to Lord Dewick and had gained the gentleman's blessing.

"Forgive me, Father, I should have come to you after I spoke with the baron." Thorn threaded his fingers through Olivia's to prevent her from edging away from him and undermining their united front. "In my eagerness, I sought out Olivia and proposed immediately."

Constance whispered loudly to Muriel. "You have a new sister."

"Well done, brother," Fiona said, pleased by the news. "Olivia will fit in rather nicely with our eccentric family."

"Congratulations, Thorn," the Duchess of Blackbern said, smiling at the couple. "Welcome to the family, Miss Lydall."

Olivia swayed a little, so he gave her hand an encouraging squeeze. "Thank you, Your Grace."

Thorn looked askance at Lady Felstead. "Well, Mother, what do you have to say about this business? I do not believe I have ever seen you at a loss for words."

To his dismay, his mother's eyes filled with sudden tears. Lady Felstead rose from the sofa and cradled his and Olivia's clasped hands within her own.

"I cannot believe you are betrothed," she said, her voice strained with emotion. "I never thought I would live long enough to see the day, my lad."

"Mother never thought you would find a lady who would have you," quipped Gideon, and everyone in the drawing room laughed.

"In our hearts, you have always been part of our family, Olivia," the marchioness said, releasing their hands so she could embrace the lady she viewed as her future daughter-in-law. "I am so happy one of my sons has the good sense to bind us through marriage."

Olivia looked at him for guidance but she was on her own. "Thank you, Lady Felstead."

His mother accepted a handkerchief from Thorn to wipe her damp eyes. "Just imagine, you will be able to call me mother like the rest of the children. With your dear sweet mother gone, I must insist on it."

"Uh—I am honored, my lady," Olivia said, overwhelmed by the easy acceptance from his family.

Only Gideon seemed reserved.

"This calls for a celebration," Chance said as both he and Tempest stood. "I will tell the butler that we need wine and glasses for a toast."

His cousin slapped him on the back as he headed for the door to find a servant.

"I am very happy for you, Miss Lydall," Tempest said as the two ladies embraced.

Thorn stepped aside so his family could each take a turn at embracing Olivia and welcoming her to the family.

"Everyone is overjoyed with your unexpected news," Gideon said stepping up to him from behind. "How disappointed they will all be when they learn that this is a ruse."

"My engagement isn't a pretense, brother," Thorn said, annoyed that his twin's reaction had been similar to Olivia's. "I have secured Lord Dewick's blessing, and Olivia has consented to be my bride."

"Is that so," Gideon said sullenly. "Fine. Keep your secrets from the rest of them. Lord knows our family has enough secrets to fill the Thames. I just want you to know that I am watching you. If you hurt Olivia in any way, I will make you regret it."

"Because you love her," Thorn replied tersely.

"Aye, I love her," his twin confirmed. "Can you say the same, brother?"

"Your father tells me that congratulations are in order, Olivia," Lady Grisdale said as she and Olivia waited to disembark from the lady's coach. "I must confess I did not believe it until Lord Dewick explained that he was in a position to apply a little pressure on Lord Kempthorn once you and the earl were discovered in rather embarrassing predicament."

She could not believe her father confessed the entire tale to Lady Grisdale. "That embarrassing predicament was a kiss, my lady. You have been married, and hope to marry my father. I warrant at your age, you have kissed a few gentlemen who were not your husband."

Her father had insisted that Olivia join the countess this evening in her private box at the King's Theatre. Not only did he wish to encourage civility between his future wife and his daughter, he also thought Olivia could benefit from the countess's insight and experience.

"I am not scolding you, my dear," the countess said with a laugh. "I am applauding your resourcefulness in convincing the elusive bachelor to come up to scratch. I have lamented to the baron for months that your average looks might not be enough for you to secure a husband. Because of your tender age, I had dismissed that you had the aptitude for trickery."

If anyone had been tricked into this engagement, it had been Olivia. Still, she kept the opinion to herself. Her father had already revealed too much to the countess. As eager as Lady Grisdale was to separate Olivia from her father, she did not trust the women.

"No trickery was involved, my lady," Olivia said, glancing out the window of the coach. "Lord Kempthorn told his family that he is quite smitten."

Lady Grisdale trilled with condescending laughter. "Oh Olivia, you can be quite naïve when it comes to men. Kempthorn took a risk in amusing himself with you and was soundly caught. To his credit, he is willing to accept his defeat with some grace. However, I am familiar with his sort. It is in your best interest to marry him as swiftly as possible before his eye wanders and settles on another lady. Oh, and you might wish to speak with his brother."

"Why do I need to speak with Gideon?"

"Lord Dewick claims you and Mr. Netherwood are good friends. If he is an ally, use him," the countess advised. "He could tell you if your betrothed keeps a mistress and how often he sees her."

A mistress. Olivia had not considered that Thorn had a mistress tucked away somewhere in London. "If Lord Kempthorn has a mistress, there would be no reason for him to marry me."

"Little innocent," Lady Grisdale mocked. "Lord Dewick is offering a generous dowry, Lord Kempthorn's family approves of the match, and marrying and bedding you will give Kempthorn his heir. So there are benefits in proceeding with the marriage. However, it is not your fault if you are unable to fulfill all of his carnal appetites. That is why many gentlemen return to their mistresses once they are married, and you should be grateful for it."

"Will Papa be joining us this evening?" Olivia asked, uncertain of her father's decision as Lady Grisdale was planting seeds of doubt of Thorn's intentions.

"He assured me that he would," the countess said. "However, trusting a gentleman to keep his promises will lead to disappointment. A clever lady accepts that all males are flawed but can be managed. As your stepmother, I will instruct you as best as I can."

It wasn't the first time that Olivia wondered how her father could love Lady Grisdale. She was as cold and calculating as a viper in a henhouse. Still, it would not do to make this lady her enemy.

"Your generosity is boundless," Olivia said, lowering her gaze to give the appearance of modesty and respect.

Lady Grisdale brought her handkerchief to her nose to sniff the fragrance she had sprinkled on the linen so she could tolerate the foul smells of the street. "Olivia, you have a bad habit of overplaying your advantages and compliments. It is just another flaw we need to work on."

In 1787, Prague had celebrated Mozart's *Don Giovanni.* Seven months later, the prolific composer oversaw the premiere of the opera in Vienna. It had taken thirty years for the opera to debut at the King's Theatre on Haymarket. Rainbault and St. Lyons had obtained the coveted tickets for the opera's first performance in April and had highly praised the production. However, it was not the repeat performance that had drawn Thorn to the theater but rather Miss Lydall.

His mother had mentioned that Olivia would be attending this evening's performance with her father and Lady Grisdale. After witnessing the countess's callous treatment toward Olivia at Malster Park, Thorn had decided to use his newfound status as her betrothed to alter the baron's plans. No one would question if he escorted Olivia to the Duke of Rainbault's box so she could enjoy the opera away from the disapproving gaze of Lady Grisdale.

There would be plenty of chaperones to ensure he behaved himself. St. Lyons and Rainbault were eager to watch *Don Giovanni* again. Chance and his wife had been invited, and Tempest had invited Lady Arabella. There would be others. Rainbault was quite popular and there was a never-ending flow of visitors who wished to be seen with the exiled prince.

If an opportunity presented itself, Thorn might even steal Miss Lydall away for a few minutes for a kiss or two. The lady would soon learn that he was willing to dedicate himself to the task. Gideon had declined to join Thorn and their friends at the theater. He offered no excuse for his disinterest, but it was for the best. Thorn's engagement to Olivia was supposed to discourage his twin from pursuing the lady. After his brief confrontation at Lady Felstead's town house, Thorn had been concerned that Gideon was determined to rescue Olivia from his lascivious attentions, but his brother had kept his distance from her. Thorn had a spy in the Lydall household who would report back to him if his twin called on the residence.

"Where is your lady, Thorn?" Rainbault inquired when he entered the theater box.

He gripped the back of the duke's seat and lowered his head so they could speak freely without being overheard. "The lady is elusive, but I am eager for the chase. My mother could not tell me which box Olivia would be seated in. St. Lyon has offered his assistance. If I cannot find her, I will visit each private theater box until I do."

As much as he had made light of his endeavor, it was no simple task. The theater was comprised of four tiers of boxes, a large pit, and a gallery. There were forty-three boxes on each tier, so he needed a stratagem to locate Miss Lydall or else he and the viscount could spend the entire evening searching boxes.

Rainbault tipped his head back and glanced over his shoulder to meet Thorn's gaze. "Gideon seems unhappy about your engagement to Miss Lydall."

There was nothing he could do about his twin at the moment that would not lead the brothers to a physical confrontation.

"Gideon has forgotten how to share," Thorn said with a contemptuous curl to his mouth that amused his friend. "He views Olivia as his alone and it incenses him that her father has placed her into my care."

"To be fair, you did force the baron's hand by compromising his daughter," the duke reminded him.

"A little more discretion, Your Grace," he cautioned. "Or else you ruin the lady and all of my good intentions."

"Miss Lydall, it appears fate persists in bringing us together," Lord Norgrave said when he encountered her and the countess near the theater's entrance.

"Good evening, my lord," Olivia genially greeted him. "Do you know Lady Grisdale?"

"I make a point of acquainting myself with all of London's great beauties." The marquess bowed. "Lady Grisdale, is it true that your heart has been claimed by another?"

To Olivia's amazement, the countess appeared flustered by Lord Norgrave's flattery. "Lord Dewick and I hope to make an official announcement soon."

The older gentleman turned to address Olivia. "And bits of gossip about you have reached my ears too, Miss Lydall. Immediately I dismissed it as idle chatter, but I heard the rumors again last evening."

"There is no need to be evasive, my lord. I assume you speak of my recent engagement to Lord Kempthorn," Olivia said, grateful the earl had not escorted her to the theater. She understood that Thorn's loyalties were aligned with the Blackberns because the duke and duchess were family. However, Lord Norgrave had done nothing to warrant her condemnation.

"So the rumors are true." The marquess's unusually light blue eyes studied her face as if searching for a sign of deception. "I would not have considered you and Kempthorn a good match, but the gentleman was very protective of you when he confronted us at Lady Purles'."

"You are not the first to note our differences," Olivia said blithely. She had given voice to the same concern but had promised her father that she would not add to the speculation of her relationship with the earl. "Nevertheless, one must follow one's heart."

"Lord Dewick is quite pleased with the match," Lady Grisdale interjected.

"When will the banns be posted?" Lord Norgrave asked.

Olivia faltered. Her father and Thorn had not addressed the wedding details since Thorn expected her to break their engagement in the near future. And when Lady Felstead had suggested that they begin to prepare for the wedding, Thorn had not exactly discouraged her but he had been deliberately vague about when and where the wedding would take place.

It was Thorn's fault that she was in this awkward predicament with Lord Norgrave.

"My father and Lord Kempthorn have not worked out all of the details," Olivia said, looking to Lady Grisdale for some guidance.

"Naturally, with two weddings to be planned there is much to be settled," the countess said.

"I have no doubt." The marquess's expression grew pensive. "Would you ladies care to join me in my private box? My son, Lord Marcroft, is awaiting my return with increasing impatience, I have no doubt. Lady Arabella is also here." He smiled at Olivia. "My daughter holds you in high regard and will likely press you for more details about your engagement to Lord Kempthorn."

The notion of visiting with Lady Arabella was preferable than sitting with Lady Grisdale. "I—"

"I have my own box, but we could spare a few minutes to greet your family, Norgrave," Lady Grisdale said cordially. "And what of Lady Norgrave? Is she here?"

"Regretfully, my wife does not share my passion for Mozart," Lord Norgrave confessed.

"A pity." The countess's gaze was sympathetic. "Is this your first opportunity to see *Don Giovanni*?"

Pleased to have discovered a fellow Mozart enthusiast, the marquess said, "No, I attended its debut in April."

"I was unable to attend," Lady Grisdale lamented. "Lord Dewick rarely attends the theater, though he promised to make an exception since this opera was so well received by the *ton*." She touched Olivia lightly on the arm. "My dear, with Lord Norgrave's permission, I will leave you in his capable hands while I visit our private box to make certain your father is not waiting for our arrival. I will also leave a note with one of the attendants and join you shortly."

"Shall we, Miss Lydall?" Lord Norgrave held her gaze with an unspoken challenge in his light blue eyes.

Olivia placed her hand on his arm and offered him a tentative smile. With any luck, Thorn would not hear that she had once again found herself in the marquess's company.

Chapter Twenty-Six

"You will never find Miss Lydall in this crush," St. Lyon said, his dark blue eyes searching the nearby boxes.

The viscount had received numerous invitations from his admirers to remain and leave Thorn to carry on his quest to find his errant lady without him. However, St. Lyons was a good friend and he had politely declined all offers. It was the last woman who had whispered into the man's ear that had tested his fortitude.

"You can always return to the wench once I find Olivia," Thorn said, when he caught his friend waving to the woman.

"You do not know what I am giving up for our friendship, Kempthorn," St. Lyons said, exhaling slowly. "Do not allow that innocent countenance to fool you. What that creature whispered in my ear was truly wicked and possibly criminal. I may never recover from the shock."

"You are likely the fifth gentleman she has propositioned this evening," Thorn said cynically.

It was no surprise that St. Lyons and Rainbault had praised *Don Giovanni*. Their own lives reflected that of the fictional libertine.

"Then the poor lady deserves my pity. Perhaps I should console her—"

"Damn you, St. Lyons . . . if you"—Thorn noted the

viscount's sly grin—"Ah, so you have not lost your sense of humor, I see. I will make you a promise, if you can concentrate on our task a while longer, I will deliver you to the lecherous lady."

"This engagement has made you tense," St. Lyon complained. He paused for a moment. "Well, more than usual."

It wasn't the engagement that was making him tense. It was Olivia. She was unpredictable and attracted trouble as easily as St. Lyons collected female admirers. Not that trouble did not also find his amorous friend. St. Lyons' carnal exploits had caused numerous unhappy gentlemen to don the horns of the cuckold.

Thorn was dismayed when he and St. Lyons entered the next box and saw Lady Millicent sitting with her parents, Lord and Lady Flewett. The young woman's expression brightened at the sight of the two gentlemen.

"Good evening, Thorn . . . Lord Bastrell," Lady Millicent greeted them, so the two men lingered to pay their respects to her mother and father. Fortunately, all of the seats in the box were occupied. Otherwise Thorn would have had to decline an invitation to stay and watch the opera from the Flewetts' private box.

While St. Lyons answered the countess's inquiries about his family, Thorn glanced out into the amphitheater and searched the boxes for Olivia. It was an endless sea of people as everyone paid their respects to friends and rivals alike. He was about to ask Lord Flewett if he knew which private box belonged to Lady Grisdale when his gaze landed on a familiar face.

Norgrave.

Thorn fought down the urge to sneer. He had not been aware that the marquess was a patron of the arts. The Duke and Duchess of Blackbern were also present this evening, though there was little risk of a confrontation. The two families usually avoided public displays. However, he would warn Chance about the marquess when he and St. Lyons returned to Rainbault's private box.

With his attention on Norgrave, Thorn murmured in his friend's ear that they should leave. As he lowered his head, he almost missed the lady in a lilac-colored dress. She was seated to the right of the marquess. Lady Arabella, wearing a light blue gown, sat at the lady's right and Lord Marcroft was seated behind the two ladies. He had not noticed her because she had shifted in her seat as she conversed with Norgrave's daughter.

She has my attention now.

Miss Lydall tilted her head and laughed at something Lady Arabella had said. Her unruly chestnut curls had been pinned high so her hair artfully framed her delicate face. His heart stuttered in his chest at her beauty.

From his vantage point, his betrothed seemed blissfully content to be seated with the Brant family. His eyes narrowed on Norgrave as he observed that the marquess's attention kept returning to his daughter and Olivia.

A feminine hand touched him on the arm. Thorn's gaze moved from the gloved hand up her arm to Lady Millicent's face. "Is something wrong?" she asked. "I had hoped that you and the viscount would stay longer."

Thorn had to tread carefully with the young lady. If she mentioned the kiss she had surprised him with while they explored Lady Purles' gallery, Lord Flewett would demand an explanation. The last time he was confronted with similar circumstances, he ended up betrothed.

Of course, to be fair, he had done much more than indulge in a few kisses with the lady.

The vision of Olivia moving against his wet fingers had left him craving more from her. Each night as he crawled into his empty bed, he had reached for his thickening cock and thought of her silky flesh and the scent of her arousal. Concentrating on the head, he stroked the straining rigid length as he thought of filling her and watching her cornflower eyes glazing over in pleasure. It was her face that he saw in his mind when his cock jerked and he orgasmed, spilling his seed on his stomach.

Just thinking about Miss Lydall stirred his cock. His lack of control was humbling.

"I cannot stay, Lady Millicent," he said, regretting the disappointment he saw in her light brown eyes. "I am meeting someone."

"Miss Lydall?" she asked, her pleasant features hardening with annoyance.

Thorn wondered if Lady Millicent had heard the news of his engagement.

Lady Flewett leaned forward. "Lord Kempthorn," she said to gain his attention. "Someone told me that you are betrothed to Lord Dewick's daughter. Is it true?"

The flash of pain in Lady Millicent's eyes filled him with guilt. He had not encouraged the young lady, but he had not discouraged her either. Or at least until she had ambushed him with that kiss. He sent her an apologetic glance before his gaze switched to her mother.

"Aye, madam, it is," he admitted.

"Well, this is good news. Allow me to congratulate you and Miss Lydall. I cannot recall the last time I spoke to her. The poor motherless girl. She was such an odd scrawny creature. I hope for your sake the lady has improved with age," Lady Flewett said.

Thorn resisted the urge to chastise the countess for her unfavorable description of Olivia. "Miss Lydall has grown into a beautiful young lady, Lady Flewett. I am extremely content with my decision to ask for her hand in marriage."

Thorn was fibbing a bit on the details. He had not asked Olivia to marry him. Her father had ordered her to accept the engagement. In hindsight, her resistance to the notion is understandable. Most ladies expected a bit of flattery and romance.

"Are you ready to depart?" St. Lyons asked.

"Aye." He bowed to Lord and Lady Flewett and to Lady Millicent. "I will pass your regards to my family. I bid you all a good evening."

Once they stepped out of the private box, Thorn's hand lifted to stop his friend. "I know where to find Miss Lydall."

"Where is she?" the viscount asked.

"Lord Norgrave's box."

"When Chance told my sister and me that you and Lord Kempthorn were betrothed, neither one of us could believe it," Lady Arabella confessed in a hushed voice so her brother and father could not eavesdrop on their conversation. "How did you keep your courtship a secret for so long?"

Olivia laughed. "It has not been a courtship in the usual sense. I have known Thorn for most of my life so we did not need to fill our days with drawing room visits and chaperoned walks in the garden. In the past year or so, our friendship . . . changed. I cannot describe it. Suffice to say that Thorn recognized our growing attraction before I did." She nibbled her lip as she mixed a bit of truth with her lies to satisfy her friend's curiosity. "My father has been quite vocal about his aspirations for me this spring, and it prodded the earl into declaring his intentions to my father."

"Chance told Tempest that Lord Kempthorn has always been guarded when it comes to matters of his heart," Lady Arabella said, truly delighted for Olivia's newfound happiness with the earl. "Could it be that he has been secretly in love with you for years?"

Lady Arabella possessed such a romantic heart. Olivia

grinned at the notion of the earl harboring an unspoken passion for her or any lady. "The earl is not one to be ruled by his emotions. I suspect he was caught unaware by his feelings as much as I was," she said.

It was then that Olivia noticed that her friend was not listening to her. Lady Arabella's attention seemed to be fixed on a private box on the opposite side of the theater. In the front seats, she noticed a handsome couple. The gentleman had dark straight hair tied at the nape of his neck in a queue. At his side, sat a beautiful lady with light blond hair attired in a brown Spanish-style dress with a very low bodice.

The gentleman stilled as if he sensed he was being observed. He raised his chin, his gaze searching the tiers of boxes until he saw Lady Arabella. His look of puzzlement eased into happiness. He inclined his head.

"Are they friends of yours?" Olivia inquired.

The other woman started at the question. She blinked rapidly as if she was struggling not to cry.

"Lady Arabella," Olivia said, keeping her voice low. "Are you unwell? If you need a moment—"

Her friend shook her head and offered Olivia a wistful smile. "No, I am fine." She brought her gloved hand to her lips and coughed delicately into her fist. "You asked about the couple. The gentleman is the Marquess of Warrilow and the lady is his wife. Theirs was a fairly recent match. I was told the couple had an autumn wedding."

Had Lord Warrilow courted Lady Arabella? Olivia tried to recall if her friend had mentioned the handsome marquess, but the name was unfamiliar to her. The same could not be said for her friend. The young lady had feelings for the gentleman and she was doing her best to deny them.

Olivia did not press her friend with additional questions about the couple and Lady Arabella's connection to Lord Warrilow.

"Lord Dewick has yet to arrive," Lady Grisdale said, providing a welcome distraction for Lady Arabella when the countess entered Lord Norgrave's private box. "At this rate, he will miss the opera."

"Lord Dewick's loss is our gain," Lord Marcroft said, silently noting the countess selected the seat beside the marquess. "Do you not agree, Father?"

"Indeed," the older gentleman said, his gaze shifting to Olivia. "Remain as our guest. We have plenty of room, and I am certain your father and betrothed would be grateful that you are surrounded by friends."

Olivia silently disagreed. Thorn would not be happy about this at all.

"I like the idea of Kempthorn owing the Brants a favor," Lord Marcroft drawled.

Lord Norgrave chuckled. "I would like to see you collect on it, Croft."

"I did not realize you and Lord Kempthorn are rivals, Lord Marcroft," Olivia said, reluctant to bring up the animosity between the Brants and the Rookes.

Lady Arabella cleared her throat to get Olivia's attention. "My brother went to school with Lord Kempthorn and his friends. I would guess that the rivalry began when they were boys."

Lord Marcroft appeared amused by his sister's diplomacy. "Boys are rather thickheaded, Arabella. That's why we prefer to settle our disagreements with our fists."

Olivia could not conceal her revulsion.

"Croft, you are upsetting Miss Lydall," Lord Norgrave said. "Most ladies are sickened by the brutish behavior of young men." He addressed Olivia. "You must forgive Croft. His civility could use some polish. I confess this is more my fault than his mother's."

"Nonsense, Lord Marcroft has excellent manners," Olivia said, feeling the need to defend the earl when his father was mocking him. "I have valued our conversations."

Lady Arabella looked grateful for her defense.

Lord Marcroft acknowledged her praise by inclining his head. "A fair beauty who sees goodness in a Brant. For that alone I could despise Kempthorn."

Olivia gaped at the earl. "Good heavens why?"

The earl's smile was self-mocking. "Because he had the intelligence to claim you before anyone else figured out what a treasure you are, Miss Lydall."

"Well said, Croft," Lord Norgrave murmured. "I suppose it would be rude to hope Kempthorn falls out of favor with Lord Dewick and the engagement is broken."

Olivia wasn't superstitious. However, the older man's words felt like a curse. She shivered.

Lady Grisdale slapped the marquess on the hand with her closed fan. "What a very rude thing for you to say. You must apologize to Miss Lydall immediately or she will think you wish her ill."

Lord Norgrave appeared properly chastened. "Forgive me, dear lady. Indeed, I wish you and Kempthorn well."

"That is a relief," Thorn said, heading toward them. His friend, St. Lyon was standing behind him. "I was about to issue challenges to you and Marcroft for upsetting my betrothed."

Chapter Twenty-Seven

"I was unaware you were attending the opera this evening," Olivia said as they walked the length of the grand saloon.

Thorn scowled at her polite demeanor. He had gone to great lengths to spare her from an evening with Lady Grisdale and Lord Norgrave and she did not seem to be properly appreciative of his efforts.

Not that they were alone. Lady Grisdale was too shrewd to allow him to stroll off with his betrothed unchaperoned. Lady Arabella had offered to join Olivia. She and St. Lyons were giving them a modicum of privacy by walking at a slower pace. Marcroft had also stood as if he intended to join their little party just to infuriate Thorn. However, the earl had separated from the two couples, announcing he was planning to visit the green room so he could flirt with the female performers.

Thorn did not care what the man did as long as he stayed away from him and Olivia.

"Rainbault and St. Lyons expressed a desire to see the opera," he said, discreetly admiring the dress Olivia was wearing. The lilac silk dress was fashioned with a demure bodice, and the simplicity of its design allowed him to admire Olivia's womanly curves rather than be distracted by rows of ribbons, bows, and rosettes that adorned too many ladies' skirts. At the hem of the skirt, there was an elegant

Greek key design embroidered in gold thread. "I thought you might like to join me in Rainbault's private box."

He anticipated her relief and pleasure at his invitation.

"No thank you, my lord," she said, pausing to admire one of the paintings on the wall.

Thorn's grin faded as her refusal registered. "Since we are betrothed, no one will question your presence at my side. The public display will confirm the rumors about our engagement are true."

"I understand, Thorn," she said, her generous mouth quirking in a way that warmed his blood and hinted that he had said something amusing. "However, if I abandon Lady Grisdale, my father will be disappointed. He still has high hopes that the countess and I will be friends."

"The countess views you as a threat for Lord Dewick's affections," Thorn said bluntly.

"It is my opinion as well."

"I wager she has been kinder to you since she was told of our engagement."

Olivia glanced up at him in wonder. "How did you guess?" She resumed walking. "My father has told her everything."

"That is not what we agreed upon," Thorn grumbled. He had allowed his own family to believe that his decision was motivated by affection. Gideon knew the truth, but only because he had played a small role in their deception.

"You can scold my father later," Olivia said, unconcerned about Lady Grisdale. "He cannot seem to help himself when he is around the countess. If she wanted to know all of the details that led to our engagement, I swear, the woman possesses the skill to interrogate the answers out of everyone. Not even a spy could resist her."

Thorn doubted it was Lady Grisdale's charm that persuaded Lord Dewick to reveal his secrets. Once she lured the baron into her bed, the man's resolve to protect his daughter had weakened. In Dewick's defense, he likely saw little harm in revealing the entire tale to the lady he intended to marry.

Thorn wished he shared the baron's confidence that Lady Grisdale could resist the opportunity to diminish her future stepdaughter.

"Lady Grisdale does not deserve your kindness," Thorn said. "However, since you are determined to remain at her side this evening, perhaps can you explain to me why you are sitting in Lord Norgrave's box?"

"Oh, that," she said, avoiding his eyes. "We encountered the marquess downstairs. He congratulated me on our engagement and invited us to visit with Lady Arabella. How could I refuse?"

Thorn opened his mouth with the intention of telling her how simple it would have been to decline the old scoundrel's offer. He promptly shut his mouth. As much as he distrusted Norgrave, Lady Arabella was Olivia's friend and Tempest's sister. It would be unfair to punish her for her father's sins.

"May I ask you a question?"

Wary, he nodded. "What do you wish to know?"

"Are you acquainted with Lord Warrilow?"

Olivia was purposefully changing the subject to avoid another lecture about Lord Norgrave. "Not really. The gentleman has shared business interests with Norgrave. Last year, the marquess was encouraging a match between Tempest and Warrilow."

"What happened?"

"Chance married Tempest, and eventually Warrilow married another lady. Why do you ask?"

"Just curious," she said amiably. "I noticed him and his lovely wife, and Lady Arabella was kind enough to tell me his name."

Thorn frowned with suspicion in his dark green eyes.

There was more to the story than she was admitting, but he had lost interest in discussing the young marquess.

An attendant announced the opera was about to commence. At the news, the theater patrons began to leisurely depart the grand saloon and return to their boxes.

"Thorn," St. Lyons called out. "Quit tarrying and kiss your lady so we can return to our seats."

Lady Arabella opened her fan as if to hide her embarrassment. Their friends turned their backs, giving them a brief moment of privacy.

He lowered his head with the thought of kissing her.

Olivia placed her hand on the front of his evening coat to halt him. "No kissing in public," she said flatly. "It just isn't done."

"Little prude," he teased, and took up her hand so he could kiss a part of her anatomy deemed acceptable. He kissed the top of her hand. "Meet me later so I can kiss you properly."

A flash of awareness and desire flickered in her gaze as she withdrew her hand from his firm grasp. "I think not. The last time I allowed you to kiss me, I found myself betrothed."

"I do not recall you uttering a single protest that night." Thorn moved closer and clasped her hands. As he brought her hands to his chest, he tugged her so she had to take a step closer. He bowed his head until his forehead lightly touched hers. "Although I do recollect hearing your soft gasps, sighs, and desirous cries in my ear."

"Oh, hush," she said, pulling away from him and glancing around the room to insure no one had overheard his brazen words. "If I had known how much trouble you would cause me, I would have stayed at Lady Purles'."

"Another lie," Thorn mocked. "Deceit is not an admirable trait a gentleman looks for in a wife."

Olivia rolled her eyes. "You are not looking for a wife."

"No, I am not," he said, his expression growing contemplative as he studied her face. "No need, I suppose, since I am already betrothed to you."

"But—"

Thorn kissed her hard on the mouth. "Meet me at midnight in the garden. Do not be late or there will be consequences."

"Thorn, I cannot—" she protested.

"You can," he countered, flashing a swift grin. "You will. Do not forget that I am aware that you used to sneak out of your father's house to meet Gideon."

Olivia's sigh was ripe with exasperation. "We were children. Our outings were innocent adventures."

Thorn knew she was telling the truth since he had spied on Olivia and Gideon on a few occasions. From a distance, he had watched them play games, share secrets, and explore the woodlands together. "Perhaps. I will see you at midnight. Oh, and one more thing."

She glared at him. "What is it? All of us need to return to our boxes."

"You are no longer a child, and you are meeting me, not my twin," he murmured. "I can promise that your adventures with me will not be so innocent."

After Thorn and St. Lyons had escorted her and Lady Arabella to Lord Norgrave's box, Lady Grisdale announced that it was time for her and Olivia to return to their private box.

They were not alone in the dim corridor. Other theater patrons were chatting with friends or making their way to their seats.

Olivia and Lady Grisdale walked together in silence. Under normal circumstances the countess made her so nervous, she had a bad habit of babbling in front of the other lady. However, Thorn's insistence that they meet later occupied her thoughts. What did he wish to discuss? Had he come up with a new plan that would allow them to placate her father *and* end their relationship?

One might think Thorn was relishing his role a bit too much!

"What did you and Lord Kempthorn discuss?" the countess asked, breaking the silence.

"Nothing significant," she lied. *Good grief, Thorn was correct. I do have a penchant for lying when it suits me.*

"I cannot believe it! The earl was rather insistent in securing a private word with you," the older woman observed.

"The Grand Saloon is hardly private," Olivia said dryly. "Lady Arabella and Lord Bastrell were also present."

It was not unusual for Lady Grisdale to assume that everyone's decisions revolved around her.

"Forgive me for overstepping my boundaries," the countess said abruptly, not sounding repentant in the slightest. "I will soon be your stepmother and I speak only out of concern. Lord Dewick favors this match with Lord Kempthorn, but I worry that it is sentimentality for Lord and Lady Felstead that influences him rather than logic."

"Have you mentioned this to my father?"

"Heavens, no!" Lady Grisdale tittered. "However, I have grown quite fond of you this past year, Olivia. Although I would not presume to replace the mother you have lost, I hope we will be friends and you will view me as someone you can turn to for advice."

Wariness overshadowed any desire to befriend this lady. Every time Olivia had let down her guard, Lady Grisdale had a nasty habit of using any knowledge she had gained from their conversations against her.

"Thank you, my lady," Olivia said.

"Your father is not a good judge of a gentleman's character," Lady Grisdale declared, obvious that she was insulting the man she claimed she loved to the man's daughter. "That is why you need me, Olivia. Lord Dewick feels the earl will honor the engagement and marry you."

"It is the natural progression of these arrangements," Olivia said, struggling to keep the wariness out of her voice. "Is it not the same for you and my father?"

"Bien entendu!" The countess glanced sideways at her, using her tongue to make a soft chiding sound. "It is that way when a man and a woman fall in love as your father and I have. Nevertheless, your arrangement with Lord Kempthorn is different, is it not?"

Lady Grisdale might be correct in her assessment of Olivia's hasty engagement to the earl, but it did not make it any less hurtful.

"You must tell me everything Lord Kempthorn says to you," the countess continued. "If the man is on the verge of ending this engagement, I will be able to tell by his words and actions."

Olivia thought of Thorn's insistence for them to meet at midnight. Perhaps he did wish to end their arrangement immediately. A part of her was tempted to seek the countess's advice, but her past experiences with the lady filled her with caution.

Instead she said, "You are always so generous, my lady."

Lady Grisdale scowled as if she doubted the sincerity of Olivia's words. Whatever she planned to say was forgotten as they entered the box. Delight filled both ladies' hearts as Lord Dewick stood.

"Dewick, I knew you would not disappoint me," Lady Grisdale said, moving toward the gentleman she intended to marry.

Olivia longed to rush to her father's side, but she slowed her pace as the countess and her father greeted each other. They were planning to build a life together, and it wasn't her place to interfere. Before she could reach her seat, a gentleman stood and turned to face her.

"Miss Lydall."

Olivia halted. "Mr. Chauncey," she said, not concealing her surprise or delight. "This is most unexpected. What are you doing here?"

"I came to pay my respects to you and Lady Grisdale. However, by the time I arrived, you and the lady were gone," the gentleman explained. "I was about to take my leave when your father entered the box. Apparently the countess left him a note with a promise that she would return, so the baron invited me to join him."

Lady Grisdale smiled at the young gentleman. "Mr. Chauncey, it is so good to see you again. I hear Dewick managed to procure you a seat in our private box."

"Yes, madam," Mr. Chauncey said, casting a quick glance at Olivia for support. "Unless I am intruding."

"Not in the slightest. The more the merrier, I say," the countess said. "Olivia, why do you not sit beside Mr. Chauncey?"

"I would be honored," Mr. Chauncey said, gesturing at the empty chair.

Olivia stared at the countess and wondered why the lady was so eager for her to remain at Mr. Chauncey's side. Unfortunately, Lady Grisdale was no longer paying attention.

"I have been looking forward to the opera," she said, seeking a neutral subject.

"As have I," Mr. Chauncey replied. "I also was hoping to see you again. I must confess that when I departed your residence I was quite disheartened to learn of your engagement to Lord Kempthorn."

There was little to be gained by admitting that she had been startled by the news as well.

"You must forgive Lord Kempthorn," she said gently. "He had just acquired my father's blessing and then he found me sitting in the drawing room with another gentleman. It is only my opinion, but I suspect he was jealous."

Mr. Chauncey looked intrigued by her explanation. "You don't say. Hmm . . . I suppose if I had been fortunate to be in his position, I would have reacted in the very same manner."

Was the gentleman hinting that he had been seeking a more intimate connection with her? Why had she not noticed his regard sooner? Olivia and Mr. Chauncey shared many interests, but he was so reserved. She assumed he viewed her as wild and capricious as Thorn believed her to be.

She leaned forward and peered down at the pit. "Lady Grisdale and I arrived just in time since it appears the opera is about to begin," she said, lowering her voice. She sensed his amusement as she deliberately avoided his gaze so she did not have to acknowledge his comment.

Her attention drifted from the orchestra to the multiple tiers of theater boxes. Where were Thorn and St. Lyons seated? The earl had mentioned they were in the Duke of Rainbault's private box but she did not know which one belonged to His Grace. Her gaze alighted on Thorn a few minutes later. He was seated one tier down and closer to the stage than Lady Grisdale's private box. She recognized His Grace, St. Lyons, Lord Fairlamb and his wife, and several others.

He wanted me to sit beside him.

Lady Grisdale would have never granted her consent, but Olivia was touched he had wanted her with him.

For appearances, you silly goose!

Seated beside Lord Kempthorn would have sent a loud declaration to the *ton*. While the countess had discouraged the earl for the sake of propriety, Olivia wondered if her father would give his consent. She glanced at Lord Dewick.

Perhaps it is not too late to join Thorn and his friends.

Olivia switched her attention back to Thorn and noticed he was no longer seated. He was standing at the back of the box. His head was bowed as he spoke to someone who was notably shorter than him. She could not tell who he was speaking with, but a glimpse of a white skirt revealed his companion was a lady.

After a few minutes of discussion, the earl escorted Lady Millicent to the front of the box. Thorn murmured something to Lord Bastrell and the viscount stood to offer the lady his seat.

Had no one told Lady Millicent that Lord Kempthorn was betrothed?

Olivia fumed as she watched the viscount move to another seat while Thorn settled in beside the young lady.

"Is something amiss, Miss Lydall?" Mr. Chauncey murmured in her ear.

"Why do you ask, sir?" Olivia asked.

The audacity of that conniving creature!

"You—uh—are tapping the blades of your fan against my knee."

Olivia gasped. "How thoughtless of me," she said, embarrassed that she was practically flogging the gentleman. "I offer my sincere apologies, Mr. Chauncey. Are you hurt?"

"No harm done," Mr. Chauncey said, his expression filled with warmth. "Although I will gladly relieve you of your fan if are worried about my well-being."

The gentleman was teasing her, but Olivia still winced.

She opened her fan and stirred the air around her face, proving she was capable of behaving like a lady. "My father would tell you that I have too much energy to sit idle, and I tend to dispel it in odd ways."

"I can sympathize," Mr. Chauncey said, leaning so their

faces were inches apart. "When I am distracted, I tend to hum."

"Oh," she said, feigning interest.

"Badly," he added, and Olivia laughed with him.

She looked away and her gaze drifted back the Duke of Rainbault's box. Lady Millicent had shifted to speak privately with the earl. Her shoulder brushed his in an intimate fashion, which did not seem accidental. Olivia frowned at the woman who had taken great pleasure tormenting her when they were children. She truly detested the woman.

After witnessing this amorous display between Lady Millicent and Lord Kempthorn, Olivia decided that she would keep her meeting with the earl. She had a few things to say to the scoundrel.

Theirs was likely to be the shortest engagement in history.

Olivia was so annoyed with Lady Millicent's brazen behavior that she had overlooked her companion. She started as she realized Thorn was staring directly at her while Mr. Chauncey whispered a humorous story in her ear.

The earl looked very displeased with her.

She held her chin up, signaling that she did not care one whit about his temper.

I dare you, her defiant pose conveyed. Not that she expected the earl to act on it when he had Lady Millicent clinging to him like a poisonous barbed vine.

The rumbling D-minor cadence of the overture filled the theater, commanding silence from the spectators. Olivia took a deep breath and switched her attention to the stage in anticipation of enjoying the opera.

Chapter Twenty-Eight

Olivia was twenty minutes late.

Thorn was unaccustomed to waiting for a lady. Olivia Lydall, nevertheless, seemed determined to prove that she was the exception to his personal rules that had kept his life uncluttered with the emotional mayhem his friends often faced when it came to women. If she thought she could punish him for some imagined misdeed, he planned on setting her straight.

If anyone deserves to be furious, it is I.

A whisper of fabric brushing against the hedge wall and a muffled oath alerted him to her approach. Belatedly, he realized that he had forgotten to tell her where to meet him in the garden. Some of the tension in his neck and shoulders eased. She might have been waiting for him near the fountain or closer to her father's rented town house.

Her curls were slightly disheveled and she was breathless when she appeared. "There you are," she said, walking toward him. "I know I am late. You never told me where we should meet."

He ignored her accusatory tone since he was at fault. "I was distracted at the time," he said, extending his hand.

Olivia walked by him and stared at the blanket he had placed on the ground. "What is this?"

Instead of heading to the center of the hedge maze, he had selected one of the corners, with hedges that were shaped like castle turrets. The gravel path circled the perimeter of the hedge walls, leaving a grass-cushioned center.

"A late supper," Thorn explained as she quietly noted the oil lanterns he had lit to chase away the gloom and the hamper of food he had yet to unpack. "I thought you would be hungry after an evening at the theater."

"It is very considerate of you," she said, still avoiding his gaze. "Where did you find the time?"

"I didn't," he said succinctly. "I had my cook prepare the basket while we were at the theater." He took a deep breath. "You are annoyed about Lady Millicent."

Olivia turned to face him and he almost took a step back. She was bloody furious. Her hazel eyes gleamed in the lamplight.

"Now why would I be upset?" she asked with false sweetness. "I am certain I am not the first lady who had to sit and watch her betrothed flirt with another lady in front of half the *ton*."

Inwardly, he cringed. Put that way, he was a coldhearted villain. Nevertheless, he was affronted that she thought he would behave so detestably. Thorn strode up to her.

"And what of your behavior, Miss Lydall?" he argued. "I had invited you to join me, and yet it was Mr. Chauncey who sat beside you in Lady Grisdale's private box."

"You dare to accuse me?" she shouted. "I had no choice but to return with the countess. Unbeknownst to me, my father had invited Mr. Chauncey to remain. What was I supposed to do?"

He gave her a mocking smile. "I could tell you suffered egregiously in the gentleman's company."

Olivia poked him in the chest. "And what of you—you

duplicitous swine! You and Lady Millicent spent half the evening with your chairs pressed so closely together, I thought the chit would fall into your lap."

Thorn thought of the lovelorn glance Chauncey cast at Olivia, and he wanted to tear the man apart with his bare hands. "Jealous, my love?"

"No more than you were when you saw me with Mr. Chauncey," she hissed. "I have lost my appetite. I am returning to the house."

He caught her by hooking his arm around her waist and hauling her backward until her back was flush against his chest.

"Let me go!"

"Stop wiggling and listen to me, damn you," he said, tightening his hold until she gasped. "You must have been blind with jealousy when you saw me with Lady Millicent. Do you know why I know? Because that is how I felt when I saw Chauncey sitting beside you. If I had confronted him, I would have grabbed him by the coat and tossed him out of the box."

The fight went out of Olivia and she sagged against him. "You had no reason to be jealous of Mr. Chauncey."

Thorn loosened his grip on Olivia so he could turn her until she faced him. Tears misted her cornflower-blue eyes, and he regretted yelling at her. "Lady Millicent has convinced herself that I will make a tolerable husband." At the sudden heat in Olivia's gaze, he added, "However, I am engaged to you."

Olivia pursed her lips. "Given the impermanence of our engagement, I doubt Lady Millicent cares."

"So eager to rid yourself of me, are you?" he sneered.

She struggled to push him away. "Yes!"

"Then why should I not seek the company of another lady?" he taunted, holding her close. As she resisted, his anger was heating and transforming into another kind of passion. "Someone who desires me. A lady who longs for my kisses."

Olivia's eyes flared. "Fine. Go to her. I do not care."

Several teardrops slid down her cheeks.

Ignoring her protests, Thorn cradled her against his chest. "Olivia . . . Olivia," he sighed. "Stop fighting the inevitable."

She tipped her head back to glare at him. "What?"

"Us." Thorn captured her face with his hands and he kissed her.

Olivia tried to pull away from him, but he was determined to win this argument. His lips glided over hers as his teased her lips to part for him. It was a silent battle of wills. She thought she could resist him because he had spent so many years building walls between them. He shattered his restraint with a single word.

Inevitable.

How could she resist fate?

Thorn had invited her to a midnight picnic in the garden with the simple notion of charming her. Courting her. He had tasted the passion between them, and privately conceded he craved more.

His jealousy and her resistance had pushed the limits of his control. It was with reluctance that he dragged his mouth from hers. "I am not interested in Lady Millicent. I never have been. I want you."

With a bemused expression on her face, Olivia watched as Thorn removed his evening coat. He discarded it, and his fingers worked to unfasten the buttons of his waistcoat. "Wait, you cannot undress—not here."

He grinned. "Why not? No one can see us."

"That is hardly the point, Thorn." Olivia brought her hands up to her face when he tugged the hem of his shirt from his breeches. "Oh no, I cannot believe you are doing this."

Thorn untied his cravat, which helped to ease the tightness in his throat. The length of linen fluttered and settled on the blanket. "Come here," he said, though he was the one who moved toward her and pried her hands from her face.

"No more lies, Olivia." He bowed his head and kissed the side of her neck. "You can share your secrets with me," he whispered, his trail of kisses following the line of her neck to her shoulder. "Admit that you want me as much as I want you."

"Thorn." Olivia groaned as if he was tormenting her. "We should not—" She pressed her face into his shoulder.

"Denial strengthens your mind," Thorn agreed, sweeping her into his arms. She wrapped her arms around his neck. He liked how she felt in his arms. "Indulgence is good for your body and soul."

With great care, he knelt down and placed her on the blanket. Olivia stared up at him, her eyes revealing her desire and innocence. Her chestnut curls shimmered in the light from the lanterns, and her well-kissed ruby lips were moist, beckoning him to taste her again. Her pale skin looked as if she bathed in moonbeams. She reached for him.

Thorn clasped one of her hands to his heart. He had never seen a more beautiful woman as Olivia Lydall. Staring into her eyes, he was enthralled. The night air was warm and scented with the fragrance of flowers, vegetation, and earth. It vibrated with energy conjured by their mutual desire.

Thorn lowered himself, using the palms of his hands to brace himself so Olivia did not bear the full weight of his body. He dipped his head and she lifted hers to meet his hungry lips. A new tension imbued his body as he anticipated touching her again.

Their mouths merged and Olivia kissed him with a boldness that was unexpected and thrilling. Without thinking, he dragged her hand lower and silently encouraged her to explore the growing rigidity of his cock. She started as her hand covered him, and he could feel the heat of her flesh through his breeches.

"Does all of it belong to you?" she whispered, slightly awed by the size of his cock.

"Why would you think otherwise?" he teased, kissing her nose.

"Once I overheard one of my governesses tell one of the maids that her lover stuffed cotton down the front of his breeches. She lamented he was all fluff and no c—"

He kissed her before she could finish. "You were too young to hear such saucy gossip."

Olivia pressed her hand against his cock and stroked him. His unruly flesh hardened. "You never answered my question, Lord Kempthorn."

The cheeky wench was torturing him and he prayed she wouldn't stop. "Keep petting my cock and you will feel its full measure, love."

Olivia had never felt more desired or out of her depth.

After her father had ordered their coachman to drive her home so he could continue his evening with Lady Grisdale, Olivia had decided to keep her midnight assignation with Thorn so she could confront him about Lady Millicent.

She had anticipated an argument that would lead one of them to end their engagement.

Olivia had been unprepared for passion to flare from ire.

Thorn was the one who was half-dressed, but she was the one who felt naked and vulnerable.

"This is madness," she said, unwilling to release the hard flesh he had invited her to touch. "I was so vexed with you, Thorn."

"And I with you," he said, rolling his hips against her hand. "See how angry I am at you?"

Olivia giggled.

"Here." Thorn shifted his weight so he could use his right hand. He reached for the buttons at his waist and unfastened them. Next he released the two that secured his fall front. Before she could move her hand away he shackled her fingers, and her hand brushed against his virile member. "You hold the proof of my desire in your hand, my lady."

Never had she ever pondered holding and coveting such intimate flesh. It was silk, heat, and strength. Just stroking it made her breasts ache and her clothes feel so confining. Curiosity unfurled within her and her legs moved restlessly as she wondered how his flesh would feel gliding against hers. It was a truly decadent thought. If Thorn was expecting her to undress in front of him, she would likely flee and seek refuge in the house.

Thorn, on the other hand, was shameless. His blissful expression told her that he enjoyed her caresses. He closed his eyes and allowed her fingers to explore his manhood. She traced the shape of him, and he shuddered. She took measure of his girth by encircling the crowning head. Several beads of liquid trickled from the opening, another sign of his arousal. In response, she noticed the growing dampness between her legs.

A soft mew escaped her lips when he drew back.

Thorn flashed a quick grin at her as he lowered his head and reached for her skirt.

Olivia instantly recalled the night he had caressed her in the coach. The wild reckless night that had resulted in their hasty engagement. She shivered and shifted impatiently as she thought of his fingers touching her as intimately has she had stroked him.

The night breeze danced over her stockings and coiled

around her bare thighs as Thorn uncovered her legs as he pushed her skirt and petticoat higher. He shifted slightly, positioning himself between her legs.

"I look forward to undressing you," he said huskily. His hand curved possessively against her right hip. "Though I doubt you would consent to lying naked beneath the night sky."

Nervous laughter bubbled inside her. "No." She tilted her head as a thought occurred to her. "Have you done such a thing before?"

He slowly shook his head. "We will be daring another day when neither of us has to worry about your father catching me fondling his daughter while I'm bare-arsed."

"My father sent me home alone. He and Lady Grisdale had other plans," she confessed, inhaling in quick shallow breaths.

"A blessing to be certain."

As Thorn moved up her body, she felt his manhood slide up along with him, lightly rubbing against her inner thigh. The weight of that rigid length bobbed as he covered her with his body.

Thorn braced one of his hands near the side of her head. "You are exceptionally lovely," he murmured. His dark green eyes examined her face, and he was pleased with what he saw. "I do not know why I did not see it right away."

"Oh," she huffed. Only the earl could compliment and insult her in one breath.

"I have offended you," he said with a breathless laugh.

Olivia wiggled against him, but froze when the blunt head of his manhood glided against the soft nest of hair between her legs. She trembled. Thorn covered his mouth with hers and kissed her deeply.

"There are different types of beauty, Olivia. You have a face that a man could appreciate every day and still discover something new to marvel at," he said between kisses.

"Different angles . . . every mood. If I had the skill and patience to be an artist, I would be eager to sketch you."

"You flatter me," she said, both pleased and uncomfortable with his compliment.

His expression hardened at her dismissive tone. "No, I have flattered to get what I wanted from other women. I am speaking the truth to you, Olivia. My betrothed."

"Oh," she whispered, moved by his words.

Thorn lowered his head and kissed her reverently. She touched the tip of her tongue against his, and it was the only invitation he needed. The hand on her hip moved up to the front of her bodice. One firm tug, and he managed to free her breast. His head dropped lower and he latched on to her nipple and suckled.

It was a remarkable sensation that seemed to spread like warm honey until it dripped downward to the aching flesh between her legs. The heat and subtle stroking from his manhood against her now-drenched slit only heightened her sensitivity. She longed to press her knees together to ease the ache.

"Thorn," she moaned, her head thrashing from side to side when he freed her other breast. "It is too much."

His breath tickled as he expelled a mischievous chuckle as he noted the gooseflesh that appeared in patches on her arms and thighs. "Not nearly enough."

The earl was devious. He understood her body better than she did, and Olivia was reluctant to dwell on how the gentleman had honed his skills. Ten minutes later, he had teased and tormented her, driving her to the brink of pleasure but always pulling her back. Every inch of her body ached and she wanted to bite him out of sheer frustration.

Thorn must have sensed her dark thoughts because he chose that moment to reach between her legs and guided his manhood so it pressed against her womanly sheath. She was so wet, the fully engorged head of his arousal sank deeper.

"Thorn."

"You are ready for me, Olivia," he murmured against her hot flesh. It was then that she realized that pleasuring her had wreaked havoc on the earl's restraint. He had been holding back for her sake, and it had cost him.

"I am," Olivia whispered, longing to free her and Thorn.

His head shot up and his dark green eyes were fierce as their gazes locked.

He moved his hips and the pressure increased as his manhood sank deeper into her sheath with each thrust. Suddenly, the resistance of her body gave way and he filled her. She winced at the unexpected fullness, but there was little discomfort.

Thorn muttered under his breath. It could have been praise or a curse.

Before Olivia could take her next breath, the earl tightened his grip on her and began to move. His hips set a swift pace as he plunged thoroughly into her womanly sheath and withdrew as her firm nipples grazed against his linen shirt. Her fingers curled around his shoulders as she seemed to feel Thorn's possession everywhere. His lips devouring her mouth. His mouth nipping her shoulder and her breast. His fingers threading through her hair, squeezing the soft yielding globes of her breasts, while his other hand gripped her hip. The uncompromising virile staff of his manhood, breaching and claiming the heart of her womanly core over and over until her entire body felt as if it were engulfed in flames.

"Thorn!" she cried out as the muscles of her sheath tightened around him.

Thorn shouted her name at the same time and plunged his manhood so deeply she gasped. He buried his face into her shoulder, and a few seconds later hard pulses of wet heat filled her. He groaned in her embrace as his hips pressed against hers, his throbbing flesh needing to claim every inch of her.

The night breeze was already cooling her damp skin when Thorn raised his head. His gaze was unfocused but he leaned closer and kissed her tenderly on the mouth. He gave her a lopsided grin as his body gave one final shudder.

"A very satisfying end to my celibacy," Thorn said before his mouth covered hers again.

Chapter Twenty-Nine

I should have bedded her a week ago, Thorn thought as he handed Olivia a glass of wine. The tension he had sensed increasing between them seemed to fade with the claiming of her maidenhead and the spilling of his seed. Although she was oblivious to the significance, theirs had been a fair exchange. She had never taken a lover, and he had never permitted himself to come in a woman. He had no interest in populating England with his bastards, nor would he start with the one woman who was responsible for his lack of control this evening.

If Olivia was quickening with his child, they would marry.

For now, he was content to let his lover believe she could break their engagement once they left Town. Besides, there was no reason to dwell on potential obstacles.

He was in too good of a mood and he had the lady sitting demurely next to him to thank for it.

Olivia sipped her wine and offered a coy grin as she stared at him. She was looking astonishingly composed for a lady who had been ravished by him twenty minutes earlier. Her coiffure had lost its fragile moorings and had fallen into an alluring tangle of curls that framed her face.

He picked up a small plate. "Another almond biscuit?" he politely offered.

She selected one and groaned. "If you keep feeding me biscuits, I will need to order new dresses."

"I can afford it," he said casually as he tried not to picture Olivia with fuller cheeks and figure, her belly round and swollen with his child. The image in his head was so clear and unexpected, he shook his head to dispel it. "Are you certain you do not want one more biscuit?"

"Absolutely not." She tossed her head back and laughed. "And you are a very wicked man to tempt me with my favorite dessert."

"Tempting you is very rewarding." He put aside the plate. "I am in a very good mood. Have I thanked you for it?"

"Twice," she said, sending him a playful look. "You may thank me again, if you like."

"I do," Thorn said, his sated cock stirring within the confines of his fastened breeches as he contemplated taking Olivia again. "Come to me."

A biddable lady, she crawled toward him then shrieked in surprise as he dragged her on to his lap.

"There. Much better," he said, indulging himself by nibbling on her earlobe. "Did I hurt you? In my haste, I was clumsy—"

She placed her finger on his lips to silence him. "I am a little sore." She paused and considered the degree of her discomfort. "Not overly much, I think. You do not want to—I mean, so soon?"

His body was willing, but Olivia had been a generous lover and there was no need for him to be greedy. He did not want to overwhelm her with his carnal demands. She was curious and eager, and he did not wish to discourage her.

"You need time to recover," he said sternly.

Olivia giggled and without prompting kissed him lightly on the lips.

"I am trying to behave, you incorrigible minx," he

scolded. "Do not encourage me or I will forget all of my good intentions."

Without releasing her, Thorn leaned forward and reached into the hamper to retrieve the box he had concealed there earlier. His fingers groped the interior until he found the item he wanted.

"Shut your eyes," he ordered. "I have a surprise for you."

Olivia dutifully covered her eyes with her hands. "What is it?"

"You will see soon enough," he said, amused by her excitement. Very few ladies could resist an unexpected gift. "You are free to open your eyes."

Her hands fell away from her face and she saw the jeweler's box in Thorn's hand. "You bought me a present?"

"No, I bought it for Lady Millicent," was his teasing reply, and to punish him she pinched him. "Of course it is for you. Did you think I would overlook your birthday?"

Her lower lip quivered with emotion. "With all of the excitement, I did not think anyone remembered it was my"—she inhaled and fought back tears—"I cannot believe you remembered."

"Maybe I heard it from Gideon," Thorn said dismissively to cover his reaction to her gratitude. He had not realized that her father and Lady Grisdale had failed to recognize the special importance of this day. It angered him that Olivia was often overlooked by those who claimed to care for her.

Including him.

"Open the box," he gruffly ordered.

Olivia did not hesitate. She took the box and removed the lid. She removed a delicate gold bracelet that looked like a chain of flowers. The center link was a larger and more ornate bloom with a rectangular-cut emerald in the middle surrounded by five small diamonds.

"It is beautiful," she said, not taking her eyes off the

bracelet. "I do not own anything finer." She clutched his gift in her fist and met his gaze with her eyes brightened by unshed tears. "Thank you, Thorn. Though I should warn you, my father may not approve of your extravagance and insist that I return the bracelet."

She kissed his cheek.

"You and I are betrothed," Thorn reminded her. "I am allowed to spoil you with a few trinkets. If your father protests, tell him to bring his complaints to my door. I will handle Lord Dewick."

The baron would soon learn he had greater concerns than Thorn giving Olivia gifts.

Chapter Thirty

Lady Grisdale often reminded Lord Dewick and Olivia that there were benefits to being engaged to Lord Kempthorn. London's Polite Society finally took note of Miss Lydall. Her connection to Lord and Lady Felstead and distantly to the Duke and Duchess of Blackbern guaranteed that invitations arrived each day, and there was a steady flow of visitors who were curious about the lady who had ensnared the handsome earl's heart.

Her father had predicted that engagement to Thorn would not discourage gentlemen callers. Olivia could not fathom how the male brain worked. When she was unattached, she strolled through ballrooms practically invisible to the eligible bachelors. Now that these same gentlemen viewed her as unattainable, she had become the most desirable lady in the room.

The earl was not amused.

Gideon thought his brother's predicament was rather entertaining. Every time Thorn grumbled about all of the gentlemen he had to trip over to get to his betrothed, Gideon reminded him that if he wished to discourage Olivia's numerous admirers, all he had to do was marry her. Thorn did not disagree but he did not appear cheered by the notion either.

It was awkward moments like this that reminded Olivia

that her engagement to Lord Kempthorn would eventually come to an end. It was difficult to hope that Thorn might be resigned to marrying her when his twin's teasing always had him fleeing out the nearest door.

Perhaps her father was correct. Olivia should concentrate on the gentlemen who sought her company. Mr. Chauncey, in particular, had been rather dedicated in his platonic courtship. It troubled her that she would rather remain betrothed to a reluctant lover than break her engagement for a gentleman who hinted that he desired to offer her more than a tepid friendship.

Not that she could find fault in Thorn's behavior. He had been the consummate gentleman since he ravished her under the midnight sky. More than ten days had passed since that fateful night. She could almost believe that she had dreamed the earl's lovemaking.

Except for the smoldering looks he gives me when he believes I am not paying attention.

No, Lord Kempthorn wanted her. Olivia just needed to remind him how rewarding it was for both of them when he gave into his desires.

Speak of the devil—or perhaps "scoundrel" was more applicable.

Sensing she was being observed, Olivia searched Lord and Lady Howland's ballroom until she found him. Her gaze locked with Thorn's. He was standing on the other side of the large room with his cousin and Gideon. She sighed, ignoring the twinge of disappointment that he was unwilling to come to her. It was pride that kept her from joining him.

Thorn turned away and murmured something to his companions. All three gentlemen laughed. Olivia glanced away. Perhaps Thorn had decided celibacy was preferable to bedding her. She whirled halfway to increase the distance between her and her betrothed and almost collided with Lady Millicent.

"I do beg your pardon," Olivia said without thought. There was no reason to be rude.

The young lady looked across the ballroom and noticed Thorn. Her lips curved in triumph as she deduced there was discord between Olivia and Thorn.

"Poor Olive," Lady Millicent said, using the old nickname that Olivia detested. "It does not look good when the gentleman you are engaged to is reluctant to greet you when you enter a room." She tapped her closed fan against her chin.

"Lord Kempthorn will join me when he is finished speaking with his family," Olivia said, her voice lacking warmth and sounding defensive. "Not that it is any of your business."

Lady Millicent gripped Olivia by the upper arm to halt her departure. "I do not know what you did to trick Thorn into this farce of an engagement. However, it is apparent to everyone who knows him that he is already regretting his decision."

Olivia knew the young lady spoke out of spite and jealousy. Unfortunately, Lady Millicent's cruel words echoed her own private fears. "I heard a rumor that you have some experience with broken engagements. You have my sympathies."

The other woman's fingers tightened on her arm. "Who told you?"

"I do not recall." Olivia shrugged and pulled her arm free from Lady Millicent's hold.

"It is unlike you to be coy, Miss Lydall," Lady Millicent cooed as her eyes hardened and glittered menacingly. "My dear friend, I insist that you tell me who has been telling lies about me."

"Let me be clear. You and I are not friends, Lady Millicent," Olivia said, standing her ground. She had been mocked and bullied by this young woman since they were children and she had reached her limit. "Nor have you ever behaved in a manner that encouraged me to offer you my friendship. Even so, I feel the need to give you a bit of advice. Your failings are not mine, no matter how dearly you wish them to be. If Thorn wanted you, he would have done something about it years ago."

"How dare you!" Lady Millicent seethed with outrage.

Olivia stepped closer. What she had to say was private. "I dare because ignoring you has never spared me from your cruel remarks. Although you do not deserve it, I see that you are in pain. You have had the misfortune of loving two gentlemen who were incapable of returning your affection. For that alone, I find that I pity you."

"When Thorn severs his ties with you, I will be there to comfort him," Lady Millicent said, her spine rigid with defiant fury. "So save your pity for yourself. You will need it. When I am finished, you will have no friends in London."

There was nothing left to be said unless she intended to challenge Lady Millicent to fisticuffs. Olivia could not think of another lady more deserving to be knocked on her arrogant backside. With her chin up, she wordlessly offered the young lady her back and strolled away as if she did not have a care in the world.

Even though her innards quivered like jelly.

Lost in thought, Olivia's unfocused gaze cleared as she noticed that Lady Grisdale stood between her and the open doorway. Olivia smiled pleasantly at the countess, while she calmly prepared to brazen her way past the older woman without creating another emotional scene.

"Lady Millicent seems a trifle upset with you," Lady

Grisdale observed, managing to sound amused and disappointed in her.

"How can you tell?" Olivia asked. "Lady Millicent always looks as if she has swallowed a toad."

The countess inclined her head toward Olivia's ear. "A bit of advice, my dear. While your advantageous engagement to Lord Kempthorn has allowed many of the *ton* to overlook your rather charming turn of phrase and lack of Town polish, you would be wise not to make enemies."

Still struggling to calm her nerves after her brief confrontation with Lady Millicent, she was in no mood to be reminded of her failings by Lady Grisdale. "I know who my enemies are, my lady," she said, meeting the older lady's gaze, letting her meaningful pause to speak volumes.

The countess's eyes widened and her lips parted in surprise. "Well, well . . . how most unexpected. It also answers a few unspoken questions I have."

Another lecture, Countess?

"It will have to wait, I fear. I have tarried too long and I promised to meet a friend." Olivia stepped away but did not lower her gaze. She could not ask her father not to marry Lady Grisdale, but from this day on she refused to allow the lady to insult her. "If you will excuse me."

It took Thorn all of his fortitude not to rush to Olivia's side when Lady Millicent stepped in front of her. A glimpse of the other woman's face and his lady's rigid stance revealed their conversation was private and unpleasant.

"What are you doing?" his brother demanded, staring at his twin in disbelief. "Should you not go to her?"

Thorn, Chance, and Gideon had been keeping an eye on Olivia ever since she had entered the ballroom. His instincts urging him to cross the large room and greet her, laying claim to her in front of Lord and Lady Howland's guests, had earned him some well-deserved teasing from his cousin and brother. Still, his pride took a little bruising as Chance and Gideon wagered on how long he could resist dashing to Olivia's side.

"How the mighty have fallen," Chance had joked, causing Gideon to laugh.

The two men had unintentionally irritated Thorn, and stubbornness had kept him from approaching Olivia. His decision had left her baffled and uncertain if she should join him. With regret, he realized she might have been hurt by his indifference. Instead of rushing to him, she had slowly turned away and had run into the one person who took delight in making her miserable.

"Olivia can handle Lady Millicent," Thorn said with confidence, earning a quizzical look from his twin. "Very well, a slight exaggeration. However, she would not appreciate it if I chased off every person who was rude to her."

After an obviously tense exchange, the two ladies parted and Olivia walked away from Lady Millicent to speak with Lady Grisdale.

"The countess is not very fond of your lady, Thorn," Chance murmured as the three gentlemen continue to watch Olivia with undisguised interest.

"I do not trust her. She has been filling Olivia's head with a bunch of nonsense. However, it is difficult to avoid the lady one's father intends to marry." Thorn said, his hands curling into fists as he resisted the urge to march across the ballroom and separate the two ladies.

"Has Lord Dewick offered?" Chance asked.

There was something in his cousin's tone that caught Thorn's attention. His gaze switched from Olivia and Lady Grisdale to the marquess. "What have you heard?"

Chance shrugged. "Just rumors, I suppose," he said dismissively.

"Olivia has left the ballroom," Gideon said.

Thorn scowled at his twin. "You wait until she leaves the room before you tell me?"

Gideon sneered. "Are you not worried everyone might believe you are enthralled by your lady if you chase after her?"

His twin knew just the raw nerve to press.

"Go to hell, brother," Thorn growled as he stalked across the ballroom to find Olivia.

Olivia had lied when she had told Lady Grisdale that she was meeting someone.

Between Thorn keeping his distance, Lady Millicent furious with her for spreading gossip about her failed engagement, and the countess's smug lectures, Olivia could not spend another minute in Lady Howland's ballroom. She had taken sanctuary in a rather small and uninspiring anteroom that connected to the card room. Their hostess had filled it with potted ferns and roses, and the earthy scents comforted her.

Olivia was not alone. The Howlands' town house was not as large as Lady Purles' and she assumed the guests who had discovered the small room had lost interest in playing cards. She had found an empty chair in one of its gloomy corners and claimed it while contemplating the notion of leaving the ball early.

Thorn deserves an icy reception from me. The scoundrel abandons me to the tender mercies of Lady Millicent and Lady Grisdale. As my betrothed, he should have come to my aid—

Olivia abruptly straightened in her seat. She hadn't needed Thorn to rescue her, had she? She had stood up to both ladies and had walked away unscathed. A hint of a smile played across her face.

"You are the prettiest bloom in the room," Mr. Chauncey announced as he halted in front of Olivia and bowed. He glanced about the anteroom, and what he noticed caused the frown forming on his lips to become more pronounced. "Ferns and roses—what was Lady Howland thinking?"

"It does have a certain charm, do you not agree?" Olivia said, rising from her chair. She curtsied and remained standing since she did not have a seat to offer him.

She laughed at the gentleman's appalled expression.

"I am teasing, Mr. Chauncey," she said, still smiling. "It is good to see you again."

"The feeling is mutual, Miss Lydall," he said, a look of concern shadowing his blue eyes. "I had high hopes of spending more time in your company. However, your recent engagement to Lord Kempthorn has spoiled my plans and dampened my spirits."

"I do not understand."

In an unexpected gesture, Mr. Chauncey displayed his gloved hands in front of him with his palms upward in an unspoken invitation for her to place her hands on top of his. It was odd for the gentleman to behave so boldly, but she considered him a friend so she obliged him by complying with his silent request.

His thumbs moved to hold her hands in place as his fingers curved around hers until their hands were clasped. Olivia peered past the gentleman's right arm but none of the other guests seemed to be paying attention to her and Mr. Chauncey.

"Did you wish to speak privately with me, sir?"

"Indeed, I do," Mr. Chauncey said. He took several deep breaths and offered her a wobbly grin. "Forgive me, Miss Lydall. I am not a man of action or clever words, so I will get straight to the point."

When he did not elaborate, she nodded to encourage him to continue.

Mr. Chauncey grimaced, and his intense expression darkened as he held her gaze. "Miss Lydall, I believe your father has made a dreadful mistake in consenting to your engagement to Lord Kempthorn."

Her lips parted in astonishment. "I beg your pardon."

"I know you love and respect your father, Miss Lydall," the gentleman continued. "You are a dutiful daughter and you would never defy Lord Dewick. Nevertheless, I must speak from my heart and warn you that the earl does not possess the temperament to appreciate a lady such as yourself. It is my greatest fear that your gentle spirit will wither in his care, and I cannot bear such a thought."

Although she disagreed about his denouncement of Thorn's character, her eyes softened with affection for the gentleman who believed he was protecting her. "Mr. Chauncey, I do not—"

"I want you to break your engagement to Lord Kempthorn," he continued, pressing forward as his hands threatened to crush her fingers. "I wish for us to marry, Miss Lydall."

"Step away from my betrothed, Chauncey." Thorn's angry voice startled her and her companion.

Mr. Chauncey had the good sense to release her hands and increase the distance between them.

Thorn was not alone. His cousin, Lord Fairlamb, and his brother were standing behind him. From their grim expressions, all three gentlemen had overheard Mr. Chauncey declare his intentions.

In an attempt to distract Thorn from throttling her friend, Olivia moved until she was standing between the earl and Mr. Chauncey. "So you finally remembered that you have a betrothed," she said, her voice sharpening as she recalled his boorish behavior in the ballroom.

Thorn spared her a brief glance of exasperation before his attention returned to the gentleman behind her. "If you were about to accept Chauncey's proposal of marriage, you are hardly in a position to accuse me of being forgetful."

"I am engaged to you, Thorn," she said, keeping her voice low. They were already drawing enough attention. "I see no reason to consider other offers, unless you disagree."

Thorn glanced down at her, and her annoyance faded as she saw the stark relief in his gaze. His fingers caressed her cheek. "I do not. I will hold you to our agreement, Miss Lydall."

It was not a romantic declaration of love, but they had an audience. Allowances must be made.

With a firm nod of her head, she glanced back at her friend. "As you can see, Mr. Chauncey, I must decline your offer." Olivia placed her hand on the earl's arm. "Shall we return to the ballroom?"

"Chance, will you escort Olivia downstairs?" Thorn asked, gently nudging her out of the way and toward his cousin. "Mr. Chauncey and I have unfinished business."

"No," she said, her voice laced with stubbornness. "I will not have you threatening my friend."

"I can speak for myself, Miss Lydall," Mr. Chauncey said lightly, his expression revealing that he was not intimidated by the earl. "Is this brute truly worthy of your tender heart?"

"You have more pressing issues to worry about than Olivia's heart, Chauncey," Thorn said silkily. "Do you wish to name your seconds, or shall I send my brother to your residence in the morning?"

Thorn intended to challenge Mr. Chauncey to a duel.

Olivia sent his brother a beseeching look. "Gideon, this is madness. Will you reason with Thorn?"

She gasped when he shook his head.

"I expect to be one of your seconds, brother," Gideon said.

"As do I," Lord Fairlamb added, holding Olivia back when she tried to approach the earl.

"I forbid this!" Olivia said, her voice rising as the other guests gave her sympathetic glances and whispered to one another.

Soon, news of the duel would spread throughout the ballroom.

Mr. Chauncey was unimpressed. With a calculating glint in his eyes, he said, "If you murder me in cold blood, Miss Lydall will never forgive you."

"I do not have to kill you, Chauncey," Thorn said, his voice thick with menace and an eagerness to commit violence. "A bullet in your leg will cool your ardor for my betrothed."

"Such arrogance," the gentleman scoffed. "Harm me and we shall see who the lady chooses."

"Is that an invitation, Chauncey?" Thorn taunted. "If so, I accept."

He punched Mr. Chauncey in the jaw, causing the man to stumble backward as he fought to maintain his balance. Several of the ladies in the anteroom shrieked, including Olivia. In response, her friend took a wild swing at the earl and clipped him on the shoulder.

Thorn landed a solid punch into Mr. Chauncey's stomach.

"Stop them," Olivia said to no one in particular.

Thankfully, Gideon and Lord Fairlamb were already heading toward the two fighting men with the intention of separating them.

"Pay attention, Lord Kempthorn," she shouted to be heard over the commotion. "There will be no duel. Do you hear me?"

Thorn turned and glared at her. "Your opinion is noted, Miss Lydall," he growled. She took a backward step away from them. "Now heed mine. Do as I have asked and get the hell out of here or there will be consequences for your defiance."

"If you bind yourself to this man, you will come to regret it, Miss Lydall," Mr. Chauncey said, rubbing his sore jaw.

"Leave us!" was Thorn's thunderous command.

Olivia flinched at his fury. Speechless, she turned and fled.

Chapter Thirty-One

Olivia had not returned to Lady Howland's ballroom.

As magnificent as Thorn's temper was, he would soon learn that he could not order her about as if she were a disobedient child or his wife. She also refused to acknowledge the irony of her actions when she hid in the cloakroom and watched the front door through a narrow gap in the door for Mr. Chauncey to appear. After his confrontation with Lord Kempthorn, she did not expect the gentleman to remain.

Ten minutes later, she saw her friend striding through the front hall.

But before she could call out his name, he was out the door.

Olivia widened the gap in the cloakroom door and slipped out of the room. She headed toward the front door and rushed after Mr. Chauncey. Thorn had done his best to intimidate the poor man, and she wanted to assure him that in spite of the earl's threats, there would be no duel.

She refused to permit the two gentlemen to fight over her and with a little persistence she was confident that she could persuade Thorn into rescinding his challenge.

"Mr. Chauncey!" she called out to the departing figure that disappeared into the shadows. The wind caught her skirt and sent it fluttering like two flags around her knees. She pushed the fabric down with her hands. "Wait for me!"

Olivia staggered after him. She slipped between two of the coaches, using them to buffer the wind and restore her dignity. Cupping her hands together, she shouted again at the top of her lungs, "Mr. Chauncey!"

The gentleman stopped and cocked his head to the side.

"Mr. Chauncey, please wait!"

The gentleman turned around and saw her. "Miss Lydall?" he said, striding toward her. "What are you doing here? The weather has worsened. It isn't safe to be running about unescorted."

Grateful that he stopped, Olivia said, "I could not have you leave without speaking to you first." Her curls caught the wind and lashed her across the face, blinding her. Annoyed, she brushed her hair back. "It is about the duel."

Mr. Chauncey shook his head with dismay. "Come along. My coach is just ahead. We can sit inside and talk."

Her throat already hurt from all of the shouting, so she simply nodded. The gentleman took her by the arm and led her to his coach. In the darkness, it looked like most of the others. Mr. Chauncey opened the door to the coach himself and pushed her inside. She sat down on the bench with the expectation that he would join her.

From the doorway he said, "I need to speak with the coachman. I will return shortly."

She waved him away as she again pushed her hair out of her eyes. A few minutes later, Mr. Chauncey appeared. The wind knocked off his hat and he disappeared to retrieve it before it rolled away into the darkness.

"It is a wild night," Mr. Chauncey said, climbing into the coach. It took him several attempts to shut the door. "What the devil possessed you to chase after me?"

"I had to speak to you before you left," Olivia said, recalling what had driven her out into the night. "Lord Kempthorn—he spoke in anger. There will be no duel."

The coach rocked on its springs as it wind howled.

Mr. Chauncey clasped his hands together as he deliberated on her words. "No offense, Miss Lydall. Kempthorn would have shot me on the spot if someone had handed him a pistol."

Olivia slumped against the back of the seat. How could she refute what she had witnessed with her own eyes? She covered her hand over her face and willed herself not to cry in front of her companion.

"There, there, Miss Lydall," Mr. Chauncey said, reaching over and awkwardly patting the hand resting on her lap. "Here." There was soft clink, and curiosity had her pull her hand away from her face. He had produced a small flask from a hidden pocket in his coat. "Drink this. It is nothing stronger than my favorite port. It will calm your nerves."

Olivia accepted the flask. "Thank you." She took a tiny sip and started to hand the flask back to him.

He motioned her to take another sip. "Violence is upsetting to a lady. It will take more than one sip to loosen the knot in your stomach."

Her husky laugh was absent of any humor. She swallowed some more port. "The knot is actually in my throat." Another sip.

Mr. Chauncey grinned. "Then by all means, empty the flask."

Olivia shook her head and realized that she did feel better. As promised, the knot that had threatened to strangle her slowly eased. "No, I have had enough."

She handed him the flask and this time he accepted it. He tucked it away in his inner pocket.

"Miss Lydall, may I speak bluntly?"

Olivia blinked owlishly at him and nodded. Now that

the danger has passed, she was suddenly fatigued. "We are friends, Mr. Chauncey. I value your opinion."

"I understand from Lady Grisdale that your father wholeheartedly supports this match between you and Lord Kempthorn." The gentleman frowned as he struggled to find the right words. "You are a good woman. You deserve a husband who will share your passions and worships you. Miss Lydall, you should aspire higher than a scoundrel like the earl."

The interior of the compartment was stifling. She longed to open the door just to feel the wind on her face.

"I promised my father, Mr. Chauncey." *And Thorn.*

His handsome face twisted with frustration. "Engagements can be broken. No one will think less of you."

Olivia yawned. "It cannot be helped," she said, slurring her words. "I am in love with him."

"Love," her male companion sneered. "And you believe Kempthorn will return this noble sentiment?"

"No, I"—she frowned and brought her hand to her head—"I feel unwell, Mr. Chauncey. I should return to the house."

She fell onto her side, her cheek striking the leather-padded bench.

Mr. Chauncey cocked his head and peered at her.

"Oh, it is much too late for that, Miss Lydall," he said, his voice sounding too distant even though she could reach out and touch him.

Olivia just didn't have the strength to even move her hand.

"Just close your eyes and sleep," Mr. Chauncey said soothingly.

She closed her eyes.

Marcroft did not flinch as tiny pellets of ice fell from the dark sky, stinging his face. Curiosity had prompted him to follow Miss Lydall outdoors. The lady had a streak of wildness in her that was likely to give Kempthorn gray hair before he reached thirty. He watched as she entered Chauncey's coach. He assumed she had sought a temporary shelter from the approaching storm. However, when the gentleman's coach drove away, a frisson of apprehension stirred the instincts that had served him well.

Something was very wrong.

Miss Lydall would not have left with Chauncey. She would have returned to Kempthorn.

There was no time to warn her betrothed. Marcroft held up his hand to protect his eyes as he crossed the dirt road. "No, remain on your perch," he ordered his coachman. He pointed in the direction the other coach was heading. "See that coach? I want you to follow it. Discreetly."

"Aye, milord," the man said as he reached for the ribbons.

Marcroft opened the door and stepped into the coach. He knew where to find Lord Kempthorn if he needed him. What intrigued him at the moment was the reason why Miss Lydall had departed with Chauncey and where the couple was heading.

Twenty minutes later, Marcroft stared through the spatter of raindrops obscuring the window of his coach and observed Chauncey's coach halt halfway down a narrow alley. A few minutes later, he scowled as he glimpsed Miss Lydall as Chauncey or his coachman carried the unconscious lady into the establishment.

Marcroft longed to follow the trio. Unfortunately, the odds of him walking out uninjured and with Miss Lydall were appallingly low. He needed assistance. Pounding his fist against the trapdoor, he waited impatiently for the coachman to respond.

"Milord?"

He loathed leaving Miss Lydall alone with Chauncey.

"Return to the Howlands' town house and be quick about it."

"Aye, milord." The trapdoor shut.

Marcroft settled back against the bench. He was not a man who often prayed, but he closed his eyes. The sweet lady deserved more than a few words uttered by a man such as him, but he knew how to help her.

Chapter Thirty-Two

Olivia's eyelashes fluttered open as awareness slowly seeped into her brain. She touched her head and groaned. Was she ill? The world tilted as she sat up and realized she was lying in a bed. Confused, she looked at the unfamiliar white walls and the worn albeit sturdy furniture.

Is this Lady Howland's house? Perhaps one of the servant's quarters?

Someone had undressed her. She wore only her chemise. Even her shoes and stockings had been removed.

Her bare feet touched the wood floor and she carefully moved from the bed to the shut door. She turned the doorknob.

It was locked.

Feeling weak, she leaned against the door and knocked. "Is anyone there?" Her throat felt scratchy and parched. She pounded her fist against the door. "I cannot open the door. Does anyone have the key?"

She pressed her ear against the wooden surface and listened.

Am I a prisoner?

"Concentrate, Olivia," she murmured as she moved away from the door and returned to the bed. She stared at the sparse room and tried to recall her last waking moments. She had been sitting in Mr. Chauncey's coach. He had offered her a few sips of port to calm her nerves since she had been so upset at the thought of Thorn challenging the poor man to a duel. It had not been his fault—

Good grief, he drugged me!

She straightened as she heard someone insert a key into the lock and turn it. A quick twist of the doorknob and the door opened. The gentleman she had considered a friend stepped into the room.

None of this makes any sense.

"Ah, good, you are awake," Mr. Chauncey said genially. "Your color has improved. For a few disconcerting minutes, I thought I might have allowed you to drink too much of my concoction."

"You drugged me," Olivia said in disbelief. She crossed her arms over her breasts because the chemise was too thin to protect her modesty. "What was in the port?"

"A personal recipe I have been working on for several years. It is a blend of various seeds that I have distilled into syrups," he explained, eager to share his work with her. "It has been a challenge to find the correct balance to suit my needs. I confess my early efforts were disheartening. Two of my volunteers stopped breathing. Another poor creature was so confused when she awoke that she climbed out a window and fell to her death." He peered at her. "How do you feel?"

"I feel ill, Mr. Chauncey," she lied. "You should tell Lady Howland to summon a physician at once to insure that I have not been poisoned by your sleeping draught."

He frowned at her, the enthusiasm dimming in his blue eyes. "You are still confused."

Her hand slid up to her throat. "This is not Lady Howland's town house?"

He shook his head. "I brought you to the Acropolis, Miss Lydall."

Olivia was unfamiliar with the establishment. "What is this place?" she said, edging away from him when he stepped toward her.

"A private club that has quite a notorious history," he said, offering her pleasant smile. "Half the gentlemen and several ladies of the *ton* have passed through the club's front doors. Only a select few are offered membership. I daresay you have met numerous patrons of the Acropolis, never knowing the dark secrets they harbored in their black hearts, even from their wives—or the vices and twisted perversions that lure them back to this club."

Olivia wondered if Thorn and his friends patronized this club. "I do not understand, Mr. Chauncey," she said, deliberately pitching her voice so she sounded meek and respectful. "Why have you brought me here?"

He tilted his head to the side. There was a time when she had thought the pose revealed his careful deliberation of each question she had posed to him. Now it looked sinister, as if he was sizing up his quarry.

"I had such plans for you, Miss Lydall."

"I do n-not—" she stammered.

Without warning, he lunged for her and seized her roughly by the upper arms. Surprised by his attack, she screamed, but the muscles in her throat were taut with fear and she barely uttered a sound.

"I am well aware that you are confused by all of this, my dear lady." His fingers dug into her bare arms and she winced in pain. "My fault, really. I should not have insisted on those extra swallows of my special port. However, I was desperate to lure you away from Kempthorn. Your tender heart makes you rather predictable, Miss Lydall. I knew you would follow me when I left Lady Howland's house. All I had to do was coax you into imbibing my brew, and I was able to whisk you away. No one knows you are here."

Olivia was repulsed by his touch. She struggled but she still felt weak from the drugged port. "Why are you doing this? Is this because of the fight with Thorn?"

The anger clouding his expression faded as he chuckled. "I did not kidnap you because I was worried about a duel. This is all about revenge, Miss Lydall. I have my orders, though I confess I am pleased with the way it all has turned out. I have been curious to discover what tasty confection is tucked between your thighs that has bewitched him so much that he is willing to kill any man who glances in your direction."

Outrage strengthened her body and her voice. "Did Lady Millicent hire you?"

"Lord Flewett's daughter?" Mr. Chauncey shoved her so she fell on the bed. "Oh dear, your poor head must be muddled if you believe I would take orders from that impudent miss."

He crawled across the mattress until he was on top of her.

Olivia did not bother screaming. Her fingers curled into a tight fist and she struck him. The blow glanced off his cheekbone. Chauncey grabbed her wrist before she could land another blow.

"Spiteful bitch!"

She cried out as he squeezed, grinding her delicate bones together. He slapped her across the face with his open hand.

"Why are you doing this?" she wailed.

"You have no clue what mischief you have wrought, do you?" he said, tightening his hold on her wrist until she feared he'd break it.

"No!"

"Oh this is rich," he said out loud to no one in particular. "You do not know—that your father has ended his relationship with Lady Grisdale."

She blinked away the tears that blurred her vision. "No.

My father said nothing to me. Why am I to blame? And more importantly, why do you care?"

"Family, Miss Lydall." He grinned down at her blank expression. "Your father ended his relationship with Nann when he realized that he had invited a viper into his bed and the lady was playing some very wicked games with his beloved daughter. She thought Dewick was so beguiled by her charms that she grew careless. Your father told her that he never intended to marry her." He wagged his finger at her. "That is the second time you have ruined the countess's plans, and she is very displeased with you. That is why she sent me to collect you."

"Lady Grisdale is behind this!" she exclaimed. "What are you? Her servant?"

He slapped her across the face. She covered her bruised cheek with her free hand.

"I already told you," he said, applying pressure to her injured wrist to gain her attention. "This is family business. It always has been. Lord Grisdale was my father."

Olivia frowned. "Not his heir."

"No. Grisdale spent most of his pathetic life denying that I was his son until he was resigned that he would never marry again. Then Nann came into his life. She was young and beautiful and she promised to provide the old bastard with the heir he coveted, leaving me on the outside again."

"Lady Grisdale never mentioned to my father that she had any children," Olivia said, striving to keep calm. As long as she kept the gentleman talking, he might forget to hurt her.

Chauncey grimaced. "The marriage did not produce any children. Nann blamed my father and his excesses, so after a few years she turned to me."

Olivia swallowed thickly. "You mean you and your stepmother—"

The man shrugged. "Nann is a beautiful woman. It was

no hardship fucking her. Grisdale would get his heir and his countess would insure that I was always welcome in her house and my purse was always filled. Regrettably, it took less than a year to figure out that Nann was barren."

"How?"

"The wily bastard impregnated one of his mistresses." The indifference in his expression revealed that he had already cut his losses on the countess's scheme. "Nann was furious and she begged me—"

Belatedly realizing someone could be listening at the door, he bent down and whispered in her ear. "Like you, I have a passion for plants. I was always experimenting with my concoctions. Mostly on animals and gullible servants, but then one day, Nann came to me with an intriguing proposal and I accepted. I poisoned the old virile bastard, Miss Lydall, and I enjoyed it. While his body was still warm, I fucked his widow. Barren or not, Nann is very skilled and knows how to please her lovers."

Olivia licked her dry lips. "You could have married her."

He shook his head. "Too many people knew I was one of Grisdale's bastards. Nann invited me to stay with her, but it wasn't long before Nann and I spent my father's fortune. Lady Grisdale required a new husband and eventually she set her sights on Lord Dewick."

"You said that I ruined the countess's plans a second time," Olivia said, turning her face away when he stroked her other cheek. "What other plans did she have for my father? Did she intend to have you poison him, too?"

The very notion curdled her stomach.

"Nann was arrogant and believed your father was too smitten to deny her anything. No, my dear, my dear stepmother intended for me to marry *you*."

"What?" she gasped.

He chuckled at her shocked expression. "The shy, biddable Miss Lydall, who had a respectable dowry that would eventually attract a husband. Nann convinced your father to increase the amount on my behalf."

Olivia's thoughts drifted to the day she had been introduced to him. "Last Season, we did not meet by chance."

He nodded. "No, our meeting was not by chance. It was part of Nann's scheme. If I married you, no one would ever question my fondness for my new mother-in-law. If I grew tired of sweets—"

Olivia batted his hand away when he tried to touch her face. In retaliation, he punished her by squeezing her wrist again.

"Stop!"

"I have always embraced my wicked nature," he admitted, moving backward on the mattress so he could pull her up into a sitting position.

Olivia gritted her teeth and panted through the pain.

"That is why I was drawn to the Acropolis," he said, tugging until she was at the edge of the mattress. "Nothing is forbidden here, Miss Lydall. Absolutely nothing. It took me only a few months to earn a coveted invitation by the owners. Do you know how I did it?"

She shook her head.

Chauncey pulled on her wrist until she obeyed him and stood.

"Because I do not deny myself anything: pleasure"—he expertly manipulated her wrist until she hissed at him—"or pain. That is why they agreed to the auction."

Nausea bubbled in her stomach.

"What auction?" she asked though she already had deduced that she would not be pleased with his response. Mr. Chauncey had proved he was clever and ambitious, and willing to kill anyone who threatened him.

"It was Nann's idea. I am offering you up as my slave this evening. The highest bidder can claim ownership for a week. When you are returned to my custody, I will hold another auction. Over and over, until I break you or I earn the dowry you and your father denied me."

"You cannot hold me against my will," she said, belatedly realizing that he had already succeeded in kidnapping her. "You cannot stop me from telling every person I meet in this horrid place that I am Lord Dewick's daughter and have been kidnapped by you and Lady Grisdale."

He clamped her jaw with his free hand. Roughly, he turned her face so he could whisper in her ear. "If I cut out your tongue, you will be quite the exotic, Miss Lydall. How many men will hand over their gold for the distinct pleasure of fucking your pretty mouth?"

Olivia trembled, believing the man she once thought of as a friend was capable of hurting her. She would throw herself out of one of the windows before she allowed anyone to touch her.

A brisk knock at the door sent her pulse racing. She sobbed, but his hand muffled the noise.

"Who is it?"

"Norgrave, my dear fellow," the marquess said from the other side of the door. "Let me in so I can see the chit you have brought to us. If I do not approve, you will have to procure another."

Olivia's breathing quickened. *Lady Arabella's father was a member of this club!* Thorn had warned her that the marquess was not the man she believed him to be, but he had spared her the unsavory aspects of his life.

"If you value your tongue, you will refrain from speaking to one of the club's most infamous members. I am told he enjoys hurting his lovers," Chauncey whispered. Her eyes widened as a coldness settled in her chest. "My roughness will seem like a caress when he is finished with you, so tempt him and *me* at your own peril."

Chauncey released her wrist and jaw and walked away from her to unlock the door.

Olivia doubled over and vomited. Her wrist throbbed as her stomach convulsed again.

"Christ, what have you done to the girl?" she overheard Norgrave ask the other man.

"Just reminding her of her place," was Chauncey's calm retort. "You would do the same if you had found her first."

"I suppose so," Norgrave said, walking toward her.

Olivia had turned her face away to avoid recognition. She felt a slight waft of air as the marquess presented her with his handkerchief.

"Don't be stubborn, my dear," he said with an air of impatience. "Use the handkerchief to wipe your face."

She took the handkerchief and scrubbed her lips. Folding it in half, she then wiped the tears from her cheeks.

"Come, come . . . I do not have all night."

Olivia winced, but she straightened and raised her chin. Her heart plummeted at the marquess's lack of surprise as he scrutinized her face.

"Very sloppy, my dear fellow," Norgrave scolded the younger man. "No one will pay well for damaged goods."

His touch was impersonal as the marquess lightly touched the side of her jaw so he could inspect her face. "The bruises are already discoloring her cheek and the swelling diminishes the lady's beauty." He gestured to the redness appearing up and down her arms. "More bruises and—did you break her wrist? Not only are you very young, Mr. Chauncey, you are very stupid. I have seen enough to believe that the proprietors of the Acropolis have made a grave mistake in granting you full membership."

Norgrave slowly raised his gaze until his light blue eyes locked on hers. "Do you not agree, Miss Lydall?"

Tears filled her eyes, blurring her vision so she could not look at the older gentleman. Her cheeks burned as the salt in her tears inflamed her bruised cheeks.

"There now, there is no reason to cry." Norgrave moved

as if he intended to embrace her, but she edged away from him.

Chauncey grimaced. "I have more than proven myself," he said through clenched teeth. "So Miss Lydall is a little bruised. No one will care."

"I highly disagree," Norgrave said, his mild polished inflection a reminder that Chauncey had forgotten his place. "In fact, I can think of one particular gentleman who will not be happy with your careless handling. Perhaps an introduction is in order."

Olivia found herself enveloped in Norgrave's unyielding embrace. She sobbed against his chest. He pivoted away from Chauncey, who was furious at the marquess's highhandedness.

"What the hell are you doing?" Chauncey shouted at him. "She belongs to—"

Someone kicked in the door and more masculine voices filled the air. Olivia was too shaken to discern what was happening. She pressed her face into Norgrave's coat as he held her. It almost felt as if the older gentleman was shielding her from the violence and the ugliness of her prison.

Chauncey's screams pierced the comforting warmth of the marquess's embrace. Olivia pulled away in time to see Thorn knocking Lady Grisdale's lover to the ground. In disbelief she watched her betrothed stomp on the man's kidneys. Her kidnapper whimpered, but Thorn was far from finished. He kicked him in the side until Chauncey rolled onto his back. St. Lyons, Rainbault, and Chance stood nearby and protected their friend's back from anyone who was foolish enough to stop Thorn from giving him the pummeling he deserved.

"You did well, Father," Marcroft said, looking grim as he noted her bruises. "You were quite convincing in your role as the debaucher of innocents. Now hand Miss Lydall over before Thorn decides to beat you bloody for touching her."

Norgrave's arms fell away as he raised his hands in surrender. "I suspect Miss Lydall has witnessed enough violence for one day." He glanced over at the two fighting men and winced. Thorn had straddled Chauncey and was polishing his knuckles with the man's face. "Bloodthirsty barbarian. It must run in Blackbern's bloodline."

Marcroft reached for Olivia and shifted their positions so she could not see Thorn and Chauncey. "No," he said. "Nothing you will see will comfort you."

"I agree," murmured his father.

The earl glanced over his shoulder to glare at Norgrave. "You are not helping." His fierce expression softened as he stared down at Olivia. "All you need to know is that Kempthorn is expressing his displeasure before he hands Chauncey to the constables waiting outside."

"If there is anything left of the gent," Rainbault said, his pride in his friend evident.

"A lady is present, Your Grace," Chance muttered.

"Thorn's lady," St. Lyons added.

The awful sounds of fist pounding flesh had stopped, and all Olivia could hear were moans and heavy breathing. Ignoring Marcroft's warning, she leaned to the side so she could peek around the earl.

One glimpse at the blood staining Thorn's hands, and her eyes rolled back into her head.

She heard someone whisper, "Croft, catch her before she—"

Olivia fainted.

Chapter Thirty-Three

Thorn was sick with worry as he carried Olivia into her father's town house.

She had not recovered since she had fainted at the sight of the blood splattered on his face, clothes, and hands, and the mess he had made of Chauncey's once-handsome face. Fortunately, Marcroft had caught Olivia before she collapsed on the unforgiving floor.

Thorn owed the Brants, and he was a man who paid his debts even if it meant angering the Rookes. It was Marcroft who had noticed Olivia leaving Lady Howland's house. He had watched her enter Chauncey's coach and had the shrewdness to follow the unremarkable black coach to the Acropolis. The earl had returned to the ballroom and reported what he had learned to Thorn and his friends. It was also Marcroft who suggested that they track down his father. Thorn was prepared to make a deal with the devil to get Olivia back, but Norgrave surprised all of them by freely offering his assistance. He used his connections at the Acropolis to quickly to locate where Chauncey had hidden Olivia, and he volunteered to distract him until the others could arrive with reinforcements.

Thorn had to admit that Norgrave had surpassed all of his expectations and had protected Olivia as if she were his own daughter. His actions did not redeem Norgrave. His sins were too numerous. Nevertheless, if there was a shred of goodness in the older man, Olivia and her friendship with Lady Arabella had inspired Norgrave to do the right thing.

She had not stirred from her slumber. Even Thorn's angry pleas failed to rouse her. Norgrave speculated that Olivia might still be under the influence of Chauncey's poison and the shock of her ordeal. He advised to let her sleep and suggested that everyone wash the blood from their hands and burn their bloodied clothes.

The butler's reaction when Thorn entered the front hall with Lord Dewick's daughter dressed in a bloodstained chemise in his arms while he himself was splattered with blood was proof that Norgrave was correct.

While Lord Dewick and the housekeeper tended to Olivia, Thorn returned to his town house. Gideon was not at home. Thorn bathed and took extra care to scrub the blood from his fingernails and hands. His knuckles were bruised and still bleeding, but his valet bandaged his hands. Gloves would hide his violent nature from Olivia. Although he quietly conceded that she knew him well enough to understand his need to protect her and punish the man who had frightened and hurt her.

St. Lyons, Chance, and Rainbault had delivered Chauncey to the tender mercies of the constables. If the man survived his injuries he would face the magistrate. Lady Grisdale had disappeared. It angered Thorn that she had escaped, but if she was a clever woman, she would put an ocean between herself and Lord Dewick.

Satisfied that he was in control of his emotions, he headed for the iron gate that separated the two properties. With or without the baron's permission, he intended to sit at Olivia's bedside until she awakened and returned to him.

Olivia awoke to find herself in her own bed. Someone had washed her and dressed her in her favorite nightdress. She might have been convinced that she had experienced an awful nightmare, but her wrist was bandaged and her cheek was tender and slightly swollen.

Olivia was unaware of how long she had been asleep, but she felt groggy and stiff. She climbed down from her bed and walked to her dressing table. Peering into the mirror, she winced at the colorful bruising. She sighed when she noticed the tiny bruises on her arms.

"Olivia!"

She glanced over her shoulder and saw her father standing in the doorway with a vase of fresh flowers.

The baron walked to one of the tables and set it down. "Kempthorn thought some flowers from the garden would please you. How are you feeling?" he gruffly asked.

"Papa," she said rushing to him. Without being asked, he opened his arms and embraced his daughter. She thought of Lady Grisdale and Mr. Chauncey's deception. Had the countess broken his father's heart? "Oh Papa," she said again, hugging him even tighter. "I am so sorry."

"There is nothing to apologize for, Olivia," Lord Dewick said, returning her embrace. "I was so worried when Kempthorn carried you into the house. I feared you had been shot."

Olivia wisely remained silent on the reasons why her father thought she had been mortally wounded. She remembered all the blood she had seen before she had fainted. "How long have I been asleep?"

Lord Dewick hesitated. "Two days."

"Two days!" She could not recall a time when she had slept as long. Not even when she had been in bed with a fever. "Am I—"

"You are fine," he rushed to assure her. "Mostly bruises and sprains. The physician assured me that your wrist is not broken, but it will be tender."

"What about Thorn?"

"A few scrapes, but mostly bruises," the baron said. "That young man has sat at your bedside for two days, Olivia. I had to bully him to take a walk in the garden to get some fresh air. Are you hungry?"

She absently nodded. "A little."

"I will tell the cook to fill a tray with your favorites." The baron lightly touched her cheek and his eyes gleamed with unshed tears. "Perhaps if you ask her, she will bake some almond biscuits for dessert."

"Papa, please do not cry," she begged, fighting back her own tears. "I cannot bear to see you hurt."

"Nor I, my sweet Olivia." He embraced her, and father and daughter held on to each other, drawing strength from the connection.

Lord Dewick was the first to pull away. "I will head to the kitchen. Do you have any requests?"

Olivia shook her head. "If you do not mind, I believe I will dress and take a walk in the garden before I eat. You did say that Thorn is there?"

Lord Dewick nodded. "If you do not see him on the terrace, check that old hedge maze. Kempthorn seems to be fond of it."

"I will."

Olivia did not move until her father shut the door. She dressed quickly, donning a simple white muslin dress. There was little she could do about the bruises on her face, but she selected a colorful shawl to conceal the marks on her arms. She left her hair down. Thorn liked her chestnut curls more than old hedge mazes.

While she had slept, Thorn had secured the gold bracelet he had given her on her birthday to her uninjured wrist. Perhaps he wanted her to awaken and immediately think of him.

Olivia put on her shoes and headed downstairs. She waved to the butler and slipped out one of the side doors that led to the back gardens.

Thorn was precisely where she expected him to be, standing in the middle of the grass circle where they had made love under a midnight sky as the stars winked overhead. He turned as if he recognized her footfalls.

"Olivia," he said striding to her. He tenderly cradled her face within his large hands and kissed her on the lips. "I have missed you."

"Papa said that you sat at my bedside for two days," she said, reluctant to release his hands. His gloves felt oddly padded, and it dawned on her that she was not the only one who required bandages.

He gave her a rueful grin. "Do not tell your father. However, when I was certain I would not be disturbed by him or the servants, I slipped into your bed and held you in my arms. It was the only way I could sleep."

She had been worried that he had stayed awake while she had slept. Her guilt lightened with the knowledge that Thorn had done what he had always done when he wanted something.

He had simply taken it.

"Have you spoken to your father?"

She nodded. "He left me to speak to the cook. I hope I can count on you to help me do justice to the tray of food that is being prepared."

"You can always count on me, Olivia."

Olivia frowned at the hint of pain he tried to hide.

"Have you spoken to Gideon?"

Thorn shrugged. "I have not seen him in days. Knowing my brother, he decided clearer heads would prevail if we had some time apart."

"And you disagree?" she pressed.

"It is for the best. All I could think about the last two

days is you." He poked at the grass with his boot. "Longer, if I'm honest."

"With me or you?"

His jaw tensed at the teasing reminder that he had not always been honest with her. "You mostly, but I became rather adept at lying to myself, too."

Olivia had so many questions. She felt as if she had been asleep for a year and she needed Thorn's guidance to navigate a world that had moved on without her. Most of her questions could wait. Before she had made the dreadful decision to chase after Mr. Chauncey, she and Thorn had left so many things unsettled between them.

She stood close to him as she contemplated her next move. "With Gideon gone, you no longer have to protect him from my feminine wiles. It must feel quite liberating to be free of both of us."

"You pick this moment to joke about it?"

Olivia shrugged as she walked to the circular hedge wall. With her wrist bandaged, she had decided not to wear gloves. Considering the decadent and inappropriate things Thorn had done to her in this very spot, her informality could be forgiven. Her bare fingers brushed the hedge wall as she savored the different textures.

"My father and I have not had the opportunity to discuss everything, but after what happened with Lady Grisdale"— she was content to omit Mr. Chauncey from their current discussion—"he will wish to return to Treversham House as soon as possible. I will likely leave Town as well. It is a prudent decision. Any gossip about our connection to the perfidious countess will fade with our departure and in a year everyone will have moved on to a new scandal."

And with luck, I will not be acquainted with any of the people involved.

Thorn stared at her. His face bore the enigmatic demeanor she had often attributed to him. "You are leaving me."

"I prefer to view it was freeing you from your obligation, my lord," she said, hoping he would notice the slight quake in her voice.

"What of our engagement?"

"My father anticipated that you would one day break it. He was angry that he caught you dallying with me as he once described it. Nevertheless, he is not a cruel man. He would not wish a loveless marriage on either of us. All he desired was that you used your family name to protect me from the gossips."

He lowered his head and sighed. "I have done a lousy job protecting you, Olivia."

"Nonsense," she protested. "As Lord Kempthorn and Mr. Netherwood, a lady would be hard-pressed to find two more handsome knights."

"Stop, Olivia."

She had struck a nerve, but she was hurting too.

"There was no reason for you to be jealous. After all, you came to me as the earl and as Gideon. What must have truly kept you up at night was wondering what your brother thought about your games. Perhaps Gideon was the man I loved and in your arrogance you gave me a very poor substitute."

"Do I have to stuff a gag in your mouth to silence you?"

"Ah, anger . . . I am familiar with that emotion. I felt it when your brother—I speak of the real Gideon Netherwood—kissed me. It was then that I knew the truth."

Thorn crossed his arms and glared at her.

"While it was a lovely kiss, I realized that your brother was not the Gideon who had caught me talking to a marble bust in my father's library or who had kissed me near the fountain." She gave him a level look. "Nor was he the rude gentleman who declared my dress ugly a minute before he tore the bodice."

She expected Thorn to apologize, but her confession seemed to baffle the earl. A few minutes later, he looked contemplative.

"Gideon's kiss revealed my deception." Thorn began to laugh. "That arrogant arse. Gideon deliberately kissed you to sabotage me and put an end to my mischief. He knew you would be able to tell the difference."

Had Gideon grown weary of Thorn's machinations?

"I am not vexed at Gideon. I applaud his cleverness. Of course you had to ruin everything by kissing me, which led to other wicked activities that resulted in my father catching us together." She grinned at him. "Perhaps it was a just punishment when my father insisted that we announce our engagement."

"Gideon was standing beside your father, looking hurt and outraged by my behavior. I wonder which one of them came up with the engagement?"

She had not considered that her father and his brother would have been pleased if she and Thorn were betrothed. "You see nothing but conspiracies. Does it truly matter? You were the one who saw it as an opportunity to keep poor smitten Olivia away from Gideon."

He grimaced and rubbed his jaw. "Is that what you believe?"

"It is what I know, Lord Kempthorn," she said, swinging her hips as she sauntered up to him. "You wanted—"

"You, Olivia," he shouted at her. "I wanted *you*. Not for my brother. I wanted you for myself. At first, I thought I could entice you with kisses. In my arrogance, I tried to bind you to me by introducing you to pleasure. I used my lips, my tongue, my hands, and my cock to enthrall you. When you stared up at me, I wanted you to see *me* first, and not my twin."

"I saw you, Thorn," she whispered.

"When Olivia?" He did not trust her, so he took a step back to distance himself. "When did you first see me?"

She frowned, guessing there was some trickery involved. Something she had missed.

"At the lake? You stood on the dock and glared at me."

Thorn shook his head. "When did you first convince yourself that you were in love with Gideon?"

She brought her hand to her mouth and shook her head. "Gideon was my friend. My own brothers could not be bothered to play with me. However, your brother was kind to me. He never found me lacking. I did not have to convince myself that I loved him. I have always loved him."

"Like a brother," he prompted.

"Yes."

He pounced. "Until he kissed you. How old were you? It was the moment your feelings for Gideon were altered and things between you were never the same."

She sent him a scathing look. "Well, it was my first kiss. I was twelve years old, and you and your brother were already charming eighteen-year-old scoundrels. Gideon had seduced my last and final governess, and the wretched creature was heartbroken. She sobbed for hours when she learned that you and your brother were leaving Malster Park for London and the chances of you returning for any lengthy visit were unlikely."

"You were intrigued."

She absently scratched at the bandage on her wrist. "I have always possessed a curious mind. Most of my governesses were practical, educated women. I have to admit that I did wonder what kind of kiss could muddle a woman's head."

"Of late, you have likely deduced that there was more to Gideon's affair with your governess than a few kisses."

Olivia laughed and stared up at Thorn, her hazel eyes twinkling. "Yes, it was you who showed me how a gentleman can muddle the brain of even the most intelligent woman. Would it please you to learn your lessons have been devastating and instructive?" Her smile faded as she lowered her gaze. "I have always viewed myself as a very sensible lady, who understood that our engagement would end one day. What I did not expect was how much I would regret our parting. I already feel quite ruined. So much so, I may never recover."

She savored the light caress of his fingers as he nudged her chin upward until their gazes locked.

"Is this your clever way of admitting that you care for me and do not wish for our engagement to end?"

Olivia frowned. "Yes, and if you mock me it is at your own peril."

Thorn held up his gloved hands. "Olivia, I nearly beat a man to death with my fists for kidnapping you and orchestrating a cruel fate that would have destroyed everything that I love about you."

She froze, uncertain if she believed him. "You love me?"

"Aye, I do," he said, gently kissing the bruises on her cheeks. "I have loved you longer than you know."

"I do not understand."

"Close your eyes," he commanded. He waited until she obeyed. "Think back to when you were that twelve-year-old girl and Gideon had come to you to say farewell since he did not know when he might see you again."

Thorn shut his eyes and tried to recall the eighteen-year-old young gentleman who was not as confident as the young Olivia had believed. He pressed his lips against hers in the most awkward manner he could imitate. What he had lacked in skill, he had made up in sincerity.

Olivia's eyes snapped open and she stared at him in wonder.

"Gideon was not the one who kissed me," she whispered.

Thorn shook his head, rubbing his nose against hers. "Even at eighteen years old, I was full of arrogance. I watched you and my brother play together, and I thought I was too superior to lower myself to play with children. Of course that did not discourage me from watching you when you were not looking. I thought you were the prettiest girl in all of England."

"You did?"

"Since Gideon and I were leaving for London, in my typical, high-handed manner, I thought I deserved a farewell kiss. I knew you were too innocent for what I wanted from you, but it did not stop me from kissing you. In a moment of cowardice, I walked away letting you believe that you had kissed Gideon. My reasons seem trivial to me now. I was too impatient to consider waiting for you to grow up. Why would I waste the prime years of my life waiting for a pretty child when London was on the horizon and I was old enough to hunger for a woman in my bed?"

"I doubt any gentleman would fault your logic," she said, lowering her gaze to conceal the hurt his confession evoked. "London is filled with beautiful ladies who are eager to flirt with handsome gentlemen who seem to offer them everything but promise them nothing. Overall, it was a very wise decision."

"Wrong," he countered. "It was a selfish decision made by a young gentleman who thought books had taught him all he needed to know about the world. I will admit that I dedicated myself to filling the gaps in my education. For a few years, I relished the decadence as I mastered my skills at seduction, but eventually I grew bored. Denial and regulating my carnal appetites was more appealing than the sort of wenches my friends bedded."

"This is the celibacy you have mentioned."

"I would test myself to see how long I could deny myself," he admitted. "A week? A month? Could I deny the entanglements of a lover for an entire year?"

Intrigued, she tipped her head to the side. "What is your record?"

"Eight months," he said, realizing he had continued to play games even without his twin. "And then I found myself standing on my parents' dock while I watched you and Gideon together. I swiftly came to the conclusion that you posed the greatest risk to the control I thought I had mastered."

"Arrogance." She sniffed.

"Aye, Olivia," he said, pushing aside the shawl she had donned to hide the dozens of finger-sized bruises that marred her flesh. Perhaps he should have killed Chauncey. "I used anger and criticism to keep you from getting closer. I did not want to remember that I had already discarded you in my youth. I let my brother bask in your affection and I resented him for it because it belonged to me.

Thorn wrapped his arms around Olivia's waist as he pulled her closer. "I am claiming what is mine."

"What?"

"I love you, Olivia. When Marcroft told me you had been kidnapped by Chauncey and was hidden away in one of the rooms at the Acropolis, I knew I would do anything to get you back—even if I had to barter with Norgrave for his cooperation."

"You love me."

Thorn's grin widened. "You cannot escape me, Miss Lydall. When your father insisted on our engagement, I allowed you and your father to believe that I only agreed because the arrangement was temporary." He kissed her. "I lied."

She frowned at him but it was a halfhearted effort. "You swore that I could discreetly break our engagement if I found another gentleman who suited me."

"I feared you loved Gideon and I was maddened with jealousy. I told you to consider other suitors in hopes that you would give up on my brother and cast your eye at another. What I failed to disclose was that I planned to be the man you fell in love with."

His hands tightened around her waist as she trembled.

Olivia shook her head, marveling at his confession. "You are not the only one who fell in love a long time ago," she said, her voice quavering. "I saw you, Thorn. Then and now. I always have. I just assumed a gentleman in your position would aspire higher than a baron's daughter. I thought it was why you—"

He silenced her with another kiss. "You were always worthy, Olivia. I was the one who did not deserve you. Now that I intend to hold you to your promise to marry me, what will it take to win your heart?"

Olivia poked the front of his frock coat. "Have you not been paying attention? You have it. I love you, Thorn."

He bowed his head and rested his forehead against hers. "Then I will spend the rest of my life making you the happiest, most muddle-headed lady in all of England," he vowed.

Olivia was so jubilant, she bounced on her heels. "When shall we tell my father that you are planning to marry me, after all?"

Thorn gave one of her curls a playful tug. "As soon as I can locate my elusive brother and order him to return home. Together, we will tell Gideon and your father of our plans to marry as swiftly as it can be arranged."

Olivia and Thorn shared a lingering kiss.

In the distance, Lord Dewick called out his daughter's name, and Thorn reluctantly ended their kiss.

"Will you meet me at midnight?" Thorn murmured against her ear.

Olivia smiled and nuzzled his shoulder. "I will be waiting, my love."